DEBORAH MOGGACH

Seesaw

Mandarin

A Mandarin Paperback
SEESAW

First published in Great Britain 1996
by William Heinemann Ltd
This edition published 1997
by Mandarin Paperbacks
an imprint of Reed International Books Ltd
Michelin House, 81 Fulham Road, London sw3 6rb
and Auckland, Melbourne, Singapore and Toronto

A CIP catalogue record for this title
is available from the British Library
ISBN 0 7493 2449 X

Typeset in Palatino by Deltatype Ltd, Birkenhead, Merseyside
Printed and bound in Great Britain
by Cox & Wyman Ltd, Reading, Berkshire

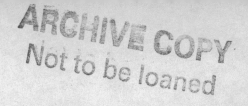

Seesaw

He sifted rapidly through the rest of the letters. The bottom one was addressed 'MR AND MRS PRICE'. He took it into the kitchen and opened the envelope. Something fell on to the floor; it pinged. He took out a sheet of lined paper, scrawled with capital letters.

FRIDAY NOON. USED BANKNOTES. NO TRICKS. WE'LL BE IN TOUCH. BYEEEE.

He stood still for a moment, holding the paper between his finger and thumb as if it were contaminated. Then he bent down and picked up the small, bright object that lay on the floor.

It took a moment, before he realised. It was Hannah's nose-stud.

Deborah Moggach was born in 1948, one of four girls in a family of writers. She has written ten previous novels, including *Porky, Stolen, Driving in the Dark, The Stand-In* and *The Ex-Wives*. Her TV screen plays include *Stolen* and the prize-winning *Goggle Eyes*. She lives in London with her two children.

To Lottie, who's worth it.

Part One

1

Their local paper sent round a reporter, a very young one.

'You must be over the moon,' she said.

'We're thrilled,' said Val. 'Thrilled to bits. We've never won a raffle before, or only bubble bath.' She and her family had won a holiday trip to Florida. To tell the truth, it was not top of her list of holiday destinations; to her, the word 'Florida' summoned up images of muggings and senility. It would be inappropriate, however, to mention this.

'Have you ever been to Florida before?'

Val shook her head. 'We've taken the kids to New York – my husband has some relatives there – but no, never Florida.'

Val wondered: did we pick the ticket or did the ticket pick us? Was it luck or fate? Later, a long time later, she pictured their piece of paper pushing its way to the surface, jostling up and leaping into the magnet palm of the TV personality who, in announcing their number, had set in motion the process that would change their lives for ever. But that was later.

There was a photographer, too. 'Nice place you've got,' he said, looking round their lounge. 'Very nice. I'll do some in here and some outside, okey-doke?'

Val's family was already restless. Morris had come home early from work; she herself had come home early from work. Getting the five of them together at four-thirty on a May afternoon had been an exhausting manoeuvre.

3

Only Becky, her younger daughter, seemed excited at the prospect of having her photo in the paper.

'So you've lived in Stanmore how long?' asked the reporter.

'Fifteen years,' said Val.

'And how long have you been married?'

'Oh, for ever.'

Morris raised his eyebrows. 'So it's such a life sentence? How can you be so cynical, in front of such a charming young lady?' He turned to the reporter. 'Twenty-four happy years and you want to know our secret? A couple who can laugh together can live together. And –' he wagged his finger, 'never go to bed on a quarrel, only on a mattress.'

The children groaned. Their embarrassment at their father was one of the few things that bound them together.

The reporter scribbled down their ages. 'Becky, eleven . . . Hannah, seventeen. You're both at school, right?' She turned and looked at Theo; she blushed. 'And you?'

'Twenty-one,' drawled Theo. 'I'm studying film.'

'That must be fascinating! Do you still live at home?'

'Christ no. I live in London.' His tone consigned Stanmore to a netherworld of suburbia, a place from which the only choice was flight.

'Let's have you here, together,' said the photographer. He herded them in front of the fireplace.

'Can you get my golfing trophies in the shot?' asked Morris.

'Dad!' said Hannah.

The photographer spoke to the girls. 'Let's have you, Becky here, and you – Harriet, is it? –'

'Hannah.'

'And you, Hannah, here.'

'Ugh!' Becky drew back. 'I'm not putting my arm round her.'

'Girls!' said Morris.

4

'Big smile,' said the photographer.

The shutter clicked. Val wished her husband wasn't wearing his check jacket; if left loose to shop on his own, Morris had terrible taste. *Florida* taste, actually. Loud shirts, seersucker, those blazers like Jack Lemmon wore. And if only Hannah would brush her hair and remove that awful, awful piece of jewellery from her nostril. With any luck it wouldn't show up on the photo, but what about the spider's web condition of her tights?

'So you run your own business, Mr Price?' asked the reporter.

He nodded. 'Price Security Systems, maybe you've heard of us?'

'No.'

'Our headquarters is not far from here – just outside Watford – but we install and maintain systems all over the country. Our turnover's up thirty per cent this past year and you want to know why, young lady? Because the world is a dangerous place.'

When the photographer ushered them outside Morris pointed to the burglar alarm above the porch – Price Security. 'Could you get it in the shot?'

'Dad!' said Hannah.

Theo said: 'Do we have to stand in front of the house? We look complete wankers.'

'We can pretend it's for *Hello*,' said Val.

'That's what I mean,' said Theo.

'Big smile,' said the photographer.

It was cold out here. The reporter's notebook rustled in the wind. She turned to Val. 'And do you work?'

'Does she work?' said Morris. 'She never stops.'

'I'm an interior designer,' said Val. 'I have an office here, and a shop in Marylebone. I'm mostly out and about.'

'She's never here to make my tea,' said Becky.

'Nice smile!' said the photographer.

5

Indoors the phone rang. Two rings, then the answer-phone picked it up. In half an hour Val had to drive out to Totteridge to meet some prospective clients. Morris had to drive into London to take the developer of some shopping mall out to dinner – a fellow Rotarian, apparently, and an amusing raconteur. In Val's view, an amusing Rotarian was a contradiction in terms.

'Cheer up, Harriet,' said the photographer.

'Hannah,' said Hannah.

In the street a car slowed down, then drove on. Val shivered; she sensed a stirring behind the windows of the neighbouring houses. Far away a burglar alarm rang; she realised that it had been ringing all this time, a thrumming in her brain. Her daughters shifted restlessly on the gravel.

'Just a couple more,' said the photographer.

The phone rang again, and stopped. Already she felt her family pulling away from her, straining to disperse – Becky to watch *Home and Away*, Hannah to retreat into her own adolescence, Theo to disappear into his opaque, student life ... she and her husband to return to their mounting phone calls and the ruptured momentum of their working day.

'Closer together. That's great.'

The shutter clicked. Standing there, she had the strangest sensation. Sucked into their own futures, her family had already disappeared. They had faded from her side; they had vanished into thin air in order to be reproduced in thousands of unknown homes. Later, she remembered this.

2

Nobody wanted to come to Camden Lock. Hannah had asked them all – Rachel, Emma, Julia. Suddenly they all had boyfriends, that was why, the traitors. They disappeared with them to the cinema. They dossed off school and met them on Stanmore Broadway; they came back into class reeking of Marlboros. They were unavailable on Saturday nights; sleepovers had suddenly become a childish activity. Emma was having sex with hers – Ollie Friedman. Her face had become closed and superior. After all those years of giggling about it she refused to tell them what it was like, how's that for friendship?

It was Sunday. Hannah always went to Camden Lock Market on Sunday. She lived in Stanmore, that was why. Sunday afternoons in Stanmore, the land of the living zombies . . . Strimmers strimming, cars starting up, cars parking. Silence. The Dante-esque limbo of suburbia; it was one of the few things about which she and her brother Theo agreed.

This Sunday Mum had promised to go over her Renaissance essay with her, for her History of Art Predictions. But Mum seemed to have forgotten. She was shut away in her study, as per usual. When Hannah passed the door she heard the tippety-tip and bleep of her mum's computer.

So she got ready, alone. She sat in front of her enemy, the mirror. She turned her head and looked at herself. Her nose-stud winked. They had been horrified, of course.

'Mutilation!' her Dad had yelled. 'My own daughter!'

'Chill,' Hannah had said, smugly.

'How're you going to pick your nose?' asked Becky, her younger sister.

Trouble was, the three pimples on her chin, they caught the light too. They were the same size as the nose-stud – no, bigger. *Gigantic*. God-why-am-I-alive. She rubbed cover-up over her horrible face. Where did her thighs come from? Not Mum, for sure. Mum was so beautiful and slim and elegant. It was Dad's fault; Dad was pudgy. Were her thighs going to get any fatter, was that possible? Two barrage balloons, she hauled them about. Even under her long black skirt, when she sat down you could see how they filled it out. Aargh! An alien growth. Her whole body was an alien growth.

Hannah left the house. She felt a wave of self-pity. If she vanished, would anyone notice? She could disappear off the face of the earth and three days later they would still be sitting there at their computers or giggling on the phone to Ollie Friedman. She walked down Cypress Drive and turned left into Ridgeway Avenue. She passed the Silvermans' house. They were her parents' oldest friends, they used to have dinner parties together before everybody got too busy. No sign of life. She passed the Barlowes' house; she used to swim there with Joni Barlowe before she was sent away to boarding school. Now, nothing stirred. The blinds were pulled down around the swimming pool as if to inform her that her childhood had ended.

Hannah walked towards the tube station. Even in the holidays Joni was usually abroad. Funny, she thought: the richer you were and the bigger your house, the less time you spent in it. Her own parents weren't that rich; they didn't have a pool. Besides, Dad was always moaning about the bills and telling them to turn off the lights. He said that any money he made he poured back into the

8

business; when she was younger she had pictured him tipping a stream of gold through a hole in the roof.

She tried to picture them all together in Florida. They were booked to go in six months' time, at Christmas. Theo was already making noises about not coming and she herself was getting too old to go on holiday with her parents. Dad would wear his shorts. And because they had won the holiday in a raffle everyone would make a fuss of them. Maybe somebody would have to make a speech! It would be so embarrassing. Everything was so embarrassing.

Actually it would be a relief to vanish. If nobody could see her, she needn't worry what she looked like. As she approached the tube station her spirits lifted. They always did, when she left home. She would live her own life, with nobody to nag her about her room. Maybe her parents would buy her a flat – they had bought Theo a flat – and she could become a hermit, issuing forth at dusk with her face veiled. She would become a legend in her own time.

Hannah took the tube to Camden Town. The hot breath of the tunnel blew her along the platform; it blew up her skirt. A woman with red hair looked at her. Hannah blushed and inspected her boots. The escalator was jammed with people, jabbering in foreign languages. Hannah's breasts were pressed into the leather jacket of the man ahead of her. He must be able to feel them! The person behind was squashed against her buttocks. Hannah didn't breathe, so her body didn't expand any more. She fiddled with the row of rings in her ear.

At Camden Town station three old men sat on the floor. They sucked cans of Triple Export. One of them winked at her – gross! He had a purple, bruised face. It looked as if it had been taken apart and reassembled. At least, surely, she didn't look as bad as *that*. Did she?

She was pushed along the street in a moving press of people. The market was crammed. Music thumped. A black guy dipped his head up and down, his dreads swaying. She touched her nose-stud, her badge of belonging. The sky was grey and heavy; it was chilly for June. The air was filled with curry smells and joss-stick smells. People pushed past her. Why did foreign girls never have any spots? Where did they get so tanned? Hannah skidded in split noodles. The waste bins overflowed. Plastic plates, heaped with orange rice, sat in doorways like religious offerings. How she loved it here! A dog, string dangling from its neck, ran past; it carried a traffic cone in its mouth. Across the canal, where the crusties drank cider under plastic sheeting, stood a shopping trolley and an orthopaedic crutch. The dead tree above was stuck with cans. It was all so *real*. So ... well, unStanmore.

She dawdled in the stalls, riffling through the clothes. She gazed at her bitten fingernails. Mum had promised to get her some new stuff for them, lotion or something. Promises, promises, huh. She pulled out a black, fringed skirt. She squeezed into a changing corner and tried to pull the curtain closed but it was so skimpy that people could see round the edges. Her face heated up. She squeezed out again and shoved the skirt back. She fingered a sixties-type waistcoat, a tie-dyed top a million sizes too small; she stepped over a guitar-case scattered with coins. Buskers – so *embarrassing*. She nearly bought a falafel, but then she pictured it crumbling to bits when she tried to eat it. She hung out.

Afterwards, she tried to remember her feelings that day. She had felt everyone was staring at her, but then she always felt that. They all stared because they *knew*. The *Big Issue* seller (he knew she came from a whopping great house in Stanmore); the buskers (they knew she had six pounds fifty in her purse); everybody (how could such a gross person be walking the earth?). She knew, really, that she didn't look any different from anyone else – long black skirt, DMs with beads on their laces, big Inca cardigan, love-beads, friendship bracelet, hair-worms. She knew this, but she always felt everyone was looking at her. Even when their backs were turned – even then they were looking at her reflection in shop windows.

Yes, but somebody was. That day, somebody *was* looking at her.

'Hey, I've been watching you.'

'Me?'

'Yeah – you.' It was a woman, wearing black leggings and carrying a clipboard. She had a portable phone. 'You're just what we've been looking for, know what I mean?' She grinned.

Hannah would always remember that face – flat, pale, freckly. A sexy, cat's face. Wide mouth, glossy with lipstick. She was slim and small-boned – another species from Hannah, another sort of mammal. She wore dark glasses; her hair was glossy red.

'We're doing, like, a fashion shoot for the *Face*. We've been looking for someone like you.'

'The *Face*?' Hannah stared at her.

'They said, find someone with a great body.'

Hannah tried to laugh. 'Great – like big?'

'A great bod and loadsa style.'

'Really?'

'Like, street style. And I mean, who wants waifs? We're sick of them, know what I mean?'

Hannah nodded. '*I'm* sick of them.' She paused. 'You don't *really* want *me*?'

The woman nodded. Hannah felt a rare sensation spread through her – pleasure.

The woman was tapping her foot. There were beads of perspiration on her face. Just for a moment, Hannah thought that was odd; it was such a chilly day.

'Well,' said the woman. 'Wanna come? We got a tight schedule.'

Hannah looked at her again. The hair, that's what did it. Glossy red hair. 'Hey, you were on the tube!'

'I was?' Her voice was sharp. 'Yeah – that's where I saw you.'

'And you followed me here? You've been following me all this time?'

The woman nodded. She pulled out a pack of cigarettes, shook one out and lit it. Her hand was shaking. Perhaps she was nervous; perhaps this was her first shoot, too. But she looked too experienced for that, too confident.

'Come on then,' she said.

'I'll have my photo in the *Face*?'

The woman nodded, jerking her head to Hannah to follow. Think of them at school! Hannah wouldn't tell them. She would just let them open the magazine, casually, and watch their expressions change.

The woman stepped over a drunk; she stepped over a cloth spread with wooden elephants.

'Are you only shooting me?' Hannah asked.

'Shooting?'

'I mean – am I the only one you want?'

The woman nodded; her red hair swung around her face. She was in a hurry. She stepped under some plastic awning; Hannah, being so big, had to duck. Out of the whole of Camden Lock they had chosen *her*! She realised: if somebody appreciates me, I could be a really nice person. I could even be nice to other people. It only takes a little thing like that.

'Come on!' said the woman. 'Over here.' She pushed through the people, shouldering her way through the racks of clothes.

'Where is it?' asked Hannah breathlessly.

'Through here.' The woman grabbed her hand; her fingernails were sharp. Such a tiny hand! How strongly it gripped hers! Hannah's hand felt as big as a ham; she felt self-conscious, being hauled along like this. They ducked under curtains of antique frocks. They pushed their way past sizzling hamburgers. The woman knocked against a stall; its jars wobbled. 'Hey!' shouted the man.

They emerged into the street. A car was waiting, its engine running. A man sat in the driving seat; he didn't turn round. The woman pulled open the back door and flung in her clipboard. Music thudded from the stereo.

Hannah drew back. A car?

'You didn't say a car.'

'Come on, Hannah! They're waiting!'

Hannah froze. She snatched her arm away.

She said: 'How do you know my name?'

The woman grabbed her arm.

3

'Hannah?' Val tapped on the door. Pinned to it was a leaflet saying *Stop Animal Testing*. It always irritated her. What did her daughter think – that the moment her back was turned her parents started injecting beagles? 'Hannah?'

'She's gone to Camden Lock,' said Becky.

'But she said she'd tidy her room first. And she's got to do her homework.'

Becky shrugged and went downstairs. She didn't care. She was eating a Passion Fruit Compote from Marks and Spencer.

Val pushed open the bedroom door. It was jammed by a sediment of clothes. The wardrobe had vomited its contents on to the carpet; in fact one couldn't glimpse the carpet at all. The room looked ransacked, as if a violent crime had taken place. Drawers were pulled out and clothes lolled like black tongues. Hannah seemed to throw everything on to the floor before she chose what to wear – why bother to choose when she always wore black anyway?

Amongst the clothes lay a silt of flyers – The Ministry of Fear at the Dome; Dead Babies at the Marquee. Val waded through the clothes and picked up three cereal bowls, encrusted with cornflakes, smeary with yoghurt. That's where the teaspoons had gone. Hannah always ate with a tiny spoon; her brother had done it too, it seemed to be one of the more curious perversities of adolescence. Why? Just

14

to be out of sync? To make some pathetic little teaspoon statement?

Val stood ankle-deep, seething. She herself had always been neat; how could she have produced a daughter like this? Peeling posters clung to the walls – *Lips, Tits, Hips, Power*! Some dopey-looking youth in leather jeans, pouting. On the unmade bed was the usual litter of cassette cases, most of them broken. Hannah was always recording her ghastly music for her friends, as if once wasn't enough. All the lights glowed in the music centre; Hannah never turned anything off, it gave her room a *Marie Celeste* look.

Furious, Val waded over to the desk. Hannah's homework books were spread out. On top of them lay *Just 17* and various paperbacks, spreadeagled – Jilly Cooper's *Riders; The Silence of the Lambs*. On top of them was a bottle of the antiseptic cream Hannah used for her unspeakable nose-stud. It was five-thirty. Hannah was supposed to be doing her Renaissance homework – in fact Val had promised to help her. Under the anger, she felt a small stirring of guilt. But then Hannah wasn't here, so how could she help her?

She struggled to the window and flung it open. The only time Hannah got any fresh air was when she opened the window to smoke out of it, hoping her parents wouldn't smell anything. Val waded back to the door and took one last look. Amongst the mess were the archaeological traces of what had once been a child's room – there was still a faded horse poster above the bed, Roald Dahl books on the shelves and Mandy the Moose on the duvet. A room belonging to a girl who had gone forever. She had been replaced by this big mutinous creature. Hannah was so large. So were her friends. Great mutants, they strode around in their boots. They moved through the house like a herd of buffalo, treating her and her husband with amiable contempt, knocking things over, grazing every-thing down to the bone and leaving all the surfaces sticky.

Val carried out the bowls and went into the children's bathroom. It smelt like a marsh. The blind was down; the room in its usual twilit state. A collection of Body Shop bottles sat around the bath, their tops off. One of them had fallen over and spilt green mucus down the side of the bath. Val yanked up the blind. She picked up sodden magazines and rammed them into the bin. Why couldn't teenagers just hibernate for five years and wake up human beings? She looked at Hannah's jumbled tubes of acne lotion and make-up, at a slimy, squeezed sachet of some free sample pulled out of Val's copy of *Options*. Why couldn't they be sent away to a special teenage place, a sort of corral, and be returned as adults who put the tops on toothpaste tubes and who didn't walk backwards out of the room when you were trying to talk to them? Who didn't gaze at you as if you were a mental retard and say 'What's your problem?'

Val went back to her study. She closed the door behind her, closed it all away. How tidy it was in here! Fabric samples were laid in a row on the table. They were damasks, in various shades of plum and ochre. She had a big job on, the complete redecoration of the Yewtree Country Hotel, Stow-on-the-Wold. Public spaces, bed-rooms, two dining rooms which she was planning to decorate on a Moorish and a Provençal theme. She had laid out the floor plans – empty stages where lives would be played out, where things could happen for which she had no responsibility. In her imagination she walked into this hotel and lost herself. She could feel the cool, marble fireplaces, the carpets underfoot. No clutter, no mess. No fluster and quarrels and perennial, grinding guilt. Nobody here was going to leave a trail of damp towels along the floor. Nobody inhabited it except herself, in her head; how airily exhilarating work was! How simple its problems, where everything could be measured with the press of a button. She sat down at her computer and pressed *Enter*.

When she looked at her watch it was six forty-five. Outside it had started to rain, a tattoo on the leathery leaves of the rhododendron bush below her window. Down in the garden a blackbird sang; its notes sounded rinsed, as if they had been squeezed clean. From downstairs came a burst of canned laughter; Becky was watching one of her *Mr Bean* videos.

Val got up and stretched. She went out on to the landing. Outside the gravel scrunched; a car drew up. For a moment she thought it might be Hannah; several of her friends could drive now, they gave each other lifts home in their parents' cars. But then she heard the swelling sound of the radio. The door slammed. It was Morris, back from golf.

Downstairs, voices murmured. Morris was talking to Becky. He would be saying 'Can't you think of anything else to do?' but in an indulgent tone. He adored his younger daughter, his Golden Girl; he had always favoured her. Becky was so lively and pretty; she knew how to charm her father, she could get away with anything. If it were Hannah sitting there his voice would be sharper. He was finding Hannah deeply irritating nowadays – her mulishness, her mutinousness. Her clumsiness. Never a man for pretence, his disappointment at his unruly lump of a daughter was obvious to anyone and that of course only made Hannah worse. Sometimes Val felt like a public relations officer, telling each of them nice things about the other and repeating to Morris something clever Hannah had said. It made her feel false and edgy, trying to pull the family together like this. Trying to make Morris love the three children equally instead of picking on Hannah, the plain one sandwiched between her more attractive brother and sister. And Hannah hadn't tidied her room – oh Lord, was the door open? Would Morris glimpse inside? *And* she hadn't started her Renaissance essay. Where the hell was she?

It was seven forty-five. Morris was in the living room, talking on the phone to Malcolm. Malcolm was his sales manager. You would think they could save it until tomorrow, when they were back in the office. Morris turned to face her; she heard the words 'rest assured'.

For a moment she thought: How nice – Morris understands my anxiety. Then she realised that he wasn't talking to her. He was discussing Rest Assured. It was a rival security firm, a multinational, that had been nibbling at Price Security for months. '. . . so Tim suggests we call a meeting?' Morris was saying. '. . . so what do we tell the shareholders? . . .'

Val mouthed at him. He put his hand over the receiver.

'Don't talk too long,' she said. 'She might be trying to get through.'

'Who?'

'Hannah. She might be stuck somewhere and want us to pick her up.'

She went into the kitchen. Why were adolescents so self-absorbed? Didn't they realise that she needed to cook the supper – indeed, it would be nice to have some help cooking the supper – because she had to go upstairs afterwards and finish the eight sheets of proposals she had to fax off tomorrow? The rain drummed on the conservatory roof. Val pulled open the freezer. She pulled out some packets. Years ago, when the children were small, she used to cook – she was good at it, she was good at most things once she put her mind to it. Now she didn't have time. She gazed gratefully at the packets. They weren't Salmon en Croute. Each was a frozen block of recovered time; a frosty rectangle of compressed freedom.

The front door slammed; she swung round. Fury rose in her – hot fury and hotter relief. 'Hannah!'

The door opened. It wasn't Hannah; it was Theo. Her son ambled into the kitchen. 'Hi, Ma.' He popped a cherry tomato into his mouth.

'You haven't seen Hannah?'

'Why on earth should I see Hannah?'

Her own voice had startled her – high and sharp. Theo hadn't noticed but then he never noticed anything about his family. Like his father, he had tunnel vision. He was obsessed with his Lightworks and everything around it was a vague blur. He had just moved into the flat they had bought him, in Clerkenwell; there, he sat all day hunched over his beloved editing machine. It had only been delivered the week before; it was the envy of his fellow students at the film school. He had the glassy, inward look of a young man in love.

She gazed at her son with abstracted pride. With his black, gelled-back hair and his father's sensual lips he looked like the leader of some Jewish–Sicilian extortion racket. He opened the fridge and inspected its contents. His face wore its fridge look – a mixture of disapproval and greed. His view of his parents as materialistic seemed to coexist quite happily with his acceptance of a £30,000 Lightworks as a twenty-first present. His contempt for their lifestyle seemed also to necessitate frequent trips home to ransack the fridge and stuff the washing machine with his clothes. He never took stuff out of his pockets so then the dryer broke and she had to call in the Hotpoint man, at vast expense, and wait in all morning till he arrived and witheringly pulled out, from the filter, strings of pulped petrol receipts and ticket stubs from the National Film Theatre.

'What time does Camden Market close?' she asked.

'Dunno. Who's eaten all the houmous and put the bloody pot back into the fridge?'

'I'd better phone her friends.'

'Why?' Becky had come into the kitchen, pink from her bath. Her fluffy blonde hair stuck out around her face. 'When's supper?'

'Hannah's not here yet,' said Val. Anxiety thrummed in her, a vibrato. 'She must have gone to Emma's. Or whatsername's.'

'Tanya's.'

'She could've *phoned*.'

'Maybe she's been kidnapped!' said Becky.

Theo snorted. He threw the houmous pot into the bin. 'How much will we have to pay them to keep her?'

A woman answered. Oh God, what was the name of Emma's mother?

'Er, is Emma there? It's Valerie here, Hannah's mother.'

Emma came on the line. 'No, I haven't seen her since school on Friday.'

'Who else should I try?'

'Try Tanya.'

Tanya was out, at her Dad's. Tanya's mother said: 'Don't they drive you round the bend? Tanya stayed out *all night* last Saturday and I was worried to death. It turned out they'd gone to Tamsin's house and then to Phillip's and she *said* she'd fallen asleep there, ho hum . . .' Her voice rose in a shrill litany of complaints. 'Went to the pub and then on to this party and she didn't have a twenty p piece to phone home, honestly . . .'

'They're so selfish,' Val agreed with this unknown woman. 'Only a phone call, why can't they lift the phone? Is it radioactive? If they knew how we worried . . . wait till *they're* parents . . .' Her voice rose, peevishly. She felt angry with herself, for griping at her daughter. She felt angry with her daughter.

She phoned Rachel's house. Rachel's father didn't know if Rachel had been to Camden Lock or not. He didn't know who Hannah was. Maybe he didn't know who his own daughter was. Fathers never knew anything. He said the whole family was out. His voice had the trapped sound of a man who was holding the fort, a fort whose internal workings were entirely beyond him. Ridiculous, thought Val, when he probably ran a multinational conglomerate. He sounded as if he were longing to get back to the TV.

Val looked at the table leg. It was plastered with Air Mail stickers. Whilst engaged in her interminable phone calls to her friends, Hannah always fiddled with things – doodling, shredding. Didn't she realise somebody had to pick the bloody stickers off? And what happened when someone had to send a letter abroad? Didn't it cross her mind?

Becky told her about somebody called Coarser. It sounded like that until Becky fetched Hannah's address book. It was full of names she didn't recognise. Coarser was actually Kauser. Probably that Indian girl whose father owned half Knightsbridge and who had her own mobile phone. Kauser's number was engaged.

Theo came into the living room: 'Don't worry, Ma. You never worried about me.'

'You were male. Are male.'

'She's probably at a pub or something.'

The news was on. '. . . *body of a seventeen-year-old girl which was found in an alley behind Wood Green Underground Station. She was wearing pink leggings and a blue anorak . . . Police say there is a strong similarity with the murder of thirteen-year-old Marie Pritchett, whose partly-clothed body was found last Thursday in wasteground near Epping High Street . . .*'

Val stared at the TV. Her husband was reading the Business section of the *Sunday Telegraph*. He looked up. 'I can smell burning,' he said.

Val went into the kitchen. She pulled the smoking, blistered pastry out of the oven. The smoke alarm weee'd.

Becky came in. 'You can scrape it off.'

'Can you think of anyone else?'

'Lots of them have got boyfriends but not on Sunday night. She's probably just forgotten.'

'What? To come home? Even *Hannah's* not that forgetful.'

Becky shrugged. Then she went into the conservatory and laid out the place mats. It was raining hard now, drumming on the roof. Becky fetched the cutlery, walking to and fro under the tattooing glass. Her sudden helpfulness alarmed Val – silly, but it did. Becky never helped if she could help it. She must be feeling worried too.

The phone rang. Val grabbed it. Her fingers were wet from washing lettuce.

'Hello,' said a girl's voice. 'Is Hannah there?'

'No. Who's that?'

'It's Ellie. Can you tell her to bring in my *Mansfield Park* notes tomorrow?'

'I'll tell her. So you haven't seen her?'

She hadn't. 'You could try Coriander.'

Confused, Val gazed at the lettuce. Was this some kind of cooking tip?

'Coriander – you know, Corry. They do Media Club together. I'll give you her number.'

Val hadn't heard of most of these girls. The whole process resembled some alarming game of Old Macdonald Had a Farm.

The unknown Corry had a comforting, mumsy voice. 'Don't worry, Mrs Price. She's such a scatterbrain. She missed Clas-Civ last week because she thought she had a Free.'

'What's Clas-Civ?'

'Classical Civilisation. She's probably met up with

some boys from King Alfred's. They're always hanging around Camden.'

Val felt dependent on Corry's reassuring voice. 'Probably.'

'Or there's been a security alert on the tube.'

Val agreed. She sighed, that her daughter's friends took security alerts, took strangers' willingness to murder them, as a matter of course.

Murder.

She scraped the tops off the pastry; charred flakes drifted on to the table. Theo came in, carrying a bag of clothes. 'I'm off.'

'Don't go!'

He stared at her. 'Chill, Ma.'

'Please stay with us. Stay for dinner.'

They would sit down and eat supper. They would impose normality, and normality might understand and bring Hannah home as usual. She ripped open a packet of watercress and dropped the leaves into the salad bowl. Everything was still all right.

The phone rang.

It was Corry. 'She's probably gone to Farida's house to copy out her notes. They do History of Art together.'

Val put the phone back. Just for a moment she felt closer to the unknown Corry, a girl she had never heard mentioned before, than to anyone else in the house. Corry understood. She would make a tactful and understanding woman.

Would Hannah become a woman?

Val's stomach lurched. She ran into the hallway lavatory, slammed the door shut and emptied her bowels.

What a melodramatic thing to think! What had got into her? She went upstairs. It was getting dark. She didn't dare look at her watch. She went into Hannah's bedroom. She waded through the clothes and closed the curtains –

curtains she had only recently opened. She switched on the bedside lamp.

She walked downstairs. The treads felt dizzyingly deeper, the stairs wider. She stepped into air, and recovered her balance. Outside, in the dusk, the blackbird still sang. *There*, it knew everything was going to be OK. Life was going on; Hannah was going on – just somewhere else, at present. She would be home soon.

In the kitchen Morris – yes, Morris – was making the salad. He couldn't make a dressing; he was pouring on the bottle of Italian vinaigrette nobody liked. But he was making an effort. Was this because he was worried sick and trying to help, or just impatient to eat? Morris worried about his blood sugar and always liked to eat on time. He said it was because he was Jewish. Their first date, twenty-five years ago, had been a trip to the cinema. When they came out they had paused in the foyer and spoken simultaneously. 'Shall we have a drink?' she had asked. 'I've booked us a table,' he had said.

Tonight he simply looked impatient. She watched him carrying the bowl to the table. How many streets were there in London, how many thousands of them? How many patches of wasteland, now darkening in the dusk?

Don't panic. If she behaved normally she might reassure herself. Theo went out into the hall. She heard the lavatory door close. Was there a smell in there, from when she had been? Now wasn't that normal, to worry about such a thing? Didn't that show that everything was OK?

Becky had laid the table for five. Mismatched cutlery, but never mind. Theo rejoined them and they sat down. They sat alert – they all did. They sat, their ears cocked like animals. Alert for the phone to ring, the door to slam.

I'm home! Breathless, drenched. Apologetic or indignant. *The bloody tube . . . bloody bus . . .* The what? Val had run out of reasons. What else could hold someone up and delay them this long? It was ten o'clock. Morris got up to fetch the wine. On the way back he paused, put his free arm around Val's shoulder and squeezed it. He did it in a wooden, theatrical way that made her jump. She didn't like it; she wanted them to act like they always did.

She turned to her son. 'How's *Digit-All* coming along?' Theo was editing a student film featuring fingers. You didn't have to pay Equity rates to fingers; you could use your own. He had told her about it last week, at uncharacteristic length and with an enthusiasm she hadn't seen since he was a child. Last week seemed echoingly far away now, in another life.

Fingers. Fingers are capable of anything.

Theo was talking. He seemed to say it was going OK. He looked at his plate. 'What's happened to the pastry?'

The phone rang. Becky leaped up; she was the first. Her chair toppled over and clattered on to the floor. They froze, silenced, and listened to her voice in the living room.

'Er, she's just having supper. I know it's late but – well, we're funny like that. Can she call you back?'

Becky came in. 'It was Thérèse. She wanted to know if you'd got the message from Stow-on-the-Something. Something about electricians. I said you were having supper.'

Suddenly, Becky seemed so adult – her tact and excuses. The last few hours had matured her. Val looked at her cooling food. *Stow-on-the-Wold . . . electricians . . .* how tinny and irrelevant they all sounded now.

Morris cleared his throat. His plate was clean. He had eaten everything, but then he always did. Sometimes this annoyed her, that he could wolf it down without tasting it, but tonight she was grateful. He cleared his throat. He pressed together his small, surprisingly female hands. He said: 'Perhaps we should phone the police.'

They didn't. Not for a while. They sat at the table. In front of them were various plastic pots – chocolate mousse, apricot fool. Sunday night bits and pieces from the fridge. Becky scraped out hers and took her mother's. Theo lit a cigarette and his father cleared his throat again. 'Let's have one of those,' he said. He hadn't smoked for five years; not since Stanley, their dog, had been run over.

Ten forty-five. It had been dark now for some time.

'Maybe we should phone round the hospitals,' said Val. 'Maybe she never got to Camden Lock – she had an accident.'

'They'd ring us.'

'Has she got any identification?' Hannah was so vague. She was always losing her purse.

'She's probably got her ID card,' said Becky. 'Her forged one.'

'Forged?'

'Saying she's eighteen. To get into clubs. Everybody's got one.'

Val glanced at her husband. Here was something else they didn't know about their daughter; they were finding out a lot tonight.

Theo blew out a plume of smoke. 'She's probably gone to the movies.'

'Without telling us?'

'She tried to phone but it was engaged,' he said. 'One of you was nattering on. And she'd met a friend and the film was just starting . . .' His voice petered out, either from exasperation with his sister or because he knew it didn't sound convincing.

'But it's school tomorrow.'

Morris stubbed out his cigarette. 'I'll phone the police,' he said.

Nobody spoke. Val's heart thumped against her ribs. To phone the police made it official; it made it so concrete and terrifying that her throat closed up. The word *police* made real all the scenarios that up until now they could pretend they weren't picturing. They would finally step over the border and leave normal families behind. Once he picked up the phone they would be caught up in the momentum of the official machinery and there would be no turning back.

Morris got to his feet. They kept their eyes on the tablecloth. They heard him go into the lounge and pick up the phone.

They were silent. Beyond the garden, lights shone in the dark. Out there, the neighbours were watching TV and running baths. Val felt her home detach itself from them; it loosed its moorings and drifted away from them, into the unknown.

'Colour of eyes?'

'Brown.'

'Colour of hair?'

'Dark brown.'

'With blacker bits,' added Becky. 'She dyed it but it was growing out.'

'*Is!*' snapped Val. *Is* growing out. She glanced at Becky. Her daughter's eyes were bright; she sat on the sofa, her knees pressed together. Now the policeman was here she had lost her tact and regressed again, back into childhood. After all, she was only eleven.

The policeman wrote it down in his notebook. Static crackled from his chest. He was a young man, made solemn by his uniform. His shoulders were damp from the rain. He was too young for the sights he must see. Through all this, a part of Val was trying to work out who he resembled – some TV actor. Then she realised it was just because it all seemed so unreal; they were acting a scene she had seen so often on television.

'What was your daughter wearing?'

Val looked at her husband. 'Do you know?'

Morris shook his head. 'I was out playing golf,' he told

27

the policeman, as if that absolved him of any responsibility.

Val thought: if I hadn't been working I would have seen her leave. Even then, would I have remembered? She blushed. What a neglectful mother she must seem, not even to have said goodbye to her own daughter. Not to know what she was wearing, not to know she had gone to Camden Lock. Not to know the names of most of her friends, who shuffled into the house, used the phone and shuffled out again.

'She's probably wearing black,' she said. 'Practically all her clothes are black.'

'And DMs,' said Becky. 'With love-beads on the laces.'

'They all wear those awful boots, don't they?' said Val, trying to sound conversational. Nobody replied.

'Does she have a boyfriend?' the policeman asked.

Val shook her head.

'You sure about that? It could be somebody she didn't want you to know about.'

'I'd know,' said Becky. 'I hear her on the phone. She snogged with Graham Lucas at Emma's party but she's still a virgin.'

Morris cleared his throat. 'Thank you, Rebecca.'

The policeman wrote something down in his notebook. Then he looked up. 'Was she having any problems at home?'

'Problems?' asked Morris.

'Rows?'

'They're always rowing,' said Becky.

'We're not!' said Val. 'Only the usual rows. Her room. Smoking. The usual things. We all get on very well.' How trite that sounded, as if she only met her children at cocktail parties. She couldn't find the right tone for this policeman simply because it was all so unlikely. On TV she would know his name and rank, people always did. Chief Constable Pettigrew or something. Somehow they always knew, on TV. 'She hasn't run away, if that's what you mean.'

'So you last saw her when? At lunch?'

Val shook her head. 'Morris was playing golf. I had to rush down to the shop – I have a shop near Baker Street – to collect something –'

'Mum doesn't believe in Sunday lunch,' said Becky.

Val glared at her. 'We don't really have it – we used to, but, well ... then Hannah became a vegetarian and wouldn't eat roasts ... and nobody was here at the same time ... there's always stuff in the fridge.' She looked at Morris and Theo. Why didn't they rescue her? She sounded such a hopeless mother. Nobody *wanted* Sunday lunch.

Morris stood in front of the fireplace. He was still wearing his Fair Isle golfing sweater. It looked inappropriate now. It seemed weeks ago that he was playing golf. She looked at his thinning hair, his tight little belly. He was shorter than she was but he was trying to look in command, the head of the household. 'So what happens now?' he asked.

'We'll put out a call to all our stations,' said the policeman. 'As you know, there's been no reports from any hospital. I don't suggest we take it any further tonight. You wouldn't believe how often this happens, with juveniles her age. It's highly likely she's just met up with some friends, you know what young people are. The last thing they think about is their parents. I will of course pass on this information to our central index, but I expect she's simply out clubbing.'

'On Sunday night?' asked Morris.

'There's that stand-up comedy place,' said Becky. 'She always wanted to go there.'

'Maybe we should wait another hour or so.' Val gazed at the policeman, willing him to agree with her. She felt ambivalent about him – his shockingly uniformed pres- ence was a confirmation that this was now a state of emergency; stepping through the door, he had changed the nature of their anxiety and there was no turning back. Yet this same young man was now the very person to whom the whole family clung – like a doctor when one was taken ill, this professional was suddenly essential to them. She urged him to say *I'm sure she's fine*. He didn't. She would, if she were him.

'I'm sure she's fine,' said Morris.

On the video, the clock glowed. 11.25 blinked to 11.26. Each pulse added another minute to whatever Hannah was enduring. Each minute – how long they seemed! – added to their fears. Maybe to Hannah's own anxiety about them. It added to the images that rose up in Val's head, like muck stirred from the bottom of a pond. She mustn't think about that. Why hadn't she phoned? Where could she be? Didn't she understand what they were feeling? What was worse – that Hannah was alone, or that she was not alone?

The policeman got to his feet. Val didn't seem able to move. Morris saw him to the door. Val thought: if I hadn't been working I would have helped her with her home- work. If I hadn't been working she would never have gone to Camden Lock. She would be here now.

And I, her mother, didn't even know when she left or what clothes she was wearing.

She said loudly: 'They're not brown.'

'Pardon?' The policeman stopped at the door.

'Her eyes.' It seemed so plain – brown hair, brown eyes. So unloving and so unobservant. Val said to him: 'They're not exactly brown. They're hazel.'

At midnight Morris and Theo drove into London, just to drive around the streets of Camden, just to do something.

They needed to be men, on the move. Val put Becky to bed.

'School tomorrow,' she said.

'I'm not going to school.'

'Of course you are!'

'Don't shout,' said Becky.

I'm not shouting, I'm trying to be normal. She knelt on one knee and kissed Becky's forehead, awkwardly. She couldn't get the angle right. 'She's bound to be back by then.'

A grey antler nestled against Becky. It was Hannah's moose. Becky had always wanted her elder sister's moose. Had she taken it to bed because she thought Hannah wasn't coming back, so now she could keep it for herself? Or was it that she needed something of Hannah's for comfort? Val didn't have the energy to find an answer.

She sat in the living room and looked at the phone, willing it to ring. Though it was June, the night was chilly. She had lit the fire. Wherever she was, Hannah would be cold; she never wore enough clothes anyway, none of her friends did. Val sat there, the *Sunday Telegraph* magazine on her knee, willing herself to cry. She had always found it difficult; she wasn't a crying person. But she didn't want to break down when the men were here; that would alarm them. Since the policeman had left they had closed ranks. At the same time she suspected that each of them, like herself, felt utterly alone. What went on in their heads was too terrible to share.

She lifted up the receiver, checked there was a dialling tone, and put it down again. She had done that about six times this evening. When she moved her arms she smelt a sharp, glandular scent coming off her body – an animal scent. Fear. Her body felt strung tight, wires within her pulling tight, yet she felt stupid with exhaustion.

AIR MAIL AIR MAIL AIR MAIL – the stickers were stuck in a jaunty row down the table leg. Val looked away.

She gazed at the living room. How cosy it looked, how safe. Gas flames flickering in the fireplace, flickering on the silver frames of the family photos. Peach curtains drawn closed against the treacherous night. Matching terracotta sofas; big Heals lamps. On the floor were scattered the videotapes Becky had been watching. Val was normally a tidy person – obsessively, according to her children – but she couldn't rouse herself to put them away. Over on the desk were the piles of correspondence which until earlier this evening had seemed so urgent – some mix-up over Morris's American Express bill, litigation about a parking ticket, documents about the trip to Florida they had won in the raffle. The letters belonged to those other people now; people who wore the same clothes she and Morris were wearing but who were no longer recognisable.

She got to her feet. It was half past twelve. She went into the hall and opened the front door. Maybe if she looked up the road, just casually, she could summon her daughter out of the ether. The rain had stopped. Next door's syringa perfumed the air. She propped the door open with the mat, so she could hear the phone, and crossed the gravel. Two porch lights still shone – the Maliks, who left theirs on all night, and the new people. The other houses were dark. Cypress Drive slumbered, unawares.

Just then she noticed a piece of paper, pinned to the tree outside her house. She stared at it for a moment. It glimmered in the light from the street lamp.

It was a message – a message from Hannah. How long had it been there – all evening? She had pinned it up, waiting for them to come out of the house.

Val stepped on to the pavement. 'LOST. FEMALE GINGER CAT KNOWN AS 'ELSIE'. REWARD FOR HER RETURN.'

Theo went back to his flat; there was nothing else he could do. Besides, though he and Hannah didn't get on that well, it seemed a good idea for him to be there in case she turned up. That was what he said, anyway; Val suspected he simply wanted to get away. He left with a muttered 'Don't worry'. Suddenly, young people seemed inadequate. She didn't have the energy to worry about how he felt. She had to concentrate, without distractions, on getting through each minute. She had felt like this in childbirth.

She and Morris went to bed. They lay like stone effigies, side by side, each pretending to be asleep. She couldn't remember putting on her nightshirt but she seemed to be wearing it. She longed to talk to him but she never found it easy, to talk about her feelings. Morris was the emotional one, the sentimental one. She wondered if he had cried; he had spent a long time in the bathroom. She wanted to comfort him but she knew the words would sound as hollow to him as they would to her. Though they were bound to each other – they were *parents*, nobody else knew how they felt – she realised that in twenty-four years of marriage they had never been through anything as frightening as this. Turbulence in that plane to New York; Theo's suspected fractured skull when he was ten – mere nothings, in retrospect. But look! They had all come out alive.

Morris was a hypochrondriac. He had a large collection of pills – for his stomach, for his insomnia. He had urged her to take some Nitrazepan but she wanted to keep her wits about her. He took two, and after a while his breathing coarsened. She thought: I shall go to sleep, wake up and find it was all a nightmare. I'll go along the landing and Hannah will be asleep in her chaotic room, her chin Tipp-Exed with spot cream. I'll shout at her *Get up*! *It's time for school*! She will moan and turn over, her back to me, cassettes sliding off her bed.

Val must have slept because now she was naked, all except for a pair of gold knickers. She put her hand inside

33

them and pulled out a key. She walked across a huge, windy room to an aeroplane and tried the key in the lock but it was too big, it wouldn't fit in. Hannah said quite distinctly: *Sorry Mum, I'm Air Mail.* Val rattled the key in the lock.

Somebody was rattling the front door. Val leapt out of bed and ran downstairs. She crossed the hall and flung open the front door. The wind blew into her face; she staggered. Outside, refuse sacks sat slumped around the dustbins. One of the sacks had split open; tins rolled across the street. Val shut the door and went upstairs.

Hannah's door was closed.

It was then that Val knew it was a dream. The whole evening hadn't happened; Hannah had simply gone to bed.

She turned the door knob. As she did so, she closed her eyes. She willed Hannah to speak in there. *What're you doing, Mum?* She pushed the door open. She inhaled Hannah. When she opened her eyes, Hannah would be sitting up in bed. *Listen to the wind!*

The bedroom was empty. The wind blew the curtains, they billowed back and forth. The wind must have slammed the door shut.

She closed the window, went downstairs and made herself a mug of tea. She heaped in sugar – she never had sugar. She sat in the living room, frail as an invalid, sipping it. Her left knee jerked up and down; it had a life of its own. She was freezing, but then Hannah must be freezing too.

Morris came downstairs and wrapped her dressing gown around her shoulders. They sat there.

He said: 'So many things, I've been thinking.'

'What things?'

'You remember Exmoor?' he asked. 'The rain?'

She nodded.

'Our honeymoon, and you were wading through the

34

mud, your cheeks red, whistling. You big strong English *shiksa.*'

'I remember carrying you over a stream,' she said. 'You didn't want to get your feet wet.'

'I asked you, *is there nothing you fear?*'

'You asked me that?'

'You said: *The only thing I'm afraid of, is to bring children into the world.*'

They sat there in silence. The room lightened. She opened the curtains and turned off the lights. It was a pearly, misty morning. The weather had changed; it would be sunny later. They heard the rumble of the refuse lorry approaching, the banging of dustbins, the shouts of the men. She went to the lavatory again; her bowels had turned to liquid. Morris made some more tea. His face looked naked and rubbery without his glasses, his lips thicker.

He rubbed his sore eyes. 'Remember when Theo got lost?'

She nodded. 'In Selfridges.' When Theo was little she had sometimes forgotten she had him. Anyone could have spirited him away. She hadn't started work then; she had been with her son all day. Still it seemed that somebody had parked Theo with her and would come to collect him later. It was a miracle that nothing more terrible had happened to him.

They sat, side by side. She looked at Morris's blue-veined ankles above his slippers. Old man's veins, though he was only fifty-five. How frail a human body is, the blood so near the surface.

'Maybe she *has* run away,' he said. 'I never know what she's thinking.'

She thought: there are so many conversations we should have had. This last year, all I've done is shout at her about her room. If I had known this would happen I would have talked to her about all the things that really

35

matter, and I would have listened to her answers. I would have told her how she is dearer to me than life itself . . . People think these thoughts when somebody has died.

Morris said: 'There's something I've never asked you. All the things we've talked about, we've never talked about this.'

'About what?'

'You believe in prayer?'

She didn't reply.

He said: 'We've shared a bed for twenty-four years and still I don't know.'

She felt her cheeks heating up. How ridiculous, to be embarrassed at a time like this. 'Do you?' she asked.

His parents had been devout – kosher kitchen, the works. They were a dignified, devoted couple, struggling to make ends meet in a small flat in Stamford Hill. At the time they had been horrified at his decision to marry her – this tall, bossy, middle-class English *shiksa*. Morris, however, had disobeyed them. His courage had impressed her. In comparison, her own rebellion had been a petty sort of affair – dropping out, going to art school, the sort of thing everyone did then. His was far more profound. Over the years his parents had thawed, and when they died they had seemed to be reconciled to her and the children she had borne their son. Still she had never known how much Morris had retained of his beliefs. How much more sustaining was his faith than hers?

He said: 'I pray. You know how I feel about it? I feel, it's like leaving a message on an answerphone, just in case there's anybody at home.'

'Hedging your bets.' Her face couldn't smile, but she shifted nearer him. 'Same here. Pathetic, isn't it?'

He nodded.

They heard footsteps upstairs, the flush of the lavatory. Becky came down into the living room.

'Is she back?'

Two rag dolls, limp in their night clothes, they shook their heads.

For other people, Monday morning began. Out in the street car doors slammed and engines started up. Val and Morris remained static, frozen in time. Val took Becky to school; Becky rushed into the building breathlessly, full of pent-up news. Morris phoned his office saying he would be late. Val phoned her shop. They didn't say why, they didn't want to say the words out loud and make it public. They put it off. Sympathy, alarm, suggestions – just yet they were too frail to bear all that. With nobody knowing they could almost pretend it wasn't happening.

She went into Hannah's room, switched off the lamp and opened the curtains. She went into Becky's room and straightened the duvet. She left Mandy the Moose on the bed. To be at home on a Monday morning added to the unreality. She walked slowly from room to room. Her bones felt brittle. She didn't have the energy to pick up things from the floor.

The phone rang. It was Theo, asking if there was any news. No friends would phone, thank goodness; they would presume nobody would be at home. While Morris was in the bathroom the phone rang again. Val picked it up. It was Morris's assistant Avril, asking his advice about some company cars that were being delivered.

A moment later Malcolm rang. He was Morris's sales manager and oldest colleague. In his breezy voice he gave her some unintelligible message about a shipment that hadn't arrived. Morris's firm installed and maintained security equipment – alarms, sensors, state-of-the-art systems. He had built it up from scratch and now it was flourishing. *Know why?* he had said. *Because it's a dangerous world out there.* He was obsessed with burglars; downstairs they had bars on their windows. She thought: we try to seal ourselves off from the chaos out there. We lock our houses, we set our alarms. We punch in codes on our computer panels connected to the police. We think we can make ourselves safe.

Morris emerged from the bathroom. Letters lay scattered on the doormat; neither of them had the energy to pick them up. She carried in some coffee to Morris who stood, gazing at their diary. *Fetch dry cleaning. Servowarm service. M.O.T.* Thérèse, at the shop, would be phoning about Stow, about the upholsterers, about the Kensington Gardens site. Rhoda the home help would be arriving at two unless she was stopped. Events were silting up around them, but they had hardly managed to brush their teeth.

Morris said: 'What are we supposed to do? What can we do?'

'I'll hold the fort. Go to work, check everything's OK. It's no use us both being here.'

He asked if she would be all right. His face had a numb look, like a heifer trapped in a lorry and taken to some nameless destination. He took off his glasses and rubbed his eyes. She felt deeply bound to him, yet miles apart. When he left, it was a relief to be alone.

She felt a curious lassitude. Whatever was happening to Hannah, she had lived through a night of it. She had lived through half the following morning. She was alive, Val felt sure of that. If – well, *something* had happened to her, Val would have felt it. She might not be a natural, motherly-type mother, but she *was* a mother. Surely she would have felt it – something in the air would have ceased.

She stood at the window, looking into the garden. The lawn was brushed with silvery stripes, like Regency wallpaper; Morris had mowed it on Saturday. They were both keen gardeners, preferring to do it themselves rather than hire somebody to do it for them; their children sneered at their neatness. 'All you do is cut and prune and bloody burn,' said Hannah. 'When you put in a plant you can hardly wait for it to flower so you can pull it out again.'

Val looked at the swing, at the bushes stirring in the breeze. The silver birch swayed to and fro, waving to her as if it were trying to draw her attention to something behind her. Hannah had hidden in the shrubbery. 'Come and find me!' she had sing-songed those afternoons when Val had not been here to call her in for tea. She had been working in other places, creating other people's homes. But still her children had grown up; this house had given them a childhood. Hannah couldn't slip from it that easily; it would pull her back.

Inert, Val sat on the arm of the sofa. She didn't know what to do. She felt like a sponge – soggy, heavy with dumb weight. She gazed at the carpet. Hannah said it reminded her of raspberry mousse. Had Hannah eaten anything? Was she in a state to eat? On the floor lay the *Daily Mail*. On the front page was a photo of the murdered schoolgirl, smiling. Val turned the paper face down.

She looked across at the family photos. The most recent one, just framed, was the print from the local paper. It had been taken last month, when they had won the raffle. The five of them stood in front of the house. Val's eyes were shut; at that precise moment she had blinked. She remembered the sensation she had felt, that her children were already disappearing before the photo was taken. She remembered the far-off jangling of the burglar alarm. She suddenly thought: we'll never go to Florida. It had seemed unlikely enough at the time. She looked at her closed eyes and felt Hannah vanishing from beside her.

Next to it was a school portrait of Hannah. It had been taken three years ago – her hair neat, her ears as yet unmutilated by rings. Her lips were parted, as if she were about to speak; braces glinted in her teeth – Hannah before she entered the dark valley of adolescence. The moment they had framed it the photo had the poignancy of loss, of the fleeting moment passed. A click of the shutter and that child was both held and gone for ever. They used computers now to age-up missing people: a gap-toothed girl became a middle-aged matron. Electronically she grew up to be a woman, even if she had been dead for twenty years.

Val went into the bathroom and vomited into the lavatory. When she came out the phone rang.

She rushed into the living room and picked up the receiver.

'Hallo?'

Silence. Down the line she could hear somebody breathing.

'Hallo? Who is that?'

The line went dead. She went into Hannah's room and lay down on the bed. Her heart thumped. Who had phoned? Was it Hannah, trying to get through? Finding she hadn't got the right money or it was one of those Mercury phones and she couldn't find the right button to press. One sort, you had to press a button inside the receiver. Even Val – efficient Val – had not managed to find it.

If it was Hannah she would try again. She could reverse the charges. But Hannah was so dozy; she had probably not thought of that. Val stopped; it made her feel queasy, to criticise her daughter now. She thought of the rows they had had, particularly over the last couple of years. She wondered if Morris was thinking the same, chastising himself for the times he had shouted at Hannah – little things, often, like not screwing the top back on a Perrier bottle so the water went flat. Hannah's face closing; the slam of her bedroom door. Val hoped he wasn't remembering these moments. Morris wasn't by and large a reflective man. She prayed he wasn't being so now.

Time passed. In her study next door she heard the bleep

and hum of the fax machine; that would be the stuff from the Kensington Gardens architects. She lay there, willing the front door to open. *Mum, I went to this all-night rave and I fell asleep and suddenly it was morning so I went straight to school.* Or: *Hi Mum, sorry and all that, me and these people have been stuck in a lift all night and the engineer's only just got us out.*

The phone rang. Val leapt up and rushed out to the landing.

'Hallo?'

'Hallo, is Hannah Price there?' A woman; Australian accent.

'Who wants to speak to her?' Val barked. 'Who is that?'

'White Cross Dental Centre here. She has an appointment at five-thirty today, for a check-up.'

'Oh.' Val felt the sweat trickling down her armpits.

'We have a little problem here. The dentist is off sick. Could we fix another appointment for the end of the week?' The rustle of paper. 'Say, five o'clock Friday?'

'Friday's fine.' Val paused. 'Did you phone earlier?'

'Earlier? No.'

Val replaced the receiver. She sat down on the landing carpet. She looked at the phone – squat, beige – the centre of her universe. Her saviour, her enemy, her lifeline. What could she do – phone the police again? But they would ring if there was any news. She didn't want to use the phone; she didn't want to block the line for an instant. Who had phoned? The police had said something about getting a photo, maybe issuing a press release. But not yet. They said this happened all the time – teenage daughters disappearing and then coming home.

Marie Pritchett, the girl in the newspaper – she didn't come home.

Val climbed to her feet. She looked at Hannah's door. The *Stop Animal Testing* poster had come unstuck. One

41

corner of it lolled over; soon the whole thing would fall off.

She walked into her study. She would read the fax, phone Thérèse at the shop and tell her honestly what had happened. She couldn't do any work. Thérèse must phone around and make some excuse.

Val went over to the fax and tore off the sheet. She looked at it for a moment, puzzled. It wasn't from the architects. It was scrawled, capital letters. For a mad moment she thought Becky had sent her a message from her school.

DO NOT GO TO THE POLICE. £500,000 BY FRIDAY AND YOU GET HER BACK. ELSE ITS CURTAINS. REPEAT: DO NOT GO TO THE POLICE. WATCH THIS SPACE. BYEEE!!!

4

When Morris got back Val was sitting beside the phone. His tall, glamorous wife had shrunk. She looked faded, like a bleached photograph of herself. He sat beside her and put his arm around her shoulder. She was rigid.

'It's not some sort of joke?' he asked. 'A sick joke?' Just for a moment he had thought that Hannah had sent it – some bizarre urge to shock them.

She passed him the fax. It shook in her hands. He flattened it out on the coffee table. His hands looked waxy, as if they belonged to somebody else.

ELSE ITS CURTAINS.

'She's not hurt,' said Val in a monotone. 'He wouldn't hurt her.' It was as if she had been sitting there chanting it to herself, sitting beside the phone for hours. 'Did you ever think of this?'

He paused. 'Maybe. Not really ... Maybe, but not in these words.' He wasn't making sense. He meant: now it has happened it seems even less believable. The word *kidnap* had hovered on the edge of his consciousness but it was too unlikely to swim into focus. Kidnaps happened in books. Was this how it was done – capital letters on a floppy piece of fax paper?

'He wouldn't hurt her,' she repeated.

'Of course not. It may be more than one person. That'd be better, wouldn't it?' One man alone with Hannah – anything was better than that. 'They just want money.'

'Do you think it's terrorists or something? The IRA?'

43

'They'd say so, wouldn't they? Besides, what have we done?'

'Who are they, to do this? Why should they choose *us*? Why did they choose *her*?'

Morris shook his head. Was it a random choice, as random as the raffle they had won? As simple as that? Put your hand in and pluck out a girl. Their girl. What made their daughter so chillingly special?

'You've seen anyone watching the house?' He felt ridiculous, like somebody in a spy thriller. 'Watching our movements?'

She shook her head. 'But then I'm not here during the day.'

Why choose them? There was no sense in it. The Greens, at number twenty-two, they were a lot wealthier – ostentatiously so. Socking great house, two BMWs parked outside. They had a daughter Hannah's age. Then there were those Lebanese on the corner. And the Schoenbaums. The Barlowes – indoor swimming pool, the lot. What weakness, within his own family, had allowed this to happen? Some canker, hidden until now, that had been eating away within his household? What had they done wrong, to set in train such an action as this?

Val sat next to him, her head bent. She hadn't brushed her hair. She was pulling at her fringe. She pulled it rhythmically, like a monkey in a cage. He thought: we are as imprisoned as our daughter. What on earth are we going to do?

'What are we going to do?' Val raised her head. Bare of make-up, her face had aged. He looked at the fax again. The top was printed: *RKL Copy Shop. Tottenham.* Maybe he could go there and ask them who had sent a fax this morning.

'What are we going to tell them?' she asked.

'The copy shop?'

'The police.'

'Ah. The police.' His brain felt dissolved into liquid. He knew he ought to be decisive, that Val was expecting him to take command. His wife was the one who usually ran things – the household, the family. But he was the man. Trouble was, he felt as if all the bones had been pulled out of his body.

The front door slammed. They froze. Footsteps tapped across the hall, then a voice spoke to the cat.

It was Rhoda, the home help. They heard the rustle of carrier bags and her footsteps entering the kitchen. Val glanced at the clock. A tiny part of his brain knew what she was thinking: it was two fifteen and Rhoda was supposed to arrive at two. Usually they weren't here, to know whether she arrived on time or not. It reassured him, to realise he could think of something so petty. Val glanced at him, either because she was thinking the same thing or because she, too, had thought for a moment that it was their daughter coming home.

'Don't tell!' she hissed.

Rhoda came in and looked at them. 'I saw the cars,' she said. 'What's up?'

'Nothing!' said Morris loudly. He hadn't seen Rhoda for years; their relationship was conducted with banknotes left in the kitchen. She had dyed her hair a shade of plum; she looked, if anything, younger than he remembered. Rhoda was a plucky woman who had raised her son alone. Morris ought to know the son's name; he must be grown up now. He must keep his wits about him.

She was inspecting them, her head on one side. 'You look awful.'

'You want the truth?' said Morris. 'Val and me, we have a bug. Maybe we ate something, who knows?'

Rhoda asked if there was anything she could do and they shook their heads. Soon they heard the drone of the Hoover, upstairs. Judging by the sound she was cleaning Hannah's room. It was ludicrous, that she could shunt the

45

Hoover to and fro, presuming life was the same as before. Ludicrous but comforting too. Maybe if Rhoda was Hoovering, Hannah was eating, normal daily things were happening to her.

He knew he should say something but suddenly he was struck with guilt. Whoever they were, these unknown people, they knew that he had favoured his other children; they sensed that Hannah was held to him by a flimsier bond. They had sensed she had been less cherished by him, less listened-to. Less forgiven. They had sensed it on some radar and pin-pointed her: his big, mutinous daughter who wore those boots that made him rage – not because he didn't love her (oh, if only he could tell her now!), but because every father wants his daughter to make the best of herself and fulfil the hopes invested in her.

Val's head was bent; she seemed to be staring at her Japanese slippers. She hadn't really got dressed. He gazed at her heavy, blonde hair. Out in the street a car alarm wailed; out in that world, would you believe, people worried that their stereos might get stolen.

'Morris. We can't just sit here.'

Morris thought: in a moment the doorbell will ring. Hannah will be standing there, one eyebrow raised. *'Just testing.' 'Testing what?'* asked Morris, pulling her indoors. *'Like, how much you love me. Like, how much I'm worth.'* Morris shut the door behind her. *'Don't say like. You know it drives me mad.'* She took off her coat, or whatever she was wearing. *'What price Hannah Price?'* she said and burst into giggles – those gurgling giggles he only heard nowadays when she was on the phone to her friends.

The doorbell rang. For a moment they didn't move. Then Val hurried out. Too late. Rhoda, wide-eyed, ushered in the policeman from last night. Today he had taken off his jacket; it was hot.

'Just dropped in,' he said. 'Heard any news?'

'We have, actually,' said Val, hurrying over to pick up the fax.

Morris blocked her. He put his hands on her shoulders and sat her down in the armchair. He stood in front of the coffee table.

'We have.' He cleared his throat. 'So what does the silly girl do? She stays the night with her friend. Whatshername. Me, I never know their names.' He laughed. Val was staring at him; he could see her out of the corner of his eye. He looked at the police officer, man-to-man. What the hell was his name? He hadn't caught it. He knew the Chief Inspector down at the station – Jack Palmer – he knew him through work; besides, they met at Rotary Club functions. He wondered if Jack had been told about this.

Val was still staring at him. 'So we were wrong, so you were right,' he said. 'Kids these days, what do we do with them? Do they think about their parents?' He was babbling. 'We sit here worrying, we're going grey with worry – look at my wife! Only just now, we've heard.'

'So she's gone to school?'

He nodded vigorously. 'And when she gets home, she'll get what for! Oh yes, she'll get a piece of my mind and no mistake!' The strange words emerged from his mouth, he had never used them before. He felt like an actor, speaking from a script.

Val's mouth hung open. The glass edge of the table dug into Morris's thighs as he pressed against it, blocking a view of the fax. It had curled into a cylinder, anyway. This large young man, Morris willed him to retreat. Val was mouthing at him but he took no notice and in a moment the policeman, whatever his name was, in a moment he was saying: 'Glad that's turned out all right then. She's been a thoughtless girl. You tell her to phone next time.' He went to the door and turned. 'It's a wicked old world out there.'

Morris nodded and closed the front door behind him.

47

He went back into the lounge. Val was saying to Rhoda: 'Isn't it time you got Becky from school?' Rhoda looked at her watch, grabbed her bag and hurried out. The door slammed.

'*Morris*.' Val exhaled his name. She stared at him. 'Why did you do that?'

'You think we can involve the police? This person, we have to do what he says. You understand?'

'But the police can help us? They're on our side! They can – oh, trace calls. Analyse handwriting. Stuff they do in thrillers. We can't *lie* to the *police*. Don't you see, that makes us criminals too.'

'Criminals? You think we're criminals? We're parents. It's Hannah we have to think of –'

'I am thinking of Hannah. We need all the help we can get. They'll find out we've lied to them –'

'They'll find out nothing,' he said. 'Sweetheart – the police's job, it's to catch them. The risk – to them it doesn't matter. They spring a trap, it goes wrong, it's bungled – they do that and what do you think'll happen to Hannah? Think!' He paused. 'Don't think.'

'We can't get the money together. We don't have it. He hasn't told us where to go or what to do. It may all be a big bluff. We don't have the money!'

'It's only money.'

She stared at him. 'Morris. This isn't like you.'

'Well, this isn't like us. Is it. Is any of it?'

He stood, looking out of the window. Out in the street, outside the Malik's house, a man was loading sacks into a van marked *Roger and Heather's Gardening Services.* Roger and Heather, they sounded so cosy but you could trust nobody now. Twigs stuck out of the sacks, like limbs. The man shoved them into the van, pushing them in, and threw in a spade and fork. Had *he* been watching their house? Overnight the world had been transformed into a place charged with malevolence. Under the cypress tree, opposite, a John Lewis van slid to a halt. A man climbed out and stood in the street. He scratched his crotch. Morris suddenly thought: we let Rhoda go alone to fetch Becky from school? One of us, we should have driven her. Anything can happen.

Val stood beside him. She too gazed at the blameless, sunny street – their street, familiar for fifteen years. His wife, did she find it unrecognisable now? He could smell her sweat; it alarmed him, that she hadn't washed. He thought: animals, that's what we are, underneath. We think we can fool ourselves. He looked at the security bars on the window, concertina'd open. Tonight he would close them and turn the lock; he would tell himself that he could keep out the evil that existed in the very bushes, in every leaf. PRICE SECURITY: on their burglar alarm his own name guarded his own home. And he had failed. He had failed Hannah, as a father, and he would be punished for it.

He said: 'We're on our own now.'

Morris went into his study and shut the door. The room smelt of Pledge; Rhoda had already cleaned it, he would be undisturbed. He sat at his desk and pulled out a sheet of paper. He took out a ruler and drew lines down the page. Just for a moment this simple act reassured him – clean paper, black lines. For a moment chaos could be reduced to simple figures – add, subtract, tot it up. He closed his eyes and pictured the John Lewis van: its back doors slid open and Hannah was delivered back to them, like furniture.

He wrote, at the top of the sheet of paper – ASSETS.

An hour later he crossed the hall. Val was moving around the kitchen like a sleepwalker, opening the fridge, closing it again. Maybe she was thinking of shopping lists but she had a blind look and moved slowly. It was so odd, for them to be here at this time of day, as if there was a serious illness in the house. Their lives had stopped, whilst outside the world went about its business. Rhoda was Hoovering upstairs. In the lounge the TV was on; he heard the theme tune of *Neighbours*.

'Have you told Becky?' he asked.

She shook her head. The phone rang. They jumped. It was a call for Val, from the shop. It rang again. Malcolm wanted to check through some items.

'. . . upgrading their CCTVs, sixteen retail outlets . . .' he said, '. . . surveillance at the Aylesbury Industrial Park . . . submit a tender for the sports complex, remember?' He rattled on, something about contracts for the dog handlers. Malcolm was his closest colleague. It seemed surreal, that he didn't know what was happening, but then this sort of thing didn't happen to them, did it? Malcolm was a breezy, balding man with strapping sons. He ran his local youth club; he played football. To Morris's knowledge, no chasms had ever opened up in his life.

Avril, Morris's assistant, phoned. She had been with him for years. She was more intuitive than Malcolm; she guessed something was wrong.

'Is it your stomach again, love?' She liked fussing over him. 'You sound ever so peaky.'

'I'm fine,' he said.

Val said she ought to fax the fabric suppliers, she ought to do about a hundred things, but she looked too numb to move – his dynamic, capable wife! Her blankness filled him with panic. Their friend Ruthie Silverman called Val 'Superwoman' – '*House, job, kids, the energy*! *You should bottle it.*' Where was Superwoman now, when he needed her?

Val sat slumped, gazing at the phone. 'Did you check the fax machine?' she asked. 'It hasn't run out of paper?'

'I've checked.'

He thought: our world, it has shrunk to a fax machine and a telephone. It's possible I'll go to a shop to buy fax paper for my daughter's kidnapper to communicate with us. The world, maybe it's always been insane and I have only just realised.

He said: 'Valerie my dear, we have to talk figures.'

That night they told the children, swearing them to secrecy. Morris hadn't wanted Becky to know the truth, she was such a blabbermouth, but Val had insisted. It was painful to watch his younger daughter struggling with her excitement, trying not to let it show.

'How awful,' she said, her eyes gleaming. 'Can't I even tell Jude?'

'No!'

Her mouth pursed, self-righteously. 'They should've kidnapped me, I haven't got any exams.' She paused. 'Still, it's not her real A levels. That's next year. Can't I tell Jude if she promises not to tell?'

'No!'

Theo reacted differently. After the shock he seemed annoyed, as if the exasperating Hannah had somehow willed this to happen. He seemed upset more on his family's behalf than hers. As they picked at some dinner – microwaved moussaka from the freezer – Morris wondered how well his family was going to cope with this, who was going to crack, who would show grace under pressure. At this point he couldn't guess, and this made him feel lonely. But then he himself didn't know how he was going to cope, he see-sawed so wildly one minute to the next, and this filled him with panic.

'I don't see how you can possibly raise that sort of money,' said Theo, 'it'd clean you out.'

'Isn't she worth it?' snapped Val.

'Will I have to go to a comprehensive?' asked Becky, who was due to move up to Hannah's school in the autumn term.

'Is nobody thinking what's happening to *her*?' Val

51

wrenched open the dishwasher and started shoving in the dinner plates.

'It's because it seems so totally unreal,' said Theo. To everyone's surprise, he got up and helped. 'It seems like a Hitchcock movie.'

'It seems like an adventure story,' said Becky. 'In this book I read they locked this girl in a cellar and tied her up –'

'Shut up!' Val's voice was shrill.

There was a silence, broken only by the snap of the flap as the cat came in, the only unconcerned member of the household. They sat there, each with their separate thoughts.

After a while Becky said: 'She's going to be in such a state. She hasn't got her spot stuff with her.'

At this, Val burst into tears. So did Becky, noisily. Theo bent down, hiding his face, and stroked the cat. Morris got up, to comfort them, when the phone rang.

They froze. For some reason – nobody knew, later – they all knew that this was it. Morris darted into the lounge and picked up the receiver. He heard the faint hum of traffic.

'You got the fax?' It was a woman's voice.

'Where are you? What have you done with her?'

'She's fine,' said the voice. It was flat, whiney. Essex Marshes. He came from Hackney; he could tell. 'You told the police, then?'

'No.' His heart was thumping in his ears; he heard the faint sound of a shop alarm. It must be a call box. 'How do we know you've got her?'

'You'll know, tomorrow. Have you, like, made arrangements? You know, about the money?'

'I haven't had bloody time!' He heard the click of the extension.

'What's that?' said the voice sharply.

Someone must have gone upstairs, to listen. He felt the

hot breath of Val behind him as she crammed her head against the receiver. 'Tomorrow I'm going to my bank manager.'

'You'd fucking better.'

Val nudged him away and grabbed the receiver. 'I want to talk to her! I want to know she's all right!'

The line went dead. Val put down the receiver. Morris looked at the two faces close to his. Becky's breath smelt of fruitgums.

'So it's a woman,' said Morris.

There was pause. Theo came downstairs, from where he had been listening. A woman – nobody had thought of that. Surely a woman wouldn't harm a girl? Surely not?

Val kept her jewellery box beneath her underwear. When Morris went upstairs she sat slumped on the floor. She must have been sorting through her jewellery, to see what was of value. Now she was reading the old newspaper that lined the drawer.

> . . . *mother of hit-and-run victim Alice Felham, 12, described how only hours before her daughter's accident they played happily in the snow in Victoria Park. Mrs Felham said 'I taught her how to make snow angels by lying down in the snow and moving her arms up and down like wings. When you get up it leaves an impression of an angel in the snow.' She described how she revisited the park today and could still see the imprints left by her daughter. 'You could still see the outline of her snow angel.'*

Val leant her head against the chest of drawers.

The next morning Morris went down to look at the mail. A letter lay on the mat, addressed to Hannah Price. He tore it open. Inside was a ticket for The Nipple Factory, playing at the Underworld Club. Part of his brain still functioned –

he noticed, from the counterfoil, that Hannah had used her mother's Visa card number.

He sifted rapidly through the rest of the letters. The bottom one was addressed 'MR AND MRS PRICE'. He took it into the kitchen and opened the envelope. Something fell on to the floor; it pinged. He took out a sheet of lined paper, scrawled with capital letters.

FRIDAY NOON. USED BANKNOTES. NO TRICKS. WE'LL BE IN TOUCH. BYEEEE.

He stood still for a moment, holding the paper between his finger and thumb as if it were contaminated. Then he bent down and picked up the small, bright object that lay on the floor.

It took a moment, before he realised. It was Hannah's nose-stud.

5

'Can you run that past me again?' asked Dennis. He looked at Morris over his glasses.

Morris told him again. He passed him the piece of paper.

'This is all very sudden, my dear,' said Dennis. They were old friends; they had been at school together in Stamford Hill, they had sat together in synagogue. Lying to an old friend was hard because they were connected to your parents, to your childhood, where to lie meant to be punished.

'This isn't like you,' said Dennis, 'not like you at all.' He gazed at the paper. There was a long pause. He wrote something down in his crabbed handwriting that had never changed. Val said he was anally-retentive. Morris had always felt sorry for Dennis, that he had knuckled down and gone into banking, that he had a clinically depressed wife. Now, however, sitting in his panelled room, he felt dwindled and cowed. It was Dennis, now, who had all the power in his hand. If he had only known.

'You're seriously suggesting we lend you this amount, against the security of your house?'

Morris nodded. He had a stomach ache, from nerves – from fear. He took out a Rennies and chewed it.

'We're talking considerable telephone numbers here,' said Dennis.

'I need to buy stock. Now. Pronto. You must understand, an order of that size –'

'You have documentation?'

'There's the problem,' said Morris. 'It's – well, hush-hush. Let's just say, a Middle-Eastern government is involved. Me, I don't mind telling, but other people are involved.'

'You didn't anticipate this? To be frank, Morris my friend, it's your methods I'm surprised by. You think they inspire confidence?'

'You know these people. They want everything yesterday. We don't deliver? There's plenty of others who will.'

'But the risk – such a risk.'

'Come on, Dennis.' Morris's mouth felt gluey; he swallowed the grainy peppermint. 'You know our turnover.'

Dennis nodded. 'And what does that tell us about the world we live in? You look in the papers, what do you see?'

They sat in silence for a moment. Morris's head raced with the questions he couldn't ask Dennis – how, even if he got the money, could he take it all out in cash? How was he going to physically extract, in time, the sort of figures they were talking about?

'It's make or break, Dennis.'

'I'll have to talk to head office. They'll no doubt have some questions. You know I'm putting my job on the line here. What about the house valuation?'

'Dennis, it's urgently I need it. I'm talking by the end of the week. You don't trust me?'

Dennis shrugged, raised his hands and put on his Fagin voice. 'Who can you trust, my dear?'

It was worse that day, much worse. It was as if Hannah had died. She was silenced and their one-way messages to her, in their heads, hung around undispersed.

The phone rang. It was Emma, from school. 'Is Hannah all right?'

Val said: 'Sorry you can't talk to her. She's asleep. It's probably 'flu.'

Putting down the phone, she felt sick. To lie about Hannah seemed to betray her all over again; it removed her even further, and made her even more impossible to reach. She must, must pull herself together and make up a story. Oh, but the energy!

The phone rang for her, countless times. The contractor on the Islington site needed new specifications, something to do with the direction of the joists. What joists? The upholsterers hadn't delivered something or other. The noises down the phone were like mosquitoes, buzzing and needling her. But she had to answer the phone. She sat for long periods gazing at it – in this room it was a sleek black Telecom Triumph, she knew every detail. Never since she had been young and in love had she gazed at a phone like this. How fierce, now, was this intimacy! Fiercer than all the passions of her past. For the voice she most longed to hear was that of a total stranger. Her enemy; her intimate.

Morris was at the bank. She couldn't leave the house; she was trapped, too. She looked at the nose-stud, lying in the ashtray. She had never seen it close before, with its butterfly stopper. She thought how one random act by someone she had never seen, who until Sunday hadn't existed for her, someone who could be one of the millions she had passed in the street – how this one person had entered into the heart of her family and taken them all hostage. She sat there. Fear had scoured out her insides. Oh, she knew what it was like to be frightened, but she had never felt this. She had never, truly, felt fear.

The table-leg had been rubbed down; Rhoda must have done it. The AIR MAIL stickers had gone. Just traces of white remained.

In a nightmare you are underwater, trying to run. You

push against the water blindly, but how slowly and heavily your legs move! In fact, they don't move at all. You know you must get there, fast; you know if you don't get there something terrible will happen. But it is happening already. And time is so short, and the water so heavy! Heavier and heavier . . . slower and slower . . . how long have you got? Just three days . . .

Morris went back to the bank, later that day. He made some more phonecalls; he set up an appointment with the manager of his business branch, in Watford. He could believe in his lie now. In fact, he felt like a criminal himself. His car collected parking tickets – he, Morris, who was usually so careful. The sheer amount of the money he sought made him reckless – in fact, for a short while he felt quite airy. Go for broke; make or break. He slammed shut the car door and turned up the radio. Music blared out. He thought: my life, I'm dismantling it piece by piece. Outside it seemed to be sunny. People seemed to be sitting in cafés, eating lunch. Women pushed pushchairs. He had lost all sense of time and yet the hours held him in their grip. They unravelled beneath him like a conveyor belt upon which he kept losing his balance.

Years ago Val had looked up from a book she was reading. She had read a lot when he first knew her. She said: 'The only thing that excuses God is that he doesn't exist.'

It had taken him a moment to work it out. 'You believe that?'

'I don't know,' she had replied.

'But you said it.'

She pointed to her book. 'Stendhal did.'

He drove to Watford; he had the meeting at his bank. Afterwards he did something he never usually did; he stopped at a pub and ordered a double Scotch. He got into the car and drove home, past peaceful houses basking in the sun. He suddenly thought: what if it's a hoax? A mad, macabre hoax to punish me for losing my faith, for not suffering as my relatives suffered? This story didn't start this week; it started at the beginning of the century in Lithuania, it started with my grandparents. I'm being punished because I survived but my uncle and aunt didn't. How could I think I would get away with it this easily?

He shook his head, trying to clear it. He must be cracking up. How could he link the Nazis with a twangy Essex voice? He switched on the radio '... body of a twelve-year-old girl ...' He switched it off. He drove towards Stanmore. He negotiated the roundabout ... change down to second ... drive down Ridgeway Avenue ... past the Silvermans' house, notice the scaffolding, they're having it redecorated, notice normal things ...

Fury welled up in him – a pure wave of hatred. That woman, how could she steal his daughter and steal his hard-earned money; how could she inflict such violence? For twenty-four years he had worked day and night to build up a future for his children; she really thought she could grab it all, just like that? She really thought she could get away with it?

He arrived home. His head throbbed. He walked through the door. He opened his mouth to say: *I've changed my mind. We're going to call the police.* Just then the phone rang.

Val darted out from the kitchen as he lifted the receiver. It was the voice.

'You got it yet?'

'Friday, it's impossible,' he said. 'The bank, how can they lend me the full valuation of the house? You know what this means? There's other avenues I have to explore.' This disclosure, to a complete stranger, of his financial resources felt oddly conversational. 'I'll have to open several bank accounts, maybe you don't appreciate that –'

'*How is she*?' hissed Val.

'– five working days they need, to clear the deposits, and then there's the problem arranging for the actual cash –'

'Tough titties. I'll give you till Saturday.' The line went dead.

The next morning an envelope arrived. With it lay three gold earrings – a hoop, a teddy bear and a crescent moon. They belonged to Hannah, of course, but he had never got close enough to his daughter to see them before. Detached from her, the three objects lay in his palm like clues to a fairy story whose end was shrouded in darkness. There was a note.

Please! They say if you don't pay them by Sat, they'll send you the rings from my other ear, but this time they won't take them out first. Please please PLEASE!

It was Hannah's handwriting.

When had she been pulled down, like Persephone, into the darkness? At what moment had her daughter been snatched from her own humdrum Sunday and plunged into another dimension – an underworld so unknowable and unthinkable? Val surely should have felt it – a breeze blowing her papers, a blip on her computer. A stutter in her car engine when she drove home from the shop. If *she* didn't feel it, couldn't dumb machinery?

'Like Persephone,' she must have said, aloud. Because Morris said: 'What? Who?', startled either because he had never been taught about Persephone – he had left school at sixteen – or because his wife had dragged him from that terrifying place they both visited, separately, and couldn't bring themselves to describe to each other. Their own private Underworld.

He knew what he had to do. He drove the six miles out

into Hertfordshire and parked in his usual space. A lifetime ago he had parked there every day. How petty were the worries that had filled his head! He looked up at the building: PRICE SECURITY SYSTEMS. He hadn't looked at it properly for years. Grimy bricks; barred windows. It was an ugly building but he loved it. Only now did he realise the extent of his attachment; in his mind he ran his finger over the brickwork as he might stroke the face of a woman to whom he must say goodbye.

He walked across the car park and into the reception area. Irene, a cigarette between her lips, was rearranging the brochures. He looked at them. SECURITY . . . When he was a boy he repeated one word over and over until it became gibberish. SECURITY . . . SECURITY . . .

He greeted Irene; he walked along the corridor and into his office. Through the glass partition he saw Avril – kind, motherly Avril, with her brassy hair and tortoiseshell glasses. She had worked with him for twenty years; in some ways she knew him better than his own wife did.

Avril opened the connecting door. She wore her emerald green jacket with the teddy-bear brooch pinned to the lapel. She stopped dead. 'You look terrible,' she said. 'Want a cup of tea?'

'Malcolm, is he around?'

She nodded.

'Could you ask him to step in here, love?'

Val put her arms around her husband. They clung together in the bathroom; they rocked together. Steam from her bath rose around them. Around them their world was dissolving away.

'I love you for this,' she said. 'You're a mensch.' She hardly ever used Yiddish words. She pulled away and looked down at him. She stroked his balding head. 'Did I tell you I love you?'

She hadn't told him this for, oh, years. There never

seemed time. And now time was running out – now she took him in her arms and gazed at him the way she used to, long ago.

'We'll manage,' she said. 'We were poor once, remember? In the seventies.' She kissed his forehead. '*All you need is love*. All you *needed* was love. We were happy then . . . we'll be like we used to be . . .'

Standing on the bathroom carpet they rocked together wordlessly. Outside, in the dark, the wind flapped the message on the tree. Way beyond the streets, way beyond Stanmore, the lost cat mewled. And somewhere, out there in the night, their daughter might be sleeping. Waiting to be awakened by the kiss of their money.

Money, what is money? One shrugs – money is as abstract as ether. It is the wind in your hair; it is dream upon dream, multiplied. It is pleasure, plucked from the air with a snap of the fingers – Waiter! Taxi! Yes, now! NOW. It is *why not*? It is *what the hell*? It is knowing that beyond your reach is reachable, beyond your grasp is graspable. It is possibilities, for anything is possible. It is a scrawled signature on a banker's draft. It is nothing . . . it is everything . . . it is what you make it . . .

Ah, but it is *heavy*! It filled his briefcase, weighing it down. It filled two plastic carrier bags. He walked to his car, weighed like a housewife with the price of his daughter. Back home he dumped the bags in his study. Val came in and closed the door behind her. The house was silent; they had given Rhoda the day off. It was Friday afternoon.

They gazed at the bags. Val knelt down and tweaked one open, her little finger raised fastidiously. The fifty-pound notes were tied together with paper bands. A thrill passed through her – an oddly sexual thrill. The notes looked as phoney as B-movie booty. It still seemed unreal; she willed herself to feel the notes' significance, to own this moment. She couldn't place it in her life. Kneeling here, doing this – it was unrecognisable. Maybe this was because so far they hadn't had to sell anything solid, anything painful – her jewellery, one of the cars, Becky's computer that she had offered in a sudden act of generosity. And yet, as the minutes ticked past, their ticking time bomb, Val had the sensation that the walls around her grew flimsier and these carrier bags gained in bulk. They sat there like a cancerous growth in a body that was starting to die.

Val and Morris waited in the quiet house; they awaited their instructions. She didn't voice her doubts to him; she wanted him to protect her. She didn't say: even if this nightmare ends, our troubles are just beginning.

6

Theo stayed the night with them, that Friday. They slept fitfully, like troops before the battle of Agincourt. Hannah seemed to be walking from bed to bed, weightlessly, urging courage upon them. They could feel her breath on their cheeks. She seemed, that night, both more tangible and more impossibly unreachable; she blurred and re-formed like a mirage.

The day dawned pearly-moist; steam rose off the lawn. It was going to be hot. Val made a pot of tea. She stirred spoonfuls of sugar into her mug. Until this week she had never taken sugar; now her metabolism had altered. She ate little, food made her nauseous, and drank the strong sweet tea they gave you in hospital when a relative had been injured. She sat at the kitchen table, waiting. She heard the flap of the letterbox and the pattering of letters like falling leaves. She went to pick them up; there was nothing there.

Upstairs, feet padded across the landing; the lavatory flushed. Outside in the street a summer Saturday was beginning. She heard the three chirrups of a remote-control car lock; Lynda next door was going to Sainsbury's. Normally she herself would be doing the same thing. Get there before the crowds; get things done. Bustle through the day blindly, blind to the earth opening beneath your feet, the hand reaching out to grab you by the ankle. Down, down . . . the ground could slide open anytime, anywhere, and nobody realised. Wasn't that extraordinary?

Nine o'clock passed . . . ten o'clock. They moved about the house restlessly, incapable of sitting still, yet incapable of doing anything that had any future to it. Val pulled the dead leaves off the fern. Nobody used the phone, as it would block the line. Letter, fax, phone? Her house felt like a flimsy fabric possessed only of orifices – dangerous orifices through which might pour, at any moment, their orders to step out of their lives and into unimaginable action.

Looking back, later, Val remembered that morning as the most frozen time of their bizarre week. Despite the lawnmower puttering next door – it was an old petrol one which periodically died, as if struck by thought – despite this it seemed as if the whole of London had been stilled. Surely everyone else was waiting too? Surely they could feel the space that had been Hannah in their midst – a girl-shaped hole in their world. Val sat on Hannah's bed, wondering if it were possible that her daughter might return. The room had been tidied; it seemed that Hannah had been swept away too – vacuumed up, never to reappear. She lit a joss-stick, as if she were in church, lighting a candle for her daughter. She blew out the flame and watched the smoke buckle. She closed her eyes tight: *if you come back, if the miracle happens and we exchange you for a bundle of used paper – if you do, I will always be able to describe what you are wearing. Why? Because from that moment onwards I shall never let you out of my sight.*

The phone was ringing. She jumped up. Theo had got there first. He put down the receiver.

'It was her. She says, are you ready? She says a fax is coming.'

The four of them stood, watching the fax. Humming casually, it slowly excreted the paper.

At first they thought it was a joke. It looked like a Treasure Island map, with X marks the spot. It was painstakingly drawn – a map of a park, with bushes and

65

paths. The bushes even had little leaves. It had been sent from a Xerox Copy Bureau in the Holloway Road. Underneath the map were written instructions to YOU, MRS PRICE! GO ALONE. I MEAN *ALONE*!!!

It was eleven thirty by the time Val was driving along Hendon Way. She slowed down at the traffic lights. Heat beat down on the roof; even with the windows open, it was stifling. Beside her, on the passenger seat, sat the two large plastic bags into which they had repacked the money. Their handles were tied together with string. How domestic they looked – just like Saturday shopping. One bag bulged with the weight of their house; the other with the bulk of Morris's business. She still couldn't believe what he had done; she couldn't take it in. He had sold his shares in his own company to make up the money; he had negotiated some vast, complicated loan to cover the sum until the money came through, something like that. She hadn't understood the details; at the time she had been struggling not to cry. For he had made this sacrifice with no hesitation and had told her about it with a breezy good-humour. 'It's only money.' Morris, who made a fuss when the girls left the lights on!

The traffic shunted forward. Val drove the six miles into London. She felt calm, almost fatalistic. She didn't believe any of it. *Ransom. Hostage.* Nobody believed in that. Morris's flurry of money-gathering had been the only recognisable action in a week which had been so surreal she couldn't connect it to her brain; it lay apart from her, unabsorbed. It seemed a preposterous, unfunny joke; even the money seemed like pretend money. Morris had covered the contents of each bag with a tea towel, tucked in, so nobody could glimpse what lay inside. One tea towel showed Scenic Buildings of Wessex; the other was a prissy floral fabric she had never liked. Soon it might be used to wipe dry kidnappers' knives and forks, could that be possible? She stopped the car at the traffic lights. Suddenly she had an urge to lean out of the window and shout to the man in the Rover, next to her: 'Doing your Saturday errands? I'm off to buy back my daughter!'

She drove towards Camden Town. A police car passed her. She stiffened. What if someone were watching? What if a policeman happened to be in the park, nothing to do with her, just some unlucky coincidence? These people would suspect a trap. There were so many things that could go wrong. She mustn't think about them.

She stopped the car and opened the A–Z map. Her hands were shaking now; they were so sweaty they stuck to the paper. So much for her calmness. She wished Morris was doing this – a man's job. No – it was a mother's job. She said the word *errand* to herself; it made it sound more casual, more Saturdayish, more possible to carry through. She located the litter park and drove there, down the hill into Camden Town.

Litter clogged the gutters. A man weaved across the road, shouting at the traffic. She stopped the Renault and turned off the engine. Ahead, the street glinted with broken glass, spattered like vomit; somebody had been breaking into a row of cars. She looked through the fence. Already, in June, the grass looked bald and worn. The little park was crowded. Bodies lay sunbathing. Drunks sat in rows on the benches; like clockwork toys, they raised cans to their lips in unison. In a wire cage, kids kicked a football to and fro listlessly, as if they had been waiting for her to arrive.

Val got out of the car and locked the door. She walked through the gate. Litter, like shed blossoms, lay under the trees. Two black youths, sitting on a see-saw, rose and fell. Someone here might be watching her. Who? Were they lying half-naked on the grass; were they loitering behind a bush? Someone must be checking that she was alone.

She walked up the path, feeling horribly visible. Far

away, a police siren wailed. On the grass a woman, wearing a bikini, rolled on to her back and sat up. She looked at Val.

'Maxie!' she yelled. 'Maxie, get over here!'

A child shouted back. The sun went behind a cloud. The bushes rustled. Beyond, the see-saw creaked.

'Hey – you! You, miss!'

She swung round. A man sat on a bench. His face was brick-red.

'Hey – miss – spare us some change?'

She faltered. May as well give the banknotes to him; he was as likely as anyone else. She closed her eyes. Music began . . . He pulled off his rags and revealed himself as Hannah, laughing and for some reason a child again.

It was suddenly chilly. The park was stirring; people were restless. The bushes made a sound like soft little hands rubbing together. Across the grass the see-saw creaked, rhythmically. On a wall was scrawled FUCK THE BNP. Val walked towards the fountain, obeying orders like an automaton. If she paused to reflect, even to hesitate, someone would know. They might not be here, they might not see, but they would know.

It had once been a handsome drinking-fountain – carved stone, four taps and saucers – but it had long ago been abandoned. Its drinking parts were stuffed with rubbish. She paused and looked around. She had driven down here from her clean, prosperous home, driven down into this netherworld that had claimed her daughter – that had swallowed her up. She looked at the caged children, the wrecked adults, the silenced fountain. She walked round the fountain, to the far side. She could glimpse the packet, jutting out.

They were whispering, she could hear them. Or was it the bushes? She pulled out the squashed Benson and Hedges packet. She felt like a derelict herself, fumbling amongst the rubbish. She turned her back to the park and fished inside the packet. She pulled out a silver key. Surely she had dreamed this already?

It was a locker key – number thirteen. Maybe it was a joke. She pulled out a folded piece of paper, the next clue in this nightmarish treasure hunt. She read it.

Val fetched the carrier bags from the car. She walked down the road to the swimming baths. The Victorian building rose up, rust-red. LEAVE THE MONEY IN THE LOCKER. She paid and went inside. Chlorine stung her eyes; she heard echoing voices and the sound of splashing water. The place was crowded with bodies. In the changing room naked women rubbed themselves with towels and wrenched caps off their heads. Their breasts bobbed; their buttocks shuddered as they strode to the lockers. She glimpsed the surprise of pubic hair. The women were washed clean of their personalities; she would never recognise any of them in the street.

She paused for a moment, alert as a fox. Beyond, she heard the clang of metal doors, the swish of curtains in the rows of cubicles. Didn't that curtain twitch? Below it, feet were visible. If she turned away a head would rear up, over the top, watching her. The back of her neck prickled.

Feeling stagey, she inserted the key into locker thirteen. Her hand trembled; she fumbled it and tried again. The door opened. Within the locker lay a towel and a swimming costume. LEAVE THE MONEY, LEAVE THE KEY IN THE LOCK. GO IN THE POOL AND STAY THERE AT LEAST 15 MINUTES. OK???

She shoved the carrier bags into the locker; she had to push them in, they were so bulky. She locked it, leaving the key in the keyhole. She pulled off her clothes. There was no room to shove them into the locker too. How stupid. If the person was that stupid, could Val trust her?

Her nerve-ends were tuned to any signs of untrustworthiness or inefficiency – if this person could botch up one thing, they could botch up something else.

'Shane! Get your bloody arms up!'

Beyond, she heard the slap-slap of hurrying feet; the struggles with children. She pulled on the yellow costume. It was too small; it cut into her crotch. Was this *hers*? The woman's? How eerily intimate, for this garment to dig into her own flesh too! She wrapped her own belongings in the towel and carried it with her.

Curtains stirred as she passed them, they stirred as if she were breathing on them. Val didn't turn. She went through to the pool and slipped into the water. Swimming was one of the few pleasures she and Hannah shared. Hannah was a good swimmer; in the water she was transformed into a graceful creature that her mother couldn't recognise. The pool was boiling with bodies. Val swam between them, heading for the deep end. 15 MINUTES. She couldn't time herself because the clock had stopped at 4.43. Time had been stilled for them too, last Sunday. Val swum a lazy, dreamy breaststroke. Maybe the clock had stopped at the moment Hannah was snatched; nothing would surprise her, ever again.

She sank beneath the surface and watched the yellowish, disembodied legs of the other swimmers. Above, they were humans – shouting, splashing. Below they were mysterious creatures, disconnected to anything recognisable. Below, down here, anything could happen . . . She was in the deep end now. Despite herself, she felt lulled by the rocking water, water that was as warm as tears, warm as the womb . . . Hannah had lain within her, she had been safe then, she had lain there, locked into Val's womb, her future years crumpled inside her like tissue-paper petals squashed inside a bud.

Val climbed out of the pool and wrapped herself in the towel. She had no idea how long she had been in the water

– time, all week so urgently monitored, had ceased to matter. She walked into the changing room.

Nobody was there. It was as if the whole place had emptied for her. A bottle of Henara shampoo lay on the floor. Behind her, a shower hissed.

Val turned, and looked. Locker thirteen was empty. Its door hung open. On the floor was a trail of wet footprints.

Val walked out on weightless legs. The sunshine dazzled her. She wrapped the spent, damp costume in the towel and shoved them into a litter bin. Passing the park, it seemed as if the same kids were sitting on the see-saw. Up, down, they creaked. She watched one of them rise whilst the other fell. She thought: I walked in rich and I walked out poor. As I sank, someone rose.

They waited all evening. Nothing happened; the phone stayed dead. Saturday night, and over the gardens drifted the scent of charred meat. The new neighbours they hadn't met yet, two doors down, were having a party. A woman laughed shrilly. In their house, however, all was quiet. Throughout the rooms, digital clocks flipped the minutes past. It was as if the house had vanished around them; only the clocks glowed and pulsed, keeping vigil with them. The four of them sat, leafing sightlessly through colour supplements. At one point Val got up and made them hot chocolate, something they hadn't drunk for years.

At ten to one they heard a taxi. It muttered to a stop in the street. Becky got to the hallway first. She flung open the door. They crowded behind her, jostling her out of the way. Val, jammed against Theo's leather jacket, smelt his aftershave.

Out in the street a woman in a white dress approached the cab. Her high heels clattered across the road. She called over her shoulder. 'Byee! Sooper party!' She got into the taxi. 'Say good luck to Grizelda!' This must have been some sort of joke; she laughed the shrill laugh again. Then she slammed shut the door. The taxi drove away.

Val closed the front door and they moved back, bumping into each other. They stood in the hall.

'She wouldn't come by taxi,' said Morris. 'Would she?'

Nobody replied. How would Hannah come home – on foot? Dropped off by a car, which would then speed away into the night? Val couldn't picture her daughter's arrival. She was filled with panic. If she couldn't imagine it, if she couldn't urge it to happen, willing it with her body and soul – maybe it wouldn't happen at all. Were the others thinking this?

'Better go to bed,' she said to Becky.

Becky opened her mouth to protest.

'Let her stay up,' said Theo. 'It is Saturday night.'

How normal that sounded! Saturday night – parties, fun. Stay up late, sleep in the next morning. That was what other people did. It sounded bizarrely reassuring.

They stood there, gazing at the inside of the front door. She hadn't looked at this side of it for years. Near the bottom the paintwork was scratched; when the bell rang their dog, Stanley, used to hurl himself at the door. In his opinion, any visitor was an enemy to his family.

Then Becky spoke. Val willed her not to speak; she knew what she was going to say.

'What happens if they don't let her go?'

Part Two

Eva was a fighter. That was one of the things Jon loved about her. She said she had almost died, being born, but she had bawled and struggled her way back from oblivion. In the beginning, when he loved her so much he could hardly breathe, when his chest ached and his soul felt unravelled by her, in those early months the thought of her fierce little fists brought tears to his eyes.

She didn't know who her father was. Her *mother* didn't know who the father was. Her mother was a half-Polish, Catholic woman called Malgosia; Eva hadn't seen her for years. She had last been heard of living in Solihull with a black gas-fitter called Rodney. 'He can gas her too, as far as I'm concerned,' said Eva.

She had been brought up in a series of rooms around north London. She said she was always finding strange men in the bathroom. For a while she had lived next to Chapel Street Market where she had run wild, pilfering fruit with her quick fingers. The same fierce hands gripped him in bed, her long red fingernails scored down his back; she brought him to life after the long sleep of his youth.

Jon was besotted with her; there was no other word for it. His upbringing seemed so timid. Pinner, of all places. Like Eva he was an only child. In contrast to her rackapulty upbringing, however, the miseries in his family were secret ones. Even his father's drunkenness had been an almost wordless process. Trying to sound colourful, Jon had once bragged to a schoolfriend about his dad's binges. Even as he spoke, he realised the inappropriateness of this word to describe the sullen silence in which his father sat in front of the TV, the only movement his hand stretching to his glass of whisky. Adultery, too, seemed the wrong word to describe his father's unexplained absences and the tense misery when he returned. Eva's impoverishment was of the feckless, yelling kind; his of middle-class gentility. He once said to her: 'Know what? You're like the inner city and I'm like the suburbs.'

He had grown up wary and polite, alert to his mother's sighs and the click of her tongue as she swung away and busied herself with chores. He grew up sensitive to women; on their side. Perhaps this was what had attracted Eva in the first place. He wanted to please his mother with his good behaviour. The only bold thing he had done in his teenage years was to remove the 'H' from his name. Jon sounded more flamboyant.

When he was eighteen his mother died. Though grief-stricken, he had felt liberated. Up until then he had done what she wanted. Now he did what he himself yearned to do; he left school after his A levels and became a carpenter. He had a vision of honest toil; of earthy, William Morris simplicity.

For a while he was content. He travelled around London in his old Transit van, working on flat conversions for firms of builders. In recent years, however, the property market had stagnated and one by one the builders went bust. He carried on alone, fixing up people's kitchens and scraping a living until a year ago when his van had finally expired.

It was then that he met Eva. A banknote brought them together; this seemed appropriate, when he looked back on it. He had gone into the Spread Eagle, up in Islington, for a drink. He spotted her straight away – cropped blonde hair, freckly face. She lit up the corner of the room.

She radiated energy; he could feel it, yards away. She and another girl were bent over a piece of paper, giggling. He took his drink over and sat beside them; he just did, he felt that bold.

She held up the paper; it was a ten-pound note. 'Want to see the Queen do her party trick?' she asked him.

'I'll show you mine first,' he said. He took out another ten-pound note – he had just been paid. He folded the portrait of Charles Dickens and slotted it against the portrait of the Queen. 'See? It's John MacEnroe.'

She snorted and grabbed her own note. She folded it and slid the folded bits to and fro. He stared. The way it was folded, a penis slid into the Queen's mouth.

'That's brilliant!' he said. 'Here, let's have a go.'

He slid it backwards and forwards. The girls laughed. He asked them if he could get them a drink.

'I'll have a vodka and tonic,' said Eva, and turned to her friend. 'Haven't you got to get home?'

The girl got up and left.

'Let's get well and truly plastered,' said Eva, and proceeded to do so. He couldn't remember what they talked about. He was mesmerised by the way she poured dry-roasted peanuts into her hand. She tipped them into her mouth and then licked her palm slowly, like a cat. Her mouth was large and ripe. She wore a stretchy lace T-shirt; he could see her dark nipples beneath the pattern. His mother would have called her common but his mother was no longer here to tell him so. Besides, what had gentility ever brought his mother?

Eva went home with him that night. He lived in a flat above a butcher's shop in Tottenham; she clattered up the stairs in her high heels and before he had closed the door they were pulling off each other's clothes. The next week she moved in with him, arriving with her belongings packed into her rusty Toyota.

That was a year ago. He had lived a quiet life, him and

his mute lengths of wood. She descended on him like a hurricane. In those early months she still had a job. She worked in a beauty salon in St John's Wood. How he envied the bodies that lay beneath her nimble fingers! She came home smelling of perfume and nail varnish remover. She brought home copies of *Vogue* with labels on them saying 'Customers Use Only' and flung herself on the bed, leafing through the pages. He listened, fascinated, to the careless authority with which she spoke of Thalgo treatments and Glyderm facials; she opened up a world of female witchcraft. Sometimes he went to pick her up. Waiting in the foyer, with its plastic flowers and framed certificates, he glimpsed her flitting into a cubicle. In her nylon overalls and white clogs she seemed as mysterious as a priestess. But she said she hated it; she hated the customers, she hated the boring routine, she couldn't wait to get away. When she came home she hosed herself down in the bathroom, washing it away, and got dressed up to go out on the town.

She dazzled him with her boldness. She went out without wearing any knickers. She grabbed his hand and hauled him off on jaunts. 'Let's score some speed!' she urged him. 'Let's dress up as sisters!' Being trained in the beauty business she was a mistress of disguise – putting on a wig, painting her face. She answered something lawless in him, something that had lain dormant all his life. She took him into pubs where they played out elaborate scenarios: she was a starlet and he produced pornographic films; she was a transsexual and he was the doctor who had just performed the operation. Anything. Anything to stop being bored. Always she was restless, tapping her fingernails, jiggling, jumping up and dragging him off somewhere else. She loved shocking people; she loved causing a stir and being the centre of attention. 'Know what you are?' he said. 'A female flasher.'

To tell the truth, sometimes she embarrassed him. And

it made him uncomfortable, the way she flirted with other men to get a reaction from him. To be honest he preferred to stay in watching TV, with her entwined around him like an eel, fiddling with his hair. He wanted to keep her safe. He loved carving beautiful objects for her – a fish, a swan, a kitchen stool in the palest beechwood. But she called him a stick-in-the-mud and besides, she hated him using his electric sander because it filled the flat with sawdust. So he gave himself up to her willingly, because she enthralled him, because he was besotted.

And then, in March, she was sacked.

'That cow Adèle, she's told everybody I've been nicking from the till.' She flung herself into a chair. 'You know the real reason? Norman's got the hots for me.' Norman, Adèle's husband, managed the salon. 'He's always round the back, checking the stock, when I'm eating my lunch. Well, yesterday he tried to feel me up and I slapped his face.'

'Shall I go round and . . . I don't know, sort him out?'

She laughed. 'You?' she shook her head. 'Sod 'em. I hated it anyway. All those fat Jewish hags, treating me like shit. Think I'm going to fritter me life away pulling whiskers out of their chins? No way.'

Jon tried to be cheerful. He said it was only money. 'What's money?' he laughed. He said they'd manage.

The trouble was, he had had no work for weeks. By April they owed two months' rent. Their car licence had expired, the insurance had expired. A final reminder arrived from the electricity and that evening he sat her down and gave her a beer.

'That all we got to drink?' she asked.

'We've got to sell the car.' He put his arm around her. 'I've looked in *Loot*. We'd get £400 for it.'

'Great!' She pushed him away. 'So what'll we do – walk?' She got up and took out her lipstick.

'What're you doing?'

'What do you think? Going to sell my body.'

She slammed out of the flat. He sat there. He didn't believe her; she had only said it to get a reaction. She liked shocking him. He told himself this, but he still felt uneasy.

Half an hour later she came back. She pulled a bottle of wine from under her jacket. 'It's only Bulgarian,' she said, as if that made it all right. 'The French stuff was too high up.'

'What if you got caught?'

'But I wasn't, was I?' She dumped it on the draining-board. 'So I take it you're not drinking any?'

Suddenly he felt reckless. He uncorked the bottle. 'Mmm, a presumptuous little wine,' he sniffed, 'from a vineyard on the wrong side of the law.'

She laughed. 'At that price, it's a steal.'

He stir-fried some noodles; he usually did the cooking, she was hopeless at it. Afterwards, in high spirits, they drove down to Camden Town. It was a warm night; the pavements were busy with people. He watched them queuing at the Midland Bank cash dispenser and thought: I've broken the law. My stomach has received stolen goods. What boundary does one cross to press a gun into somebody's back and relieve them of their cash?

'Hi! Eva!'

He jumped. But it wasn't the police. It was Denise, a girl who worked at the salon.

'I've missed you,' she said to Eva. 'There's no laughs anymore.' She turned to Jon. 'How's the music business? Signed up any new bands?'

'I'm not in the music business,' he said. Eva nudged him. 'Well, not anymore. Not as such.'

'So what're you doing?' asked Denise.

'He's getting into property,' said Eva.

Denise laughed. 'You mean he's a burglar?'

'No' said Eva. 'He's a property developer.'

When Denise left he turned to Eva. 'Why did you lie about what I do? Are you ashamed of me?'

'It just sounded more interesting.'

'Property? More interesting? Anyway, you made *me* lie.'

'I promise I won't again.'

'Yeah, but how do I know you're telling the truth?' He tried to make a joke of it. Patting his pocket he said: 'Just checking my wallet's still there.'

Back at the flat he couldn't give it up. He asked: 'What else have you told Denise? Do you always lie to people?'

'I hated her. She was a pain in the arse, she was always wittering on about her wedding.'

'You hated her because she was going to get married?'

He remembered that evening and his feeling of unease. Eva stepped outside his boundaries. Sometimes he found that exhilarating, sometimes unnerving. She lied – would she lie to him? She stole things without a moment's guilt – and her mother a Catholic. Perhaps that made it easier; you just said some Hail Marys and did it again.

She did stranger things, however – things that startled him. She seemed capable of such hatred. He should have been warned. One day, soon after she moved in, he had found a bracelet of woven hair.

'What's this?' he had laughed. 'Voodoo?'

'Oh, that's from Louise. She's a cow who was married to a bloke I was screwing. So I was in his house one day and I found her hairbrush. I pulled out the hairs and made them into that.'

'Why?'

'I wore it on my left wrist. If you do that it's like a spell. The person dies.'

He had stared at her. 'Did she?'

'Don't know. Don't care.' She flicked her lighter and lit the bracelet. 'It doesn't matter now. I've got you.' The bracelet shrivelled; a coil of black smoke rose into the air. 'Haven't I?'

He had tried to dismiss it as childish jealousy. Sometimes, however, she alarmed him more profoundly. Months before all this happened, before their lives changed, they had been walking down Dean Street on their way to a club. A red Ferrari was parked in the road. She had stopped, taken out her nail-file and scored their initials, 'JE', on the bonnet. It had set off the alarm. She had tottered off on her high-heeled boots, laughing. 'How could you?' he asked. 'Easy!' she laughed, clattering her nail-file along the railings. 'Easy-peasy.'

She wrote their initials everywhere, 'JE' entwined. It was them against the world – more so, now they were alone together with nothing to do. She said: 'Ever walked along a beach and lifted up a stone? There's these two worms lying there, curled together? That's us.' Life was so bloody unfair. Why did other people have money, what had they done to deserve it? She was a child pressing her nose against a sweetshop window, she banged her fist against the fortifications that blocked her off and left her outside in the cold. Behind those walls lived that safe, secure and alien species: the rich. In St John's Wood she had powdered their faces and smoothed cream into their necks; she had snapped them into sunbeds, entombing them, and wrenched wax off their legs like pulling bark from a tree. He knew because he had seen her waxing her own. She had listened to their complaints about rude waiters and unreliable cleaning ladies. She had leaned towards the rich, breathing in their perfume. The lucky ones, the pampered women. There was a sheen to them, as if they had been polished. In her pink overalls she had spent her days on the fringes of a world she could never penetrate but which kept her in a state of permanent arousal, chafing at her. If only he could help her! Sometimes her resentment made him uneasy; at other times it filled him with pity. In some stupid way he felt responsible; it was all his fault.

One night they were lying in bed, listening to the rain sliding down the window. They were lying in bed because it was the only way to keep warm. She said: 'When I was little, every week me mum gave me pocket money – a quid. She told me to put half of it into this special, like, metal money box on the wall. She said if I did it each week, then I could take it out and buy something really nice at the end. Except, there wasn't an end, was there? 'Cos I never saw me money. It was the fucking electric meter.'

Jon's eyes filled with tears. 'That's the saddest story I ever heard.' He held her tightly in his arms; she lay rigid. He drew back and looked at her flat, amoral face, the face he loved. Freckly skin, cat's eyes. There was something Slavic about her face, she said it must be from her dad, whoever he was. He was something foreign she knew nothing about.

'Fuck 'em,' she said. 'Fuck 'em all.'

When they were happy it was all right; their little room was their everywhere. After all, some things are free. They made love, they danced to her Tamla Motown cassettes. She spun around the flat in her nightie – a surprisingly girlish, winceyette garment with flowers printed around the hem. She sat him on the side of the bath and, gazing intently into his face, painted his eyelids and turned him into a temptress. But as the weeks went by and their money ran out their happiness started seeping away. Their little room closed them in; there was nothing to *do*. She snapped at him; they bickered. His head throbbed. He should be looking after her, that was what men did, but he was helpless. They couldn't go out; some days they couldn't even afford a drink. They had nothing to come home from so they stayed at home. When he lived alone he had often been short of money but it was only now, in

83

Eva's restless presence, that he felt the grinding boredom of poverty – the lack of distractions, the lack of variety.

He felt unmanned; they didn't make love for a week. They lay in bed all morning, with nothing to say to each other, whilst the rush hour traffic down in the street filled their room with fumes. How purposeful was the world outside! They felt as elderly and inert as pensioners. *He* felt that. He no longer knew what she felt. She sat watching TV for hours, stubbing out one cigarette and lighting another. She spent hours in the bathroom changing the colour of her hair – plum, orange, blonde – using tubes of stuff she had stolen from the salon. She glumly inspected herself in the mirror and said, 'This looks shit.' She disappeared to dye it another colour and left the bathroom a swamp of squeezed tubes and stained bathtowels. She was sluttish about her own mess but critical of his and snapped at him when he dropped crumbs on the carpet. What was he going to do with her?

When he couldn't bear it any longer he went out and walked down the high street. The busy shops mocked him. Their windows displayed videos he couldn't buy, even if he had a video recorder. Jobless, he felt separated from other people by a transparent screen. He felt heavy with lassitude. He could hardly bring himself to buy the local paper and open the *Jobs Vacant* section. He felt useless, separated from the human race; he felt like a car whose engine has been removed. He dragged himself home. When he climbed the stairs, he smelt the dead meat in the butcher's back room.

Things came to a head at the end of May. Their landlord sent them a Recorded Delivery letter giving them an ultimatum. Pay up or get out. A parking summons arrived for Eva – she always used the car if she could, she hated walking. She squashed both the letters into the pedal bin, pushing them into a mush with the teabags.

'You're crazy!' he said.

'Fuck 'em.' She looked at him. 'That is, if you can.'

He turned away and filled the kettle. As he did so he thought, quite distinctly: I am going to lose her.

Chance? Coincidence? Who believed in it? Eva believed in predestination; she read their horoscopes each week in *TV Guide*. When they met, she said it was foretold in their stars – some planetary conjunction he had never worked out. Its force drew them together.

Chance – a hand plunges into a hat and pulls out a raffle ticket. A hand plucks a sheet of newspaper, bowling along the grass. Was it chance or fate – what happened the next day? It was a Monday, the day that changed their lives, and the lives of people as yet unknown to them and as removed from them as if they lived in another time zone.

It was a chilly morning, and they had been walking round looking at cards in newsagents' windows. *Room to let. Suit non-smoking gentleman.* Even when he was not homeless, these cards filled him with despair. Eva pointed. 'Look! *Must like alsatians!*' She wore her mock-leopardskin jacket and red leggings. Her bright, bugger-you-all outfits touched him; she blazed down the street. She was in a restless mood that day, as skittish as a colt. She shot glances at passing men. While he looked at the newsagents' windows she inspected her reflection in the glass. He could find nowhere for them to live.

They had two pounds; two pounds in the world until they collected their benefit the next day. They had half a tank of petrol left in the car, paid for by his Visa card which he had no possibility of repaying at the end of the month. If he repaid the minimum . . . but then the interest . . . his head ached. They spent the two pounds on a kebab. They carried it to the little park, behind Safeways, and sat down on a bench. The ground beneath the tree was scattered with litter. When he tut-tutted she patted his head.

'They're petals, thicko.'

He smiled, surprised. It was May; spring had crept up on him stealthily. It was so damn cold, that was why.

'I want to be hot,' she said. 'I want to jump on a plane and boil on a beach. Me sap's rising. Let's get in the car and drive to Spain!'

'Sweetheart, we've got to sell the car. Don't you understand?'

She didn't reply. Nearby, a see-saw creaked up and down. Two children sat on it; one rose, the other fell. He thought: I should be taking her to a restaurant and filling her up with cocktails. What sort of man am I?

They sat in the scruffy little park, amongst the other people who measured out their lives in public places – drunks, the very old, a man who stood alone, talking to a broken-off sapling. Jon thought: what on earth are we going to do? In four weeks we'll be homeless. In four weeks *I'll* be homeless. She is going to leave me. My life will topple like dominoes; it's only a matter of time before I'll be out on the streets arguing with lamp-posts.

Suddenly, as if in response to this, a chill wind blew. It blew a newspaper towards them, its sheets separating and billowing out. He bent down and picked up a page. It was the *North London Advertiser*; he read its jobs section each week.

There was a photograph on the page. Eva looked at it. Her red fingernail followed the print. 'See what I mean, Jonny?' she said. 'About unfair? See what I mean?'

The photo showed a family. They were posed outside a large house. 'THE PRICE IS RIGHT' said the headline. '*Pictured above, the lucky winners of last Saturday's Rotary Club Prize Draw – Mr and Mrs Morris Price of Cypress Drive, Stanmore, with their children Theodore, 21, a film school graduate, Hannah, 17, and Rebecca, 11. When asked about their prize, a family holiday in Florida, Mrs Price said "We're thrilled to bits." '*

Eva's fingernail jabbed at it. 'Why them? Tell me that. Why fucking them? They've got all that and they win a holiday in fucking Florida.'

'Don't swear.'

'Why fucking not? Look at that house. Look at the size of it!' She scrumpled up the kebab paper and dropped it on the ground. 'Let's go and rob them! While they're away.'

'So now we're going to end up in prison.'

'We *are* in prison!' She stood up, brushing the crumbs from her leggings. 'Jon, we can't go on like this.'

'We? You mean, you and me?'

'Us. This. What're we going to do?'

He couldn't answer. They got up. Shivering, she drew her leopardskin jacket around her shoulders. He shoved the newspaper into a bin. They walked away, but after a moment he realised that he was alone. Eva had stopped.

At the time he feared she was thinking about him, and whether she was going to leave. Not whether – when. She was so alive, so vibrant, he often wondered what she saw in him. He had asked her once, and she had said: '*Because you've got the most gorgeous bum in Britain.*' Her finger stroked his buttock. '*Because I trust you. Things that have happened to me, you wouldn't believe. You're the only person who's been really nice to me, all my life.*'

He heard Eva's breathing; quick, shallow breaths as if she had been running. But she was standing still. There was no sound except the creak-creak of the see-saw. Then she walked over to the litter bin and pulled out the crumpled page of newspaper. She folded it and put it into her pocket.

She was in a strange mood all afternoon. When they got home she didn't switch on the TV. She stood at the window, jiggling like a schoolgirl who wanted to go to the lavatory. She had threaded bits of red cotton around the tufts of her hair. When he spoke to her she didn't react. She looked right through him, as if he wasn't there. She was plotting something – at the time, he thought she was plotting her escape. She went into the kitchen and started watering the spider plants – she never did that, it was he who had kept them alive. She did it abstractly, with a cup; half the water spilt over the edges of the pots.

He came up behind her and put his hand on her shoulder. She jumped. He said: 'Don't worry. We'll work something out.'

She turned round. Her eyes were bright. Her face was illuminated from within; she *crackled*. She put down the cup and grinned at him. 'Don't worry,' she said. 'We have.'

2

You think you know somebody. Hundreds of nights you have lain in their arms, your breathing their breathing. You have come into their body, come inside their body, its moist throbbing has been your throbbing. You have talked, millions upon millions of words; you have heard their heart's secrets and the shames and embarrassments of their childhood. You have washed them when they have been ill. You have seen them asleep, their mouth lolling open like a corpse. You have seen them ugly and naked when they are sobbing; you know how they brush their teeth, little spits and gurgles. You have lived with them, you know a person other people have only glimpsed, you think you know them and suddenly it's as if you are standing in a room and the walls have collapsed around you.

He said: 'You're joking. Tell me you're joking.'

It was two o'clock in the morning. Eva sat on the bed. She smoothed out the photo on her knee. 'See, we take her. Not the little one, she's too young. Not the brother, of course. We take *her*.' She pointed. 'This one.'

They had been talking for hours and still she didn't call the girl by name. She just said 'this one'. She was smoking; ash fell on the photo. She brushed it off. Her hand was trembling.

'It's not, like, we're going to *harm* her. We're not going to *do* anything to her.'

'I can't believe you can even think like this.'

'You see it on TV all the time.'

'This isn't TV,' he said. 'It's real. Well, it's not real because we're not going to do it.'

'– the IRA and things. Cop shows. You write a note, you cut the letters out of bits of newspaper –'

'Eva –'

'You arrange a drop.'

'A drop? What are you *talking* about? A drop?'

'It means –'

'It's driven you barmy, being stuck in here, watching TV all day. I know it's my fault –'

'It's so simple!'

'We're dreaming this,' he said. 'Let's go to bed and when we wake up –'

'We can't keep her here, of course. Hey, we'll put her in your uncle's shed!'

Her cheeks were flushed; her face looked hectic. He thought: I don't know her at all. Down in the street there was the sound of breaking glass. He felt utterly alone.

He gazed down at the photograph. The mother of the girl had her eyes closed as if she, too, could not believe what was being planned. The newspaper was creased across her face.

'One of us stays with her.' She lit another cigarette. 'We'll take turns.'

He looked at her through the smoke. 'I can't believe you're serious.'

Actually, he *was* starting to believe it. Trying to connect up this person with the Eva he knew, he was slowly and unwillingly seeing a resemblance. His Eva stole leggings from Kensington Market – in fact she was wearing them now. His Eva was lawless. She vandalised strangers' Ferraris. She had given him a blow-job on the tube – Northern line, between Euston and Camden Town; it was a long run because Mornington Crescent station was closed. But that had been a lark, an erotic dare. A dare by his darling dare-devil. Until now, all those events could simply be considered adventures.

She was still talking. 'Give them a week to pay up . . .' She was revving herself up, talking herself into it. She was flushed with her own momentum.

'Eva. Shut up!'

She looked at him. 'Don't be such a wimp. You a man or what?'

When he woke, the next morning, she had gone. No note, nothing. The car keys were missing from his jacket pocket. He went into the bathroom and opened the cupboard. Her make-up had gone.

He sat down, heavily, on a chair. He felt as if he had been slugged on the head with a sock filled with sand. Slowly, very slowly, he made himself a cup of tea. There was just one teabag left. He stirred in three spoonfuls of sugar.

Last night had not been a dream. She had meant every word. She had tested his love and he had failed her. She was out of his orbit now; she had spun away into another dimension and left him.

You a man or what? He had lost the only woman he had ever loved – his soulmate, 'JE' stamped through his bones like greetings through rock. She had entrusted him with her secret, she had opened her heart to him. She had revealed to him an ugly part of her innermost self and how had he reacted? With shock and revulsion.

He sat there for a long time. What a wimp! Yes – he was crying. How could a wimp like him hope to hold on to a bewitching creature like Eva? She had brought him alive only to leave him for dead. He deserved it; he was useless, worthless. He sat there whilst down in the street the rush-hour traffic thundered past, shaking the mirror on the wall. Every minute took her further away from him. He knew where she was going – up to Derby, where her old boyfriend Lyle lived. She had been talking about him a lot lately. Lyle had money; he owned a car-hire firm. Lyle was a *man*.

Jon got up and made another cup of tea, lifting the old teabag out of the bin. Maybe she hadn't meant it. This kidnapping thing was just a moment's madness, a sudden flare-up. A reaction to their grey, pinched little life. After all, she was always grabbing him and suggesting things: *Let's go to Spain*! *Let's do it in the lift*! She was desperate. Anything to relieve the tedium of living with him, a failed chippie who couldn't even get it up anymore. He threw the teabag into the bin; within it, the rubbish was starting to smell. The whole flat was already starting to smell, as if with her departure it had died.

It was a joke. She had just suggested it as a joke, and his dreary reaction was the final straw. How pedantic he was! How unadventurous! How could she have stuck with him for a whole year? No wonder she had decided to leave.

Jon knew he was prone to self-pity. Even his mother, who worshipped him, had accused him of that. His schoolfriends had taunted him and called him a cry-baby. He flung himself on to the bed and buried his face in the pillow. It smelt of Eva – her perfume, which was called *Escape*.

Some time later in the morning – he could tell because the traffic noise had died down – he got dressed and went downstairs. He had nowhere to go but he had to move around. Outside it was a blindingly sunny day. The world carried on, mindlessly. In the butcher's window moist mincemeat lay in metal trays. The cuts of meat looked naked, as if they had just flinched.

Lyle wouldn't have reacted like this. Nor would those other blokes she talked about. A shadow lay across the pavement. He looked up. Above him, a sign had been erected: 'LEASEHOLD SHOP TO LET'. One of the lads was unloading carcasses from a van – stiff, pallid pigs, slit from throat to crotch. Jon pointed to the sign. The boy said: 'Yep. It's Tesco's up the road. They put the kibosh on us.'

The butcher's was closing down and he hadn't even spoken to them until today. They didn't even know that he lived upstairs. How huge London was! How could he start to exist in it, all alone? How could he begin again, without her?

He walked around for a while. With no Eva beside him, clutching his arm, he couldn't think where to go. Without her to remark on them, how boring people looked! He passed the park where they had sat side by side, only the day before. *They're petals, thicko*! She had transformed his life.

Jon sat down on the bench. Beside him, a man ate a sausage roll. It must be lunchtime. The man said: 'About bloody time.'

Jon said: 'Pardon?'

'Spring. About bloody time.'

He went back and climbed the stairs to the flat. He inserted his keys, mildly surprised to find that he hadn't double-locked the door. He let himself in. A woman stood there, naked except for a pair of knickers. She had shiny chestnut hair.

He went up to her and put his arms around her.

'I've been there!' Eva wriggled out of his embrace. She pulled off the wig and flung it on to a chair. 'I saw them!'

'I thought you'd –'

'I'm sweating like a pig.' She pulled off her knickers, grabbed his hand and led him into the bathroom. 'Hose me down.' She stood in the bath. He picked up the rubber shower attachment and started spraying her.

'I got there really early, see,' she spluttered. 'I found the house, it's just like the photo, it's fucking enormous! I, like, parked and waited. I felt like a spy, in me wig and all. At half past seven the bloke came out, the father, and drove off to work. Then at eight twenty the mum came out, suit and all, briefcase, must be off to work too. She had the little girl with her, she must've been taking her to school. They drove off.' She got out of the bath, grabbed a towel and started rubbing herself. 'At half past eight *she* came out. Our one. Big girl, carrying school books. I felt, like, I was a hunter or something. Know what I mean? So I got out the car and I followed her down the road. She didn't notice. Teenagers, they don't notice anything, you know? They're, like, just thinking about what they look like. I followed her along to the main road and she waited for the bus, and, get this, I got on too! Three stops. And she got off at this poncey-looking school, St Mary's. Private, of course. And she went in.' Panting, she paused for breath.

He gazed at her. He put his arms around her and buried his face in her wet hair. 'Oh, Eva . . .'

'See, it's started! We've started. You proud of me? I knew, just by looking at her — I knew we can do it! She's, like, slow and dim-looking. She wouldn't even mind. She could be in fucking Outer Mongolia and she wouldn't notice! We can do it, you and me!'

Her towel fell to the floor. She wrapped her damp leg around his thigh; she slid her tongue into his mouth. With one hand she pressed his buttocks against her, into her, grinding him against her. She moved to and fro. He felt himself swelling. They staggered, knocking against the door, and slid on to the bathmat. Her fingers yanked down his zip. He lay on the floor, his head rammed against the lavatory; she pulled off his T-shirt and ran her tongue down his chest, lower, lower. She licked the hair down his stomach, where it grew thicker; she licked him like a cat licking her prey. Her saliva made him wet and slippery. She took him into her mouth; with her other hand she gently kneaded his balls. He sobbed with relief. He pressed her wet head into his crotch, harder.

'My love,' he muttered. 'My love . . .'

*

Afterwards they lay, damp and naked, on the bed.

'You'll never leave me, will you?' he murmured.

'We're partners,' she whispered. 'We're partners in crime.'

He ran his finger down her flattened, freckly breast. He had never known anyone like her. Her body was taut and boyish. It felt wired-up; an electric current under her skin, under his fingertips. When she shifted against him, he shuddered.

She said: 'I went back there, to the house, after she'd gone to school. I had a good look at it.' She licked his ear luxuriously. 'I looked round the side. They've got a bloody conservatory, the buggers. I've always fancied one of them . . . like, nothing matters, in a conservatory . . . summer, winter, rain, shine, it can't get to you, none of it . . .' She lay across him and licked the other ear. She breathed hot breath into it, as if she were breathing out her dreams.

'Why did you take your sponge bag?'

''Cos I got up at five, dum dum. To be in time. I had to put on me warpaint when I got there.'

'Promise you'll never leave me. Ever.'

She stopped him by tracing her finger over his lips. He opened his mouth and sucked her forefinger. Miraculously, he felt himself hardening again. She straddled him, and silenced him with her mouth.

He woke with a start. Footsteps on the stairs. It was late afternoon; the sun slanted into the room. There was an unfamiliar shadow across the wall; it was the 'TO LET' sign, outside, blocking off the light. When he was a boy he had once inked in an I, on one of those signs, to make TOILET; that was the extent of his youthful criminal activity. The door opened and Eva came in, carrying a plastic bag.

'I've just signed on,' she said. 'Better get your skates on or they'll be closed.'

He climbed off the bed. She took some groceries out of the bag. 'Got us some stuff to eat,' she said. 'And this.' She pulled out a box and wrenched it open. Inside was a mobile phone.

He stared at it. 'You bought it?'

'Only had enough for the deposit. But I know the bloke at the shop.'

'Why've you got it?'

'Why do you think, thicko? For us. So we can call each other up.'

That day, 24 May, he stepped from one life into another. They had done nothing yet, no action that turned them into criminals. But in his mind he had already stepped outside the law. It transformed his world, exhilaratingly. Within him, a motor started up. In those early days, when as yet they had done nothing wrong, when it was still a game, the very streets possessed a tingling excitement that he hadn't felt since he was a child playing hide and seek. He was bonded to Eva; she was his, he was hers, it was like their first passionate weeks together. They were welded together sexily by their secret.

'We've got to do it fast, while we've still got this place, got a base, got a phone,' she said. There was a payphone outside on the landing. 'So we can contact each other. We've got to think how we're going to take her.' She always said *take*. Not *kidnap*. As if the girl were an apple they could pluck off a tree, easy as that. And still neither of them called her by name. 'We can't, when she's walking to school. The streets look as if they're empty, but they're not. Stanmore's full of bloody curtain-twitchers – like, bored housewives, *au pairs*. I'll show you.'

They drove there the next day. His heart thudded – and he wasn't doing anything wrong! Still it thudded. He felt thrillingly alive. He glanced at Eva. She had slicked back her hair with gel; she looked as sleek as an otter. How sharp her nose was, how quick her senses! They were animals, the two of them. He drove past the 'Neighbourhood Watch' sign and parked down the road under a cypress tree. The houses sat back from the road – each detached, each different, each rising from their gardens with the four-square solidity of wealth. He gazed at number eighteen; it was half-timbered, set behind a semicircular gravel drive. Normally he would have passed it without a glance, but it was no ordinary house now. Eva leaned nearer him, whispering. There was no need, but still she whispered.

'See, the streets look empty but there's always somebody around – like, servicing things. Looking after these rich buggers.' She pointed. Down the road, a man clipped a hedge. A Hotpoint van drew up and parked. A black woman, probably a cleaner, walked towards them carrying a shopping bag. People hummed around these houses like drones around the big, prone bodies of queen bees.

They sat in the car, watching. Normally he wouldn't have noticed these people, either, but today he did. It was like one of those drawings in a puzzle book, when you had to count how many objects were hidden. Once you knew how to look, you spotted them. He thought: children see things like this, and so do criminals. A van marked 'White Horse Laundry' stopped and a man got out. He wore a blue uniform – it looked unnervingly official. A window opened and a woman shook out a duster; today she was transformed into a potential witness. 'My mum used to clean for people like this,' whispered Eva. 'Socking great house, jacuzzi, you name it. East Finchley. Three years she worked for them and they never even told her she could make herself a cup of tea. Like, it didn't cross their minds. She was fucking invisible.'

He gazed at the house – their house. Bars criss-crossed the downstairs windows. He burned with the unjustness of it all. He switched off something in his head: he didn't think of them as people, the owners of this house. He didn't give them faces or think of them by name. He didn't allow himself to think of them as perfectly innocent – maybe even pleasant. He couldn't start to do that. It was too late.

'Fifty thousand,' said Eva. 'We don't want to ask too much. Fifty grand'll do us and they'll hardly feel it.'

'Hang on. We haven't – well, *done* it yet.'

'We will. See, what's on our side is surprise. It's not like she's, like the daughter of a famous film star. Or Fiat or something – like, they'd be expecting it. I got these plans up my sleeve, exactly how to do it. I'll tell you when I've worked them out.'

He gazed at her, intoxicated. Her face was radiant, she blazed with energy and confidence. Now she had a purpose she seemed to have grown in intelligence; people grow cleverer, he realised, once they are doing something that absorbs them. They use every brain cell. He thought of the war, how people utilised every bit of their garden, even the forgotten weedy bits, to grow vegetables.

It was Thursday and they were sorting out the hut. That was why he had thought of vegetables. The hut stood on a vast area of allotments, way beyond Acton – an expanse of half-abandoned plots surrounded by distant factories. Eva pointed out of the window. 'See, it's perfect! Specially on weekdays. Just a few old boys digging away and I bet they're all half-deaf. Half-blind too.'

The hut belonged to his Uncle Charlie, who had died in March. Charlie had been a solitary man; nobody else had ever come here except Jon, who loved it. He had loved his uncle, too – a benign man, a confirmed bachelor before that meant a man was gay. Charlie had introduced him to the joys of carpentry; his workbench stood in the corner, covered by a cloth.

Eva wrinkled her nose. 'Christ it's filthy! We'll sweep it out and make up the bed, over there. We'll need two sleeping bags – we've got them, haven't we? Lucky it's getting warmer.'

It still seemed unreal – a boy scout's jaunt rather than anything more serious.

'. . . one of those little camping cookers,' she was saying. 'And a kettle, we can use the one we found in the flat.'

Jon gazed at the mud-encrusted gardening tools, at the tins of Growmore and Slugdeath. Unlike Eva he loved the smell in here; it was honest and earthy. He still hadn't caught up with the reality of what they were doing until Eva, ticking off the items on her fingers, said to herself: 'Oh yeah – and we'll need a blindfold.'

3

On Friday Eva announced that they were going to drive to Stanmore Broadway. It was near the school, she said. 'She's in the sixth form. She's not going to stay in school in her *lunch hour*. I never did.'

'Yeah, we know what *you* used to get up to in your lunch hour,' said Jon. 'I'm amazed you didn't get expelled.'

'I was. Twice.'

'But this is a private school. Maybe they keep them locked in.'

'Jesus, you're negative. You want to be rich, or what?'

'We're going to bundle her away in broad daylight?'

'We've got to grab the moment. Like I said, we've got surprise on our side.' Eva inspected herself in the mirror. She was wearing the chestnut wig. Actually it suited her – a glossy bob that curved around her chin and gave her the appearance of a twenties flapper. She put on a pair of dark glasses. 'Lucky it's sunny, eh?' She passed him his pair. 'Even if we don't, we'll get to know her. Like, what she's up to.'

Jon thought: I don't want to know what she's up to. I don't want her to become a human being. Eva, leaning close to him, glued a moustache to his upper lip. Her face inspected him impersonally, as if he, too, were hardly human – just an object. He smelt the tobacco on her breath.

He stared at himself in the mirror. 'You're a genius.'

Grey wig, grey moustache, dark glasses. He was not only unrecognisable, he was convincing. He almost convinced himself. She had borrowed the wig and moustache from her friend Elaine, who did costumes for commercials. Jon gazed at himself, turning his head from one side to another. He looked older, distinguished, vaguely homosexual. He looked like a professor from California. In fact, he preferred this version of himself.

He said: 'Know something? It's easier to do something – well, that you don't usually do. If you don't look like yourself.'

She raised her eyebrows. 'Why do you think women wear make-up, dum-dum?'

They drove out to Stanmore. It still felt like a game – more so, now that he was in disguise. They had even gone to a toyshop and bought a replica gun – a plastic pistol that felt convincingly heavy. It was a Browning HP, made in Japan. The box said *Pricise Details and Rearistic Finish*.

It was noon. They drove down to Stanmore Broadway. With the gun hidden in the glove compartment he felt like an outlaw riding into town. Eva switched off the engine. They sat there, next to a parade of shops. How clean and shiny this place looked, compared to their own high street! Mercedes convertibles were parked outside dress shops; an assistant carried bags out from a delicatessen. There was a coffee shop and a lingerie shop; it was a place for women with time to kill. He yearned to release Eva into this world, to liberate her from the squalid and monotonous reality of their lives. He could buy her a convertible! Watch her hair fly free! They could go anywhere, do anything!

He gazed at her profile. Her lower lip stuck out; he knew that stubborn expression so well. She was psyching herself up to go through with it.

Time passed. He watched a woman coming out of the health club. She was suntanned; her hair was immaculate. She had the unmistakable look of the rich – as if she had been buffed up with chamois leather. She looked wealthy through and through, as if her very insides were pampered, whereas Eva just looked as if she wore make-up. He thought, suddenly, that their ludicrous plan was totally disconnected with this world, he could never link it up. It would never work.

'Stop daydreaming.' She snapped her fingers in front of his face. 'Look!'

Several girls seemed to have appeared. They were obviously schoolgirls, though they didn't wear uniform – in the sixth form, Eva had told him, they didn't. How big adolescent girls were nowadays – bulging with hamburgers and hormones. They were a different species. That was how he must think of them – like another breed of human being. How strong they looked! He imagined trying to hold one of them down, in a struggle. She would reduce him to a pulp.

Jon and Eva sat there, rendered invisible by their car, and watched. The air grew thick with Eva's cigarette smoke. The girls drank Coke from cans and leaned against bollards. They gathered in groups, talking to boys. They were flirting. They shrieked with laughter, soundlessly. Minutes passed. Their particular one didn't appear. At one forty-five the girls drifted off, back towards school.

'What was the point of that?' he asked. 'What now?' More and more he relied on Eva to know what they were doing. It absolved him from responsibility.

'What do you think, dickbrain?' she replied. 'We go to the school, at four.'

They arrived well before four, to secure a parking place next to the gates. St Mary's School for Girls was a large Victorian building with Portakabins clamped to the sides. They parked; Eva switched off the engine. She wound open the window. Other cars drew up behind them – BMWs, Range Rovers. The street filled up. Women got out and chatted to each other. Their old Toyota was so rusty, compared to everyone else's cars; wouldn't they be noticed? But Eva seemed oblivious. She sat there, her eyes fixed on the gate.

A white dog scampered up to their car and cocked its leg against their wheel. 'Oscar!' shouted a woman and hurried up to them. 'Sorry!' she said, and pulled the dog away.

Eva sat, very still. He looked at her jutting lower lip. In profile she looked more foreign: a volatile young woman from another country. Slav? Croatian? Half of her, the father's half, was foreign even to herself. He thought: she is anchorless in the world. That's why she's dangerous.

A far bell sounded. She stiffened, like a foxhound hearing a hunting horn. Girls streamed out through the gates – little ones first because they were faster. They wore blue and white flowered school dresses. They raced out, chattering and expectant. He thought: they all have parents to go home to, soon they will be safe. The older girls walked more slowly. Behind him, car doors slammed and engines revved up.

Eva jabbed him in the ribs with her elbow. 'There she is!' she whispered.

Two girls were approaching the gates. He recognised one of them from Stanmore Broadway. The other one was Theirs. He recognised her instantly from the photo – maybe because he had been staring at it for days. She was a big, slow, pear-shaped girl – big hips and legs. A mass of unruly black hair. She wore black clothes, as if it were mid-winter, and she carried a stained Indian bag bulging with books. Through the open window he heard her voice. '. . . Mansfield Park . . .' The other girl stopped and gave her a sheaf of papers. They turned to go, in different directions.

'Bye!'

'See you at the Underworld!'

'Is everyone going?'

'Yeah – Emma, Julia . . .'

'See you there at nine!'

'Byeee!'

They walked away. Eva had tilted the rear view mirror to watch Their Girl, who walked to the bus stop and joined the queue.

'The Underworld?'

'It's that club, thicko.' She swerved to overtake a lorry. In the glove compartment, the gun slid from one side to another. 'Off the Charing Cross Road. She's going there, tonight.'

'You mean – we sort of ambush her on the way there? Like, on her way to the Tube or something?'

She shook her head. ''Course not. It'll still be daylight, anyone could see us. Anyway she might be given a lift. Who knows? No. We go to the club, of course. We do it there.'

She drove around Apex Corner and speeded up the dual carriageway. The sign said 'Central London'. She was driving fast. Jon didn't speak. He felt weightless with shock.

He had seen her. *Her*. Their Girl, Hannah. He repeated the name to himself – *Hannah*. She had stood so close to their car that he had seen the pimples on her chin; bumpy ones she had tried to cover with make-up. He had suffered from spots, too, when he was her age. When she had spoken she had kept her chin tucked in; he had done that too, trying to hide his own pimples. She had patchy brown and black hair with a rebellious little plait in it, one of those plaits with coloured thread in them.

His chest felt blocked. 'We can't do it,' he said.

Eva didn't hear. 'It's Friday night, it'll be crowded. I've been to the Underworld. It's dark, and ever so noisy. You can do anything in a crowd, it's easier than in an empty street.' She hooted at a van, accelerating behind it. 'See, it's much better than by force.'

'What do you mean?'

'You move in on her, you dance with her, you chat her up. Then you take her outside and I'll be waiting, in the car. Easy peasy, piece of cake.'

It it wasn't so terrible he could have laughed at it. Later on he tried to, but Eva didn't see the joke. And it wasn't that funny; in fact it wasn't funny at all.

He was in the Underworld, nursing a bottle of Becks. Around him bodies heaved up and down; the place was packed. Lights pulsed. Music thumped out of socking great speakers, *fuck the fuzz* . . . He wished he were back in the flat listening to Art Tatum. He hated discos; he only came to them because Eva liked to dance. And tonight Eva wasn't here. She waited outside, in the dark, a spider spinning her web.

He had already spotted their girl. Between the heads he could glimpse her; she was lit rhythmically – green, white, red. She was over the other side of the room, jiggling and dipping to the music. He recognised one other girl, the one from the school gates; maybe some of the others were her friends. Most of the dancers were her age – in fact, he was the oldest person there. Much the oldest, he suddenly remembered, in his ridiculous disguise. His scalp itched, under the wig. He felt conspicuous, and very much alone. His throat was sore; he was getting a cold.

He edged closer to her, pushing his way through the crowd – no harm in that, surely? *Fuck the fuzz* droned the voice, or was it something else? He moved nearer; his foot skidded, the floor was wet with beer. Now he could see her more clearly. She was heavily made-up – black eyes, a row of earrings that winked in the lights, something winking in the side of her nose. She wore a cobwebby top with straps that fell off her shoulders; she hitched them up. She looked awkward and young – more so, oddly enough, now she was wearing make-up. He thought: you shouldn't be here. Somebody should take you away from all this. Then he realised, with a start: that's what I'm supposed to do.

The song changed. *Getta getta getta something . . . gotta gotta gotta something else . . .* He jiggled up and down, alone. He knew he looked silly, in the wig and all, but curiously enough he didn't mind; his disguise removed his personality. *Gimme gimme gimme something . . . manjax akimbo something or other . . .* The lights pulsing on their girl's face turned her into a traffic signal – stop, go, stop.

He moved nearer. He was close now, nearly touching. The green light transformed her into a ghost, drowned in the underworld; her eyes flickered through him without interest. *He* could be a ghost, for all she noticed. How could he start to flirt with her, for God's sake; how could he possibly do such a thing?

He took a breath and shouted: 'Don't understand a word of it, do you?'

She couldn't hear. She shrugged and nodded.

He shouted. 'Heard of this chat-up line? Bloke goes up to a girl and spills a drop of Perrier on her sleeve –'

'A what?' she shouted.

'Perrier. Then he says, *Let me help you out of those wet clothes.*'

She smiled politely. She hadn't heard. Her face flicked to green.

Just then he sneezed.

'Bless you!' she shouted, and smiled.

That did it. He turned, and pushed away through the crowd. He fought his way to the corridor that led to the exit and leaned against the concrete wall. His lungs wheezed; his eyes watered. He pushed the iron bar and stepped into the street. Under the 'NO ENTRY' sign the car waited. He went up to it, flung open the back door and sat down.

Eva swung round. 'Where is she?'

'I flunked it.' He wrenched off the moustache; it tore his skin like a plaster. He held it between two fingers. The hair was damp; his nose had been running. How repulsive!

'You flunked it?' she demanded.

'I couldn't do it to her.'

'Kidnap her?'

He thought: what's a worse crime than kidnapping? Pretending to find a shy, overweight young girl attractive.

'Lie to her,' he said.

There was a silence. *Bless you*, she had said. She had blessed a complete stranger; how could he do anything to her after that? At the end of the street a clamping van appeared and parked, waiting.

'Shit,' said Eva.

Suddenly, reality hit him. He thought: we are both insane. How could we really expect to kidnap an unknown girl and – hysterical, this – hold her to ransom? This isn't a film. In films people don't get colds, they don't have to move the car because it's parked on a double yellow line. In films, a teenage girl is an actress being paid to play a teenage girl. And she doesn't have to keep hitching up her shoulder straps.

Eva got out of the car.

'What are you doing?' he asked.

'If you can't, I can. Come back in fifteen minutes.' She flung him the car keys and jerked her head at the clamping van. 'They'll be gone by then. Come back and wait for us.'

Us. She walked away to the front of the building. As she rounded the corner he saw her face flare briefly in the crimson neon light: *The Underworld*. And then she was gone.

It took him a long time to drive round the block – so long

that he lost all sense of what was happening and reverted to simply being Jon trying to pick up his girlfriend from a disco. Normality welcomed him back. Charing Cross Road was jammed with Friday night traffic and he missed the turning. He nosed down a narrow one-way street and got stuck behind a Westminster Council dust-cart, loading up with refuse bags outside a restaurant. He got stuck behind a taxi disgorging Japanese men. How could she believe her words: *wait for US*? What was she planning to do – take the girl by force? Pretend she was a lesbian?

He wasn't surprised to see her standing alone on the pavement. He opened the door and she flung herself into the passenger seat. 'Drive!' she hissed.

'Where?'

'Home!'

After a moment he realised that nobody was following them – no outraged manager, no tousled girl. Eva was simply excited. He drove up Tottenham Court Road and stopped at the traffic lights. She sat beside him, jiggling with impatience; on her face the light changed from red to green.

'I followed her into the toilets,' she said, 'her and her friend. They started to make up their faces in the mirror so I went into one of the cubicles and listened. Our one, Hannah, she said, *Did you see that old guy, really unattractive?*'

'Unattractive?'

'Yeah. She said, *really sad-looking . . . He tried to get off with me!*'

Stung, he changed gear. She had said that, had she?

Eva went on. 'She said, *Did you see him dancing? Really pathetic! He danced like an accountant.*'

And he had liked her. He had pitied her!

'Then she said she was really bored and was this other girl, Emma or Jemma or something, coming to Camden Lock with her on Sunday. She said she couldn't, she was going somewhere with her boyfriend, so our one said, *Well I'm going, even if nobody else is. Sunday afternoons at home, it's like the land of the living dead.'*

They were stuck behind a bus. Jon gazed at the shop windows; they were filled with computers – rows of blank screens. Toshiba. Amstrad. How *could* she have called him *really sad-looking*? Fury rose in him. *Dances like an accountant.* He thought: I save her from being abducted and she calls me unattractive!

'So that's where we do it – Camden Lock,' Eva was saying. 'I'll wait at the end of her street and follow her to the Tube. You wait in the flat. I'll phone you when she appears. I'll phone you again when we get to Camden Town. We arrange a pick-up point and you drive there! Easy!'

Jon drove across the Euston Road. People, their heads down, scuttled through the wind that whipped around the Capital Radio building; even the car shook. He said: 'What happens if she's given a lift? What happens if I can't park the car in the right place? Or people see us?'

'Nobody'll notice. That's the point of Camden Lock. It's fucking pandemonium. A person could *die* and nobody would notice.'

There was silence. He wished Eva hadn't said that. Up ahead, the full moon hung in the sky. It looked shockingly big, as if inspecting them from a few feet away. It gazed into his face and knew that he had changed. He had become harder. *Really sad-looking*, eh?

He drove up through Camden Town, past the lit windows of the kebab restaurants, past the emptying pubs. Men staggered in the streets, bellowing at the cars. They howled at the suffused sky. Jon drove northwards, under the hanging moon.

4

When Jon was little he could blank himself off. He sat under the table pretending he was dead – *being* dead – and waited for someone to realise what had happened. Nobody ever noticed so in the end he clambered out. But that solitary time was potent. He could be somebody else, he could voyage on his own. When he grew older and his parents were quarrelling he could lock that muscle in his brain; he could sit there while they shouted, he could blank himself off and take a trip through misty mauve landscapes in his head. When he grew up he did the same thing in the Tube, in the rush hour. It drove Eva mad, that he could detach himself and leave her alone. She battered at him to let her in.

The muscle locked, now he was parked here in Camden Market. People pushed past the passenger door; they bumped against the bodywork. The windows were closed; he was sealed in with his music. To his right the traffic moved slowly; the street was choked with people. To his left the crowd pushed past. He felt like a log, jammed in a river whose current flowed sluggishly on either side.

Ten minutes had passed. Every now and then, through a gap in the crowd, he glimpsed a nearby stall – a black guy, selling cassettes. The man's head bobbed up and down to the thump of the music; between the people, his head flickered like a freeze-frame film. A van was parked in front of Jon – an old Transit van, like the one he'd owned. There were stickers on the back window. 'FREE

TIBET', said one. It looked as if somebody had been picking at it with their fingernails. Below it, a yellow sticker said 'CREATE RANDOM KINDNESS AND SENSELESS ACTS OF BEAUTY'.

Five minutes passed. He was illegally parked; soon a traffic warden would move him on. Suddenly he willed Eva not to arrive, for none of this to happen. *Senseless acts of beauty*. What did it mean; what did any of it mean? The words rolled around his head.

He and Eva, they couldn't be doing this. His engine was running; he could just pull out into the traffic and drive away. The cassette clicked to a stop and jutted out; he turned it over and shoved it back in. *Random kindness.* A random piece of paper, blowing across the grass . . .

And then the back door opened. He heard a voice.

'You didn't say a car.'

'Come on, Hannah! They're waiting!'

'How do you know my name?'

Something bumped against the car. 'Come on, Hannah!' Eva's voice rose. 'Mum says you've got to come home!'

'What?' Suddenly the girl shouted. '*Help!*'

Nobody heard her. Through the open door Jon heard foreign voices, jabbering, '. . . *sprechen itchen* . . .', '*on hunraca oftin* . . .'. Nobody understood what was happening.

He revved the engine. In the driving mirror he saw Eva push the girl into the back seat. 'Drive!' she barked.

'Help!' yelled the girl.

Jon reversed. He pulled out into the traffic. In the mirror he saw the girl struggling with Eva. She yanked at the wig; it slithered off in her hand.

He pressed his foot on the accelerator; his passengers were flung back in their seat.

They had her! The girl lay curled in the back seat, covered with a blanket like a captured animal. In Africa they immobilised baby elephants with an injection. Eva's syringe was the gun; that's what turned this girl to stone. Eva, squashed in the back seat, pressed the pistol against the blanket. Jon overtook a bus and drove through Chalk Farm. It had happened; they had done it. He couldn't begin to believe it. The only thing that felt real was his cold – it had got worse; his throat was choked with catarrh.

A noise – a grunt – came from under the blanket. Eva said: 'It's all right, love. Don't move and you'll be fine.' *Love*? Eva never called anybody love. 'We're not going to hurt you. Not if you do what we say.' Her voice was crooning, like a little girl speaking to her doll. She sounded as if she had been practising this in front of the mirror.

He glanced over his shoulder at the blanket. It was motionless. The girl must be stiff with fear. He drove towards Acton, through grey, empty, Sunday afternoon streets. Eva had made a plan, of course, but as he hadn't believed they would actually capture the girl he hadn't taken it in. Though it was chilly, it was Sunday and the allotments would be at their most crowded. What were they going to do until darkness fell?

He looked in the mirror. Eva had put the wig back on her head. She readjusted it and lit a cigarette. Under the blanket, the girl coughed in the smoke.

Jon said: 'Hey, E –' He stopped in time. They had agreed not to call each other by name. They had also agreed that he mustn't turn round; the girl should never see his face, she should never be able to identify him afterwards. Eva she had only seen when heavily disguised. He had to remember all this now, all those words he had only half-heard. It was like barely listening to the safety instructions on a plane, and suddenly the aircraft catches fire and you have to remember them. He couldn't ask Eva about their plans, of course – not with the girl there. They must look as if they knew what they were doing.

What was she thinking, under that humped tartan blanket? They had performed a bodily act of violence. They had bundled a complete stranger into their car; they had broken the rules of human behaviour. The girl had struggled; she had cried *help*! But because he himself had done nothing – it was Eva who had grappled with her – because he had simply sat behind the wheel and driven the car like a normal person on a normal day, he still felt detached. Despite their careful preparations, the whole thing seemed too bizarre; he hadn't caught up with what they were doing.

He drove along the Harrow Road, past the barred and shuttered shops. A dog trotted across the road; he swerved. 'Ow!' A muffled yelp, from under the blanket. She had been rammed against the door handle.

'Sorry,' he said. Now he remembered. *We'll take her to the allotments. If there's people around we'll wait until dark . . .* It was five fifteen. It was June. Night wouldn't fall for hours. *We'll take it in turns . . . food . . . key for padlock . . . key for main gate . . .*

They had got her now, a big frightened breathing creature. Days stretched ahead. What was she feeling? What on earth were they going to do with her?

He sneezed. No 'bless you' came from the blanket.

As it turned out, they got her into the hut without any trouble. There were only a few people working in the allotments, all in the distance. The hut was on the edge, well away from the others, and surrounded by overgrown plots nobody used. Jon drove the car right up to the sagging wooden building and parked beside it, blocking anyone's view. Eva bundled the girl out. Jon started to help but he couldn't put his hands on her body, it might shock her. Blindfolded, she stumbled into the hut and Eva sat her down on a stool.

The girl didn't speak. Her chest rose and fell. She sat very still, like a frightened rabbit. Eva busied herself arranging things; she unpacked the carrier bags, pulling out the jar of Nescafé and the toilet roll. She still had the focused, intent look of a small girl setting out doll's-house furniture.

'What are you doing with me?' asked the girl. She sat there, clutching her ink-stained Indian bag. 'Who are you? I want to go home.'

'You can't. Not yet,' said Eva.

'It's a joke, isn't it?' The girl turned towards Jon. 'You're Ewan, aren't you.'

'Who's Ewan?' asked Jon.

'You're Emma's brother, I know you are. Listen, I'm sorry about Tania's party. I didn't mean it, what I said. Everybody fancies you really. Can we stop now? Mum and Dad'll be frantic.'

She sat there, her knees pressed together. The stool was so small, she looked as if she would topple over. The blue silk scarf was wrapped tightly around her head; beneath it, her mouth was tight. The heavy lower lip started to tremble. She looked as if she had been told to play blind-man's buff and was slowly realising that everybody had gone home.

Eva said: 'It's not a game, love. But you won't get hurt if you do what we say.'

Outside it started to rain, a drumming on the corrugated-iron roof. The girl clutched her bag. 'What's that? Where am I?'

'Somewhere safe,' said Eva. Jon wanted to pat the girl's knee, to reassure her, but he didn't dare in case she jumped. When he was young he had brought home a wounded mouse and had stroked it so lovingly it had died of fright.

'What are you going to do to me?' the girl asked.

'Nothing,' said Jon. 'Nothing, honestly. Not if your parents do what we say.'

'They'll get you! They'll find me! My dad's a very important person, he knows lots of people! He'll get the police –'

'Oh no he won't,' said Eva.

'He runs his own business, he's got fifty people working for him, he could just click his fingers –'

'Rich, is he?' asked Eva.

'Course he is! He could hire private detectives and helicopters and anything!'

'That rich, eh?' Eva stared at her intently.

'He could do anything! He'll find me!'

There was a silence. How loud the rain was! It rattled like pebbles on the roof. Eva leaned against the wall, looking down at Jon. She fiddled with the chestnut wig, twisting it around her finger as if it were real hair. Jon wished she would take it off. Sitting on the rolled-up mattress, he gazed up at her. Her eyes were narrowed; she was thinking hard.

It was cramped in the little hut, with the three of them, and they hadn't even set up the camp bed yet. Over the noise of the rain he could hear the girl's quick breaths. She was biting her nails. He wanted to speak to her but he didn't know what tone to use: whether to be comforting – his natural instinct – or to be severe enough to keep her cowed. Through the window the sky was charcoal-grey, as if dusk had already fallen.

Eva pulled the shawl out of a carrier bag. 'Let's put this up.'

He got out the hammer and nails; she held up the shawl against the window. He raised the hammer and turned to the girl. 'There's going to be a banging. Don't worry.' He felt like a doctor, explaining to a patient that there was going to be a little discomfort. 'We're just putting up a curtain.' He banged in the nails; the girl flinched. 'Then we'll light the lamp and I'll make us some coffee. OK?'

Eva frowned at him. What had he said wrong? The girl's hand was rummaging in her bag. 'Can I have a cigarette?' she asked.

Jon nodded, and then realised she couldn't see him. 'Sure.'

She fumbled blindly, pulling out various items – tissues, a wallet with a picture of Garfield on it. Her personal belongings looked pitiful, like the belongings of the victim of a car crash. She pulled out a paperback book, *A Dictionary of Art and Artists*; she pulled out a packet of Marlboros.

'Here, I'll light it for you,' he said, and struck a match. He thought: two smokers in this little hut, how are we going to breathe? He looked at the book. 'You like painting then?'

She nodded, blowing out smoke. 'I did,' she said. 'When I could see.'

This remark was so unexpected that Jon laughed. Eva glared at him. They lit the oil-lamp. At once the hut looked cosy. He knew what Eva was thinking: this mustn't get too bloody cosy. She gave the girl a plant-pot saucer and guided her hand to tap the ash from the cigarette – she suddenly seemed fastidious in this respect. Then she said, in a clipped voice: 'Take that thing out of your nose.'

The girl froze. 'What?'

'That stud. Take it out of your nose.'

The moment of cosiness vanished. The girl trembled. 'Why?' she asked. 'What are you going to do to me?' She must be thinking that they were preparing her for something indescribable, something sinister and painful, like removing a patient's jewellery before an operation. She took a drag of her cigarette.

Eva took the cigarette from her hand and stubbed it out. 'Hurry up,' she said.

Or maybe the girl thought they wanted to steal it. She clamped her bag between her knees, to free her hands, and fiddled with her nostril. Her hands were trembling so violently that it took a while to unscrew the stud. 'Just tell me what you want it for.'

'To prove we've got you,' said Eva. 'To prove to your parents.'

'You can't! Please! They'll freak out.'

Jon said: 'Then they pay us to get you back. Simple.'

She turned blindly towards him. 'What happens if they can't pay, what then? What happens if they *won't* pay?' Her voice broke. 'Oh, please. I want to go to the lavatory. I want to go home!'

Helplessly he stared at her. Two dark patches appeared on the blindfold, like blood seeping through a bandage.

From beneath it, tears slid down the girl's cheeks.

The other gardeners had long since left, bicycling or driving home through the rain. It was seven o'clock. When they opened the door, rain pattered on to the leathery dock leaves that choked the path. Eva took the girl to the toilet, a Portaloo next to the allotments' office. Jon watched them – a hunched blanket with four legs. *Umbrella*, he wrote, adding to the list of things they would need. *Beer. Toothpaste.* He wrote *Potty.* What a funny word; he hadn't said it since he was a child. They would need a potty for the hours of daylight. They could put it in the wardrobe that was leaning up against the back of the hut; it was hidden from the other plots. Uncle Charlie had kept his tools in there until the roof started leaking. *Potty.* How embarrassing. He hadn't thought of this side of things; of the practicalities of it. Even to himself he thought in euphemisms – *it* not *the kidnap.* In the hut he and Eva had had a hushed conversation about plans, but it was tricky to talk with the girl there and they couldn't leave her alone for a moment because she might pull off the blindfold. He was relieved that Eva hadn't suggested tying her up, but that may have been because they had forgotten to buy any rope. In the hut, there was only some frayed bailing twine.

Jon had volunteered to stay the night; he would sleep on the foam mattress and the girl on the camp bed. Eva had agreed. 'I'm not staying here!' she had whispered. 'The *spiders*!' One of them had to go home, partly because there was no room in the hut for three people and partly because a car, parked here all night, would look suspicious. Although they were surrounded by factories, somebody might notice. More importantly, the next morning one of them had to fetch supplies and send the ransom note. Eva had got the girl to tell them the family's fax and phone numbers. 'Leave it to me,' she had whispered to Jon. 'I'll take care of everything.'

She brought the girl back, took the car keys and paused at the door. He thought she was going to kiss him – after all, they had pulled it off! They had done it! Wasn't she thrilled? But maybe she was self-conscious with the girl there. She just left.

The sound of the car engine faded. Hannah fumbled in her bag for her cigarettes. 'What's happening?'

'I'm staying the night here with you,' he said. 'Don't be frightened. I'm quite safe.'

'I'm not frightened.'

'Oh.' Obscurely disappointed by this, he said sharply: 'You shouldn't smoke at your age. It's very bad for you. Your clothes get to smell of it.'

'I know. I could smell her too.' She put the cigarette back in the packet. 'I'll have it later.' She felt inside the packet. 'Only two left. They've got to last all evening. What are we going to do?'

He knew what she meant. 'Eat. I've got some tinned ham and baked beans –'

'I'm a vegetarian.'

'Baked beans then.'

118

'What's the time?'

'Seven thirty.'

'They'll be starting to worry. They'll be phoning up my friends.' Her voice rose. 'How could you do this to them? They'll be terrified.'

'But you're not.'

'I'm not frightened of you. But she bloody terrifies me.'

He thought: she terrifies me too. She's done something I would never dare do. Why? Because all her life, she's had nothing to lose.

'Who are you two?' the girl asked. Her belligerence was surprising; he hadn't expected this. He had thought she would be frightened – no doubt she *was* frightened, but she was making a courageous effort to cover it up. 'What are you doing this for?'

'What do you mean?' he asked.

'Like – who are you collecting the money for? You're not the IRA, are you? What's your cause?'

He paused. 'We haven't got a cause.'

'What?'

'We're the cause. Just us. We're doing it for us.'

She let out her breath. 'That's really sad. Aren't you ashamed of yourselves? You want to steal money from my family just because you want it? Why?'

There was a silence. The rain seemed to be easing off, or maybe they were just talking more loudly. 'That's what people do, steal things,' he said. 'Car radios, insider trading. Look at the papers. People do it all the time.'

'That's no excuse. That's pathetic.'

He fiddled with the carrier bag. She must sense he wasn't a kidnapping sort of person – who was? It confused him, this unexpected display of character. Who was in control here?

Jon pulled open the bag and took out a loaf of sliced bread and the tin opener. There were some bananas, too, and Kit-Kats. It was the sort of Boy's Own, knapsack-and-

119

fresh air sort of grub one would take hiking. Father and son would sit down together, ruddy and bonded. Except his father had been too busy shagging his secretary to take Jon hiking. A wave of self-pity swept through him. He remembered the rows – hushed voices through the wall; his father's slurred speech and the creak of the drinks cupboard door. He pictured the photos of this girl's parents. He thought: they don't look like that. I bet they're happy.

Except they're not happy now.

She was talking. 'Why did you choose me?'

'I can't tell you that.' He mustn't give out any information.

'We're not even that rich. Most of my friends are much richer. Nadia's got her own car. Why me? It's not fair.'

That was what Eva had wailed. He said: 'Nothing's fair, is it? In life.'

'Oh God. You going to go on like that? It's bad enough being locked up here.'

'Don't get stroppy, please,' he said. 'We've got a long haul ahead of us.'

'That's why I'm stroppy.' She paused. 'How long?'

He hadn't a clue, but he had to assert some sort of authority. Eva would know how to deal with this. He was missing her already. And their big warm bed. 'That depends on your parents.'

'Knowing my dad, he'll probably pay you to keep me here.'

'What?'

'We're always rowing. About me being messy and rude and not helping wash up. And being horrible to him, and my horrible music. He likes Becky much better. She's cunning, the little cow, she knows how to manipulate him.'

Jon stared at her. 'You mean, he wouldn't want you back?'

Under the blindfold the mouth split into a grin. 'Ha ha! You've got me for ever!'

'It's that bad?'

'He'll make me think this is my fault. Everything's my fault. He always manages to do that.' Suddenly the lower lip trembled. 'I don't care. I want to go home! I want to watch *Neighbours*.'

He sneezed, loudly, and thought: so do I.

She said: 'I don't even know your name.'

'No.'

'But you know mine.'

He nodded. 'It's Hannah.'

'That's not fair.' She started whimpering. 'Please, let me go home.'

When they had finished eating it was still only eight forty-five. This kidnapping thing seemed so dramatic when they planned it but he had never actually imagined what it would be like, if they pulled it off. *This*.

It was getting chilly. Outside it was raining softly. Hannah had been silent for some time. He felt they were on a little wooden ship, a Noah's Ark for two, alone on a vast ocean. It was amazing, how quickly one could feel utterly cut off from the world. He had made up the camp bed with difficulty; it was an old-fashioned one with rusty iron legs that slotted into canvas tubes, he'd had it since he was a child, it had belonged to his father. Hannah lay on it, covered with the tartan blanket. Outside some bird was singing, liquid notes that tumbled down. How free it was, compared to them! He realised: I'm as much a prisoner as she is. At intervals, a long way away, came the rumble of a Tube on the Jubilee line. When he lifted the shawl at the window to see if it was dark yet – it wasn't – he saw the illuminated centipede pass in the distance.

Hannah said: 'I wonder if they've been able to eat any supper.'

'Your parents?'

She nodded. 'I bet my sister has. The little pig. But they won't.'

It suddenly hit him, the profound wrongness of what they had done. He had wrenched this girl out of her life; its half-finished tasks remained half-finished. He had stopped her normal life as if she had been struck unconscious by a car. But this was no accident; he had done it on purpose. For the first time he really thought about her parents. He, Hannah and Eva knew what had happened; they were united in this respect. But the family in the photo – what nightmare must they be living through at this moment? And there were many more hours to go before they would hear any news. If only Eva could hurry up and contact them now, to put them out of their misery – or to change it into a different kind of fear.

Hannah lay still. With her face blindfolded, he couldn't tell if she were sleeping or not. It was unnerving. Without seeing the expression in her eyes, he couldn't guess what she was thinking. Already her moods had changed wildly. Sometimes she was stroppy; sometimes she cried. She was only a kid. She was kidnapped; he, unbelievably, was a kidnapper. Neither of them knew how to behave. In films kidnappers were violent, their victims trembling and trussed up. Sometimes, God forbid, bits were cut off them. Gazing at the motionless blanket he wondered how far Eva would go. *She bloody terrifies me.*

He pictured Eva bent over a hairbrush, pulling out the hairs and stuffing them into her pocket. Her nimble fingers, her busy little fingers, plaited them into a bracelet. She tied them together with a bead, red as blood.

Hannah turned towards him. 'What do you do when you're not doing this? Or do you do this all the time?'

'No.'

'What do you do? Am I allowed to ask? What on earth can we talk about?'

'What do you do?' he asked. 'Like, at school?'

'A levels.' Suddenly she wailed: 'I've got my Predictions in three weeks!'

He thought: I should have gone to college. At school they thought I was quite bright. I only dropped out to punish my father, and get away from him. 'You're lucky,' he said.

She laughed, harshly. 'Lucky? Oh yeah? Not the first word I'd use right now.'

'I mean –' He stopped.

'What happens if I fail? See, I need to get an A and two Bs if I want to get into Sussex next year.'

'What's in Sussex?'

'The university, of course.'

'Wish I'd gone to university. I'd like to have studied History.' Trouble was, it was impossible to read with Eva around. She kept interrupting him; the more engrossed he was in a book, the more annoyed she became. In fact, during a row about something entirely different – she was goading him about some former girlfriend, she was wildly jealous about his past, not that there was much to tell – during that row she had torn up his copy of *Moby Dick* and thrown it out of the window. It was a library book.

There was a long silence. *Quite bright.* If he were honest, and here in the hut there was nothing else to be – if he were honest, he had only been quite average. He could imagine, when he left school, that by the next week none of the teachers could remember what he looked like. An unmemorable boy.

Then he thought: for a criminal, being unmemorable is an asset. In fact, it's almost a job requirement.

He suddenly remembered the high spot of his schooldays. It was at primary school. He had constructed a sundial – he was good with his hands – and underneath he had written a poem.

Time is slow
Time is fast,
Time will last and last and last.

He was seven. His teacher, Miss Mason, had read it out. 'Quite profound, Johnny,' she had smiled.

How pathetic, that this was the high spot. He had forgotten it until now.

Don't be pathetic, Eva had said. And Hannah had said it too.

What else had he done, of note? Removed the 'H' in his name. And this. *This* was something. Oh yes, this was something all right.

He had a sudden desire to recite his poem to Hannah. It seemed appropriate, in the circumstances. But Hannah was silent. She sat hunched, biting her nails. He wanted to tell her not to, but it wasn't his place to do so.

Silly really, when he was doing this.

'Test me.' Hannah rummaged in her bag and brought out her *Dictionary of Art and Artists*. 'That'll be something to do.'

He opened it, leaning near the oil-lamp so he could see. ' "Signorelli",' he read.

'Er . . . Italian painter.' She paused. 'I think he was the pupil of somebody famous. Forgotten who.'

' "Pupil of Piero della Francesca." Who's he?'

'Don't you know? Ever been to Italy?'

He shook his head, then realised again that she couldn't see. 'No. Been to Spain, though. Twice.'

'He's one of my favourites. There's a wonderful Nativity in the National Gallery. Ever been there?'

'No.'

'Get back to Signorelli.'

' "1441–1533 ... his work finds its most complete expression in the famous fresco cycle at Orvieto Cathedral, which depicts his vision of life, death, resurrection and damnation." '

She paused. 'You feel guilty about this?'

He didn't reply. ' "Seurat, Georges." '

'Su-e-ra,' she said, correcting his pronunciation. 'French. Painted bathers with little spots.' Her hand wandered to her chin. 'How am I going to *wash*? Go on.'

' "Born 1859. His experiments with form, colour and line were part of a lifelong search for a sense of order ..." Here's the spot bit. "In his theory of Divisionism each colour is composed of tiny particles of pure colour which also reflect the colour of light." He's lost me there.'

'I have this stuff, see. Oxycreme. I have to put it on my pimples.' She stopped. 'Still, I don't really care because I can't see myself anyway.' She rubbed her eyes, through the blindfold. 'If it wasn't so tight, it'd be quite peaceful. Like, I can't see how horrible I look.'

'You don't look horrible.'

'The worse is when I catch sight of myself when I'm not expecting it – like in a shop window. When I've not got myself ready.'

'Everyone's like that at your age. I used to worry I was too white and weedy.'

'So that's what you look like?'

He smiled – then, realising she couldn't see, he laughed. That's what happens with blind people, he thought: your reactions have to be turned into a noise. It turns you into a new, hearty sort of person. 'No, I'm not white and weedy. I'm slim and incredibly good-looking.' And she couldn't see, by his face, if he was joking.

'It's funny,' she said. 'I know you in a different way than other people do.'

'Like, the real me.' He laughed again. 'You know the real me.'

There was a silence. He got up and tweaked aside the shawl; darkness had fallen, at last. Far away, a dog barked. Since the struggle in Camden Market a lifetime seemed to have passed; it seemed impossible that it was still the same day. He turned back, to look at Hannah. She had turned away and lay on her side. He didn't like it when they stopped talking.

He said: 'They aren't bad, honest – your spots. I know – I'm the one who can see them. But I'll get you that stuff. I'll put it on the list.'

'Just sometimes, when I'm dancing – that's when I forget what I look like. I get into this altered state.'

'I'm lousy at dancing.'

'Are you?'

'Yeah – according to you I dance like an accountant.'

'What do you mean?' She shifted around to face him.

He gathered his wits. Should he confess that she had met him? But it didn't matter, did it, because he was in disguise. 'I was that bloke at the Underworld on Friday. You know, oldish. The one who talked to you. The one who sneezed.'

She sat up straight. 'You?'

'You must remember me,' he said bitterly. 'You told your friend how unattractive I was. You said I danced like an accountant.'

There was a long silence. Outside, an owl hooted. 'Yeah – I do remember someone shouting at me. He had grey hair. But I never said anything afterwards. I didn't even *see* you dancing.'

'But you talked about me in the toilets.'

She shook her head. 'I talked about going to Camden Lock, I remember that. And then Emma and I measured our chins – which was the biggest. That's all.'

Jon digested this. Slowly it dawned on him: Eva had made it up. She knew he was wavering, that he was having doubts about going through with it. So she had

126

made him angry with the girl by making up that stupid remark – a remark that had wounded his stupid, stupid pride.

The worst thing was his pettiness. And the fact that Eva understood him so well. The bitch! Oh yes, he could believe she had done it all right. Knowing Eva, it all made sense.

He suddenly felt very tired. He unrolled the foam mattress. At that instant he knew that she had stolen the money from the beauty salon. Maybe Norman had had the hots for her, but she had made up the story about slapping his face. It was just her sort of lie. Utterly believable. Like the lie about Hannah.

He had to trust Eva; they had to trust each other. He suddenly thought: I don't even know what the real colour of her hair is. We've slept in the same bed for a year and I've never asked. What else don't I know? They were in this together, as deep as they could get. This wasn't petty pilfering; it was *crime*. Crime was more intimate than sex, terrifyingly intimate. And he hadn't prepared himself. Before today, the worst thing he had done was to claim benefit when he was doing cash jobs. But this was the real thing – too real for reality. He must pull himself together and face it: soon the police would be searching for them; they could be locked up in prison. Hannah could escape. Eva could betray him. In the chaos that lay ahead, anything was possible. Already he stiffened when he heard the sound of a car engine, and willed it not to stop. That was what criminals must feel, all the time, and he was a criminal now. He was guilty of giving enormous pain to unknown and blameless people. Soon, if all went according to plan, he would be guilty of large-scale theft. And he had no idea how Eva would react. This was almost as alarming as everything else.

Hannah lay curled up in a foetal position. He wished she would talk. He tried to be practical. To say something solid would reassure himself as well as her. 'I'll take you to the toilets soon. And there's a tap outside, so we can wash. When we go to bed I'll have to lock us in, I'm afraid.' He suddenly realised he would have to put something solid against the window, too, so she couldn't look out of it when he was asleep. 'When I've put out the light you can take off your blindfold. Is that OK?'

She didn't reply. His words seemed to have had the opposite effect from what he had intended. Low, whimpering noises came from the blanket. She was crying.

5

The next morning, Hannah had caught his cold. Jon felt absurdly guilty. The intermittent friendliness of the previous night had vanished. She sat on her bed, wiping her nose on damp lengths of toilet paper.

'When's that horrible woman coming?' she asked. 'I need some Karvol.'

'She's not horrible.'

'So kidnapping me's nice, is it?' She blew her nose wetly. 'Just because she's your wife or your girlfriend or whatever. Just because she's pretty and slim and hasn't got any spots. I should know, I just hear what her voice sounds like. If you closed your eyes and listened to her, you'd know what I mean. Her voice is all whiny and hard and fancying-herself. She's bloody psychotic.'

He closed his eyes, but all he could see was Eva's satin-smooth stomach and her dark, puckered nipples. He felt a sudden, dizzying wave of desire. 'She's had a terrible childhood,' he said. 'Her mother had a string of boy-friends. Then she married again and he molested her. You know, abused her.'

'Poor diddums. So what're you both doing to *me*?'

'Then she was put into foster-care.'

'That's no excuse. My dad, his uncle and his aunt died in Auschwitz. Six million people like him were gassed in the bloody camps. That hasn't made him go around locking people into huts.' She paused for breath. 'You're much nicer than her. So what does she see in you? Apart from you supposedly being slim and gorgeous. I can't see you, but I can see something *in* you. Maybe because I can't see you. What does she like about you, or is it just sex?'

Jon paused in the middle of rolling up his mattress. It was a question he had often asked himself. Was it just because he did the cooking and the shopping; because he doted on Eva and let her boss him around? She had told him, once, that he was unlike any other man she had ever known: he was gentle and understanding, he didn't get drunk and beat her up, he didn't just want her for her body.

Didn't he?

'Know who she reminds me of?' said Hannah. 'Lady Macbeth. We're doing it for A level. In fact, you might like to know, I've got a double period this morning.'

She fell silent. Far away he could hear the rumble of traffic. It was rush hour. Soon the schools would be filled with pupils, with one desk left empty. Soon the factories would be busy with people, toiling for years – for a lifetime – just to make the unimaginable amount of money he was aiming to extract like oil from this adolescent girl. Ten miles away, in Stanmore, two parents would be experiencing emotions that were inconceivable to him.

He opened the door. It was a dewy, misty morning. The allotments were ringing with birdsong. How beautiful it looked, how innocent! Despite everything, he felt his heart lifting to greet the sun. Spiders' webs, spun between the weeds on his uncle's plot, glistened with drops of mercury. There were no human beings in sight; it was Monday, and still early.

He led Hannah out, with her mug of tea, and sat her on an upturned bath. Already she looked paler; she emerged like a veal calf that has been kept in the dark. Because he knew he would never physically hurt her – nor, he presumed, would Eva – because he knew they were simply playing a dangerous game of dare with the highest of stakes and would bale out rather than carry through

130

any threat – because of all this he felt less guilty than he had expected and was grateful to Hannah for behaving with what seemed like normal teenage stroppiness. He also felt grateful to her for sleeping so soundly – in fact, her snores had kept him awake. He felt intimate with her, having become more acquainted with her bodily functions than with those of his closest friends. He felt bonded to her, having lain next to her in their little hut – his captured damsel, his blind Red Riding Hood.

He gazed at the dock leaves, struggling through the thistles. They were refreshed by last night's rain; he could almost hear them rustling as they grew. When he had first met Eva he had said: 'Let's run away and live in the middle of a wood. Just imagine it! You and me in a little cottage. I could make all our furniture, we could grow our own vegetables –' He had stopped. Eva was painting her nails; she looked at him with pity: 'Don't be pathetic.' Just what Hannah had said.

He took a gulp of tea. Hannah said: 'I've got to call you something. What shall I call you?'

He remembered a boy he had admired at school. 'Eliot.'

'As in T. S.?'

'What? Oh, yes.'

' "The Waste Land". That's where we are, aren't we? Somewhere in the middle of nowhere.' She sniffed. 'But where is it? Even with my cold I can smell biscuits.'

So could he. Up-wind from them, behind the industrial units, stood a Peak Freans factory. 'I can't tell you where we are. I'm not that stupid.'

Way up in the sky, a lark trilled. He gazed at the trembling dot. This waste land, lost in the hinterland of the city's edge, surrounded by blind industrial units and factories, was strangely affecting. Around him stood the little huts. They were constructed out of left-overs – car doors, window frames, corrugated iron and sheets of plastic. Doggedly assembled from the flotsam and jetsam of people's lives, they were a tribute to skills that few people possessed anymore – humble skills that he admired, that he himself had learnt. Now he and Hannah had been washed up in this lost shanty-town. '*The dirt! The spiders!*' cried Eva. She hated making-do; she liked to buy things, shiny and new, she lusted after luxury. But he found it soothing here. In the middle of the vast and indifferent city he and Hannah had disappeared into their own secret countryside. Days lay ahead of them.

He gazed at his uncle's weed-choked plot and thought: I'll dig this over and plant some seeds. Suddenly, with the thought of work, his skin tingled.

Hannah sneezed.

'Bless you,' he said.

'Don't be a hypocrite,' she replied, sharply, and blew her nose.

Later that morning Eva arrived. She wore her blue blouse and black leggings; she looked crisp and metropolitan, like an office worker arriving for her shift – she *was* arriving for her shift.

She said: 'I phoned, to make sure they were there. Then I sent the fax. And I posted the nose-stud.' Sneezes came from the hut. 'It's all going according to plan. We'll know, tomorrow, if they've fucked us around and told the police.'

'How?'

'Because it'll be in the papers, dum-dum.'

'What'll we do if that happens?'

She didn't reply. He urged her to answer. In one of the distant factories a tannoy sounded. He stiffened. *The police are evacuating the area . . . They are setting up road blocks . . . they are closing in . . .* He jerked himself back to reality. Eva was unloading things from the car. He looked at her firm little buttocks, shiny in lycra, as she bent over. He thought:

you cheated me. You told me something Hannah never said. But he didn't speak.

She had brought her Walkman and cassettes. They went into the hut and gave them to Hannah, who ran her fingers over the tapes, feeling them. 'What are they?'

'Sting. Madonna.'

'Ugh! Madonna! I thought it was bad enough torture, being locked up in here.'

'Shut the fuck up!' shrilled Eva. She turned to Jon. 'You let her talk like this?'

'You can stop me doing everything else,' said Hannah. 'You can't stop me talking.'

'I said shut up!' said Eva.

'What's the matter?' He realised, with surprise, that Eva was more jittery than he was.

She said: 'You, young lady, had better behave.'

'Why should I?' said Hannah. '*You're* the ones who're behaving badly.'

There was a silence. Far away, on the Jubilee line, a train rumbled. Eva turned to Jon. 'Why haven't you tied her hands? She can pull off the blindfold when you're not here.'

He pointed to the planks which he had nailed against the window. 'She can't see where she is. And when I knock on the door, she puts on the blindfold. We've worked out this system.'

'I don't trust her,' said Eva.

'Think *I* trust you?' Hannah's voice rose. 'Have you talked to my parents? Have you told them I'm all right? Well, not all right. How long have I got to stay here?'

'As long as it takes. Yeah, they know you're safe. But any messing around – you try anything, see? – and, like, you'll be sorry.' She turned to Jon. 'Why've you got your eyes closed?'

He was listening to her voice. Hannah was right – it was flat and whiny. Normally he gazed at Eva's ripe lips moving; normally he was distracted by her beauty. He looked at Hannah; under the blindfold, her mouth twitched.

It was time for him to leave. He wondered how the two females would get on together. Eva was rubbing some earth off her shoe. Already she looked restless. What was she going to *do*?

She gave him the car keys. As he started the engine he realised: since we captured Hannah we haven't touched each other, once.

He was unprepared for the effect it would have on him, the real world, once he entered it. Driving towards Tottenham that sunny Monday he felt disconnected and numb, as if he had jet-leg; he felt like a foreigner who had emerged, blinking in the daylight, from a different time-zone. He drove slowly, keeping his distance behind a bus. Yet he felt alert, too; his body had changed composition, as if he had been given a blood transfusion. He had become another creature. He *was* another creature: he was a criminal. He drove with care because he didn't want to draw attention to himself. He parked the car and walked round the block into the high street; he felt people's eyes looking at him. Even the sausages, hung in the butcher's window, seemed accusatory in the way they dangled. No wonder Eva had seemed jittery; now he knew how she felt. For it was only now, when faced with the normal world, that the abnormality of what they had done finally hit him. It was like a chemistry lesson he remembered at school; they had unstoppered a jar of crystals and it was only then, when they were in contact with the air, that the crystals changed colour.

On the landing, the phone didn't ring. In the flat, nobody lay in wait for him behind the door. Everything looked normal; the sun shone on the washing-up, stacked on the draining-board. He felt as if he had been away for a month – a lifetime. The man who had lived in this flat was someone he could no longer recognise. He busied himself with tasks. It felt odd, rifling through Eva's underwear to find some knickers for Hannah, but no odder than anything else. It was two o'clock in the afternoon but he ran himself a bath, as if he were an invalid. Afterwards, rubbing himself dry, he looked at himself in the mirror. A beaky young man gazed back at him – tousled brown hair, weak chin, smooth, hairless chest. Thirty-two years old. An unknown young man who was in the process of extracting £50,000 from total strangers. *Extracting* sounded better than *stealing*; it sounded more abstract. On the other hand it could suggest pulling out teeth from the roots.

He walked down to the garden centre to buy some seeds. Two policemen approached – young ones, in shirtsleeves. Jon's blood thumped in his ears. He walked past them, averting his head to look in a window. In the shop he gazed at the packets of seeds – Aquadulce Broad Beans, Nantes Carrots. Behind him a woman said to her friend: '. . . doused him in petrol and left him for dead.' He picked out some packets at random. When he walked to the counter he knew, quite clearly, that they all knew what he had done. The customers stood with their backs to him, pretending to inspect the geraniums, but they knew. Already the police had been informed; already they were closing in on the allotments. A toddler, sitting in its pushchair, looked at him with frank interest; its clear blue eyes gazed into his soul.

He hurried back to the flat. His shirt, damp with sweat, clung to him. He realised, suddenly, that he needed to get back to the hut and to Hannah. He couldn't wait. For it was only there, amongst the blameless vegetation, that he could find some measure of peace.

It is amazing, how human beings adapt. How they

establish their small routines and adjust to the seemingly unadjustable. How after a couple of days it seems life was always like this.

For a routine was established. Eva seldom came to the allotments, she hated the place. Mud and weeds and this eerie sort of camping, it wasn't her scene; she stayed away, she did the other stuff. Jon and Hannah were alone, those long summer days when the lark trilled above them; those short summer nights when the dog barked, far way in those lost and unimaginable streets where normal people must live.

He adjusted to her blindness, sleeping during the middle of the day, when there were people around, and staying up during the night when he took her on nocturnal walks. He led her along the cinder paths, between the cabbages and beans. Sometimes he closed his eyes, too, and lived through his senses. He picked a sprig of mint and held it to her nose. 'Smell this,' he said. In the daytime he smelt mulligatawny soup when the wind blew one way from the Heinz factory; when it blew from the Peak Freans factory he smelt biscuits.

'Feel this,' he said in the hut. He passed her a polished piece of wood. It was a length of yew his uncle had been planning to make into a box. 'It's centuries old. Feel the peg-holes. They didn't have nails then. Feel the grain in it, feel how it's never chilly.' He knew he was being boring but he had a captive audience. 'Wood has this warmth inside it. Think of the hands that have felt it.'

He felt a curious sense of liberation. He cut planks of pine, for shelves, and sanded them down. Unlike Eva, Hannah didn't make a fuss about the mess. Her mum made a fuss, she said. 'She's always yelling at me about my room.' The she stopped. 'I wonder if she will when I get home. *If* I ever get home.'

He emerged in the late afternoon to dig over the plot, wrenching out the thistles, pulling out their long white tap roots and flinging them away. Way beyond the fence the factory hooters sounded and the gainfully employed downed their tools and left the allotments to their silence. He and Hannah were the disappeared; they were alone in the world. Only once, late one afternoon, did he straighten up from his gardening to find an old man standing nearby, watching him.

'You want to double-dig that,' he observed. 'Way you're doing it, the weeds'll come back up.'

Jon glanced at the hut. Would Hannah hear them? Would she call out? But nothing happened. The old man inspected the earth.

'You young people,' he said, 'it's all instant results, innit? Know what you want?'

'What?' asked Jon, willing him to go away.

'Something for nothing.'

As the days passed Hannah's moods fluctuated. Sometimes she was angry with him, for what he was putting her through – for what he was putting her parents through. How could he do this to them, when they had done nothing?

'How much am I worth?' she kept demanding. 'How much have they got to pay?'

Finally he told her.

'£50,000.' She repeated it. 'You greedy bloody pigs. Why should you get all that, why should you get something for nothing? How am I going to face them?'

'It's not your fault.'

'They wouldn't mind paying it for Becky. Miss Bloody Spoilt Brat. Everyone loves Becky. Oh no, they wouldn't mind paying it for her. Or Theo. He's a *boy*. He thinks he's the bee's knees, he thinks he's God's bloody gift. Mum dotes on him. They bought him a Beetle for his eighteenth birthday. Catch them buying *me* a car.' Her voice broke. 'Well they won't now, will they? Oh God, why am I being

137

horrible about them to *you*, of all people? See how horrible I am?'

He patted her on the shoulder. She jumped. Sometimes he still forgot that she couldn't see. She was wearing his grey sweater today, and the same long black skirt she wore all the time. She sat there, a big girl, her greasy skin bare of make-up. It was a one-way business, talking with somebody whose eyes one couldn't see; it blocked the expression from her face and put him both at an advantage and a disadvantage. Blind, she seemed to sense things deeper. He tried to accompany her by keeping his own eyes closed.

'If only I looked like my mother,' she said. 'I wish I was blonde. Even when she's wearing jeans she looks glamorous. She makes me feel like a lump. I want to be pretty.'

'You are.' He kept his eyes shut. 'And you're nice inside. I should know that, by now. You're ever so plucky. I bet they wouldn't be as brave as you're being. Who cares about looks? Maybe we should all go around with our eyes closed, then we'd know what people are really like.'

He thought about Eva. It was Thursday. They hadn't really touched, let alone made love, for nearly a week. He was realising how necessary sex was to their relationship, how it was only making love that drew them close. Their entwining bodies had a life of their own. Suddenly it seemed as if all they had been doing together was generating heat, to keep the loneliness away.

He said: 'Come on, let's get back to work.' He opened the book. ' "Caravaggio." '

'Italian, fifteen something –'

' "1571–1610" ,' he said.

'Born very poor but suddenly his fortunes changed. Like yours really, except he had talent. See, he was commissioned to do some paintings for the . . . what was it, the Contarelli Chapel. At the height of his success he killed a man in a brawl . . .'

'Great! Go on.'

'. . . dramatic use of light . . .' Coaxed by him, she grew calmer. They became almost friends again.

His own moods fluctuated too. Sometimes he felt surprisingly serene in the little hut, companioned by this blind girl with whom he felt increasingly intimate – after all, they were both going through the most extraordinary experience of their lives, an experience nobody else would ever be able to understand or share. But sometimes he was seized with panic. What was going to happen? Even if everything went according to plan, could he really cope with it? Already he felt nauseous with guilt. And then there was that other, deeper feeling – fear. He was deeply, truly frightened. More frightened, he imagined, than Hannah had ever been since the struggle in Camden Market. For no possible punishment awaited her.

On Friday it was cold and blustery. He asked: 'Are your parents religious?'

'My mum was brought up C. of E. but she's never done anything about it. She worships at the altar of style.' Outside, the wardrobe door banged in the wind. 'There was a great fuss when she married my dad. His parents were ever so strict. They were horrified he was marrying out.'

'Is he still religious?'

'He says nobody can ever stop being a Jew. However much they try. He worships at the altar of guilt. He probably thinks, deep down, this is happening to punish him.'

'What for?'

'For surviving.'

They were silent. Outside, the door banged. She said: 'My hair feels disgusting. I wish I could wash it.'

He said: 'My father punished himself by becoming an alcoholic.'

'What had he done wrong?'

139

'I never knew, but I thought it must be my fault.' He had never told Eva this; they didn't have these sort of conversations. 'I haven't seen him for years. He made my mother so unhappy that after she died I didn't speak to him again. He moved up north. In fact, I think about him in the past tense.'

'So you've been punishing him too.'

He paused, considering this. 'I think he was unhappy because he didn't believe in anything.'

She said: 'It'd be convenient if you didn't believe in God either.'

'Why?'

'Because if you don't believe in Him, He can't see what you're doing.'

The wind blew through the cracks in the hut. Jon struck a match, to make some tea. The flame flickered. Hannah inspected her fingers; she still did this, after all these days blindfolded. She chose one and started to gnaw it.

'It's our last night,' he said. 'Let's get well and truly plastered.'

'Like your father did?'

'No. Not like him.'

6

'What's wrong?' asked Eva. 'What's happened?'

'We can't go through with it.'

Funnily enough she didn't flare up. She gazed at him with a small smile, as if he were a retard. 'You look wrecked. Got a hangover?'

He nodded. He and Hannah had drunk a bottle of Martini Bianco the night before. He didn't want to think about it, any of it. He wanted, violently, to let her go.

Eva said: 'Listen, loverboy. It's Saturday. It's our last day. We're all feeling a bit antsy, know what I mean?' She ran her finger down his thigh. 'Just stay cool.'

They were sitting in the car, next to the hut. His fork stood in the freshly-dug earth. He could have buried Hannah in there and nobody would ever know.

He willed himself to wake up and discover it had all been a dream. No crime, no punishment. He would open his eyes and see their familiar wallpaper, with the stain near the ceiling. He would sit up in bed, and his biggest fear would be that he had left the car on a double yellow line.

Oh the sweetness, the innocence! His life prior to this week was bathed in a golden glow. Nothing could ever bring that back, he had passed beyond the point of no return. His life was divided into a Before and an After. He would have to cope with this feeling for ever, just as people had to learn to live with chronic pain.

He said: 'Let's just let her go. Unpadlock the hut and bugger off. Let's do that!'

Eva wasn't listening. 'I'd better go,' she said. 'Got a lot to do . . .' She ticked off her fingers: 'Map . . . swimsuit . . .' She turned to him. 'Wish me luck.'

I'm sorry I'm sorry I'm sorry. He sat next to Hannah in the hut.

'It's all right,' she said. He jumped. He hadn't realised he had spoken out loud.

'I'm sorry,' he said.

'It's a bit late for that.'

The mobile phone rang. They both jumped.

It was Eva. There was interference on the line; her voice roared and receded like waves on a shore. 'I've done it,' she said. 'I've got the money. I'll see you later.'

They had to wait until dark before they released Hannah. Until then there was nothing to do. The afternoon seemed to last for ever. It seemed to last longer than the whole preceding week. Eva visited briefly, flushed and distracted. She smelt of chlorine. She said she had had a swim while she waited, otherwise people would have noticed her. She had seen Hannah's mother, wearing the yellow swimsuit, getting into the water.

'It's in the boot,' she whispered. 'It's all there, I've counted it.' Then she left, to take it to the flat. She drove off, crashing the gears.

The hours dragged by. The afternoon had the restless, already-vacated feel of the hours before one is about to go on a long journey, when the bags are packed and one doesn't know what to do. Jon started to rake the earth but even this simple task seemed too exhausting. He entered the permanent twilight of the hut and lay down next to Hannah. The Walkman was clamped to her ears but he could hear no scratchy beat. He had been trying to interest her in jazz, with little success. He had a stomach ache. He knew he should feel relieved, but knowing this didn't make it any better.

He closed his eyes. In the darkness, Hannah spoke.

'Come, seeling night,

Scarf up the tender eye of pitiful day.'

'What?'

'*Macbeth*,' she said. 'This downy sleep, death's counterfeit.' She paused. 'First thing I'm going to do is have a bath. God. I feel so dirty.'

He thought: so do I.

When he woke up it was truly dark. Somebody was rattling at the door. He jumped up and fumbled with the padlock. Eva stood there. Behind her, the moon had risen.

'OK,' she said. 'Let's go.'

In the car, none of them spoke. He drove along the North Circular; on either side, houses slumbered under the sodium lights. It was half past midnight. Hannah and Eva sat in the back, as they had done on the journey from Camden Lock a thousand years ago. He fiddled with the radio. '. . . soldier in Northern Ireland . . . body of a young girl . . . Celtic Rangers . . .' He found some music – country-and-western. 'Your cheatin' heart . . .', sang a woman with a swooping, elastic voice.

They arrived at Apex Corner. Above them loomed the signs: A1 HATFIELD AND THE NORTH . . . M1 WATFORD. Even at this hour traffic thundered around the vast roundabout, but the Burger King Drive-Thru was closed and the parade of shops shuttered up. There is nowhere more anonymous than a huge roundabout; that was why they had chosen it. He parked next to a darkened shop called 'Simply Bathrooms'.

'What's happening?' Hannah's voice was sharp. She seemed a stranger; it felt as if they had returned full circle to the beginning again. It was like the end of a holiday, when people change back into their travelling outfits and hang around awkwardly at the airport. Like this, but much more strange. Their plan was to lead her down the concrete walkway, down into the sunken pedestrian underpass beneath the roundabout and leave her there. Now they were sitting here, however, he felt alarmed. How could they just ditch her? It seemed more brutal than snatching her in the first place. What happened if, after all they had gone through, she got murdered on the way home?

He wound down the window. The air smelt of exhaust fumes. Beside the car, steps led down into the mouth of the underpass. The walls were scrawled with graffiti: 'SHANE IS A PLONKER'. Even through the traffic fumes he could smell urine. 'MB AND GM ARE BUM CHUMS.'

'Come on!' hissed Eva.

He started the engine. 'There's a taxi rank at Edgware station,' he said. 'We'll leave her there.'

'A taxi?' Eva's voice was sarcastic. 'Very nice. How about giving her a going-home present too?'

'I just mean, it's the least we can do.'

They parked down the road from the station. In the distance a taxi waited, its sign illuminated. Edgware was deserted. He got out and opened the back door. Hannah climbed out, clutching her ink-stained shoulder bag. What should he do – shake her hand? Social etiquette didn't cover this particular situation.

'Count to ten,' Eva told her. 'Then you can take off the blindfold. OK?' She paused. 'We'll be watching.' Jon couldn't work out what she was threatening. Maybe she herself didn't know.

He laid his hand on Hannah's shoulder. 'Take care,' he said. She stood on the pavement. A chilly wind blew her black skirt up; she brushed it down. 'Look after yourself.' He was dismayed at what he was saying, the inadequacy of it. She didn't reply. Behind her a sign in a shop window said 'HURRY! LAST DAY.'

'I'm sorry,' he said, and got back into the car.

When they finally got home it was two o'clock. Jon could hardly climb the stairs; Eva grabbed his hand and pulled him through the front door. She yanked the curtains closed, knelt down and pulled out two carrier bags from under the bed. They were large ones: Top Shop and French Connection. She put her arms around them and fondled them like babies.

There was still a crack in the curtains; the people in the flats opposite could look in. He pulled the curtains closed. Eva was kneeling on the floor. She pulled out wads of banknotes; they were tied with paper bands. They looked as unreal as movie money. He remembered the first time he had seen Eva: sitting in the pub, giggling over the ten-pound note.

'Come and get them,' she grinned. She started stuffing them down her T-shirt.

He stared. 'There's so much of it! I've never seen that much money before.'

'You mean, like £500,000?' She looked up at him impishly, and stuffed a bundle down the waistband of her jeans.

'Like what?'

'Like this. Like half a million.'

He was silent. Down in the street an ambulance passed, its siren ringing. He said: 'What did you say?'

'Aren't I a clever girl? She said her daddy was rich, remember? Remember her bragging? So I thought – why the fuck not?'

'But we agreed –'

'You going to complain?'

Half a million pounds. He sat down, heavily, on the bed.

'Half a fucking million,' she said. 'Don't I get a kiss?'

Numb, he gazed at the bags. He had to make a massive

readjustment; he could feel his brain clanking like machinery. Until now, £50,000 seemed unimaginably large.

'Hey, you!' Her fingers clicked in front of his eyes.

He gazed at her, awe-struck. 'You're quite something.'

'Aren't I just.' She pounced on him, and wrapped her thin strong arms around his neck. 'Don't you love me now?' She pressed her face close to his. He smelt the tobacco on her breath. *I could smell her too*, said Hannah.

Eva's fingers pulled at his zip. She yanked it down and slid her hand inside his jeans. She whispered: 'I suppose a fuck is out of the question?'

Part Three

1

Hannah's deep sleep lasted twelve hours. When she awoke it was Sunday afternoon. Her sight had been restored – how shiny her posters looked! The sun, sparkling on her glass animals, hurt her eyes. Her bedroom had been tidied. Now it was cleared, she noticed how many of her childish things still remained. The clutter of her recent life had been swept away or stacked on her desk. It had reverted to the room of her youth, she was still a child, wrapped up safely under her jungle animals duvet. Downstairs she could hear the clatter of pans . . . Sunday lunches back in the past. When she woke up she would get on her bike and search for Theo and his gang; she knew where they would be hiding . . . in the boarded up hut in the recreation ground, just beyond the swings . . . Once they had taken her prisoner there, they had barricaded the door and pedalled away . . . it had taken her ages to wrench open the door and get out . . . boys were so cruel . . .

She opened her eyes again and realized what was happening. Her family was waiting downstairs to celebrate her return from the dead – from the could-be-dead. She looked at her clock; it was two thirty. She lay under her duvet, willing them not to come upstairs yet, willing them not to know she had woken. If she closed her eyes the blackness rose up again, but when she opened them it drained away. Already, separated by her sleep, the events of the past week seemed as unlikely as the adventures she had embarked on in her dreams, if only she could remember them . . . the rec, the swings . . . In fairy stories it happened – a prick of a needle, a long slumber, and the heroine wakes up to find everything transformed. She gazed at her poster of James Dean. He had died too, long ago – he had died before she was born. But still he gazed back at her, his eyes narrowed through his cigarette smoke. He understood the change that had taken place within her.

She could smell food cooking; the lost, roast-beef scent of her childhood. Long ago, when her mother was a proper mother, home all day, she used to cook Sunday lunch . . . years ago, she had lain in bed and her father had read her stories, just as she had been lying in the dark during the big sleep of the past week . . . lying there, listening to the man read to her . . . the Resurrection . . . the Day of Judgment. She had heard about the man's childhood too, things he had told nobody else. They had talked for hours, speaking their secrets into the darkness. Just now he felt more intimate with her life, more familiar to her, than the voices of her family downstairs.

She ought to get up, but she couldn't. Enveloped in warmth, she lay in her womb-like bed. How soft the mattress was! Her feet didn't stick out at the end. When she turned, no camp-bed bar dug into her hip. How comforting were the things she had taken so heedlessly for granted. Her own soft bed. Her eyesight.

It was so simple, not to move. How simple it had seemed too, the joy last night when she had stepped out of the taxi. The four of them, illuminated in the doorway. 'Hey, can someone pay my fare?' she had called. The scrunch of her feet as she ran up the drive and into her mother's arms. Hugs, tears, laughter . . . Hot chocolate, a hot bath, tender questioning . . . for the first time in years she had felt swamped by simple love. It had been there all the time, a bedrock beneath the squabbles.

The door creaked open. Becky came in. She carried

Mandy the Moose. 'I knew you were only pretending,' she said.

'I *was* asleep –'

'Get up, I'm starving. Mum's cooked a proper lunch, everyone's waiting for you.'

Hannah felt the stirrings of guilt. She pushed back the duvet.

Becky put the moose on the bed. 'You can have her back now.'

Hannah looked at the lolling grey object. 'I don't want it anymore.'

'It's not *it*. It's her.'

She picked it up and gave it to her sister. 'I'm too old for it now. You can have her.'

As Hannah was going downstairs the phone rang. She picked up the receiver on the landing. It was Tanya. 'Hi! So you're better?'

'I'm fine,' said Hannah.

'What was it, 'flu? Have you been in bed all week?'

'Sort of.' Tanya didn't know! None of them did. Hannah swelled with excitement. Just wait till Monday, till she told them! 'I've been, like, lying in the dark.'

'I do that, when I get a migraine,' said Tanya.

'I just need to get used to walking around again.'

Tanya laughed. 'Rejoin the land of the living. See you tomorrow.'

'Did you have enough to eat?'

'Were you frightened?'

'They didn't hurt you? They didn't lay a finger on you?'

'Did they tie you up?'

'How did you go to the loo?'

'Becky!'

'What did you *do* all the time?'

The questions were fired at her from all directions –

more questions than last night, when she had been too tired to tell them much. It was both confusing and gratifying to be the centre of attention. Normally she was the cause of complaint – *Your room! Your clothes!* Now every single moment of the past week was of intense interest to the four members of her family gathered around the table. Even Theo gazed at her with the full-voltage look his face wore when he spotted a Harley-Davidson in the street. Her father carved the joint. Hannah flinched as the moist red beef curved and fell on to the serving dish. Everything was so vivid; it was like emerging from a cinema into broad daylight.

'Did she really have a gun?' asked Becky. 'Were there any spiders?'

'You say it was a hut,' said her father, passing her a plate. 'Is that all you saw?'

Hannah nodded. 'The window was boarded up. It was just – like a hut for garden tools.'

'How long did it take to drive there? Have you any idea of the location?'

'Think of clues!' said Becky.

'I heard a train, sometimes.'

'A train?' said her mother.

'And a factory hooter.'

'You've described the woman,' said her mother. 'Have you any other clues to their identity? Doesn't this sound strange, like an Agatha Christie. Did they never address each other by name?'

Hannah shook her head. 'He told me he was called Eliot, but it wasn't his real name. I'll think of everything I can, to tell the police. Maybe they can piece it together.'

Her parents exchanged a glance. At the time she didn't understand what they meant. Theo was talking.

'I can just see it.' He moved his hand in front of his face. 'Panning shot around Camden Lock, jostling crowds, very Chabrol, cut to woman in red wig –'

'It isn't a film,' said Becky. 'It's much more exciting.'

'It felt like a film,' said Hannah. Actually this wasn't true. It was the lunch that felt like a film – mouths mouthing at her, voices echoing, Technicolored vegetables heaped on her plate. It was odd, to *see* what one was about to put into one's mouth.

Her father looked heavier; puffier, somehow. Her mother looked gaunt. There were tiny lines around her mouth. Maybe they had been there before and Hannah hadn't noticed; she hadn't really looked at her parents for years. 'What about you?' she asked. 'It was you I was worried about. I knew *I* was all right.'

'It doesn't matter,' said her mother. 'Nothing matters, now you're back.'

'But I feel so awful. You've paid all that money.' She speared a carrot. '£50,000. How did you find it?'

There was a silence. Theo said: 'Fifty? It wasn't fifty. It was five hundred.'

'Five hundred pounds?' asked Hannah.

Her father said sharply: 'Not now, Theo –'

'No, fathead.' Theo drained his glass of wine. 'Didn't you know? They paid £500,000, just for little you.'

Their mother made a clucking noise with her tongue. 'Theo, this isn't the time –'

Theo pushed back his long black hair. 'They're totally cleaned-out. Dad's had to sell his shares in the business.'

Hannah couldn't stop trembling. It wasn't cold; in fact it was stifling. Lunch had been cleared away. Her mother turned a handle and winched down the blinds to shut out the sun. *Aren't us humans funny?* she had laughed once. *We spend all this money building a conservatory, and then a whole lot more installing blinds to turn it back into a room.* This afternoon, however, nobody was laughing. It seemed ominous, as if she were closing off the outside world so that nobody could hear what they were saying. Her father lifted Amy, their cat, off the table and lowered her to the floor.

'Coffee, sweetheart?' asked her mother.

Her dad had sold his own business! He had built it up from nothing, it was his life's work. What was he going to do now?

'Thanks.' Hannah took the cup. It rattled in its saucer.

'Coffee for you, Theo?' Her father passed him a cup.

It was she who had caused it, she who was responsible. *Don't worry*, he had said, *it's only money*. It was half a million pounds. She had ruined him; it was all her fault.

Her father cleared his throat. 'We're not going to tell the police.'

Hannah stared. 'What?'

'What's the good, if you have no clues? If this is all you know?'

'But Dad – maybe I can think of something else.'

'Now listen, all of you,' he said. 'This whole thing, we keep it to ourselves. Me and your mother, we've agreed.'

Hannah looked at her mother. She sat there, her head in her hands. Her fingers dragged down her eyes at the corners. She looked at her husband. 'I agree. I didn't, but I do now.' She turned to Hannah. 'If you'd been hurt, well, that'd be different.'

'You want everybody staring at us?' said her father. 'You want the whole world to know something that's no business of theirs? People pitying us and whispering about us, you want our story in the papers?'

Hannah felt sick. 'You mean, you're ashamed of me, of what's happened?'

'Darling, don't be silly,' said her mother. She tugged at her fringe. 'We just don't want people banging on our door –'

'She could sell her story to the *Daily Mail*,' said Becky. 'We could get lots of money!'

'Shut up,' said Theo.

154

'Malcolm knows, in strictest confidence,' said her father. 'In fact he's lent me a large percentage of the cash; as luck would have it he sold one of his properties last week and he's helped me out. And we'll have to tell your headmistress . . . make some arrangement about school fees –'

'What about me?' wailed Becky.

'I'm sure we'll sort something out.' Their mother tugged at her fringe. It alarmed Hannah. The last time she did that was when Granny Wilson had had her operation for bowel cancer.

'Can't we tell Granny?' she asked.

'Nobody,' said her mother. 'It's our secret.'

'We shall have to face some major changes.' Amy jumped on to the table; her father put her on the floor. 'Your mother and I, we're working out what we're going to do. But we face it together, all of us, and we face it alone.' The cat jumped up again. He ignored her. 'The only important thing is that we have you home safely. That's the only thing that matters.'

Her mother nodded. No – she was just pulling at her fringe.

The next day Hannah's headmistress, Mrs Beestock, invited her into her study. She asked if she needed the services of the school counsellor. 'In strictest confidence, of course.'

Hannah shook her head.

'You seemed to have behaved with great spirit,' said Mrs Beestock. 'From what I've read, however – the Beirut hostages and so on – you may experience an unexpected reaction later. Delayed shock, something like that. So please remember, I'm here if you need me.'

At lunch Tanya, Emma and Julia crowded round her. Why had Mrs Beestock called her in?

'Oh, just to talk about catching up with work.' Hannah peeled the lid off her yoghurt.

They lost interest. Julia told them about some party she had been to on Saturday night, how they had smoked dope through a bong and watched old *Blackadder* vidoes. Hannah thought: I could open my mouth and silence this room. I could say: *I wasn't ill last week. I was kidnapped. I spent six days blindfolded in a hut.*

Power swelled up within her; power to stop their chattering, to drop the spoons from their fingers. Eating her yoghurt she imagined them gazing at her, awe-struck. At a stroke, she was superior to them all. A week ago she had felt so inadequate – so big and spotty, so lacking in a boyfriend. She had felt excluded from their giggling confidences, from Emma's sexual know-how. Now, at a leap, she had sprung way ahead of them – not just ahead, but out of their orbit altogether. She had been projected into a criminal, adult universe they had only read about in the papers. She had been there, and from now onwards it would be they who seemed childish.

Actually it wasn't as pleasant as she had hoped. Her secret, lodged within her, leaked a corrosive fluid like a battery leaking acid. In English she gazed at the notes she had borrowed from Tanya; the words jumped like gnats. *Jane Austen's irony . . . compare and contrast . . .* How could she possibly be a schoolgirl again, sitting at this ink-stained desk? She gazed out of the window. She remembered Sunday, just eight days ago: the last day of her childhood. Walking to the Tube station she had imagined vanishing from the face of the earth . . . *I'll disappear and nobody will notice . . .* How simple it had seemed! How pathetically infantile.

At four o'clock the bell rang. She collected her bags and walked through the gates. Out in the street she saw her mother, sitting in the car.

'What are you doing here?' Hannah hissed.

'I've come to collect you.'

'I'm not a baby!' She glanced around, to see who was watching.

Her mother said: 'From now on, darling, I'm not going to let you out of my sight.'

For several days she was treated gently, as if she were convalescing from a major operation. Nobody nagged her to help with the dishes or get on with her revision. Her father treated her with a tender solicitude she hadn't known for years. She lay on her bed, separate from the rest of the household, while the sunlight inched across the wallpaper. Even Becky was instructed not to disturb her. She felt simultaneously isolated and the centre of attention, like royalty. She felt like an explorer who had been to a remote country nobody else had visited, somewhere with its own bizarre landscape, and she had returned home with no photos. Try as they might, none of her family could understand what she had been through. The only person who could was the man whose voice and presence had shared the hut with her; only he knew how she felt. Did he feel the same, wherever he was?

She closed her eyes and the sounds rose up: the hiss of the tin-opener as it pierced a lid, the scratch of his match and gentle pop-pop of the Calor-gas ring. The sound of him clearing his throat before he read aloud from her book; the way he hummed under his breath as he moved around the hut, swilling out mugs in the plastic bowl . . . the way he whistled when he was sawing wood . . .

The scents . . . the sweaty scent of his armpit when he leaned over her to reach the shelf . . . the cheap soap that reminded her of hotels . . . her own body odours that he must have been able to smell, they were so strong . . . the cloying perfume of that woman, when she came into the hut . . .

The feel of things, the *thingness* of them . . . the way she

157

learnt to use her fingertips as her eyes, like a snail's horns
. . . the feel of the nylon sleeping bag when she buried her
face in it, dampening it with her tears . . . the feel of his
hand, dry and strong, as he guided it to the china mug-
handle . . .

Why hadn't she attempted to see his face? *Can't you
describe anything?* her mother had asked. At night she
could have grabbed the torch and shone it on him. How
feeble she had been! At first she had been frozen by fear.
Even if he didn't wake up, he would *know*. That horrible
woman would know. If she just lay there, motionless,
nothing would happen to her. Time wore on and she
realised that he wouldn't harm her, but by then she had
subsided into a curious passivity. She had lain there
inertly like a bathroom sponge, absorbing the sensations
around her. She had sunk deeper into her memories;
during her week of hibernation the foreground of her life
had stepped back and the background stepped forward.
But nobody would understand that. They thought that
having a criminal thing happen to you must be terrifying,
thrilling, those sort of words. Big words. They didn't
realise that nothing stays big for long.

She should have roused herself from her inertia and
tried to identify her whereabouts, for her parents' sake.
Lift that blindfold, love, and you're dead, ordered the woman.
And she, Hannah, had obeyed. What a coward! She had
learnt many truths in the hut. One of them was that she
was not as rebellious as she had thought. It was easy to be
mutinous in the safety of your home; quite a different
matter when you had had a gun pressed against your ribs.
True rebellion meant more than wearing a nose-stud. She
should have done a Colditz and used her ingenuity –
worked loose one of the planks in the window, maybe, so
she could see the car number-plate. Then her parents
would call in the police and, who knows, maybe they
would recover the money. They weren't blaming her for

this. Nobody blamed her for anything. But this only made her feel more guilty.

Hannah lay in the bath. She had been having a lot of baths this week. She scooped foam over her pubic hair and gazed at the meringue of froth. The real reason lay much deeper. She could hardly admit it, even to herself.

'I feel I've known you for ever', he had said. 'Isn't that strange?'

The real reason was, she couldn't bring herself to betray him.

Hannah slid under the water. She didn't want to think about it. She closed her eyes and tried to concentrate on what they were doing, him and that woman. Were they living it up in Spain? Drinking champagne at the Ritz? She still couldn't believe that they had stolen so much money. The amount was so huge it was abstract, it was beyond imagining. Normal robbers did physical things like breaking into cars and houses. In her home no windows had been smashed, nothing had been removed. The atmosphere had altered – there was a low thrum of anxiety in the air, her parents spent a long time behind closed doors, murmuring to each other and speaking on the phone. She caught the words 'selling the Renault'. Her mother was at home most of the time but that simply made it feel safer than usual. No, eighteen Cypress Drive remained the same – sunny, carpeted rooms, mumbling pipes when someone ran a bath. It remained the same, comfortable home in which she had spent her childhood; the suburban security against which she had recently rebelled – *Ugh! Stanmore. So boring!* – but which now, to her relief, sealed her in from the violent outside world.

So it seemed, anyway, during that convalescent week. So it seemed, until the bombshell dropped.

On Friday evening Theo came over for dinner. Her father was no longer a practising Jew – 'Well I've learnt it now, haven't I?' he used to joke. However, the one thing he insisted on was that they all gathered for dinner together on Friday evening. Theo arrived, looking blanched from a week spent editing his fingers film. Their mother had cooked a chicken for them and a vegetable risotto for Hannah. In the past she used to microwave meals from Marks and Spencer's but this week she had shopped at the local greengrocer's. Hannah hadn't liked to ask her: is this because you want to be a diligent mother or because you can't afford to go to Marks and Spencer's any more?

Tonight her mother chopped courgettes like a housewife. In fact she was starting to look like one; her heavy blonde hair was pulled back in a clip and she wore a tracksuit. Despite the reassuring smells of cooking, she looked tense and abstracted. She snapped at Becky to help lay the table, then suddenly hugged her awkwardly, pinioning her daughter's neck against her side. She poured tonic instead of soda into her husband's whisky. More surprising even than this, he gulped down a mouthful before he noticed.

As they ate, Hannah watched her father. He cut up his chicken with care, into small pieces, before spearing it with his fork. She knew, by the intent way he did it, that he was preparing to make a speech. He hadn't said anything yet about the money side of things; he hadn't forced any economies on them and in fact he had been less petty than usual about turning off the lights. He hadn't even told them what was happening about the firm. He probably considered that Hannah was now recovered enough for them all to hear the truth.

When he had finished eating he cleared his throat. 'Can I have one of those?' he asked Theo, and took a cigarette. This was alarming enough, but still Hannah wasn't prepared for what followed. Unless possessed of the most powerful imagination, you cannot be prepared for terrible news – no amount of rehearsal in your head can anticipate the effect of the real words spoken aloud.

He said: 'This isn't going to be easy for any of us. The details, I won't bore you with those – your mother and I, we've spent all week going through our sums and trying to avoid this decision. But we have to act fast.' He turned to Theo. 'Your flat, it's mortgaged up to the hilt and do I want to make my son homeless?'

Theo inspected his cigarette. 'So what are you suggesting?'

'There's one step we hoped we'd never have to take, but it now seems unavoidable.'

Becky burst into tears – caused, no doubt, by her father's formal tone of voice as much as by his words. He moved the ashtray, lining it up with his plate.

'Just tell them, for God's sake,' said their mother.

There was a snapping sound; they all jumped. It was Amy, escaping through the cat flap. 'I phoned Blenheim and Neaves this morning and they're sending someone round.' Puckering his mouth in the smoke, he stubbed out his cigarette.

'Who's that?' asked Becky.

'We're going to have to sell the house,' said their mother. 'I'm so sorry.'

Their father said: 'We need the capital. Even then, it's not going to be easy.' He paused. 'They've arranged to put it into their auction at the end of the month.'

2

'Where've you been?' Eva looked up. She was crouched on the floor; estate agents' brochures were spread around her. 'Hey, look at this!' She pointed to a photograph. ' "Renovated to the highest specifications, luxury three-bedroom flat within a stone's throw of the King's Road" – that's Chelsea! "En-suite marble bathroom with jacuzzi"!'

Jon knelt down on the floor and looked at the photo. 'We don't have to get a renovated one,' he said. 'I can do the renovations. I'd like that.'

'You crazy? You want to stand halfway up a ladder covered in frigging emulsion?' She pointed to another sheet of paper. ' "Penthouse duplex" – duplex means two floors – "panoramic views . . . Poggenpohl kitchen . . . two en-suite bathrooms" – two! One for you and one for *moi*.' She moved his hand away. 'Ugh, your hands!'

'It's just earth.'

'You been down there again?'

'I needed to plant the beans.'

She burst out laughing. 'Beans! We've got half a million pounds and you're planting beans! We can *buy* beans. We can buy enough fucking beans to last a lifetime. We can buy solid *gold* beans.'

'That's not the point.' How could he start to explain it? He decided on another approach, one she might under-stand. 'It might look suspicious, that we've been seen at the allotments for a whole week and then we suddenly stop. It might look odd.'

She nodded, mollified, and shuffled the brochures into

piles. 'Let's go and see this one,' she pointed, 'and this one. You're so boring, you never say. Where do you want to live – Chelsea? St John's Wood, so I can crow over those old hags with their cellulite thighs?'

He didn't say because he didn't know. Panic, like a drawstring, pulled his throat tight.

'We can get more for our money if we move out a bit – like, the Green Belt. Finchley, Harrow.' She chuckled. 'Stanmore.' She nudged him with her elbow. 'Stanmore! Geddit?'

He climbed to his feet. 'I get it. Want some tea?'

He went into the kitchen, pushing his way through the pile of cardboard boxes. There was no room to move any more. Sony, Whirlpool, Toshiba – the empty boxes filled up the kitchen. Wedged inside the boxes were the white styrofoam shapes that had cradled their new microwave, TV, video. He couldn't throw them away because he and Eva would soon be moving out of the flat and then they would have to pack up everything again. It was Friday, and the place was silting up with the results of their week-long orgy of spending. Correction – *her* spending. He had just bought some jazz CDs. But Eva! He never knew she had such a hunger within her. The force of it! Dazed, he had followed her around John Lewis from one department to another. They had stood at the lifts; she had jiggled impatiently and then grabbed his arm and pulled him to the escalators. She couldn't wait. She wanted it all nowNowNOW. He was mesmerised by her; he marvelled at her knowledge. 'Have to get a telly with Nicam.'

'What's that?' he asked.

'Digital stereo, dickbrain.' She grabbed his arm and led him down Oxford Street. 'The only place to get underwear, my dear, is Fenwicks.' All these years she had been reading magazines, storing up information about consumer durables and fashion designers – all these years she had been longing for things that were out of her reach. In different circumstances, he would be touched.

Her exhilaration seemed untinged by guilt; she blazed with gratification. The first day she had come home, laden with carrier bags from Bond Street. She had stripped off her clothes down to her new underwear and pulled him down on top of her. She lay beneath him on a rustling bed of tissue paper. She lay, her thin arms flung above her head. She didn't caress him; she simply surrendered herself, shuddering as she climaxed. Her thighs gripped him and her hands, above her head, clenched and unclenched a ball of tissue paper. Afterwards she had slept, flushed and replete, amongst her glossy carrier bags.

To her it was simply a big adventure, the biggest adventure of her life. It was a massive gamble they had managed to pull off. She didn't trouble herself about the losers; in fact, in a curious way she seemed to think she was owed the money. For twenty-eight years she had struggled and suffered. Life was so unjust; why should some people have everything and others nothing? 'It's our turn now,' she had told him, and on the second morning she went off to a beauty place near Selfridges and had the works – massage, facial, waxing, whatever. 'I'm lying there with this girl doing me and I just gave her a wink. I wanted to say, "This was me, once." '

'You didn't say anything, did you?' Jon's heart jumped. 'Be careful, for God's sake.'

'You think I'm stupid?'

She wasn't stupid; in fact she was surprisingly businesslike. He had never seen her in this mode before, but then they had never been in this situation. She had worked it out beforehand, what they were going to do with the money. During that week they opened eight building society accounts, four in her name and four in his, and deposited the bulk of the money in those. He had insisted they did these trips alone; her presence made him jittery. At the Abbey National he had stood at the little window. The girl – 'Stella' said her badge – counted out the banknotes twice, moistening her thumb with a little sponge. She glanced at him, then down again. She had a button under her desk! She was going to press it! Surely the man waiting behind him could sense that it wasn't his money? When he emerged into the sunshine he paused, expecting somebody to step out of the shadows and put a hand on his shoulder.

That Friday night they went out to dinner; they went up west, to Chinatown. Sizzling prawns were placed in front of him. Eva chattered away; maybe they looked like any young couple discussing their plans for the future. He speared a prawn. It didn't belong to him; even the prawn knew that, it was curled up in distaste. Two waiters stood, watching.

'Don't you want them?' asked Eva. She picked up a prawn and slotted it between her shiny red lips. 'Mmm . . .' Oil slid down her chin.

One of the waiters said something to the manager. He picked up the phone.

'What's up with you?' Eva stared at him.

'Nothing. Just got a stomach ache.'

The manager put down the phone. He strolled over. Jon stiffened. The manager passed their table and went to talk to the people behind them.

On the way home the car kept stalling. Eva said: 'Wait till we get our Porsche.'

'We must be careful. We don't want people to get suspicious.'

'What people?'

'Friends,' he said. 'Neighbours.'

'We haven't got any.'

It was true. They didn't know their neighbours; the high street was utterly anonymous. People must live above

Radio Rentals but all he saw were shifting shapes behind the curtains. As for friends – since he had met Eva his few mates seemed to have melted away. He had a suspicion that most of them didn't like Eva; they thought she was bad for him. She herself seemed to have no close girlfriends; she didn't get on well with women. The only men she knew were her ex-boyfriends – an unsavoury, violent lot by all accounts – with whom she had long ago broken off contact. She seemed to depend entirely on him. *Two worms under a stone, that's us.* He had sometimes wondered about her lack of friends, but just now their isolation was to their advantage. Still, they had to take care.

Back home he said: 'And I think we should rent a flat, not buy one. Not just yet. We don't want anyone to wonder how we got together that sort of money.'

'What's the matter with you? All bloody week, all you've done is make objections. This is supposed to be *fun*. It's mé who has to do everything – book the bloody restaurant, get the bloody holiday brochures. It's me who has to work out how the video works.'

'It's so complicated. Who wants to pre-set ten different programmes over the next twelve months? It's crazy.'

'If you had your way the most exciting thing we'd do is buy a new set of tea-towels. Just in case anybody noticed. You're such a fucking damp blanket, Jon.' She paused. 'Why've you got your eyes closed?'

Her voice is all whiny and hard. He had a strong desire to go to Stanmore. He needed to stand outside the house, in the darkness, and watch the windows. Just to check that Hannah had got home safely.

'Can't work this frigging thing.' She was pressing buttons on their remote-control, trying to adjust the TV. The table he had constructed from a cross-section of oak – the little coffee-table he loved – was cluttered with remote-controls. Half their time seemed to be spent reading books of operating instructions. If only Eva were in the right mood, he would tell her things were getting out of hand.

'I'm just saying, we must take it easy.'

They froze. Footsteps were coming up the stairs. They looked at each other. The footsteps passed on by; it was just the people who lived in the flat above. During that quick flash of understanding he wondered if she, too, was frightened all the time . . . If for Eva, too, nowhere felt safe. He didn't dare ask, in case she said yes.

'We mustn't quarrel,' he said. 'Else, what's the point?'

'I'm not quarrelling.' She lunged towards him and dug her fingernails into his neck.

'Hey!' He jerked his head away. 'That hurts.'

She was so volatile; her moods swung alarmingly. *She bloody terrifies me*, Hannah had said. For the past few days Eva had been like tinder-dry grass, ready to burst into flames. He slept badly – fitful dreams and sudden awakenings. He dreamed Eva came up to him in the street, took out her nail-file and scored him open, from his face down to his crotch. He looked down and watched his insides spilling out. Tap-tap went her high-heeled boots as she tottered away.

Tap-tap . . . footsteps on the stairs . . . tap-tap . . . a knock on the door. He woke up, drenched with sweat. It was only the 'TO LET' sign outside; it had loosened in the wind and was knocking against the wall.

The next day, Saturday, he went to the allotments. Eva wanted him to come to a car saleroom but he said he ought to be seen working there and hurried out of the flat. He needed to get away from her; she pressed up so close to him, she demanded so much. Life seemed to be spiralling out of his control. What they had done was still too extraordinary to digest; at the same time he felt he was suffocating – oh, he couldn't describe it. He didn't want to think. The only way he could quell the panic was to exhaust himself by digging.

He arrived at the allotments and got out of the car. It was a grey afternoon; it had rained in the night. There were only a few people around, in the distance. Plastic windows flapped on the greenhouses. He walked across to his hut and stopped. There, in the earth, were fresh footprints.

They led up to the hut. Somebody had stood there, trying to peer in the window. The mud was trampled flat. They weren't his footprints; these had been made by large boots. Police boots.

He stared at them. He felt the blood draining from his face. Far away, a siren wailed.

Jon closed the door and sat down in the hut. He sounded like a rodent; his teeth were chattering. He stared at the spade, leaning against the wall. It looked threatening, ready to clout him on the head. It was dark in here, the planks were still nailed against the window. He had removed the two beds and the other evidence of occupation, but now that seemed a pitifully inadequate thing to do. How could he believe they would get away with it?

Time passed. He sat there, unable to move. The police had been here, nosing around the hut. They were closing in. There had been nothing in the papers, no reporting of a kidnap victim being found. At the time he had felt slightly reassured by this – without seeing it in print he could almost believe it hadn't happened – but he knew in his heart of hearts that this made no difference to anything. The police would still be investigating. It was only a matter of time. They were bound to track him down. He and Eva had committed a major crime and they weren't used to being that sort of criminal, they hadn't been taught how to do it. He certainly hadn't. Certain sorts of people broke the law, and others didn't. He had grown up believing this.

Except it wasn't true, of course. A criminal is the same as anyone else, they just see the world differently, like a negative of the same photograph. That packet of Karvol, for instance, sitting on the shelf – he had forgotten to remove it. To anyone else it meant nothing, it was just capsules for nasal congestion. But to him it was incriminating evidence. Those footprints outside – in the past, in that lost past he could never now regain – they would have just been footprints.

He sat there, trying to gather his wits. He could jump in the car and warn Eva, but perhaps the police had already arrived at the flat. What could he do – get in the car and speed off – drive away, anywhere, anywhere but here? Drive until the tank was empty. And then what?

Jon got to his feet and let himself out of the hut. He didn't look round; he concentrated on padlocking the door. He walked, head down, to the car. He was just opening the door when he heard a voice.

'I been watching you.'

He turned round. The old man stood there – the man who had talked to him the week before. He pointed to the freshly-dug plot.

'Your digging – see?' He bent down, stiffly, and picked up a piece of greenery. 'This little bugger, that's ground elder. He pops up again, see. Know why? Because you haven't got him out – need to get every little piece of root out. Burn it.' He gave Jon a plastic bottle of weedkiller. 'Anything still pops up, you squirt him with this.' He gestured around. 'Otherwise he spreads like nobody's business. Like into other people's gardens. See what I mean?'

Jon looked at the man's boots. 'Did you come here earlier?'

*

169

Jon drove home. He knew he should be feeling relieved, but he still felt shaky. He hadn't caught up with his earlier shock. Parking the car, he realized that he never would. The fact that a policeman hadn't made those footprints was irrelevant. They might not have come today but they could come tomorrow, next week, next month . . . next year, sometime, never.

He locked the car and walked round the block, into the high street. It was still windy; rubbish stirred in the gutter. A disembowelled tape from a cassette was strewn across the pavement; it wrapped itself around a lamp-post, shivering in the sunlight. Suddenly he longed to bundle back the present, stuff it back into the past and rewind it. If only it were that simple – if only he could start again!

He passed the butcher's window. The trays were laid out. Liver lay sunk in blood. He thought: what I've done, I can never undo. Hannah has been released, but Eva and me – we shall never be free, as long as we live.

'Where's the coffee table?' he asked.

'It's in the cupboard. Look, Jon – don't you just love it?' Eva ran her finger over the new table. The marble was mottled green; it rested on brass legs. She said she had gone to Hampstead, while he was away, to look at flats. She had seen it in a shop and bingo! 'Just imagine it, in our new place.'

Jon said: 'That was the first table I ever made. I found the oak in Epping Forest. Don't you like it?'

'It had a cigarette burn on it.'

'Your cigarette, actually.' He looked at her. They mustn't quarrel. Too much was at stake, now.

He decided not to tell her about his alarm at the allotments. She might freak out. On the other hand, she might just laugh at him. And he wasn't in a state for either of these reactions.

*

On Monday he could stay away no longer. He drove to Stanmore. It was mid-afternoon. Cypress Drive was deserted. Black bands of shadow lay across the street, as solid as the trees that created them. Cypresses held such a hush in them, the hush of cemeteries; even in the car he could sense it.

He drove slowly past number eighteen. There was no sign of life – no sign of the drama that must be taking place in there. But a board had been erected outside.

'HOUSE FOR SALE BY PUBLIC AUCTION.'

Part Four

1

Sometimes, when she sat in a train, Val used to look at all the little houses flashing past and gone for ever; she would gaze at them and wonder who lived there, what did they do, how could there be so many of them. Britain was full of people she would never meet, she couldn't possibly meet them all. How did they spend their time, day after day? What did they *do*?

Well, she was learning the answer to that: they queued. That's what people did. Outside it was a sunny September morning; the shops were bathed in golden light. Here in the post office, however, nobody was restless. They stood in line patiently while a very old woman fumbled for her pension book; while a very young girl with two coffee-coloured babies, both crying, argued about some recorded delivery letter. The cigarette smoke made Val's eyes water. How long-suffering people were! It was Monday morning and the queue stretched to the door. They coughed, they shifted from one foot to another and gazed at the display of cards saying 'Happy Anniversary, Husband'. But nobody demanded to see the manager and ask why the other two windows were closed, what sort of service do you call this?

Val was collecting her family allowance. She hadn't set foot inside a post office for years, not until recently. In the past Thérèse, or one of the other girls who had worked for her, had gone to send off the parcels. Val had been too busy. But now she was a housewife again, trying to budget the family finances, and she needed the cash because she hated asking Morris for money.

At last she arrived at the window, its smeary glass so barricaded by reinforced plastic that the man beyond was barely visible. 'It's a wicked old world out there,' the policeman had said. Well, now she was in it. The man paid out the money, easing it through the slit. She folded the notes into her wallet. Forty pounds eighty pence per month – according to the government, that was what Hannah was worth. Val had a mad urge to swing round and announce to the queue: *And according to us she's worth half a million.*

Val crossed the street to the supermarket. Its windows were fortified by sandbags of disposable nappies; it was one of those downmarket places that look vaguely closed even when they are open. But it was her local shop, the only place she could reach on foot, and Morris had the car. He had to have the car, to get to work. They lived in a hinterland between Harlesden and Kensal Rise. If she took the bus she could get to Sainsbury's in Kilburn, but the buses were so infrequent and then one had to haul the bags home. How did people manage, with public transport? She had been learning, over the past two months, but the time spent waiting in the rain! The thumping of one's heart as one hurried up the street, tensed to see the bus flashing past and disappearing in the distance! She had to leave so much time for everything.

Since she had sold the Renault her map of London had altered. She was forgetting her intimacy with its one-way system, its parking places and the cunning short-cuts from Baker Street to Knightsbridge, from Notting Hill to Hampstead, avoiding the congestion and whizzing up side streets with the other *cognoscenti* . . . She was forgetting her daily, invigorating game of cat-and-mouse with traffic wardens. In the past a bus was something she got stuck behind or which flashed its lights at her when she drove down its bus lane. Now she possessed a travel card; she was becoming knowledgeable about bus routes and Tube stations, she was becoming familiar with *Poems on the Underground* and advertisements for secretarial agencies.

On a good day she felt as if she had stepped back into the mainstream of life. She was already becoming more compliant, more one of the herd. People didn't chat as much as she remembered, no whistling conductor took the tickets. Nowadays the Tube was full of litter; surveillance cameras testified to the treachery of strangers. But on a good day she told herself this was part of life's rich tapestry, Burger King cartons and all; she was rejoining the human race. On bad days – no, she couldn't admit to bad days, not even to herself. She couldn't afford it.

She searched the shelves for cocoa powder. It was Becky's first day at school, an event that filled Val with foreboding. Though she hadn't done any baking for years she was determined to make her daughter a chocolate cake for tea. Becky was starting at the local comprehensive, up the road. Her natural anxiety about this was mixed with resentment because Hannah was remaining at St Mary's; Mrs Beestock said that her removal, on top of what had happened, would be too disruptive in the middle of her A levels and had helped out with a bursary from their hardship fund. Not only had Becky been longing to join her in the big school, but now she was transferred to the state sector she went back to school ten days earlier than her sister. 'She's got longer holidays, it's not fair!' she wailed.

It wasn't fair, but her outburst had distressed Hannah and their delicate equilibrium had collapsed into slamming doors and muffled sobs. Then Hannah had put on her music, loudly, and the people upstairs had banged on the ceiling. Now they were living in a maisonette they had

177

to consider their neighbours – a new sensation for the girls who had spent their lives in the airy freedom of a detached house. Oh, how complicated it was! Val had wanted to yell to Hannah: 'Turn that bloody music down!' She had wanted to shout at her like she used to, in their old life when Hannah could be treated as a normal adolescent. But she couldn't do that, now. One of the many casualties of the recent events was that, when dealing with Hannah, she could no longer distinguish between the normal turbulence of adolescence and the abnormal turbulence of someone who had been traumatised. And so she had to treat her with extra gentleness, and then Becky accused her of favouritism, and then . . . and then . . .

Val put the cocoa powder into her basket. She couldn't find any bars of bitter chocolate. This shop didn't sell things like that, or freshly-squeezed orange juice or unsalted butter. It sold the sort of things she didn't think people ate anymore – condensed milk, tinned pilchards and cartons of long-life orange juice that Becky said tasted like wee-wee. Gone was the heady cornucopia of Marks and Spencer's, the breezy nonchalance of flinging-it-into-the trolley; gone were the days of taking-it-for-granted, the easy luxuries of the rich – except Val had never felt rich. For many years she just hadn't thought about money. Money was abstract; it was simply figures she wrote in her cheque book. Maybe that was truly being rich – who knows?

She carried her shopping bags down the street. Even the carrier bags were flimsy; everything cut-price seemed to remind one of the fragility of life. That unknown couple thought she was rich. As she walked she glanced around. Sometimes she had a prickling feeling that they were still watching her; the power of such random malevolence couldn't be dispersed simply by the passing over of money. Logically she knew this was nonsense; they had ruined her family, they had cleaned them out. It was over. They had got what they wanted. But for her family it wasn't over, it was just beginning. And because that couple had caused it they were still with her; they couldn't be shaken off. They breathed their evil breath down her neck.

She couldn't talk to Morris about this. It was her job to keep everyone together and maintain some sort of equilibrium. Morris had been shocked that she had given up her work.

'Sweetheart, you can't do that,' he said. 'You'd go crazy.'

'I need to be at home, for the girls.'

'The girls? *They'll* go crazy.'

She herself had been shocked by the force of her feelings but she had had to surrender to them. They were too strong to resist. She was a mother who had allowed her daughter to be snatched. She had failed to keep her safe. How could she continue in her old life? Overnight it had become utterly meaningless. And now she had succumbed to her maternal instinct she was finding it surprisingly satisfying. After all, what were paint charts compared to one's own flesh and blood? She was amazed how irrelevant her work seemed now, how quickly it had fallen away and how painlessly she had dismantled her career. She had closed the shop and ceased trading. She had put Thérèse in charge of the current projects and simply cut the knots she couldn't untie as if she had died. There was a fine carelessness in the way she had done it, a noble exhilaration. Maybe she too was suffering from delayed shock.

She had packed her old life into storage, as they had packed away their furniture into a repository in Colindale. She had put all that behind her. Here she was, a housewife, shopping on a Monday morning amongst the other people who were out and about at this time of day – the very old, the very young, the loitering men who had long since given up any hope of a job. Unlike Morris she came from solid yeoman stock – her grandfather had been a farmer in Derbyshire – and she had decided to re-invent

179

herself as an earth mother, an unlikely role in some people's eyes but she was working at it. She had to. She pictured herself with her sleeves rolled up, boiling chicken bones to make soup – even, God forbid, darning. It wasn't like that, of course – it wasn't remotely like this – but in her darker moments it was this image that sustained her.

Crewkerne Road was a long street of Edwardian semis, mostly divided into flats. It was largely inhabited by Asians. A street like thousands of others, the sort of street she had seen from trains. Malcolm, Morris's sales manager, owned several properties in this area and had rented them this maisonette at a nominal sum. On the ground floor there was a front room overlooking the houses opposite; there was a kitchen and a tiny dining area. If the four of them ate together, they had to leave the door open to fit the fourth chair around the table. Upstairs there were two bedrooms and a bathroom that seemed to be constantly occupied as it contained the only lavatory. Out the back there was a small garden, partitioned off from the strip belonging to the people upstairs. It was a patch of trampled grass the size of one flower-bed back in Stanmore but at least it was a garden. When Becky complained, Val said this in the jaunty tone she was using a lot nowadays. *At least it's a garden. At least we've got our health . . . At least we're alive . . . at least . . . at least . . . Count our blessings, make the most of it.* She inserted her doorkey; she remembered the newspaper story she had read, the day after Hannah disappeared: *I taught her how to make snow angels by lying down in the snow and moving her arms up and down like wings . . .*

Val opened the front door. The place was silent.

'Hannah?'

She felt a spasm of panic. It was eleven twenty. Hannah didn't go out without telling her exactly where, it was one of the rules. She dumped down her shopping and paused at the bottom of the stairs.

'Hannah?'

Something brushed against her leg. She jumped. It was the cat. Val went upstairs, paused, and pushed open the door to Hannah's and Becky's bedroom.

The curtains were closed. In the darkness she could just make out a Hannah-shaped mound under the duvet. Val's moment of relief was followed by a wave of irritation. Hannah had promised to get up early and tidy the room; Becky had been complaining shrilly about the mess creeping into her side. Val stared at the chaos. *We do all this for her – she could at least keep her half of the room tidy*! And she was supposed to be finishing her Aristophanes essay for her Clas-Civ next week; Val herself had just read *The Frogs*, so she could help her.

She mustn't get angry. If she did, Hannah would flare up: 'I know it's all my fault!' Hannah had always been touchy. Before all this happened, if Val advised her not to eat a Toblerone Hannah would wail: 'You mean I'm fat! That's what you mean, isn't it!' Or: 'You mean I'm spotty! I know!' But now the balance was thrown. It was thrown off-course by the enormous weight of what had happened. Hannah's long lie-ins might not be caused by normal adolescent torpor; they might be a necessary recovery process. Indeed, they might be a symptom of profound, delayed shock. She couldn't ask because that would imply criticism and then Hannah would react. Oh, it was so difficult. That morning she had read a piece in the newspaper about Vietnam vets: how they blamed the war for everything that had gone wrong with their lives, since then. She thought: it's been three months since the kidnap; how will it be for us in a year's time? In two? Will it lessen or will it always throw this distorting shadow over our future?

Val's head started throbbing. She and Hannah had both been getting headaches recently. She stepped through the clothes and gazed at her sleeping daughter. Only Hannah's whitewashed forehead was visible. It glimmered, ghost-like, in the gloom. All that mattered was that her precious daughter had been returned to her. Like a miracle, Hannah had been delivered up from the underworld into the sunlight. Who cared then if she messed up her room? No price was too high, even the price they had paid. Who cared, even if the price rose?

Hannah stood in the doorway, yawning. She opened her eyes wide. 'What are you doing?'

'Baking a cake.' Val bashed the butter and sugar together with the spoon. Already her arm ached; she had forgotten how tiring it was. 'Want some breakfast?'

'No thanks.' Hannah filled the kettle. How large she looked, in this little kitchen. There was hardly room for the two of them; they had to squeeze past each other. Hannah wore her STOP ACID RAIN nightshirt and airline socks – the grey British Airways ones that were given out with the headphones. How casually they had once hopped on planes bound for Pisa or New York!

'Want some coffee?' Hannah asked, scratching her hair. The week after her kidnapping she had cut it short. Val secretly thought this was a mistake; her lustrous, thick hair was her best feature and with it cropped chin-length Hannah's face looked heavy and more Jewish. But who was she to question her daughter's motives? She suspected some sort of self-chastisement. Hannah no longer wore her jewellery either – no nose-stud, none of those little earrings that Val and Morris had hated so much. She was trying to please them, trying to be a good daughter.

Hannah, fetching the coffee jar, indicated the wall. 'Know what those tiles remind me of? Varicose veins.'

'They are hideous, aren't they?' Val bashed the butter. Being poor meant having to live with other people's taste. Poverty wasn't picturesque. Her image of herself, the earth mother, in a simple cottage kitchen was wildly inaccurate. Poverty was lack of choice and lack of power. It was being marooned in a maisonette with flimsy partitioned walls and woodchip wallpaper and a Draylon suite in the lounge. When she had first arrived this place had professionally pained her. Her instinct was to rip it all out and start again, but they couldn't do that, the property belonged to Malcolm.

Hannah was silent. Maybe she was thinking the same thing. Val longed to comfort her, to tell her for the hundredth time that it wasn't Hannah's fault. It was they, not Hannah, who should feel guilty; none of them had had to endure her terrible experience. Val wished they had picked on her instead. It weighed so heavily on Hannah; she seemed to be struggling with so many conflicting feelings – the burden of gratitude, guilt and obligation. Last week Val had been helping her with her E. M. Forster essay and one sentence had leapt off the page: *It is easier to give than to receive.*

Val beat in the eggs. She had tried to reassure Hannah that this place was only temporary, just a stop-gap, and soon they would move to somewhere nicer. They would get their furniture out of storage and Hannah would have a room to herself again. But since Morris's news last night she was beginning to have her doubts. She'd had no idea their financial situation had worsened. He had volunteered to speak to Theo, who so far had got off lightly. Theo still had his flat, he still had his beloved Volkswagen convertible.

'What's the matter?' Hannah was looking at her.

'Nothing.'

Hannah passed her the mug of coffee. 'There's a book on my reading list I've got to get.'

'Fine. We'll go to a bookshop.'

'No, don't do that. I can borrow it from Tanya or somebody.'

'But they're miles away.' It was true. Hannah's friends all lived out near Stanmore, it would take hours to get there on the bus.

'I needn't buy it,' said Hannah. She was always trying to save them money. 'I can see if it's in the library.'

'We'll have to sign on or whatever. Get a library ticket. I'll come with you.'

'It's all right. I can do it myself.'

'No, I'd like to.'

They both knew what she meant. She wanted to accompany Hannah everywhere, she didn't want to let her out of her sight. Over the past three months their relationship had changed profoundly. She fussed over Hannah, but ineptly, mis-timing it and irritating her. She took offence, snapped at her daughter and then apologised awkwardly. They were so *female*, closeted together like this. In some mysterious way the lack of space seemed to intensify their gender. What a suffocating mother she had become!

Hannah stood at the window, looking out. The fence cast a shadow over their square of grass. Val thought: my poor daughter. She's seventeen. This couldn't have happened at a worse time. Just as she is rebelling against us and wriggling free, just as she is trying to assert her independence *this* happens. And now she's trapped at home and I can't bear to let her out of my sight, as if she were six years old.

She poured the mixture into the tin and passed the bowl to her daughter. 'Here, you can scrape it out. Like you used to, when you were little.'

Hannah wrinkled her nose. But she took the bowl.

'I'm looking forward to Florida, aren't you?' said Val. 'Sunshine at Christmas! At least we can have a proper holiday.'

Hannah didn't reply. They were walking down to the

high street. First they were going to find the library, then they were going to get Becky from school.

Val wondered if it had been tactless to mention Florida. Apparently it had been the photograph of them, the prizewinners, which had started all this. But she wanted to cheer Hannah up by saying something positive. Hannah seemed increasingly unreachable. She had put on weight, too – a bad sign. Maybe things would improve when she went back to school.

It had been a long, long summer holidays. Everything they had wanted to do seemed to require the spending of money. It was amazing how everything seemed to boil down to money when one didn't have any. Her cheerful suggestions that the three of them had a picnic on Hampstead Heath or visited the Tate Gallery were met with a polite lack of enthusiasm. Her daughters wanted to go out with their friends but they now lived too far from here – Stanmore was five or six miles away – and Val didn't have a car to ferry them around. Besides, most of their schoolfriends were away.

They walked past Elite Remoulds, a graveyard of heaped tyres at the end of their street. Val stepped over the oil that had seeped on to the pavement. Hannah was dragging behind; she had done this for years, distancing herself from her family. Morris had always found it infuriating; if they slowed down, Hannah slowed down too. Val moved back, and got into step with her daughter. We only have each other, she thought. If we've learnt anything, it's this.

'Wonder how Becky's getting on,' Val said. 'It's as if she's in hospital having an operation.' Hannah grunted. It was probably a tactless remark but she wished Hannah would be more responsive. During the first few weeks here she had been polite and helpful; on her best behaviour. In her more flippant moments Val had thought it had almost been worth it, to get such a well-mannered daughter back. But now ... in many ways it was worse than before, because she couldn't snap at Hannah or even ask her what the matter was. In silence they walked past BB Minicab Service and one of those corner shops whose half-empty shelves gave it a third-world, makeshift look as if the owners had just arrived or were just packing up to leave.

They reached the high street – a long, traffic-choked thoroughfare. They walked past the shops – past Geekay Styles with its lurex evening gowns; past Al-Rahim Fancy Goods. Its window displayed faded packets of fishnet tights and clocks painted with pictures of the Virgin Mary. They passed the greengrocer's stall, heaped with sweet potatoes, and the Afro Cosmetics and Wig Centre where veils of human hair hung from hooks. She said: 'I'm getting quite fond of this place. It's a lot more interesting than Stanmore Broadway, don't you think?'

Hannah grunted.

Val said: 'You know, I never liked our house as much as your Dad did. He was the one who wanted it. I wanted somewhere old, with character.'

'I liked it.'

'You were always saying how suburban it was!'

'Did I?'

'You always said it was so boring, if only we lived somewhere with street cred.' She laughed. 'Well, here we are.'

'You think I wanted this?'

'No. Just joking.' She squeezed Hannah's arm awkwardly. 'Trying to cheer you up. Is anything the matter, darling? I mean – anything different?'

Hannah shook her head. She plodded along, gazing at the pavement. How heavy her profile looked! Her cropped hair stuck out like a shelf. Val's heart swelled with pity. She would never know the extent of Hannah's suffering that lost week. She felt a wave of hatred against the two people who had stolen more than their home.

They had stolen her daughter's normal, rebellious adolescence. By singling out Hannah they had robbed her of her natural development. They had placed upon her a burden unimaginable to anyone else – her family, her friends – and by doing this had thrust her into a separate universe. How lonely she must feel!

'Here we are,' said Hannah.

'This is the library?' It was a stained sixties building, its windows plastered with posters. *Problems with your Landlord? Let's Kick the Racism out of Football.* They went in. Val hadn't been in a public library for years. She remembered them as hushed, musty places. This place had strip lights like a job centre. Surveillance cameras eyed them. *HIV Positive?* No! thought Val, I'm not. She couldn't see a sign of any books, only a shelf of videos – *Lethal Weapon 2. Henry: Portrait of a Serial Killer.* There was a litter of leaflets on the floor. A Rastafarian sat reading *Loot*.

'Where are the books?' whispered Val.

They found a few shelves of books but they were labelled 'Urdu' and 'Women's Studies'. Val went up to the librarian. 'We're looking for a book called *The Birth of Greek Comedy.* Where might we find it?'

'Like, stand-up comedy?'

Behind her, Hannah sniggered. Val said to the girl: 'No, not like stand-up comedy. Ever heard of Aristophanes?'

'What?'

'He plays in this little pub up near Kensal Rise.'

'Mum!' Hannah pulled her away.

'Forget it,' Val said to the girl. 'We'll go to a bookshop.'

'There aren't any bookshops here,' whispered Hannah. 'Except the porno one.'

They went outside. 'What's the world coming to?' asked Val.

'It's always come to this. It's just you never noticed.'

A criticism! Val's heart lifted. 'I wasn't exactly locked away.'

' 'Course you were. You only met people who wanted a new Siematic kitchen every year.'

Val felt absurdly cheered. They were bickering! Just for a moment everything seemed back to normal. They went into a newsagent's to buy Becky a comic. 'Do you want one of your horrible magazines? Or one of mine so you can pull out the free anti-wrinkle cream and give it to me?'

'OK.'

They looked at the racks. There were no glossy magazines – no *Interiors*, no *Vanity Fair*. They were living in another Britain now, whose inhabitants read the *People's Friend*, puzzle books and a bewildering selection of TV and satellite guides. Today she found this invigorating, just because she and Hannah seemed suddenly intimate again – an ordinary mother and daughter, needling each other.

And then it was all ruined. They waited at the school gates. It was a vast building – her little daughter, in there! At four o'clock swarms of alarming-looking youths emerged – huge black girls who were probably Becky's age but who looked like grown women; white boys with the faces of old men, who lit up cigarettes as they walked down the street. The noise was deafening. And then there, amongst them, was Becky. She looked very small in her new brown uniform.

She walked up. Her face was set. 'Let's go,' she muttered.

They walked down the street and around the corner. Once she was out of sight of the school Becky burst into tears.

'It was horrible! I don't want to go there, I want to go to St Mary's!' she sobbed. 'I want to be with my friends!'

Hannah flinched as if she had been stung.

Val said: 'Darling, I'm sure it's –'

'They made fun of my voice, they said it was all posh! These big girls got me in the loos and pulled my plaits!'

She jerked away from Val's arm. 'I want to go home! I want to go to St Mary's! I don't want to be here!'

Val glanced at Hannah. Her face was closed.

Back home, even the chocolate cake failed to console Becky. Her normally resilient, bouncy daughter only ate a mouthful. Hannah left her piece on the plate. Val could comfort neither of them; they sat, hunched, in front of the TV. And neither of them could even be alone, because they shared a room.

A few minutes later the phone rang. It was Morris. He asked about Becky but she shook her head fiercely; she didn't want to speak to him. Then he said: 'They've sacked Avril.'

'They've what?'

'She's been with me eighteen years.'

'They couldn't!' said Val.

'This morning, she was due back from holiday. I went into her office – they've moved the Xerox equipment in there.'

'Oh Morris . . . What can I say?'

'Nothing.' His voice was clipped and impersonal. 'It's fine.'

'Oh darling –'

'I'll be late back. I'm going to go round to Theo's, to talk to him about what we were discussing.'

'Sure you don't want me to come?'

'No. It's better man to man.'

The phone went dead. Why couldn't he involve her? His voice had sounded so cold. She looked at the girls; they sat watching TV with studied concentration. They didn't even dare ask her what had happened. Her poor children. Her poor husband – her jokey, sentimental, volatile husband, he had pulled down the shutters. It was so complicated. Why couldn't this misfortune draw them closer? In the early days she had a vision of them being united by what had happened. Making-do, clinging together, a little team . . . In the early days she and Morris had clung together in the steam . . . *Oh I love you for this* . . .

She went outside and sat down on the step. The garden faced south; it had the sun all day. This was one of the rallying things she had told them when they arrived: *Look, we can sit here and get a suntan!*

It was true, what she had told Hannah: she had never really liked their house. What she missed was the garden. And the conservatory. All her life she had wanted a conservatory; they had only built it two years ago. She missed her lemon tree that had just produced its first fruit; it was still green when they had had to sell the house. She looked at the trampled grass. She looked at the larch-lap fencing, which still smelled of creosote. It alarmed her that she had done nothing to this garden, nothing at all.

What's money? he had said, holding her in the steam. *It's only money* . . .

Hannah and Becky came out. *Home and Away* must be finished. They asked if they could go to the shop – probably, she suspected, so Hannah could buy some cigarettes.

'Sit down,' she said. She gestured up at the sky – a blue, vaulted dome, criss-crossed with vapour trails. 'Look – at least the sky is free.'

'Ugh,' said Hannah. 'You sound like a really sad sixties folksinger.'

She laughed. 'I was a hippie once. Full of hope and ideals.'

'Bet Dad wasn't.'

'Wasn't a hippie, or wasn't full of hope?' She patted the step. 'Sit with me a moment, my little chicks.'

But they shook their heads and left.

2

Avril was a victim of the new rationalisation. Avril, his friend, ally and faithful PA, had been rationalised out of a job. That Monday Morris had phoned through to Iain Capshaw, their new Managing Director, but he was tied up in meetings all morning. Inflamed with fury Morris finally collared Malcolm in the corridor.

When the firm had been taken over they retained Malcolm as Sales Manager; even they could see he was too able to be made redundant. He took Morris into his office. 'They didn't tell you?' he commiserated. 'That's truly out of order. Look, I'm meeting Iain in an hour, I'll rap his knuckles. He'll pass the buck to head office, of course, the slippery so-and-so.'

'It's no way to treat Avril,' said Morris. 'Or me.'

Malcolm's phone rang; he buzzed his secretary to take his calls. He was a busy man but Morris and he were old friends and he always found time for him. Their relationship, however, had altered. Since Morris had been bought out by his rivals, Rest Assured Security, he had lost control of his own company and been effectively stripped of his power by being removed into that grey and lowly no man's land known as Consultancy. Their new MD, the thrusting young sleazeball Capshaw, had said that of course they would retain Morris's services. 'It's your know-how that has made Price Security what it is today', he had said with his patronising smile. So now Morris was no longer Malcolm's boss; Malcolm was his. Morris had to report to him, and as part of the general overhaul and modernisation of the firm he had been ordered to prepare what he considered a totally unnecessary and creepy questionnaire for their customers. *As part of our ongoing commitment to offer the most efficient and competitive service we are requesting our most valued clients to spare us five minutes of their time to fill out the following . . .*

'You know what I'm doing? I'm wasting my time,' said Morris. 'I've been put out to bloody grass.' He laughed bitterly. 'Know what a consultant is? Someone who's never consulted.' His arm twinged. Angina! So now he was going to get a heart attack! 'We ran a tight ship, Malc, but it was a friendly ship, you agree with me? Why did we keep our staff? Because they were loyal, they were part of the family. What does it to do morale, to sack Avril? Not to mention the others.' Rest Assured had moved in ten of their own staff – mid-Atlantic clones spouting management gibberish. Was it any wonder his heart ached? Maybe he should see his doctor. 'Nobody trusts anyone anymore, they're frightened for their jobs, they hate wearing those ID badges, they hate all this performance-related nonsense –'

The phone rang. Malcolm lifted the receiver and put his hand over it. 'Sorry, old chap – got to take this call.'

Morris walked back to his office. He never received urgent calls anymore.

Over the summer the place had been refurbished; the homely, admittedly shabby corridors had been redecorated with rag-rolled walls and uplighters. Rest Assured had installed air conditioning too; the place had the hushed, denatured atmosphere of a conference hotel. Through the windows lay the familiar Hertfordshire countryside but indoors the building was unrecognisable. It wasn't his own place any more. He felt like a kindly-tolerated visitor, an elderly retainer kept on out of pity. Even their receptionist had gone – chain-smoking Irene, who had been there for ever and knew everbody's birthdays. Her domain, the lobby, was now a no-smoking zone. It was floored in marble. She had been replaced by a telephonist who said, when people range: 'Rest Assured Security, Jodi speaking, how can I help you?' and then barraged them with Vivaldi. Behind the desk sat a security guard, one of an interchangeable number of expressionless young men who nobody knew because they worked in shifts. Morris thought: why do we wear name badges? Because nobody knows anyone anymore.

He settled at his desk and gazed at the draft questionnaire. *As part of our ongoing commitment* . . . He gazed out of the window. His office overlooked the car park. His old parking place, marked *Managing Director*, was now occupied by Iain Capshaw's BMW convertible. Metallic green, it gleamed beetle-like in the sunshine.

One of the new girls from Accounts tapped on his door and came in with his tea. If it were Avril, she would say: 'Becky's first day at school, the poor love!' This girl, whose badge proclaimed her to be called Kimberley – what sort of name was that? – gave him tea in a plastic cup.

'Where's my mug?' he asked.

'I'm sorry.' There was a twange in her voice. Cockney or Australian. Something. 'Do you have one?'

'Of course I do,' he said peevishly. 'It's got Snoopy on it.'

She promised to investigate and went out. The twinge had gone but now his stomach ached. He wondered what she knew about him; what the new staff had been told. His official reason for stepping down was that he had a heart condition and it was doctor's orders that he took it easy – an explanation that had been accepted with a surprising lack of comment. Over the past months he had often wondered if Malcolm had told anyone the truth. He had told nobody – not even Avril, his old friend and confidante – about the kidnap. But he didn't trust Malcolm and he had caught some odd looks in the corridors. Sometimes he suspected that everybody knew and they were gossiping about him behind his back. Gossiping and pitying him. Oh – the shame of it! He had let his own daughter be stolen; helpless and impotent, he had let his family's security be spirited away in a couple of carrier bags. How could a real man allow that to happen?

Beneath this lurked a sinister feeling that had taken him some time to identify, it was buried so deep. It was a feeling that he had been targeted – that the forces of evil had marked him out with their rifle-sights. He couldn't confide in Val; she would consider him paranoid. There were some things only another Jew could understand.

He couldn't confide in his brother David. During that terrible week he had thought about asking David for a loan – he was a venture capitalist, he had plenty of money – but he couldn't bring himself to do it. A profound rivalry had existed between them since they were boys; David was the last person in the world to whom he could bare his soul. He missed his parents. He could have told his mother about this, about how he felt that in some profound sense he deserved what had happened. He remembered his mother's bitter monologues as she tucked him up in bed, her dark, haunted eyes with the bruised brown beneath them, how she raised her hands in the air as if she alone were plugged into the unimaginable tragedy of life. She would understand.

At night, he had such violent dreams. His doctor had prescribed stronger sleeping pills but they had only plunged him deeper. Lately he had woken up trembling with agitation. He didn't tell Val; he didn't want to upset her. They were trying to pull together, to make the best of it. 'It's not so small,' she said, when they moved into the maisonette; 'look, it's got this big extension at the back! And the garden faces the sun.' She said: 'We were poor when we started out; we managed then, didn't we?'

But Val had never been truly poor; she was an educated woman from a solid, even prosperous family. She hadn't known the fear of it. And twenty years ago they were young and ambitious, like their contemporaries; they were making their way in the world together. Now he didn't have the energy or the hope; it was utterly different, the second time around. Even their friends, after the first supportive week, were falling away. This was partly because he and Val had moved out of their neighbourhood, he had resigned from the golf club, the old ties were cut. But it was more than that: there was a mutual feeling of embarrassment. People didn't know what to say to them; it was as if there had been a death in the family. What gross mismanagement on Morris's part had consigned his family to penury? And so many things they used to do with other couples – Bernie and Adèle, Harold and June – things they had taken so blithely for granted, they involved the spending of money. Sharing a holiday; going up west to see a show and having a bite to eat afterwards. Nobody phoned them up and suggested that now.

They were out of sync with their contemporaries, thrust back into a struggling student past without having the energy to cope with it. Of course people had been kind and tried to help them out, but then there was the obligation ... Take Malcolm: Malcolm was not just his boss, he was also his landlord now. He was charging them a minimal rent, he was making a loss. It made Morris deeply uncomfortable, to be beholden to him. And on top of that he would have to confess to him that Becky had scratched the bath by dropping some metal object in it ... a fitted enamel bath, it would have to be replaced ... Oh, his head ached, his heart ached ...

It's only money he had said, holding his wife in his arms. Steam rose up around them. *What is a daughter worth? ... more than all the riches in the world ...* But nobody knew how serious it was, not even Val . . . nobody knew what a nightmare it was becoming. Val didn't realise how much he had been calculating on her income. Her announcement that she was giving up her work had pole-axed him, but how could he argue with her when she seemed in such turmoil? She seemed to believe, deep down, that her daughter had been stolen to punish her for working. By allowing it to happen it was she herself who had committed a crime. Giving up her career was an act of atonement. Who was he, of all people, to quarrel with this? It would only make matters worse. And now, because of this, their son was to suffer . . .

'You all right?' The girl stood there, looking down at him.

He jerked up his head. 'Fine.'

'I found your mug.' She smiled at him. She was a pretty girl – pale brown hair, pink cheeks. She put down his mug of tea and left the room. A fresh, flowery perfume hung in the air.

The bastards!, thought Morris. If I could get my hands on them! He dropped sugar lumps into his mug and stirred the tea so roughly it slopped on to the desk. They are destroying my son's future; they are destroying my daughter's education.

He picked up the phone and rang Val. 'How did Becky get on? Can I speak to her?' He heard the TV in the background.

'Oh, fine. Er – not just now. She's not here.'

He told her about Avril. She sounded shocked, but how distant her voice seemed – distracted, as if she were thinking about something else. He suddenly thought: do we really know each other at all? They talked for a moment, then he rang off.

Over the past months she had changed. His smart, amusing, capable wife – the beautiful woman of whom he had been so proud – she had changed into a worried

196

housewife, restless and abstracted. It didn't suit her, to be at home all day. She didn't know what to do. She kept trying to jolly them along, making the best of everything, but her heart wasn't in it. Her eyes looked hectic and glassy. She wasn't a natural mother. She needed to be whizzing up the M1, whizzing off to meetings; she needed to be out in the world. In the maisonette she was like a caged animal. There was nothing to do. He had nothing to do, either. After work he had always liked pottering around, fiddling in the garden, fixing things. In this place all they could do was watch TV. And they couldn't admit this to each other. There were so many things that were unsayable; they had to protect each other. For the first time in twenty-four years, silence had entered their marriage.

He couldn't put it off any longer, this visit to Theo. After work he got into the car and drove towards London. He drove through Stanmore, his old route home. He hadn't seen their house since they had moved out at the end of June; none of them had. They had kept away on purpose but he wanted to see what it looked like. Some Arabs had bought it; he knew that the place was being refurbished. As he drove down Stanmore Hill, however, he slipped so easily into the past that for a moment he believed that nothing had changed. It was a warm September evening and he was driving home as he always did. Becky and Hannah would be watching TV; they would be lying on their stomachs surrounded by their magazines . . . Outside in the garden the Michaelmas daisies would be blooming, a blur of mauve amongst the blood-red clots of the heleniums. Rhoda, their cleaning lady, would be gone by now and maybe Val would be home, her Renault parked in the drive . . . Indoors she would be dumping down her Marks & Spencer's shopping bags and clattering around the kitchen, calling the girls to help . . . She would be standing in the conservatory, her head on one side, frowning at the plumbago . . . The scrape of the plant pots as she moved them around, she was never satisfied . . . the puff-puff as she misted the ferns . . . The girls were younger now, they were out in the garden, Theo was there, riding his bike round the lawn . . . their laughter echoing in the slanting sunshine . . .

He parked the car, turned off the engine and stared. His house stood in an expanse of mud. Building materials were stacked in what had been the front garden. In the driveway stood a skip and a Portaloo. There was no sign of life; the house had been gutted. The side wall of the lounge had been knocked out and a half-built extension rose up to the first floor.

Morris got out of the car. He walked up to the house. Through the gaping hole in the side it seemed to breathe out cold air, like an opened tomb. He made his way down the side; he balanced on planks which had been laid across the mud. Out the back, the far part of the garden still remained. He could see the blur of the Michaelmas daisies and the children's swing, with its bald patch beneath it. But everything else was chaos. He looked through the conservatory window. Inside the floor had been dug up; Val's Mexican tiles – most of them broken – were stacked against the wall. A pit was lined with plastic. It took him a moment before he realised: it was the beginnings of a swimming pool.

'A pool, wow.' Theo passed him a bottle of beer. 'I didn't know Arabs swam, I thought it was against their religion.'

Morris sat down. He hadn't been to Theo's flat for some weeks, basically because Theo hadn't asked him. Theo had his own life. The flat was in Clerkenwell – a whitewashed, bare space with movie posters hung on the walls. It had been converted from an old industrial building; outside, lorries thundered down Farringdon

Road. The door to Theo's editing room was ajar; Morris could glimpse the machinery within. The big grey computer was lit like a shrine.

'We drink this straight from the bottle, right?' Morris asked.

Theo nodded. 'You a real man or what?' He tipped back his head and drank. The stubble moved, on his Adam's apple; Theo never seemed to completely shave. Morris thought: my son, my firstborn. He felt a wave of love.

'How's things?' asked Theo. 'How's Mum?'

'She manages. You know your mother.'

This feeble reply seemed to satisfy Theo. Morris wondered how affected his son had been by what had happened. In a way, Theo's self-absorption was refreshing. After the smothering guilt and anxieties of home it was like emerging into the open air. Theo, lounging there in his black leather jacket, was the only member of the family who had been virtually unscathed. So far.

Theo said: 'I've got some great news. This mate of mine, Jordan, he's got a commission from Channel Four. A documentary about ticket touts. He's forming this production company and he wants me to edit the film.' He smiled his rare smile. 'Nice one, eh?'

Morris put down the bottle. 'I'm afraid, that may not be possible.'

'Why not?' Theo pushed back his hair, frowning. Hannah used to say he was spoilt; she said her father let Theo get away with everything. She said it wasn't fair.

Morris took a breath and began. 'I would do anything, my dear boy, not to ask you to do this. You must believe me.'

'What are you talking about?' Theo reached for his cigarettes.

'You're aware that when we sold the house it went for thirty thousand pounds less than the market value?' said Morris. 'You go to auction, that's a risk you take. At the

199

time we had no choice. But it made nonsense of my sums. And I had to sell my shares at way below their value. So what did I do? I took out another loan, on top of the loan from Malcolm and the loan from the bank, which I have to repay by the end of the month.'

'You've kept very quiet about this.'

'Why should I worry you all? What good would it do? Plus of course there's the original loan, you understand? Added to which, well, I had calculated on your mother bringing in an income . . .' His voice trailed off. 'What happens? I have Dennis breathing down my neck. Believe me, would I want to involve you in this? My own son? But we have to share our troubles.'

Theo exhaled cigarette smoke. 'You want me to sell the car?'

Morris shook his head. 'No, my boy. I need more than that.' Outside, a church clock chimed. A church, in the middle of this wilderness? He said: 'You know how this pains me. I must ask you to sell your editing machine.'

It was dusk when Morris arrived in Crewkerne Road. He sat in the car. For the first time he realised how much this street, with its heavy, red-brick houses, resembled Arnthorpe Road – the street where he grew up. He could be sitting outside his childhood home in Stamford Hill. So I've come full circle, he thought. I'm doing it all over again. My children must learn to struggle just as I struggled. Maybe it's no bad thing. They have it so easy, these kids.

He looked at the lit window on the ground floor. It was a bay window, jutting out over the concrete front garden. The curtains were closed; behind them his family would be waiting for his return. The radio burbled: '. . . *traffic still solid on the Westway elevated section . . .*'

Morris told himself: it's not the end of the world. Film school graduates, are they all so lucky to possess an editing machine? So they manage; even in this climate they manage. He himself had started with nothing, a poor boy from Stamford Hill. He had worked his way up from being a rep, trudging from shop to shop with his electrical samples, sitting out the lonely nights in hotel lounges. He had worked his way out of that by sheer determination and guts, by his refusal to spend his life being a wage-slave, a cog in the wheel. By the time he had met Val he was building up his own business – already, by then, he employed three staff in an office above Sketchley dry cleaners, Crouch End.

But it was a present. For Theo's twenty-first birthday. A key to the door, to the future . . . his son had thanked them for his Lightworks with tears in his eyes, he had taken them out for a curry, their own son who had never taken them anywhere, who considered them embarrassing old fuddy-duddies, he had raised his glass to his parents and not cared that everyone was staring; he had said, with an odd formality: *I shall remember your generosity all my life . . .*

Morris got out of the car. He let himself into the hallway. Silence.

'Hallo?'

Val would be wondering how Theo had taken the news. She would pour him a Scotch – Morris noticed that she bought whisky by the half-bottle now, one of the false economies that poor people practised.

'Anyone home?' No cooking smells; that was odd.

Morris went into the lounge. Val sat there, alone. She looked up at him. She seemed to have shrunk. For a moment she didn't speak; she just tugged at her fringe, as she had done that terrible evening all those months ago.

He said: 'What's the matter? Where are the girls?'

'Upstairs.' She closed her eyes and pushed back her hair. 'Hannah's just told me something.'

His heart stopped. 'What?'

A moment's silence. All his other worries vanished – his

son's future, Becky's new school, how they were going to manage. None of that mattered.

Something terrible had happened to Hannah. He knew it; he had been waiting for this. He realised it now.

'Tell me, Val – what is it?'

Val raised her head and looked at him. 'She's pregnant.'

He seemed to have a glass in his hand. Val had passed him a whisky. He set it down on the table. Upstairs there was silence, as if the very rooms themselves were holding their breath.

'The man in the hut?' he asked at last. 'The man who kidnapped her? He did it?'

Val nodded. She stared at the carpet.

Morris asked: 'You mean, he raped her?'

Val hooked her hair behind her ears. She didn't reply.

'She was raped?' he asked again. 'Oh my poor baby.'

Val raised her head. 'No,' she said. 'That's what I thought, but it wasn't like that. Maybe that would have been easier to bear.' She stopped. '*No*. It wouldn't.'

'What happened?'

She turned away and addressed the radiator. 'They had sex, as she put it. And now she's pregnant.'

Part Five

Outside the owl is hooting. In my darkness I know when night has arrived; this is the sixth night. We're deep in a forest; I believe this, that we're closed off amongst the trees, even though I can hear the murmur of the city. On our walks I can sense space around me but I feel there are trees beyond, stretching for miles. We're far, far away. Being blind, I've retreated. Eliot says he closes his eyes too; more and more he's been doing this. He moves around the hut touching things, feeling them with his fingertips. He's keeping me company. He has entered this darkness with me – the big dark. Speaking into the blackness we've told each other things we've told nobody else, ever. We're all ears. I'll never know him the way other people do – I'll never identify him – but this frees us; I know what's in his heart.

A few days ago he told me a poem he had written when he was little.

> Time is slow
> Time is fast,
> Time will last and last and last.

That's what it's been like, here.

It's our last night tonight, he says. Tomorrow I'll be gone. We're drinking Martini Bianco out of our mugs. Under my skirt I'm wearing his girlfriend's knickers; they're stretchy lace but still too tight. Slim bitch. He has washed my knickers and my tights. He's intimate with my bodily smells, isn't it strange? This stranger? In the early days I hated him for what he was doing, keeping me here, but now my feelings change violently, see-sawing. We've been through so much together, I'm as intimate with him as he is with me, it's not a one-way thing. We're both prisoners, yet in a funny way it's liberating. Slowly, as I've grown accustomed to my blindness, I've shed the things that have worried me; how can I care about my looks when there is nothing to mirror them back to me?

Yesterday – I think yesterday – I said, 'I hate my spots. I hate my big rubbery lips like my dad's.'

He said: 'They're not rubbery. Some man's going to be driven crazy by them.' Wasn't that nice? I feel I've been stripped bare and he's recreating me as a woman. He said: 'It's like – you say your thighs are fat. Someone will love you soon and know what he'll say? That they're the most beautiful thighs in the world. See?'

'I can't see.' I reply sharply, to hide my pleasure.

We talk about the woman whose knickers I'm wearing. He says: 'I've never been dazzled before – not like that. She dazzled me. It's love, see – love is blind.'

He doesn't say more, he suddenly remembers where he is and what he's doing. Often, we both forget. Because in a way we're in it together. We're both frightened. Tomorrow it's all going to end – well, begin – and I think he is as alarmed as I am. Our lives are going to be changed for ever. Nothing will be the same – for him and that cow, as well as for my family. Am I worth it? Sometimes I feel guilty and utterly worthless; sometimes I feel that anybody's life is beyond rubies, even mine. Sometimes I feel, during this long darkness, that I'm a pupa cocooned in my sleeping bag; when I burst out I'll be unrecognisable – a moth? A monster? A grown-up woman? I can't tell any longer because there are no eyes to mirror me back to myself – only his.

Outside the owl hoots. It must be very late. I drain my mug and hold it out. Glug, goes the bottle; my mug weighs heavier. I put it back on my knee.

'I've remembered another limerick.'

'Go on,' he says. We've told each other all our jokes.

'The Archdeacon's wife of South Mimms – ' I stop.

'Go on!'

'It's disgusting.' I take a breath. 'The Archdeacon's wife of South Mimms / Had really an outsize in quims / But the Dean of the Diocese / Had elephantiasis / So life wasn't just singing hymns.'

He laughs. 'Who told you that?'

'Julia. She got it from her brother.'

'Julia – the one who always eats her pudding first in case the world ends?'

'That's right.' *He knows all about my friends. Julia used to do this when she was a little girl; she liked puddings so much. She says she's stopped now but I've seen her at lunchtime.*

For a while we don't speak. The air is humid; it's been a hot, lethargic day. I'm sitting, my back resting against the wall as usual; the bar of the camp bed digs into my thighs. Outside I can almost smell the lush vegetation growing.

'What's it like, sex?' *I ask.* 'Tell me what it's like.'

'The first time I touched a girl's breasts it was so dark I could hardly see her face. It was a party in Potters Bar. My friend Neville's place.' *I know about his friends too. And his parents' marriage in their chilly house with its cuckoo clock and lino. He doesn't tell me where it is, he's not that stupid. I don't know the normal information but I know the things that matter. With my eyes closed I can picture his house so clearly; I've furnished it, every room.*

'Go on,' *I urge him.*

'I had my hands on her bra. Then I saw she was looking over my shoulder at her friends. Saying look what he's doing. I should've kept my eyes closed.' *I can sense him raising the mug to his lips – I can sense with a sort of radar now. I hear the sound of him swallowing.*

'What's it like?' *I want to know. I want to step out into the free-fall of it, way beyond my friends. Already I've stepped out of their lives.*

'It can be everything, or nothing at all,' *he says.* 'The power of it's frightening, but so is the meaninglessness.'

'What do you mean?'

'Like – you know, drunken fumbles. You can't even remember her face.' He pauses. 'Once – before, you know, her – I shacked up for a few months with a girl. It was late at night and my clothes were in her washer-dryer. I remember thinking – if we make love I can stay awake long enough for it to finish its washing cycle. Then I can put the dryer on and my clothes'll be ready in the morning. That's how much it meant. There could be a baby born from that. See what's frightening?'

'But it's not like that all the time?'

'No,' he says, after a moment. 'It's not.'

Far away, the dog barks. I guess it's nearly dawn. There's a feeling of rising heat, of nature opening up. Time is irrelevant; sometimes I sleep half the day and stay awake half the night. But soon I'll be slotted back into life. I feel as if I'm waiting to begin a great journey. I want to go home – of course I do – but I'm terrified too. I'm drunk. My head swims.

'You'll find out,' he says.

'Emma has but she won't tell me what it's like.'

'Emma's the one who's done it?'

'Yes.'

'We'd better get some sleep,' he says. He asks me if I want to go to the toilet and I say no. He turns off the oil-lamp; there's a small phut. I pull off my blindfold and open my eyes. It's pitch dark. It's not the morning; it's still the middle of the night. My head reels.

I ask: 'What happens tomorrow – if – ?'

He knows what I mean. If someone springs a trap. If they don't give him the money. All those dramatic possibilities that might happen in a thriller. His voice comes from the blackness: 'She doesn't know this but I'll tell you. Whatever happens, I'm going to let you go.'

I hear the unzipping sound of his sleeping bag and a rustling sound as he undresses. I wriggle out of the tight, alien knickers and pull off my skirt. I pull down my T-shirt over my knees and unzip my own sleeping bag. The nylon is warm, from where I've been sitting on it all day. Below, on the floor, I can hear him

*shifting around to make himself comfortable. The sound reminds
me of Stanley, in his basket. He got run over. Eliot's heard about
our dog. He said he always wanted one and I said* Is it worth it,
when they die in the end?

*'Night,' he says. His fingers touch my shoulder. They travel
down to my hand. He shakes my hand, formally. We both laugh
out loud – you can't just smile, not in the dark. Then he
withdraws his hand. 'This sounds stupid, given the circumstances, but I'm going to miss you,' he says.*

*There's a silence. I listen to his breathing, waiting for the soft
exhalation his lips make –* a phew *as if he's just finished a
tongue-twister. He makes this unconsciously, just before his
breathing deepens. He doesn't know he makes this sound – only I
know, and the known yet unknown women with whom he has
slept.*

*The sound doesn't come; his breathing stays shallow. He is
still awake, not moving. I wonder what he's thinking. I lie there,
my eyes open. My head swims, from the alcohol. The back of my
skull aches from the knot of the blindfold. Far away a siren wails.
Its sound echoes through the forest that surrounds us, between
the tall trunks of the trees that separate us from what is going to
happen. Tomorrow I'll see myself again and I need to be changed
by this – otherwise, what's the point?*

*I take a breath. I say the words, but not with my mouth. I say:
'Show me.' I know I don't speak aloud, I wouldn't dare. But he
knows what I'm thinking, we know each other's thoughts. He
must know, because there's a pause, then the sound of his
sleeping bag unzipping.*

*I climb out of my camp bed and ease myself down beside him. I
feel his sleeping bag, spread open like a filleted fish. I lie down
beside him, half-on and half-off the mattress. He pulls me close.
Awkwardly, in the cramped space, I put my arms around him.
He is wearing a T-shirt and shorts; he feels surprisingly slender.
I can feel his jutting shoulderblades. He smells of sweat, like I do.
I bury my face in his hair and we rock together, holding each*

other for comfort. We don't kiss; we just grip each other in the darkness.

How long this goes on I don't know – us lying there. He strokes my hair. For a moment I'm embarrassed – my hair's so greasy, it hasn't been washed for a week. His breath warms my neck. My T-shirt has ridden up but he doesn't touch me down there, he just strokes my hair and smooths my forehead. All week his body has been abstract – a thing I've sensed and heard. Now it's solid in my arms. This seems only natural, after what we've been through. I relax. A week ago, in another life, I entered the Underworld and all this began. Another Hannah got ready for Camden Lock, zipping up the skirt that's lying beside me.

Time passes. Thin grey needles appear between the planks nailed against the window. I still can't see his face. I stroke it like a blind person, feeling with my fingers the sharp bridge of his nose and the lashed hollows of his eyes. His eyes are closed. I can feel the strong root, growing out of him, that's pressed against my thigh but we both pretend it's not there.

But my body begins to heat up; my throat is dry. I feel like a fleshy, tropical flower opening. He is hot too – damp with sweat. Our noses bump as his lips brush mine.

After a moment I say it aloud. 'Show me,' I whisper.

He takes my hand and guides it down. Then he stops. 'I can't,' he whispers in my ear. 'I mustn't.'

'Show me what it's like,' I whisper in his ear, smelling the scent of his hair. 'After all this, don't you owe me something? Show me what it's like.'

And so he does.

Part Six

1

Such dreams he had, such nightmares. More and more Jon put off going to bed. He sat in the lounge, gazing over the rooftops of Kensington, while Eva hummed in the bathroom. If he closed his eyes the dreams rose up in his throat, blocking his windpipe. Last night he had dreamed about the hut again. It was big and airy and carpeted. He had pulled out the two sleeping bags and buried them in the earth; he had tried to run away but when he turned he saw the soil moving, as they stirred beneath it. He had woken, fighting for breath. The flat was so hot – it was in a luxury block and though it was warm for January the heating was up high; he couldn't fling open the window because it was double-glazed.

'Coming to bed?' Eva stood at the door, wearing her silk wrap-thing. She wriggled her hips and smiled at him. Her pointy little cat's face was tanned – all of her was tanned. She had enrolled at some health club in Chelsea and spent hours there limbering up or lying under a lamp. She spent her days having herself serviced, just as once she had serviced others. She looked pampered and sheeny; she looked rich. She *was* rich. So was he.

She gestured around the room. 'Know what we need? Pictures.'

'You mean, the odd Piero della Francesca.'

'What?'

'Italian,' he said. 'Old.'

'Don't want anything old.'

'Anyway, even *we* couldn't afford one of those.'

213

She ran her fingers along the wallpaper. 'Nice, though, isn't it?'

The wallpaper was embossed and silky. The curtains were silky, too; pulled back with tasselled things. The chairs were reproduction Sheraton, with the same silky stuff on their seats. In the early days he had felt as if he had stepped into the wrong flat – a minor diplomat's residence, something like that. He had done a job in a place like this once. Despite the lavish furnishings and the chandelier hanging from the ceiling, however, the place did look bare, as if they hadn't moved in yet.

'Trouble is, we're not allowed to bang nails into the walls,' he said.

She went into the bedroom. He got up and switched off the lamps. He removed the magazines scattered around the carpet. Though the room was large he felt like a trapped animal, pacing to and fro. They were up on the fourteenth floor – thirteenth, actually, though it wasn't called that – and London lay spread out below, but he still felt caged. The furniture came with the flat and nothing quite fitted; there were such big spaces between the settees and the walls. The spaces caught him unawares.

It was getting worse. Months had passed, seven months since June; he had hoped it would get better but now he was getting headaches as if a weight was pushing down on his skull. They had only had a few visitors but he had sat there, tense, willing them to leave. Denise, the girl from the salon, had come for a drink with her new husband.

'Wow, this place is amazing!' she said. 'How did you get it?'

Eva had hooked her arm around Jon's. 'I said he was in property.' She had given him a squeeze. 'Aren't I a lucky girl?'

He had sat there wordlessly, waiting for Eva to betray them by saying something careless. Afterwards she accused him of being boring, no fun. Weren't they supposed to be having fun? Hadn't they got what they wanted?

He climbed into bed. It was a brass bed; they had always wanted a brass bed, that was why they had chosen the flat. He had put his oak table on one side and Eva's marble one on the other.

Eva's deft fingers slid down his thigh; they stroked the skin behind his balls. She whispered into his ear. 'Jonny, isn't there something we should be talking about?'

He lay still. 'What?'

'Something beginning with B.'

'Burglars?'

'You've got crime on the brain.' She ran her fingernail down his stomach. 'Know something? You need to put on some weight, you're getting really skinny.' She nuzzled him. 'B for baby, dum-dum.' She brushed her knuckle down his cheek. 'Don't you think it's time? We got the money, we got the space. When it's growing up we can move to somewhere with a garden. Know something? I don't even mind the stretch marks. You said you always wanted a kid.'

It'll be born diseased. It'll be born deformed, like a victim of nuclear radiation. He stared into the darkness. He knew, with utter certainty, that any child they produced would be contaminated.

'Yeah. Fine,' he said.

'Wow. Don't be too enthusiastic.'

He squeezed his eyes shut and put his arms around her. 'Sorry,' he said.

'Know what? You've been really odd recently. Sitting around in the dark. You scared me out of me wits last night.'

'You think we should get married?'

'Hark at him, the romantic!'

'I want to make you happy.'

He spoke automatically. He was still unnerved by his

vision. He stroked the curve of her hip. He thought: we have blood on our hands. He closed his eyes and let her feel him, blindly, with her blind fingers.

The next day he went out. He thought: the idle rich, the idle poor, we all have time on our hands. Downstairs the lobby lamps were lit day and night; the painting on the wall was a splash of crimson. The security man, porter, whatever, sat behind his desk and nodded as Jon passed. He made Jon uneasy. The porter knew they were imposters; he must know. They weren't the sort of people who lived here. Jon's boots clack-clacked across the marble floor. Behind him, the man lifted up the phone and dialled.

Outside it was a warm, grey day. It was the warmest January since records began; nature was turning herself inside out and playing havoc with the climate. There were TV programmes about it. The street was hushed with money; opposite reared up houses, blindingly white, wedding-cake white, their windows criss-crossed with burglar grilles. The pavements were empty; it was like Stanmore. Rich people, he was realising, are seldom at home. They are always somewhere else. Nobody knew anybody here; it seemed to be all foreigners.

Kensington wasn't his sort of area, he didn't feel at home here, but Eva thought it had class. Maybe she felt safe, locked into their anonymous block of flats with its prison-guard downstairs. But Jon felt helpless here; even if he could use a bag of nails he couldn't buy one, the local shops sold Belgian chocolates or party dresses. It had no connection with his past. Sometimes he thought it was all a dream and he would wake up above the butcher's shop and everything would be back to normal. He even thought of the stairs with affection – the brown lino, the unknown phone numbers scrawled on the landing. He would be back in his life, queuing in the post office, his only acquaintance with crime the *frisson* when Eva stole a bottle of Bulgarian wine.

He pulled on his helmet, mounted his Yamaha and roared off. His spirits lifted. *The danger of wanting something is that you might get it.* Well, he had wanted this, and he had got it. He loved his new motorbike. He only felt safe when he was roaring from one place to another. If he drove fast, full throttle, he could outrace his demons. They caught up with him at traffic lights and then he raced off with them in pursuit.

He still felt shaken by the vision of his babies, the night before. They had smooth white skin where their eyes should be. *For the guilty shall perish, the fires of hell shall consume them.* He had committed a sin – several great sins – and doubting his own punishment was one of them. Hannah had understood that, a mere girl of seventeen. She had offered him her body and her wisdom. He had taken advantage of her – what a quaint phrase but it was the only way he could describe it.

He roared up Kensington Church Street. He thought: how can Eva believe we'll get away with it? Sooner or later it will catch us up, even if it takes years. What was that folk song he used to listen to, when he was working at his carpentry? 'For the fish might fly and the sea run dry and the rocks melt in the heat of the sun.' Nature was turned inside out, summer in January, the planets in disarray . . . blame it on the ozone layer, they said . . .

He rode to the allotments. The place was deserted. A Tuesday morning in winter, it was not surprising. Nowadays, however, he preferred it when there were people around; it gave the gardens an air of normality, with himself part of them.

He dismounted, heaved his bike on to its stand and pulled off his helmet. Celandines starred the edge of the path; the dandelions were already in flower. He looked at his plot, where the soil had heaved in his dream. Between the stalks of the Brussels sprouts the earth was laced with chickweed, like a delicate bedspread.

He had to get away from the flat. It was only here, far from Eva and the oppressive luxury of Kensington, that his head cleared. He had long ago removed all traces of Hannah. Last month he had finally dismantled the wardrobe, the site of her deepest embarrassment; he had smashed the wood and burnt it on a bonfire.

She still remained, however. She was the smell of mulligatawny soup, drifting across the allotments. She was still there in the hut, shifting her legs awkwardly under the black skirt as she adjusted her position on the camp bed, her lips pursed as she lifted the tea mug to her mouth. She was the tightening in his guts when he thought of their last night together . . . the skin of her thighs under his hand, her stubbly shins . . . *I haven't shaved since last week* . . . well, she hadn't been expecting this, had she? When he closed his eyes, her tongue slid experimentally into his mouth. *After all this, don't you owe me something?*

Jon dug vigorously. He plunged the fork into the earth and levered up potatoes. They hove into view, bald as bodies. Clammy soil clung to their sides as he exhumed them. He had planted these potatoes when Hannah sat in the hut; they were the products of her imprisonment.

Eva didn't want potatoes; she wanted his baby. Over the months she had changed. Now they could go out, anywhere in London, she didn't want to. She wanted to stay at home. Their crime had closed them off from the normal world; his wacky adventuress had become clinging and domestic, following him around the flat and freezing on the rare occasions that the phone rang. Their fear lay unspoken between them. It lay behind the stir of the curtains when the balcony window was open; it lay in the hushed, carpeted corridor outside, in the hissed breath of the lift door closing. It made its own silence.

Jon remembered thinking this, as he rode home. That the change in Eva was simply due to fear. She said he was no fun but she was less fun too. She wanted them to get married and have children. They could move into a house like a normal couple and put this behind them; it was understandable, really.

When he got back Eva was in the kitchen. He dumped the carrier bag on the table.

'Ugh!' She inspected the potatoes. 'They've got blight or something. Look.' She lifted one out, fastidiously, between her finger and her thumb.

'They're always like that. It's just sort of warts.'

'Ugh! A slug!' She dropped the potato back in the bag. 'I like the ones from Marks & Spencer's. They've been cleaned.'

He went into the lounge. It looked like a stage set; the two golden settees sat facing each other, waiting for their occupants.

'Christ it's hot.' He pulled open the sliding window.

'The thermostat's stuck,' said Eva, following him. 'I told you. The bloke never comes to fix it.'

'That's what we pay them for.' His voice sounded peevish, like a rich person's voice. 'The service charge, it's daylight robbery. You phoned Mr McCormack?' He was the managing agent.

'It's always engaged.'

Jon gazed across the rooftops. 'Life was simple once, remember? Ten pence in the meter, bob's your uncle.' He smiled. 'All that pocket money, you poor thing. Should've called it socket money.'

'What?'

'When your mum made you feed the meter, remember?'

'Oh.' She paused. 'Yeah.'

He looked at her. She gazed back, her eyebrows raised,

challenging him. Then she swung away and walked back into the kitchen. 'I'm ravenous,' she said.

For a moment he didn't move. Then he went into the kitchen.

'Eva.'

'Now, what'll we have?'

He grabbed her shoulder. She ducked, and moved aside.

'You were lying, weren't you?' he said.

She opened the fridge and squatted on her haunches. 'Salmon roulade.' She took out a packet and read its label. 'Finest scotch salmon wrapped around a mousseline of spinach.'

'You were lying about the meter.'

'Why should I do that?' She took out another packet. 'Lincolnshire sausages with garlic.'

He gazed at the top of her head. Her hair was longer now. She had dyed it blonde but the brown roots were showing through.

'Tell you what,' she said, 'I'll even mash your blooming potatoes. Sausage and mash.'

'You lied about the meter so I'd feel sorry for you.' He didn't add: so that I would love you more.

'Don't be stupid.' She nudged him aside and turned on the tap. She filled the sink with water. She tipped the potatoes into it; earth rose to the surface, a black scum.

Jon gazed at her back – her slender shoulders in a green T-shirt – as she busied herself at the sink. That night he had held her tightly in his arms. *That's the saddest thing I ever heard.* He had told himself he would never leave her.

The potatoes knocked together as she scrubbed them. 'I can cut out the bad bits,' she said, without turning round.

He thought: she has never been loved. Nobody has ever loved her, that's why she has never had any friends. That's why she has to lie.

He would always remember that moment in the

kitchen, how something shifted within him. He realised: I got it all wrong. Before all this happened, way back in Tottenham, I thought I was going to lose her. It wasn't like that at all. It was she who thought she was going to lose me.

'Put on the kettle, silly,' she said. 'Make yourself useful.'

Jon didn't move. He thought: she stole the money to keep me. All these months, she's been trying to buy my love.

Eva turned around. She touched his cheek with her wet finger. 'You silly-billy,' she said.

And he knew, sinkingly, that he was right.

Blood poured from the wound in Christ's side. The paint gleamed fresh, as if the crime had been committed an hour ago. Christ's face, however, showed no sign of emotion. His eyes were closed, as if He were asleep up there. It was painted by the School of somebody in 1493.

Behind Jon, on the other side of the room, stood an attendant. Jon could feel his gaze following him as he moved from one painting to another. He looked at a painted panel: a man vomiting devils; they pushed and clamoured out of his mouth, struggling into the daylight. Rocks rose up behind him – spaces where evil could crouch, hidden, as it crouched in the spaces behind his settees. Fra Angelico ... Signorelli somebody ... To Hannah, they were probably familiar. Guilt and suffering ... wherever he looked, figures huddled at the base of the cross. They pressed their hands to their faces, swooning with grief. Only Jesus remained serene.

Know what this place needs? Pictures. He went downstairs to the shop. Trouble was, he didn't want to buy a picture for the flat. He didn't want to go back to the flat. He picked up a book. It was called *The Art of the Renaissance*. There was a picture of the Madonna and Child on the cover.

Mary gazed at him, her eyebrows raised, as if she were asking how he could hope for forgiveness.

He bought the book for Hannah and paid with his credit card. Seven months, and he still wasn't used to spending money with ease. Eva had laughed: 'You should see yourself when you're at cash machines – like you stand close to it in case the whole fucking world wants to see your pissy little pin number.' He couldn't explain that signing a credit card wasn't so bad, it was abstract, but with real money . . . when the warm crisp notes slid out of the slit he felt he was stealing. He *was* stealing.

He went outside. Yesterday he had dug up potatoes in his shirt sleeves. Overnight, however, the temperature had dropped. An icy wind blew across Trafalgar Square. He pulled on his gloves and climbed on to his motorbike. He thought: I'm trapped with a woman I didn't know. *Close your eyes*, said Hannah, *and listen to her*. As he roared off he thought: Eva no longer terrifies me. The truth is, I feel sorry for her. Tears of self-pity stung his eyes, or maybe it was the wind. Today he felt too numb to know the difference. He thought: we're locked together, Eva and I. Crime, like the birth of a deformed child, has bound us together for life.

He needed to see Hannah, to convince himself that she was all right. Maybe if he saw her, a normal girl continuing with her life, he could return to some sort of normality himself. He needed to make decisions, the sort of decisions he was capable of making a year ago when he was part of the human race. He roared north, through Hendon. It was three twenty. He passed Apex Corner, glimpsing the canyon below; a gaping mouth led into the underpass. When he was a teenager he had read books on criminology; murderers often revisited the scene of their crime, they were drawn there by a morbid fascination. Several times he had returned to Stanmore, riding around the streets, hoping to glimpse her.

He rode up Cypress Drive and slowed down. Over the months the house had been extended and the front garden concreted over as if to smother the evidence of the past. Today three cars were parked there. On an earlier visit he had glimpsed the new owners; they looked Middle-Eastern. This afternoon there was no sign of life. It was three forty-five.

He rode on to St Mary's and parked near the school gates. He would see that she was all right and give her the book, to help her with her exam. In a few months she would be sitting her A levels. To Hannah he would just be a motorbike messenger, his face hidden behind the plastic visor. He would be a nobody, a faceless sheen.

His heart thumped. Girls were streaming out of the gates – small ones wearing the familiar blue uniform, larger sixth formers in their own clothes. Minutes passed. Doors slammed, cars drove away. In another lifetime he had sat here with Eva, the old Eva who had vanished for ever. They had sat here, scheming. How naïve they seemed, now he looked back on them! It was four ten. Sealed in his helmet he watched girls silently chattering. *See that man? He kidnapped Hannah Price.* They passed his bike. *He lives in Kensington, they've cordoned it off this afternoon.* Above the wall the bushes shivered in the breeze. The police were crouched the other side – *see, they always come back to revisit the scene of the crime, like a dog returning to its vomit.*

Four twenty. Everyone had gone. He was just about to leave when three girls came out of the school building. He recognised the red-headed one; she had been at the Underworld that night. Tanya? Emma? He had forgotten.

He stepped forward, holding the parcel. He lifted his visor an inch. 'Excuse me, I've got a parcel for Hannah Price.'

The girls stopped. 'Hannah?' They looked at each other. 'You want Hannah?'

He nodded.

'She's not here anymore.'

'What?'

'She left school last term,' said the red-headed one.

He paused. 'Where's she gone? Where can I find her?'

'They live in Harlesden,' said the tall one. 'Crewkerne Road.'

'What number?'

'Ssh!' The red-headed girl nudged the other one and shook her head. They hurried away, glancing at him over their shoulders.

Jon climbed on his bike. He twisted the handle, revving up. So she had gone. He had caused Hannah's removal from school – the upheaval of it! Leaving her friends, disrupting her A levels. *I've got my Predictions in three weeks!* She must have moved to a school nearer their new home.

He rode through the suburban streets; the lights flickered on one by one. Like a distant, evil dictator he had pressed a button and far away a bomb exploded. The havoc of it, the destruction! A house had been sold, a girl had been removed from school. Innocent people scurried around, small as ants, trying to rebuild their lives.

It was dark when he found Crewkerne Road. A burnt-out car sat under a street lamp. Three dogs trotted purposefully across the road. He switched off the engine. Terraces of houses, bathed in sodium light, stretched into the distance.

'Hey mister, give us a ride!'

'Wicked bike! How fast it do?'

Jon looked down. He was surrounded by small boys.

'How much it cost?'

A dog joined them, yapping at the wheels. He willed them all to go away. Two older boys sauntered across the street, skipping sideways to avoid a passing car, and walked up to the bike.

Just then he heard a woman's voice. 'Becky!'

He swung round. Down the road, a figure stood illuminated in an open doorway.

'Remember the *Standard*!'

'OK.' A girl skipped off down the road. She was accompanied by a bigger girl.

'And come straight home!' called their mother. The door closed.

Jon grabbed the parcel and followed the girls on the other side of the road. They both looked as if they were wearing school uniform. At the end of the street they went into a corner shop. He approached cautiously. He pulled down his visor and looked through the window.

Becky stood inside, choosing sweets. *Miss Bloody Spoilt Brat*, according to Hannah. She moved past the window. She had grown older than her photo; she looked almost adolescent. There were two small bumps on her chest. He didn't dare look at Hannah yet – not now he had found her. There was a luxury about delaying it. He inspected the window display – copies of *Viz* and *Your Wedding*, faded by the sun. Relief flooded through him. See – Hannah was all right. She was a normal girl, choosing sweets with her sister.

The other girl stepped into view. She wasn't Hannah. She was a big black girl, in school uniform. She nudged Becky and pointed to a magazine.

A few moments later they came out, carrying paper bags. Their jaws worked as they chewed. Jon tried to gather his wits. He stepped nearer them and pulled up his visor, just an inch. 'Rebecca Price?'

She stopped. She was a pretty girl – blonde, gelled hair; gold rings in her ears. There was a hard, insolent look to her. He held out the parcel. 'Got a delivery for your sister.'

'What do you want me to do with it?' she demanded.

'Give it to her.'

'When?' She looked up at him coldly. There was a cluster of pimples on her chin.

'Now,' he said.

'I can't.'

'Why not?' he asked.

'She doesn't live at home anymore.'

He stared down at her. 'Pardon?'

The black girl said: 'She's moved away. She –'

Becky kicked her. 'Shut up, Joelle.' She backed away. 'Fuck it. Forgotten the *Standard*.' She swung round and hurried back into the shop. The other girl followed her.

He stared through the glass. They were huddled together, talking. They looked at him. He jerked his head back.

Gripping the parcel, he ran up the street. His head was bursting; he wrenched off the helmet. Hannah had left school. She had left home. What on earth had happened? When he arrived, panting, at the end of the street he saw his bike. It lay on its side.

'Hey! You!' he yelled, but the boys were melting into the darkness. Somewhere, beyond a wall, he heard the crash of broken glass.

2

There's only so much a man can take. Morris knew this was no excuse. There was no excuse at all for what happened, that hot spring day and the weeks that followed, but the words kept rolling around his head quite separately from his conscience. *There's only so much a man can bear.*

Winter hadn't really existed. The soupy warmth of January and February had left people feeling unsettled, as if nature had cheated them out of their own shivering come-uppance. The rightful balance had been disrupted – bulbs had flowered in November and migratory birds had been bewildered into lingering. Then spring had clamped down, icy as steel, freezing the buds and erupting into storms that spun tiles off roofs and overturned bus shelters. It made no sense, any of it. The climate, like his family seemed to have lost its moorings. Blame it on the ozone layer, people said. We've only ourselves to blame.

Then, quite suddenly, a perfect day dawned. It was the beginning of May and the sun blazed through Morris's window. He sat at his desk adding up columns of figures. They were only estimates for the new building work but there was a certain satisfaction to them. You totted them up and look! They made sense. Arithmetic was as satisfying as he imagined carpentry must be – the slotting in, joint fitting joint; the way it dovetailed into a whole.

Over the months his attitude to his job had changed. As the chaos in his home life had deepened, so the office had become his refuge. His work was so undemanding.

Months ago he had found this humiliating. Now, however, he welcomed it because he didn't believe he could concentrate on anything more weighty. To think that he had once coped with the cut and thrust of running this outfit! Now it was his bolthole. He felt like an ageing time-server, a shadow of his former self, but he had to admit that there was a certain serenity in the life of a clock-watcher. He remembered Clarence in Dispatch, long since dispatched into redundancy under the new regime. Clarence with his crossword and his unending mono-logue about his tropical fish.

Morris got to his feet and took the papers to the photocopy room – Avril's old office. Kimberley stood there, sorting through a folder of documents. Her scent overpowered the warm, inky smell of the machinery. She wore jeans and a yellow T-shirt; her pale brown hair was pulled back with a ribbon. There was a healthy, schoolgirl glow to her.

'Hey, I'll be hours,' she said. 'Leave 'em here. I'll copy them for you.'

He thanked her. She was the only one of the younger employees who seemed to have time for him. A robust, sporty sort of girl, she had told him she belonged to a volleyball team. Volleyball! She came from New Zealand, that explained it. Good, old-fashioned values. *Mens sana in corpore sano*. He thought: she's the sort of girl people would like their son to marry.

At twelve thirty he walked across to Accounts. Kimber-ley sat alone, frowning at her screen. She looked up. 'The photocopier's jammed. Bob says he'll fix it but he's gone to lunch.'

Cards were propped up on her desk. 'When was your birthday?' he asked.

'Today.'

'Today, and nobody's taking you out?'

'Not till tonight.'

'Not till tonight!'

'No sweat.' Once he had found her twangy voice irritating. Now it seemed charming. She indicated her screen. 'Got to do the petty cash for Margot.'

'A day like this and you think of petty cash? You think of *Margot*?' He paused. 'Who is Margot?'

'She's my new boss. She joined last week.'

'The woman with the voice like Bette Davis?'

'Who's Bette Davis?'

'You've a lot to learn,' he said. 'Forget Margot, my dear. We're going out for lunch.'

He took her to the Bluebell Wood. It was out beyond Watford; they bought sandwiches and a bottle of champagne on the way. When they got out of the car she gasped at the blue mist blurring the feet of the trees.

'Wow!' she said. 'It's like, the world's turned upside down, know what I mean? Like – the sky's fallen on to the earth!'

'I used to bring my kids here when they were little.' He pointed. 'That tree, they used to climb it.'

Such a tender green, the leaves above him! They made his heart ache. He heard the sound of children laughing.

'I've never seen an English spring,' she said. 'I only came here last June – like, my winter back home. I cheated winter out of getting at me.'

'And you know it cheated us? We never had it.'

Carrying the picnic, they walked through the wood. She weaved from side to side, avoiding stepping on the bluebells. Their scent made his head swim. Birdsong rang in the trees; the sun warmed him. A sensation swept through him – such a forgotten sensation it took him a moment to identify it.

They sat down on the grass. The sensation was happiness. Up in the sky a plane droned – a piston engine, must be from Elstree airfield. It was the sound of his own youth – innocent summer days.

'New Zealand, I imagine it like this,' he said. 'Time-warped in the fifties. No crime, no drugs. Somewhere to park.'

'Yeah,' she laughed. 'That's why I left.' She shook her head. 'Actually it was more than that. My dad died when I was little, then last year my mum passed away so I felt – well, footloose.'

'Your parents, you loved them?'

'Of course.'

Of course. How simple.

He uncorked the champagne. She squealed, holding out the plastic cups.

'Where's my mug?' he joked. 'Remember?'

She nodded. 'You old grump.'

'Separation anxiety,' he said. 'I loved that mug. So, my dear, happy birthday. How old are you?'

'Twenty-four.' She drank. 'Bugger Accounts. I really want to quit that place and train to be a nurse. I can say that to you, seeing as you're not the boss anymore. Fun, isn't it, playing truant?'

He nodded. The advantage of his so-called job was that nobody would miss him if he wasn't there. He, a man who once could have sacked the lot of them. He laughed.

'What's the joke?' she asked.

'Nothing,' he replied. 'Everything and nothing.' He looked at her as she drank. She was a big girl – pink and wholesome. She radiated youth and simple high spirits. He said: 'Know where you should be? With a handsome young man in a BMW convertible.'

'Iain? Give use a break.' She tore open a packet of sandwiches. 'We call him the Slimebag.'

Morris was pleased. 'You do? What do you call me?'

'Morris.'

Was this a sign of respect, or simple lack of interest? It

was a pleasant sensation, to feel curiosity. At least it was a sensation.

She passed him a sandwich. 'Roast beef for you.' She munched her cheese and celery.

'My daughter, she's a vegetarian too.' He thought: she minds about eating a piece of veal but she doesn't mind about destroying her parents. 'Funny, what you young people care about.'

'Aw, don't sound so elderly.'

'I feel elderly.'

She balanced her sandwich on her knee. 'I like older men. I adored my dad.' She drained her cup. 'I feel safe with you.'

'Safe, she says! Nothing's safe.'

She nudged him. 'Hey, give over. It's not that bad.' She held out her cup. He filled it up, then he wedged the bottle between his knees.

'So you brought your kids here?' she asked, munching. 'Did you have fun?'

'You want the truth? What I remember, it's Theo, that's my son, he made Hannah cry. He taunted her into climbing this tree but she couldn't do it, she had no co-ordination. Then she hit him and he hit her harder and all hell broke loose.' He pointed. 'See through those trees? That's my golf club. Ex-golf club. I remember thinking: oh to be playing a round of golf. You know what a game of golf does? It makes sense. You think – if only life could be like this.' He paused. 'Oh it's been a hell of a year.'

'I know about your daughter.'

He stared at her. 'You do?'

'Of course,' she said. 'We all do. Nobody says anything, so British. I know she was kidnapped. Malcolm got us together the day I joined and told us not to talk about it.'

'Is that the truth?'

She nodded. She had wolfed down her second sandwich; she wiped her hands on her jeans.

He wasn't as shocked as he had thought. In fact it was a relief, to talk about it. He said: 'The price, it was even higher than we expected.'

'What do you mean? They cleaned you out?'

'Oh yes, they did that.' He took a breath. 'Something else happened. My daughter, she got pregnant. She wasn't raped, nothing like that. But the man who kidnapped her, he got her pregnant.'

'No kidding!' She stared at him.

Speaking the words out loud made them solid, as if they belonged to somebody else. 'So what happens? She moves out of our home.'

'Why? When?'

'Last November.'

'But why?'

'Why? She couldn't face her parents, that's why. My wife and I, we thought she'd been having a terrible time but then, as it turned out, she hadn't. Had she?'

'She still could've had a terrible time.'

'But it changed things.'

'For you, or her?'

'It just did,' he said.

'Did you support her?'

'Did we support her? My wife, she did. But Hannah, she couldn't take that.'

'Silly girl. Surely she'd need you more than ever?'

'You'd think that. I'd think that. But nothing's that simple.'

'Sounds simple to me.' She bit an apple; mist spurted from it. How refreshing she was! 'Seems to me she should be grateful you paid all that money. She should try to be nice.'

'But did she? My own daughter – I lost her once and then what happens? All over again, I lose her.'

'Where did she go?'

'To Notting Hill. You want to hear all this?'

'Go on. Shoot.' She wiped juice off her chin.

He paused. 'So she moves in with an ex-girlfriend of my son's. To this flat in Notting Hill. Then she has this little boy, Tobias.'

'She happy? You see her?'

'Sometimes.'

'What – sometimes she's happy or sometimes you see her?'

'Both.' He put down the sandwich; he couldn't finish it. 'Mostly it's my wife, she goes.' Somebody else had been sitting here; the bluebells were crushed flat. 'This knock-on effect, it's like dominoes. You played dominoes? My son, he'd just got his first job, editing this TV documentary – a colleague of his, he was making it – but he had to sell his editing machine and so, what happens? Things fall apart, that's what happens.'

'What things?'

'He gets drunk one night, he crashes his car. Then, in February, he gets caught with cocaine in his pocket. My son, he's a drug addict!'

'Because he's got some cocaine?'

'He's a criminal! So what do I do? I bail him out.' With his shoe he stirred the bruised leaves. 'My little daughter, she's thirteen now, she's at this school and you know what she learns? She learns how to smoke and skip classes and shout at her mother in filthy language.'

'Yeah, but she's a teenager now. She'd probably be like that anyway.'

'So you swore?'

She laughed. 'Like fuck.'

He rubbed the side of his nose. 'I sold my house to some Arabs. Ah, Arabs . . . So I'm prejudiced, I'm Jewish, I can't help it . . . Sometimes I feel – they've broken me. Those people, that wickedness. They've broken my family.'

'Don't be a prawn.' She refilled his cup. 'So – you're broken. You've got an illegit grandchild. So what? You're still alive. You've got a healthy baby. Let's celebrate. Seems you've been a bit short on that lately. Anyway, it's my birthday.'

They drained the champagne. Kimberley stood up. She pulled at his arm. 'Come on. Let's play some golf.' She wrenched a stick out of the leafmould and found a conker – a dark, soft one from the autumn. Laughing, she swiped at it with the stick.

'No no!' He climbed to his feet, grabbed the stick and put his arm around her. 'Your back, it's straight like this . . . hands together . . . that's right . . .' He felt her shoulderblades shifting as she swivelled. He felt the bump of her bra strap against his arm. 'There . . . and swing!'

It was a flimsy stick, more a twig really. The next swipe, it snapped. He looked at it, in her hand. 'Sad, isn't it?' he said. 'Story of my life.'

She burst out laughing and collapsed on the ground. She lay on her back, her arms outstretched. He thought: months it's been since I heard laughter. Months since I have been silly. He eased himself down beside her – his joints ached – and lay on his back. They gazed up at the chestnut tree; its canopy of leaves with the sky pressing between them, solid. His heart pounded. How many weeks was it since he and Val had made love? Five – no, more. Neither of them had the will. It wasn't just their money that had been stolen. He thought: my wife, can't she realise how happy we could be, lying side by side like this? But nothing was this simple, not anymore.

He looked at Kimberley's profile. Her eyes were closed. Beside her the bracken was unfurling – silvery sheep's crooks. He looked at her ear. Its downy lobe caught the sun; within it, ah the secret whorls and caverns . . . There was a world in there, in miniature. He gazed at the lobe. Nothing had punctured it and mutilated it with studs. His throat tightened.

She murmured: 'What are you looking at?'

'You want to know? The bracken. They're like little crochet hooks. I'm watching them unfurling. You know there's fur on them?' A moment passed. Finally he spoke. 'Your ear,' he said softly. 'I'm looking at your ear. Never have I seen anything so perfect.'

'It's just a regular ear. I've got another one too.'

Above them a bird sang; its notes boiled over and tumbled down. Something welled up in him; he felt tears pricking his eyes. He leant towards her, he couldn't help it, and kissed the lobe of her ear. It felt cool against his lips. He took the lobe into his mouth and held it there.

She rolled towards him. He heard the soft, moist sound of the bluebells as her hip crushed them. She removed his glasses and laid them on the grass.

'You poor old bugger.' She smiled at him.

And for the first time in – oh so many months – he put his arms around another human being.

3

Becky opened the fridge and took out a Fruit Corner. 'Joelle thought she was pregnant last week.'

Val stared at her. 'But she's your age!' Joelle was Becky's best friend – a big, benign black girl, already heavy with the weight of womanhood.

Becky peeled off the lid. 'It's OK. Her period was late.'

She wandered back into the other room. The doorbell rang. It was her friends from school, arriving to watch *Neighbours*.

Val was cleaning the oven. She sat back on her haunches. Becky liked to shock her and Morris with horror stories from school – pregnancies, pupils being frisked for weapons, drugs in the cloakrooms. Just as shocking, however, were the facts that she knew to be true – the lightning turnover of teachers, the debilitating cutbacks, the lack of sports. At a recent swimming gala three children in Becky's class had had to be rescued by the lifeguard because they couldn't swim at all.

Whoops and laughter came from the lounge. With Becky's friends in it, the maisonette seemed very small. In their old house Val could escape from teenagers; here she could only retreat upstairs into the bedroom or busy herself in the kitchen.

She scrubbed the floor of the oven. She thought about the protective envelope of wealth and wondered, for the thousandth time, if Becky's removal to a large comprehensive had accelerated her loss of innocence or whether it was an inevitable happening. Becky had always been tougher than Hannah – sharper, more manipulative.

Becky came back into the kitchen, opened the fridge and took out a bottle of Coke.

'Does Joelle's mother know?' asked Val. 'Shouldn't she get fixed up? She shouldn't be sleeping with people at thirteen anyway.'

'You mean she should wait till she's seventeen and get pregnant then.'

'Oh, *touché*.'

'What?'

'I suppose they don't teach you French expressions,' said Val.

Becky left. It was a hot day in early June – a year, almost to the day, since Hannah's abduction. Val wiped her forehead with the back of her wrist. At times she forgot she was the mother of a teenage mother, that Hannah was one of the statistics that had once made alarming head-lines in the papers. Over the months Val had become knowledgeable about things which previously she had only read about in the *Daily Mail* – those *Why oh why* columnists and hand-wringing features about Generation X. Theo was now on the dole. Through him she had become painfully intimate with the labyrinthine benefits system, UB40s and all. Also with the laws of possession, police records, all the paraphernalia of drug-related crime. Her handsome son, the apple of his father's eye! Through Hannah she had learnt about the crumbling edifice of the welfare state and the subterfuge of sub-renting a council flat. Hannah and Tobias were living in a high-rise block in Notting Hill. Until this year council tenants had been a separate species – the only person Val knew who lived in such a flat was her home-help, Rhoda, and she had finally bought hers.

Val peeled off her rubber gloves. She gazed at the tiles. *They remind me of varicose veins* said Hannah. She missed her daughter desperately. Becky was becoming so bolshy and getting a third child through adolescence, when one had done it twice before, was so exhausting. Besides, with the other two she had been out of the house most of the time, working, and had employed other people to clear up the mess.

As Morris said – *children*, throwing up his hands, *children, nothing but worry*. Becky had a hard, knowing look to her nowadays. She had become so pert and – well, common. Last week she had announced she was going to leave school at sixteen and become a beautician. A *beautician*. Theo seemed to have given up on the film-making, he said nobody could get the finance anyway, and seemed to spend his time lounging around Soho cafés with dope-smoking drop-outs who sponged off their girlfriends. And Hannah, who this week should be sitting her A levels, whose friends were sitting theirs, who should be looking forward to Media Studies at Sussex University – Hannah was stuck on a graffiti-daubed estate, alone with a baby. Her carefree student life had been stolen from her; independence and fun and first love-affairs had been stolen from her. Hannah's future had been hijacked by two criminals who were walking free. How could any of them cope with this sort of injustice?

No wonder Morris seemed to have aged ten years. Val had realised, only this morning, that his hair was now completely grey. Their marriage was another thing that was being hijacked – a slow, painful process but she had to admit it. Morris had changed. Her sentimental, sensual husband, who used to embarrass their children by holding her hand in public and boasting about their happiness – *a couple who can laugh together can live together* – he was turning into a bland, courteous stranger. A man who shared her bed but who didn't touch her, whose sorrow had solidified inside him like a cyst that had grown thick protective skin around itself. They didn't even quarrel anymore; they had lost the intimacy of anger. Over the past few weeks it had got worse; he seemed more preoccupied than ever. Perhaps he, too, was thinking about this anniversary. It was one of the many areas that were closed to discussion.

She walked past Becky's room – a pit, like Hannah's used to be. She remembered Morris joking, back in Stanmore: *'Anyone who needs to enter Hannah's room ought to get vaccinated first.'*

She couldn't imagine him saying that now. Val stood there. The wallpaper blurred. Tears filled her eyes – she, Val, who never cried.

When Morris came home from work she said: 'I went to see Hannah and Tobias this morning. We took him to the park.'

'How were they?'

'She seems to be coping terribly well. Much better than I did, with a baby.'

Morris took his *Evening Standard* into the garden. Val followed him. Rap music thumped from the open window next door.

'She'd love it if you went to see them.'

'I do see them.' He took off his glasses and rubbed his eyes.

'Not for ages.' She paused, then she ruffled his hair. 'I was thinking of that Yiddish proverb you told me, this morning.'

'This morning? Did I?'

'Not this morning. Ages ago. But I was thinking about it this morning.' Their conversations were getting like this – cumbersome. She soldiered on. 'About, why hair on top goes grey but pubic hair stays brown.'

Morris's head jerked up. 'Why were you thinking that?'

'Isn't it, because here it's all trouble –' She touched her

head – 'and down here it's all pleasure? What're the Yiddish words?'

Morris paused. '*Mekheye* and *tsoras*,' he said, and opened the paper. He was only pretending to read it, however; he hadn't put on his glasses.

She wondered if he had worked out how long it was since they had made love. Two months. It was after they had been invigorated by watching *Singin' in the Rain* on TV.

She said: 'Are you all right?'

'I'm fine.' He put on his glasses and turned the page.

'You seem a bit . . .'

'I'm fine. So when do you want me to see Hannah?'

'I'm not making you,' she said. 'I didn't mean that.' Sometimes she wished Morris drank – really drank. Then they could get sloshed together. 'It's just – I don't know. Maybe we could go this weekend. It's so nice and sunny. We could all go out.'

'I can't.' He turned the page. 'VANDALS WRECK PETS' CEMETERY'. 'I've been meaning to tell you, I won't be there this weekend.'

'Why not?'

'I have to go to a conference in Derby. The Germans are coming over, we're making a presentation.' He turned the page. 'I'll have to stay away overnight.'

She looked at his grey, thinning hair. He seemed to be inspecting an advertisement for Comet Discount Warehouses. Pleasure flooded through her.

'That's wonderful!' she said.

He looked up. 'Why?'

'Because they're sending *you*.' She stopped. Maybe that was tactless – oh, she had to tread so carefully! She meant: it shows they still think you're important.

'It's just for the Saturday night,' he said. His face looked pink; it must be the sun.

Val smiled at him but he missed it; at the same moment he looked down at his paper.

It was strange, waking up in an empty bed. For weeks she had felt Morris wasn't really there; still, the absence of his body gave her a jolt. It was a beautiful day, already hot. As she got dressed Val felt that curious sensation again, the sensation she had felt the day of the photograph – that her family had dissolved from her life and she was alone. This time it was true; Becky was staying at a friend's house. There was nobody here.

She also felt mildly surprised that Morris hadn't given her the phone number of his hotel in Derby. In the past, when he had travelled on business, he had been particularly diligent over this – in fact, phoned her so often for a chat that it had become a family joke.

Val felt sad. They were growing apart; they no longer communicated. All the clichés they had applied to other couples whose marriages were in trouble – friends who they had smugly discussed from the safety of their own contentment – those clichés applied to them now. They didn't fit, however; no clichés do. They felt like someone else's stiff clothes that chafed under the arms because they hadn't been worn in yet.

Perhaps they never would fit. Perhaps this was just a blip, an inevitable result of the strains and traumas of the past year. Val herself felt distanced from her husband, it wasn't a one-way thing. A year ago, when it happened, they had both behaved nobly. It was the long haul, with no end in sight, that was the real killer. The guilt and remorse, the problems with their children. The grinding claustrophobia. Their bedroom looked out on the street. The red-brick houses faced her – cars, concrete, an unlovely view that remained unchanged, whatever the season. Now she was alone she could admit it: she hated it here. She hated their mean maisonette with its graceless little rooms and plastic doorhandles: the view without a leaf in sight.

Val pulled on her jeans. She roused herself: don't give up. If I give up, we'll all go under. She thought: I shall go to the garden centre and buy some geraniums. I'll put them on the front window ledge, a symbol of hope.

Later that morning she set off. Becky wasn't due back until lunchtime. Val walked past the tyre graveyard and down into the main road. She remembered her feelings so distinctly, that hot Sunday morning. She was thinking about when she worked, and didn't have time to sit down and read a book. For a year now she hadn't worked and she still didn't have time for things like that – for reading a book or buying geraniums. Life itself kept her busy, it had spread into every corner of her day – housework, and fixing things so that they didn't have to call somebody at vast expense, and hours spent waiting for public transport to take her to visit Hannah and Tobias, or to take her down to Windsor to visit her mother who now Val was freer seemed mysteriously to need her more. That was what women did, women who didn't work. How on earth had she ever had time for a job?

These thoughts went through her mind as she walked down the high street, past the bus depot and the library, which now closed three days a week – always, inevitably, the day when Becky needed to go there. She remembered that morning with the heightened clarity she remembered that other Sunday, a year ago, when Hannah disappeared.

She turned left and walked down the hill. Looming up on her left stood the church, a red-brick, Pentecostal-type place. 'JESUS SAVES', said the sign. Does he really? thought Val. Theo, when he was a teenager, would have asked: 'What building society does he use?' Theo used to like puns. She didn't know what he would say now and this made her melancholy.

As she passed, the church doors opened and the

congregation spilled out. They were all black. They wore the sort of outfits white people only wore to weddings – hats, yellow dresses, two-piece silky suits printed with poppies. In the past this had lifted Val's spirits but today she felt excluded, not just by her race but by her solitude. How happy these families looked; how well-behaved! God-fearing little girls wore white ankle socks, with ribbons in their hair.

'Mrs Price?'

Val turned. It was Joelle's mother. They had met a couple of times at school functions. She was a formal, handsome woman; she wore a pink pillbox hat and matching suit. Val found her intimidating – the old Val wouldn't have, but she did now. Next to her stood her daughter Joelle and her son.

'How's Rebecca?' she asked.

'She went to a party last night.' Val turned to Joelle. 'Did you go?'

Joelle nodded. 'It was crap.'

'Joelle!' said her mother.

'Sorry.' Joelle bit her lip. Val wondered if her mother had known about Joelle's suspected pregnancy. She also tried to remember the woman's name.

Around them, hats bobbed. People greeted each other with old-world courtesy. Joelle's mother turned to Val.

'And how's your other daughter?'

'Hannah? She's fine.'

'And the little boy?'

Val said something, she couldn't remember later because when Joelle's mother spoke everything was wiped from her mind.

'I didn't see him last week, your little grandson,' she said. 'Maybe they left him in the car.'

'What do you mean?' asked Val.

'Your daughter,' she said patiently. 'She came into the café last week, with Mr Price.'

'Hannah did?'

'I was going to say hallo, but then they'd gone.'

Val's mind worked laboriously. This woman, she remembered, worked in catering. Becky said she wiped the tables.

Val said: 'Where was this?'

'Where I work. Hatfield House. There was a big coach party, so I couldn't get to greet them. She's a nice-looking girl, isn't she?'

The woman turned away to greet somebody else. Val backed off. She made her way round the corner and stood there, staring at a rubbish bin. 'KEEP BRENT BEAUTI-FUL', it said.

She thought: Morris hasn't seen Hannah for weeks. He hasn't taken her to Hatfield House.

She thought: Joelle's mother, she doesn't know what Hannah looks like.

She's a nice-looking girl, isn't she?

Morris came home as the sun was sinking. He didn't notice the geraniums because she hadn't bought any.

Val watched him as he dumped his bag in the lounge. He sighed with the effort. He had his back to her. He wore his lightweight blue suit, the one she had bought for him. He gazed out of the window. It took her a moment to realise that he was talking.

'. . . they've published this survey, ninety-two per cent of alarm calls turn out to be false, would you believe it? We hadn't realised it was so high. This delegate, from the Association of Chief Police Officers, he gave us the figures . . .'

She gazed at the plump folds in the back of his neck. The skin bulged over his collar.

'. . . the Germans, they're developing this thumbnail-sized camera, the photos can be sent down the phone to private security guards, we're going to have to get our skates on . . .'

It was a linen suit. There were creases across the back of the jacket. Left to himself he would have bought an awful polyester mix because it was easier. She had bought him linen because she thought it gave him class.

'. . . Probe FX, that's this Walsall-based company, they demonstrated this anti-theft dye . . . invisible, it's released from overhead sprinkers . . .'

'What the hell are you talking about?' she said.

Morris stopped. He didn't turn round.

She said: 'Who is she?'

4

'*It is easier to give than to receive.*' Hannah was leafing through her old A level notes. The words opened up and spoke to her, like mouths, from the page. How could E. M. Forster know this when he had never been a parent? Never been kidnapped, either. She gazed out of the window. Down in the courtyard three kids were wrestling with a supermarket trolley. One of them won and trundled it away, out of sight beneath the block of flats.

It was Monday morning. Today she had made a decision: she was going to finish her A levels. Tomorrow she would go to the Westway Community College and see if she could enrol in September. It was unfinished business; damage to be repaired.

A levels. What a quaint phrase that seemed now, a blast from the past! She was nearly nineteen but she felt vastly older. She was a mother. Her breasts were two boulders aching with milk. She would have to wean Tobias before she went to college but oh, it was so seductive, feeding him. When he suckled he gazed into her eyes with such transparent need; he gazed into her soul. His fingers worked at her breast, kneading it. Needing it. Once she thought her body was fat; now it seemed like a ripe, full fruit. It was his; his body was hers. When he was satisfied his eyes clouded; all weathers chased across his face. He was her everything . . . the lover she had never had . . . he was her saviour, her torment and her joy. He was her one-way flight from adolescence; at his birth she had leap-frogged over all the embarrassing stuff – the snogging, the giggling, the feelings of inadequacy and *does he fancy me*?

'You're missing out!' wailed her mother. 'You're missing what girls your age ought to be doing.'

'Yeah,' she had replied. 'Thank God.'

She had vaulted past that and there was no turning back. Even her skin had cleared.

The flat was in a council block in Notting Hill. She was sub-renting it from one of Theo's ex-girlfriends, someone called Annette who was away in Thailand. It was in the sort of estate which, until she lived in it, she had only seen on TV dramas; that scene when the police charge along an upper walkway, break open a door and surprise the black people inside. When they had come here for the first time her parents had been appalled by this place but in fact the neighbours were a lot more friendly than back in Stanmore. Yasmin, the little girl next door, was besotted with Tobias and spent half the day in Hannah's flat manhandling him proprietorially. Music thumped in the small hours of the morning to companion Hannah when she was feeding her baby. Lottery fever had gripped their floor because the old boy at the end had won £78. Hannah filled in her numbers each week. She thought: if this was a TV drama I would win back the £500,000. I would present the cheque to my parents, they would forgive me and everything would be all right.

It wasn't all right, of course. She was responsible for everything that had happened. If she hadn't gone to Camden Lock, if she hadn't been swayed by her own idiotic vanity – *You want to take my photo? For a fashion shoot?*

All that was bad enough. But then, just as her parents were closing ranks and rallying round, giving up their most treasured possessions without a word of complaint, treating her kindly as if she were an invalid, repeating *no, it doesn't matter, none of it matters now we've got you back safe and sound* . . . then she had broken the news and sent them reeling.

She had had to get away. She couldn't live at home. Her parents still didn't understand that, even after seven months. She had to release them from their own turbulent feelings towards her; she had to release herself and set them all free. Her struggle with loneliness was at least a clean struggle, unmuddied with guilt, far away from the watchful claustrophobia of home where every word and object reproached her. It was hard, living alone with a baby, but in a curious way she needed it to be a tough haul; E. M. Forster understood. Didn't her parents understand that taking from the state was easier than taking from them?

She went into the kitchen and put on the kettle. Outside, on the balconies opposite, washing hung up to dry. She felt intimate with the changing display of underwear belonging to the people who lived there. Compared to Stanmore, life here was so exposed. People quarrelled and chattered, even indoors you could hear them shouting through the walls. Down in the courtyard men tinkered with dead vans. Children ran wild, like the dogs which gambolled under the sign saying 'NO DOGS'. She put a teabag into her mug and poured on the water. Other people's meals, too; she smelt them. She felt as intimate with their cooking as with their public display of knickers.

Hannah sat down and picked up her Clas-Civ file. Its cover was embellished with old doodles and messages to Tanya, who used to sit next to her. In his carrycot, Tobias sneezed – a tiny, surprisingly adult sound, a sneeze-in-miniature. She gazed at him. She was flooded with love. How strange it was, to bear the child of a man she had never seen! There were plenty of single mothers living here, but they all knew the identity of their children's fathers – indeed, criticised them vociferously. *The sod, the bastard*! At times she felt like the Virgin Mary, impregnated by a spirit. A voice, a stubbly cheek, a tongue, a penis – parts of a man who was there and yet not there. Sometimes she searched the faces in the street – one of them might be him and she would never know. Tobias would never know. One day she might be standing in a queue, or squashed in the tube, and smell his scent as he stood near her. And he, of course, would recognise her.

Hannah looked down at her son. He was hot; his hair was plastered to his forehead. His hair was black – the only resemblance to herself that she could discern so far. Whether he looked like his father she would never know. What a dizzying thought!

She gazed at him. How pure he was, how simple his needs! He was simply loved; simply unacquainted with the corrosive nature of evil. Nothing had happened to make him feel guilty. His brow was unfurrowed. He lay there, two fingers inserted in his mouth.

She closed her file and bent down to pick him up. As she did so, someone hammered at the door – the bell was broken. Tobias's face crumpled.

She picked him up, put him over her shoulder and opened the door. Becky stood there. Her face was white.

'Becky! What's happened? Shouldn't you be at school?'

Becky pushed past her. She started sobbing – noisy, ugly gulps. Tobias started yelling.

'Becky! What is it?'

It was a startling noise, as if Becky's guts were being pulled up through her throat. She always cried like this; there was something histrionic about her grief. Hannah sat her down on the settee. She tried to put her arm around her but Becky leaned away. 'What's happened?' Tobias yelled louder. She gripped him with one arm. 'Come on, Becky!' She looked at the silver dolphin in Becky's ear; it was one of hers.

Becky's sobs stopped. She wiped her nose with the back of her hand. 'They've been having this awful, awful row.'

'Who?'

'Mum and Dad. I had to get away, they were shouting all night. I hate him! I want to kill him!'

'What's he done?'

'I'm not going home, ever! I'm going to disappear and nobody's going to find me.'

'Don't be stupid. That's already happened to them once. What's Mum going to think, when she goes to fetch you from school? She'll have a fit if you're not there.' She passed her the mug of tea. 'Have a sip. Calm down. Tell me what's happened.'

'He went away for the weekend. He came back last night and they had this huge row.'

'What was it about?'

'Dad's got a girlfriend.'

5

'Where have you been all day?'

'The allotments.' Jon put his helmet on the table. His brown hair stood up stiffly; he brushed it flat with his hand. Eva's heart turned over.

'Hey, we were supposed to be looking at houses,' she said. 'You promised.'

'God, were we?' He kissed her forehead. 'Tomorrow, let's go tomorrow. Sorry sorry sorry.' He smelt of sweat.

He went into the bathroom; she heard the hiss of the shower. Jon was the only bloke she'd ever known who turned on the shower before he took off his clothes. He copied it from American movies. Daft bugger.

Eva stepped out on to the balcony. The sun was sinking over some turretty building. Jon knew what it was – some museum or other. It was June. In a month they would be married. He would be hers. They would be married and everything would be all right.

She sat down and lit a cigarette. She looked at the tubs: each had a bay tree in it, and some geraniums and that trailing thing, what was its name? Jon had been miffed, that she'd hired a professional gardener to plant them; he said he could have done it himself. Oh yeah? For a start he would never have got round to it, heaving up the stuff in the lift. And anyway, why work his balls off when he could save himself the trouble and get somebody else to do it? He had sulked for days. Sometimes she thought he was barmy. They had money – why not enjoy it? But she loved him; Christ she loved the man.

He must never know how much she needed him. He would be bloody terrified. She used to have him in her power but over the past few months she had felt him slipping away – God knows why when he had got everything he wanted – but she was going to get him back. They would get married; she would get pregnant. They would take out all their money and put it together to buy somewhere permanent – this place was just rented. Maybe he was nervous of this final commitment. She mustn't push him – see how well she had handled that just now? She hadn't blown her top. He mustn't feel trapped; he mustn't get a whiff of it.

Eva ground out her cigarette and flicked it over the balcony. He was impressed with the way she was handling their finances. Sure she had spent a bit – the second-hand Merc, the furniture – but there was still £450,000 left. So far they had been living off the interest from the building society accounts. She had it all worked out. They would buy a house for half the money max and they would pool the rest and invest it. For months she had been reading the business pages of the *Evening Standard*, she was getting familiar with PEPS and Unit Trusts. They would get a small income, but they could live on it. She would set up her own business from home – aromatherapy and massage. Jon was a shit carpenter, that was why he had never got any work, but he could be a man of leisure. She would look after him. She would have him. He would be hers.

She had played it down, this domestic stuff. He thought she was a goer. She *had* been a goer – she had got a kick out of shocking him. Like, the drugs and stuff. But something had happened to her over the past few months. The money should have brought them together, they should be having a ball. But Jon was being so weird. He sat in the dark. He disappeared for hours on his motorbike. She was starting to panic. She needed him; she had nobody in the world but him. She wanted to lock him up and have his babies. This place wasn't happening for them; he wasn't settled here in Kensington. They had been living here nearly a year and it was like he wasn't settled at all. She would do anything to keep him; she would hang wallpaper and dig the garden. She *wanted* to. She, Eva!

She loved him to death. She loved him so fiercely she could pull him inside out and lick his intestines. She had never met a man who had really reached her, who actually seemed to like her. He was so gentle, he was such a great lover. Loverboy loverman lovelylovely. He understood her body. He could make her come, deep inside, again and again, and if he came first he kept with her, he kept going. And when he was doing it he looked at her – he looked into her soul. He even liked what he saw there – *she* didn't, but he did. He understood the black places, he knew all the crap inside her. He had heard all her secrets; he was her only friend. If he left her she would die – yeah, but she would kill him first.

Later she remembered all this, how she sat on the balcony and dreamed about their future. Tomorrow they were going to Harvey Nichols to buy her a wedding outfit. She knew exactly what she wanted: a cream silk suit, Jasper Conran, a designer like that. Then they were going to Chelsea Register Office to finalise the details. It was going to be an exclusive occasion, like just a few friends. Her mum and his dad were definitely not on the guest list.

Someone below was having a barbecue; smoke drifted up. A taxi hooted down in the street. She remembered thinking: he's been hours in the shower.

She got up and went into the bedroom. Jon was sitting there, hunched up. He was so thin now; his backbone jutted out like a necklace was hidden under his skin. She sat beside him and touched his shoulder. He jumped.

'You'll catch a chill,' she said.

When he turned – the look on his face! It was like he had never seen her before.

'What's up?' she asked.

'Nothing.'

'Come on Jonny, what is it? You've been ever so strange.' She stroked his thigh; he flinched. 'What is it?'

He didn't speak. He gazed at her teddy bears, propped against the pillow.

'I know, you're shagging someone else.' She kept her voice light. 'That's what you do when you pretend you're at the allotment – like, fertilising your carrots.'

He swung round. 'What?'

'Just kidding.'

He paused. 'I went there last week.'

'Where?'

'To where the Prices live.'

'The Prices?'

'The people whose money we took. They moved to Harlesden.'

'You went there? But that's daft! They might see you!'

He shook his head. 'They weren't there.'

'Why did you go? You mad or something?'

'I wanted to see if she was all right. Hannah. I knew she'd left home, I'd found that out months ago, I've been there before.'

'When?'

'It doesn't matter,' he said.

'You want to get us arrested?'

'I wanted to know what had happened. To be frank, I didn't care if they knew who I was.'

'*What?*'

'But they weren't there.' His voice was dead odd – flat. 'I banged on the door and the woman upstairs said they'd moved out. She said they'd had this huge row last week. She'd heard it through the floor.' He rubbed his forehead with his forefinger, up and down. 'The dad left the next

254

day. And then Mrs Price, she moved out with the other daughter, the younger one. They've broken up and it's all because of us.'

'Where've they gone?'

He shook his head. 'I don't know.' His voice sounded choked. 'I can't bear it.'

His body shuddered. Shit, he was crying! She had never seen him cry. She put her arms around him but he sat rigid, he didn't budge.

'Come on Jonny, it would've happened anyway, it's nothing to do with us.'

He jerked away. 'Oh no? Nothing to do with us?'

'So it's our fault,' she said. 'Was it my fault, what that bloke did to me?'

'What bloke?'

'Mum's boyfriend, Arnold. I told you –'

'That's nothing to do with it,' he said.

'He fucking dislocated my jaw. I was twelve years old! I had to tell this doctor – I had to explain to him what I had to do to a bloke, for it to dislocate my jaw. You know what that feels like, huh?'

'What do you mean – that life's a shithole so you ought to screw everybody else?'

'Shall I tell you what happened?'

'You told me.' He raised his head and looked at her. 'Trouble is, I don't believe it.'

'You what?'

'I don't believe the things you told me. You only said them to make me sorry for you.' He wiped his nose with the back of his hand. 'And the real trouble is, I don't even care any more.'

'Jon –' She stopped. The old stomach cramps began; she hadn't had them for years. She held her breath, willing them to stop.

Jon was looking at her but his eyes were blank. Tears

slid into the corners of his mouth. 'I didn't care if they saw me. I didn't care if I was caught.'

'Don't you care about me?'

'I can't forget them.' He wasn't listening to her. 'I've tried, but I can't.'

'What about me?'

He paused. 'She told me to close my eyes and listen to you,' he said. 'But it's worse when I open them.'

The next day he was gone. She had taken the car to the Mercedes place for its service. When she got back the flat was empty. She felt it when she stepped through the door.

'Jonny?'

She rushed into the bedroom. There was nobody there. The bathroom door was ajar; his spongebag was gone. In the wardrobe, his travelling bag was missing.

She went back into the lounge. She yanked open the desk drawer and rummaged amongst the documents. His passport wasn't there. On the table sat his mug of coffee; it was still warm.

Afterwards she tried to remember what she did. She was numb. It was like when you stubbed your toe and just for a moment the pain hadn't reached your brain. First she vomited down the toilet. Then she tried to roll herself a joint but she couldn't stick the fucking Rizlas together. That was when she started to cry. During all this she managed to pour herself a vodka and tonic. Ice, even. She tried to raise the glass; the ice cubes rattled against the sides.

The buzzer buzzed. She must have got up to answer it. A voice said: 'Delivery from John Lewis.'

Just for a moment she thought: it's a joke! All of it. In a moment I'll hear the lift and Jon will be standing there carrying a gift he's ordered – like, a surprise for our wedding.

It was a big black bloke. He carried a cardboard box. 'Where shall I put it?' he said. She pointed to the floor. He put it down. 'Want to check it's all there?'

She hadn't been lying, not really. Well, a bit. Things had happened to her, she was sure of it, when she was young. She'd repressed it – that repressed syndrome thing. She must have been abused because that was why her mum had felt guilty and put her into care. That must have been the reason, whether she could remember anything or not. Didn't Jon love her enough to believe her?

'Sure you don't want to check it?' the man asked. He spread out a sheet of paper. 'Sign here, love.'

Her hand wouldn't work. Finally she managed a jagged up-and-down mark and he must have been satisfied because then she was alone again. The box was a Gaggia coffee machine. They had always liked espresso coffee and look! Now they could make it themselves.

She went back into the kitchen to refill her glass and it was only then that she saw the note. It was propped against the bread bin.

Dear Eva. Sorry I'm a coward but I've been a coward from the start. It's best this way. Don't try to find me because I've gone a long way off and I won't be back. Sorry. Best luck for the future, and love, Jon. PS Please give my belongings to someone who might need them like Oxfam.

She went back into the lounge and pulled open the drawer again. She rummaged amongst the chequebooks. His building society account books, the four ones in his name, had gone.

Late that afternoon she went to collect her car. They had put a plastic cover over the seat; it stuck to her back. Though the roof was open she was clammy with sweat, as if she was running a fever. She drove out to the allotments in Acton. She didn't know why; she wasn't thinking too clearly. He wouldn't be holed up there but she had to do something. She drove through a city that didn't have Jon in it. He had taken his fucking passport. He had vanished without trace, like he had been kidnapped. No – like he had kidnapped himself. *Kidnapped*. It was a funny word when she applied it to herself. She thought: so this is what it feels like. A person, they vanish just like that. The earth swallows them up.

She hadn't been to the plot for a year. Jon spent a lot of time there; he brought back the vegetables he had grown. He showed them to her proudly. The bastard. How could he do this to her? He'd been weird, oh she had noticed that. Maybe he had totally freaked out. Maybe he had gone to the police and given himself up. Like, he'd finally cracked. Maybe at this very moment he was telling them about her and giving them their address. These thoughts crossed her mind but just now she didn't give a toss. Soon she would, but not yet. She just needed to see where he had been all this time. Maybe she would find a clue to where the bastard had gone.

The gates were open. It was six o'clock. In the distance old geezers were stooped over their spades. She smelt soup – the wind was blowing from the Heinz factory. It brought it all back – the rush of it, the fizz in her veins. She and Jon, partners in crime. The lift and swoop if it – two of them, against the world.

She drove up to their plot and parked. For a moment she thought she had come to the wrong place. But there stood the hut with its padlocked door; there was the tap and the stained old bath.

She looked at the plot. For a moment she sat there thinking: it's here, isn't it? Somewhere here. Where the fuck is it?

The place was choked with weeds. Knee-high nettles

and thistles. It was a fucking jungle. Nobody had been there for weeks.

She didn't get out. She just sat there, with the engine running. Then she must have left but she didn't remember driving back to the flat. She was back there, though. She was rummaging in the fridge. Only two days ago Jon had come home with a bag of stuff from the allotment.

She pulled out the carrier bag. It was bundled inside the crisper, in the bottom of the fridge. She took out a lettuce, some tomatoes and a bunch of watercress. The lettuce was too clean. And even she knew you didn't grow watercress on an allotment.

Shit! Shit *shit*!

He hadn't been to the plot, had he. All fucking summer. He had gone somewhere else, and he had just bought the frigging vegetables on the way home. Bought them in a shop. For months he had been telling her lies. For months he had been planning something – all this time, when she had been wittering on about their future. Wedding, house.

What the fuck had he been doing? Where had he been? With another woman?

Trembling, the fridge rumbled into life. She closed the door. The cramps in her stomach tightened. She sat folded up on the floor; she seemed to have lost the use of her legs.

She sat there and remembered one of their rows, more than a year ago, before all this had happened. She had been prodding him about Susan, one of his past girlfriends, and working herself up into a right old state. She had shouted at him: *If you ever leave me I'll hunt you down! I'll find you even if it takes me years. You can go to the ends of the bloody earth but I'll get you in the end!*

6

On a Sunday in September Hannah was summoned down to Windsor. Her mother and Becky were living there; they had moved in with Granny Wilson. From all accounts this was a far from ideal arrangement; over the summer tempers had become frayed. Maybe this was why her mother had asked her to lunch. 'Come down, please,' she had said on the phone. 'I want to talk to you. And do bring Tobias,' she had added like an afterthought, as if Hannah might otherwise have left him alone in the flat.

Hannah took the train. As the houses sped past, her spirits rose. Her parents' marriage had broken up, her mother was unhappy, Becky had been wrenched away from yet another set of schoolfriends – all in all, it was a mess. She knew it was selfish, to feel so light-hearted, but over the past three months an extraordinary thing had happened; her guilt had vanished. It was her father, now, who was the transgressor. The heat had been removed from her and placed on Dad. Her father was an adulterer; a faithless husband who had reneged on his responsibilities, run away with a girl half his age and gone to ground in St Albans. Of course Hannah was angry with him, she knew she should be, but she also felt profoundly grateful – a feeling she could only confess to her son, who wouldn't understand. As she sat in the train she bent over him and exhaled her secret into his scalp – how fragrant his hair was! She breathed out her guilt and breathed in his innocence.

Granny Wilson had never seemed like a granny. She

was a wafer-thin woman, still a beauty, who wore ski pants, played bridge and vigorously dug the garden. She lived in a large Edwardian house; her husband had been a solicitor. She had lived there for ever; Hannah's mother and her aunt Sophie, who had emigrated to Canada, had been brought up there. Hannah's mother had returned to her childhood home.

It was her mother who opened the door. She seemed to have shrunk; diminished, somehow. Her lips were creased, as if a drawstring had pulled them tighter. She kissed the top of Tobias's head. 'He looks more like his father every day.'

'What?' Hannah stared at her.

'Just joking.'

They went in. Hannah smelt the familiar scent of furniture polish and her grandmother's cigarettes. What a strange thing for her mother to blurt out! Val wore jeans, and a T-shirt saying *Windsor Park Garden Centre*.

'Where's Granny and Becky?' Hannah asked.

'Out. They'll be back later. I need to talk to you alone.'

Hannah gave her Tobias. Her mother held him awkwardly, as if the postman had given her a parcel for next door. Her mother didn't know what to do with babies. She had never been a motherly sort of person. Granny Wilson hadn't been, either; perhaps that was where she had learnt it.

They went into the lounge. It overlooked the garden. There was a swing at the end where her mother used to play, just as Hannah herself had played in the garden in Stanmore. She felt as if the world were rolling backwards.

Val gave her back Tobias and poured them some Cinzano.

'I ought to heat up his bottle first,' said Hannah. 'I'm trying to wean him. I'm starting at the college next week.'

Her mother ignored this. 'Have you seen her yet?' she demanded.

261

Hannah shook her head. 'Kimberley? Apparently she's left the office. She's training to be a nurse.'

'No wonder he fell for her. Your father's such a hypochondriac.' She followed Hannah into the kitchen. 'It's like a paedophile getting it together with a primary school teacher.'

'Mum!' Hannah hooked Tobias on to her hip and searched for a saucepan. Her mother didn't help.

'It's bad enough to commit adultery, but with somebody called Kimberley! How could he?'

'It's a perfectly normal name,' said Hannah. 'One of the actresses in *Neighbours* is called Kimberley.'

'That's what I mean. So you haven't met her yet?'

Hannah shook her head. All she knew was that her father was living in Kimberley's flat in St Albans. They were sharing it with two Australian nurses. If it weren't so painful it would be fascinating, to picture her Dad in this unlikely harem.

'Apparently she wears Snoopy T-shirts,' said her mother. 'You know, when I first met your father Granny said he was common.'

'Mum! You never thought that.' Hannah gave up on the saucepan. 'You said Dad was romantic and emotional and un-English. You found that very attractive. You said Granny and Grandad were terrible snobs.' She sat down, unbuttoned her bra and hoisted Tobias on to her nipple. 'It's just the male menopause. He'll come to his senses.'

She knew it was deeper than that. Her father was having a sort of nervous breakdown. What had happened last year had broken him, he had lost his faith in the human race. The terrible unjustness of it had driven him off-balance, and this Kimberley person was his only comfort. She was a new daughter, a fresh one to whom nothing distressing had occurred, who hadn't yet had the opportunity to disappoint him. But Val couldn't see it like that.

Val was talking – Hannah thought of her as Val now, rather than her mother. She said: 'I can never forgive him. Just when we needed him most, he deserted us. How could he do that? You can be married all those years and never discover what the other person's really like, you're never really tested.' She spoke in a flat voice; Hannah had heard it all before. 'I thought he loved his family, I thought he loved us.'

'He does!'

'And underneath he's just a selfish bastard. You know what's terrifying? That I've never noticed. He's been like that all the time and I've never noticed.' Val brought in the Cinzano bottle and sat down at the table. 'It would have happened sooner or later. I'm grateful, really, that I've learned the truth.' With her thumb she pushed the ice out of the rubber tray. It rattled into the glasses. 'I want to divorce him.'

'You can't!'

'I want to be free of him.' She passed a glass to Hannah. 'I want to come to London with Becky. I can't live here with my mother. Windsor! It's so boring.'

'That's what I used to say about Stanmore.'

'Living off her, being beholden to her, being a daughter. I'm too old for that.'

For many months Granny Wilson hadn't been told about the kidnap. When she had finally been admitted into the secret, Morris had been too proud to tell her the truth about their finances. It was only after he had gone that she had realised the state they were in; she was now supporting Val and Becky.

'We get on each other's nerves, we're too alike. I want to come to London and be an independent woman, like you.'

'Me?' asked Hannah.

'Look, you're managing.'

Hannah stared at her. So it was she, Hannah, who had

got it right! On this mad see-saw, their positions had suddenly been reversed.

Val drained her glass. The colour had returned to her cheeks. 'You've changed,' she said.

'So have you.'

'So's your bloody father. Know what he was wearing last time I saw him? A tie-dyed waistcoat!' She pushed out some more ice. 'What do you think I should do?'

Hannah thought: eighteen months ago I was a teenager, being shouted at about my mess. Now I'm a mother to my own mother, dispensing advice. 'Don't be too hard on him. I've spoken to him on the phone, he's in a terrible state.'

'Easy for you to excuse him.'

'You think this is easy, any of it?' Her voice rose; Tobias stopped sucking. 'You and Dad *were* happy, we all were. That's why I feel so terrible, for what I've done.'

'Not you. Them. I hope the money bloody chokes them. I hope it's making them miserable, wherever they are.' She glared at Tobias.

'It's not his fault,' said Hannah.

'I hope they're destroyed with guilt for what they've done.'

'They don't know what they've done,' said Hannah. 'They don't know us. They're probably in Rio de Janeiro or something.'

'I hope they rot in hell. Along with your father.'

'Don't!' She wanted to block Tobias's ears. She loved her mother but she suddenly felt full of rage. Why had she sat there at her computer when she should have been a proper mother, helping Hannah with her homework? Why hadn't she protected Hannah from wreaking this havoc? She, Hannah, wouldn't behave like that with her own son. The world was reeling, parents weren't parents anymore, they had blown away, as insubstantial as dandelion fluff . . . *one o'clock, two o'clock* she used to blow.

She would teach it to Tobias. Suddenly she longed to be alone with her son.

Val squeezed a piece of lemon into her drink. 'Once, your father and I were having tea at Fortnum's. I lifted up a piece of lemon, for his cup, and said, "Shall I give it a little squeeze before I pop it in?" ' She drank. 'We used to laugh, your father and I.'

'I know you did. You must remember that. Don't let this spoil everything you had.'

'I know you found him – oh, embarrassing and pompous sometimes. But when we were young he was really very funny.'

Her mother was silent. Hannah saw, with horror, that tears were sliding down her cheeks. Her mother, crying!

'When I first met him, when I was at art school, I used to bike everywhere. I used to bike from my flat to St Martin's.' She wiped her eyes. 'This is rather rude but I think you're old enough.'

'Go on,' said Hannah.

'I said to him, "Isn't it a miracle, I jump on this bike, a slip of metal, and ten minutes later I'm in the Charing Cross Road?" Your Dad, he shook his head and said: "I'll tell you what the miracle is. I jump on you, a slip of a thing, and two minutes later I'm in Paradise".'

A drop fell on Tobias's hair. Hannah wiped her eyes. She indicated her son. 'At least we've got him. Something good's come out of all this.'

Her mother drained her glass. 'The only point – the only possibility of living with what's happened is if it makes you a better and wiser person.' She gazed at her glass. Hannah noticed, for the first time, the wiry grey threads in her hair. 'Your father and I, I'm afraid we haven't dealt with this very well, either of us.'

That afternoon Hannah returned to her flat. She stood in the kitchen. Down in the courtyard there was a tree; just a single tree, surrounded by concrete. A plastic bag was caught in its branches. As the seasons changed the bag had stayed there, entangled – first in the bare branches and then blowing amongst the leaves. Some of the leaves were already turning yellow. She thought: when Tobias is a grown man that bag will still be here. We're flotsam and jetsam, adrift on the storm. Only that plastic bag stays anchored.

Part Seven

1

The funeral was in Warrington. That was where his father had lived the last however-many years. His only surviving relative, his Aunt Lavinia, said: 'What a shame, Jonny. What a waste of a life.'

It gave him a jolt, to hear his name. It was a year since he had changed it but nobody here knew that. He had stepped back, just for a day, into his past.

'Rent arrears and emphysema,' said Lavinia, sipping white wine. 'Every penny he drank away. What's it all about, Jonny? He brought your mother nothing but misery. In fact, I think he killed her off.'

'Lavinia!' said her husband.

'Not in the literal sense, of course.' She took a sandwich. 'Shame you and he never made it up. In fact, lucky you phoned me last week or you'd never have known. We had no idea where you were.'

'So what've you been up to?' Her husband, Alan, turned to him. 'Last thing I heard, you were beetling round London in a Transit van.'

Two years ago I kidnapped a girl and ransomed her for half a million pounds. I moved to Kensington with my girlfriend, did a runner on the eve of our wedding, changed my name and went to ground in Sussex.

'I live in Sussex,' he said.

'Still at the woodwork?'

He nodded. Alan moved away. He was probably thinking: there's boring old Jon for you, boring as ever.

269

The only exciting thing he has ever done was remove the 'H' from his name.

It was when Jon got back that it hit him. He was unprepared for his reaction. When his mother died he had felt anger and grief; when his Uncle Charlie died he had mourned him because he loved him. This time he felt dislocated. For the next few days he tried to work. He lived in a rented cottage near Gatwick Airport. It was June, he had brought his workbench into the garden. He was making some bookshelves for a client in Horsham; he sawed at the lengths of pine while the planes roared overhead, the great bellies of them, and brushed him with their shadows.

What a waste of a life. That pretty well summed up his father. He had cheated on his wife because he was too feeble to resist temptation; his life had been a series of shoddy prevarications and teachery. And the worst thing was that he, Jon, had never truly spoken to him – to make his peace with him or even to have a flaming row. He had kept putting it off.

Unfinished business. The two words nagged at him. He hammered pins into the lengths of moulding. He thought he could lay the past to rest here; that he could slough it off like a skin. He knew he was fooling himself. When he picked up a seed packet the old nausea rose. 'Where've you been?' Eva had asked. 'The allotments.' The treachery of it, the cowardice. Oh, he was his father's son all right. *You want to know the truth? I haven't been to the allotments for weeks. I've been riding around the home counties, searching for somewhere to live so I can escape from you and you'll never find me.*

If Eva ever found him she would kill him. That was what she had said. *Go to the ends of the fucking earth and I'll track you down.* Over the past year his fears had faded – that the police would track him down, that Hannah's parents would find him. He told himself he was rid of Eva, that he was free. But she was in the air, as deadly as a gas. She haunted him at night, pushing through the curtains in his bedroom and leaping on him like a panther. Sometimes she was disguised in the chestnut wig. He was walking down an alley and he heard her high-heeled boots; when he turned she slipped out of sight. One night the red wig was busy between his legs. He was on the Northern line; a plane, roaring overhead, was the rumble of the tube. When she looked up, her mouth was smeared with blood. She grinned, her cheeks bulged. When he looked down there was a painless hole between his legs.

It was June. He had left Eva a year ago; she hadn't found him yet but he had taken care to cover his tracks. Arriving in Sussex he had reinvented himself. He had changed his name to Eliot; he had concealed his past. At first he had considered it a disguise, like the games he and Eva used to play. In those days, when he was dressed as a different person he could do things he had never dared before. He could sashay round the West End as Eva's sister; he could even enter the Underworld and attempt to snatch an unknown girl. But this time, when he had done it in earnest, it had been another sensation altogether. The old Jon seemed false and alien. Eliot felt like the true him – the nicer, stronger him, the real person he had been searching for all the time.

He told himself this. He had tried to begin again. He was even seeing a new woman – Hazel, a nice woman, the sort of woman he should have met long ago. She worked at Gatwick Airport; she was a stewardess and flew to foreign cities. She sent him postcards. He propped them up above his sink – postcards showing Central Park at sunset, the Piazza San Marco. He looked at them when he was doing the washing-up. Hazel could fly anywhere; she was a free spirit.

Three days after the funeral they slept together for the

first time. She welcomed him into her like a door opening in a room flooded with light. Afterwards she stroked his cheek. 'Are you really here?' she asked.

He nodded, in the darkness.

She said: 'You're the nicest man I ever met.'

He turned away. 'Don't say that.'

'What's happened to you, Eliot?' she whispered. 'Won't you ever tell me?'

He turned to her. He took her hands and laid them against his eyes. Her warm, dry hands – he pressed them into his sockets, he pushed them into his eyeballs; he pressed them hard into his brain . . . the blackness spread in . . .

She kept her hands there for a long time. Lights exploded behind his lids. His fingers lay over hers, the same length as hers; they lay together like bodies.

The next day dawned dewy and translucent. Birdsong rang out, drowned at invervals by the roaring planes. Hazel left early, kissing him at the door. He listened to her car engine; he heard the gear-change as she slowed down at the crossroads. He felt his heart thawing in the sunshine, like sensation returning to a numb limb.

He went into the living room and phoned Directory Enquiries.

'What town?'

'Watford,' he said. 'It's near there.'

'What name?'

'Price Security Systems.'

A silence. He gazed at the holdall on the floor; it contained the sum total of his father's possessions. He hadn't unpacked them because he didn't know what to do with them. The family photos; that was all he would keep.

The telephonist said: 'Price Security Systems? There's nothing of that name here.'

*

272

He mounted his bike and roared down the lane. He rode through the streets of Horsham. He passed the building societies behind whose windows his money lay slumbering like monsters. *You're the nicest man I've ever met . . .*

He roared along the M25; it was still busy with commuter traffic. The words rose up again: *what a waste of a life.* He roared along the fast lane, chasing his own shadow.

WATFORD. It was half an hour later. He slewed across the lanes and down the slip road. Where did Hannah say her father worked? Somewhere near Watford. Tring? South Mimms? No, that was the limerick. *The archdeacon's wife of South Mimms . . .*

He tried to recall their conversations. *I wonder what Dad'll tell them at the office.* It was a small factory – where? On an industrial estate? He racked his brain for clues.

He drove into Watford, stopped at a hotel and went into the lobby. He found a telephone booth. Directories were stacked under the phone. He picked one up and fumbled it open at 'P'. *PricePricePricePricePricePricePricePricePrice PricePricePricePricePricePricePricePricePricePrice Price . . .*

Residential. Idiot. He opened the Business directory. *Price-Beaters . . . Price-Busters . . . Price-Rite . . . Price-Wise . . . PricePricePricePricePricePricePricePrice . . .* His brain felt scrambled. *What's the Price? . . . Paid the Price? . . . Paying the Price? Eh? Eh?*

He closed the book. They had disappeared off the face of the earth. Just as he had.

To track Hannah down, he had to find her father. It was dangerous but now he was beyond worrying. Otherwise what could he do – wander the streets of London hoping to glimpse her? The woman in Harlesden was no help; all those months ago she'd had no idea where the Prices had

273

gone. She didn't even know who owned the downstairs maisonette, she had only just moved in herself.

He could no longer picture Hannah's face, it had faded from his memory. Besides, he had only been familiar with its lower half. Like the Cheshire Cat, all that remained was a mouth. She had vanished into something abstract, into an ache in his conscience. How on earth could he find her?

He almost gave up. He sat on his motorbike, in the hotel car park. The sun moved behind a cloud. He thought: well, I've tried. The old Jon spoke in his head – the cowardly Jon, his father's son, who let evil happen because he was drawn along weakly in its slipstream.

He rode out of town, into the countryside. Hedges streamed past him. The sun came out. He slowed down at a T-junction and there, in front of him, stood a cottage.

It was set back from the road. It was old – thatched – with creepers growing up the brickwork. A wishing well stood in the garden.

He switched off the engine and sat there. Sunlight reflected back from the windows. *Just you and me, in a cottage in the woods*. How simple life had seemed, once. A workshop where he could produce objects of use and beauty, a woman humming under her breath in the next room. He had thought he had managed it; the place he rented, it even had trees at the end of the garden. But Eva was right. *Pathetic*, she had said. *Get wise*.

He dismounted from his bike and walked up to the gate. A gravelled drive led to the cottage. He looked at the wishing well. It had a matching thatched roof – bit twee, really. He squeezed his eyes shut. *Make a wish*. He thought: all these months I've been sleepwalking. When I open my eyes, I'll wake up.

He opened his eyes. It was then that he saw something, stuck to the wall of the building. It was a burglar alarm. Even from here he could read it. 'PRICE SECURITY'.

Later, he remembered that moment. A car passed,

music thumping then receding. A bird, hidden in the bushes, sang so loudly it sounded like a schoolboy mimicking a bird. PRICE SECURITY. He would knock on the door and ask them the address of their alarm company. Simple as that.

He walked up the drive. Maybe that was a phone number on the alarm – once he got nearer he would be able to decipher the small print underneath the name. Who knows? He went up to the front door. No – the small print said *systems*. He rang the bell and waited. Plastic bricks lay scattered on the gravel; somebody had made scrabbly marks with a stick.

Just then he felt the strangest sensation. Behind the door the Price family waited, all five of them. The faded photo of them stood there. *All this time we've been waiting for you to come back*, they mouthed at him. *You wished for us? Well, here we are. You think you can make up for what you've done, mmm? You think you can find us? Don't you realise, we don't exist anymore. You've stolen our lives away – look, we're nothing but paper.*

He wanted to surrender himself to them, just as last night he had surrendered himself to Hazel. He would sob on their shoulders and tell them where the money waited, untouched. *I've not taken out a penny*, he would say. *I've been living on my earnings like an honest person – look, Hazel knows I'm honest! I thought if I didn't touch it at least I wasn't doing anything harmful. Silly, when it makes no difference to you. But it did to me.*

He rang again. The child had scratched signs in the gravel – a criss-cross puzzle. If he knew the clues, it could tell him the secret of all this, how to unravel the past . . . the Price family, photographically frozen before their tragedy, would spring into life and carry on as if nothing had happened. Released by him, Hannah would go home from Camden Lock and finish her essay . . . they would eat dinner and wash up . . . Hannah would return to her virginity . . .

Nobody was home. The wind blew, rattling the window panes. Jon suddenly felt foolish. What on earth was he doing, standing in the middle of Hertfordshire? How could he wave a wand and exorcise the past? Even the bloody wishing well was a fake.

He didn't know how long he stood there, but it couldn't have been more than a few minutes. He didn't notice the police car drawing up. The first he heard was the crunch, crunch of footsteps on the drive and then these two officers were standing in front of him.

'Can we help you, sir?' one of them asked.

He stared at them. 'What?' The policeman had polished red cheeks, like a yokel. Jon looked at the road. A patrol car was parked by the gate. He said, quite calmly: 'I knew you'd come in the end.'

He shouldn't have said that. They exchanged glances: we've got a nutter here. The red-cheeked one said: 'Could you explain what you're doing, sir, on private property?'

He said airily: 'I can explain everything.'

Just then he heard a car arriving. It stopped at the gate. A woman jumped out.

'What's happened?' she yelled. She opened the gate and drove up. She switched off the engine and got out. The back of the car was piled with shopping and children. 'Stay there!' she barked, and strode towards the police officers. 'What's happened? Who's this?' She was a square-jawed woman with a commanding voice.

He said: 'I wanted to get the phone number of your burglar alarm.'

They looked at him. One of the children starting yelling. The woman swung round. 'Shut up, Piers!'

'I know it sounds strange,' he said. 'But I've just been burgled myself, see. They took everything, even my jazz CDs.' His voice rose. 'How could somebody pick on a complete stranger? What's the world coming to? So I happened to be passing by and I heard that Price Systems were good, so maybe you could help me and tell me where you got it. That's all.' He turned to the two policemen. 'Arrest me if you like. I don't care anymore. Something like that happens and – well, what's the point of it all? Can anyone tell me?'

There was a silence. He must have been shouting. The children gazed at him through the car window. The woman looked at him for a long time, then she turned to the policemen. 'It's OK. I believe him. He looks pretty traumatised to me.' She took out her doorkeys. 'I should know, I've worked in hotel management.'

Finally they left. He helped her unload the shopping bags and carry them into the house.

'I've always dreamed of a place like this,' he said.

'Dream away.'

He dumped the bags on the kitchen table. 'That was really nice of you.'

'Hamish makes me put it on. The blithering alarm. He's not trusting like me, his father deserted him when he was little, he thinks the whole world is out to rob him and kidnap his children. Huh, wish somebody would. *Caroline!*' The little girl had pulled open a Sainsbury's bag. Jon pictured banknotes spilling out. 'Hamish makes me set the damn thing every time I go out. It takes ages – codes and control panels and whatnots, you need bloody GCSEs to understand it.' She pulled out a leg of lamb. 'You got caught by the low-beam intruder thing. It's connected to the police station. We've already had three false alarms. After six you have to start paying them to come out.' She went over to a drawer, pulled it open and took out a leaflet. 'They seem to be called Rest Assured now but it's probably the same lot. Hamish would know. He specialises in knowing things like that.' She pushed back her hair and smiled at him sideways. 'How about some coffee?'

'Sorry. I've got to go.'

She turned away abruptly. 'All right, all right.' She pulled out a cabbage. 'Least it'll be something to talk about tonight. God I hate living in the country.'

It was six o'clock when he arrived at the address. 'REST ASSURED SECURITY SYSTEMS' said the sign. It was one of those low, windowless, vaguely industrial buildings within which one could imagine anything happening. There were only a few cars left in the parking lot.

He went into the lobby. A youth in a beige uniform was watching TV. Jon said: 'I'm looking for a Mr Price.'

'Price?' His skin was so pimply that for a moment Jon couldn't locate his features.

'Mr Morris Price.' It startled Jon, saying his name out loud.

'Oh, him. He's gone.'

'When? Where?'

The youth shrugged. 'Dunno. He doesn't work here anymore.'

A notice on the desk said 'DISPATCH RIDERS PLEASE REMOVE YOUR HELMETS'. Jon took off his helmet.

'You don't know where he's gone?'

The youth shook his head. 'Never met him.'

Jon went outside. Beyond the parking lot stood some warehouses and a Texaco garage. Opposite, fields were bathed in the evening sunlight. He looked up at the sign, 'REST ASSURED'. Hannah's father must have sold his own business. Before Jon had arrived here the news had been as abstract as the report of a disaster in a far-off country. He was hit, all over again, by the enormity of what he had done. Two years ago he had sat in a park . . . a see-saw creaking, blossoms scattered like litter . . . a newspaper had bowled along the grass and set in motion a series of events that had caused the takeover of a business in Hertfordshire ... the break-up of a marriage ...

He walked towards his motorbike. Behind him he heard footsteps. A man came out of the building and made his way towards his car, a BMW convertible. He stopped, and looked at Jon's motorbike.

'Nice wheels,' he said.

Jon looked at the car. 'Just thinking the same about yours.'

'I used to have a Harley, for my sins.' He was tanned and good-looking, in a preeny sort of way. '1000cc. Rode it across the States, coast to coast.' He pointed to the Yamaha. 'What's the price on these now?'

Jon told him. He had an absurd desire to tell him exactly how he had got the money. He said: 'Talking of prices, it's a Mr Price that I'm looking for. He used to work here.'

'Morris? He's taken early retirement.'

'Where can I get hold of him?'

The bloke frowned, opened his briefcase and took out an organiser. He punched some buttons, squinting in the sunshine. 'Flat A, 14 Abbey View Road, St Albans.'

Jon was memorising this when the man walked off. He heard a bellow.

'*Shit!*'

Jon hurried over to the BMW. The roof had been slit – a clean gash, sagging on one side.

'Fucking vandals!' said the man. He dropped his briefcase and ran his finger along the side of the car. There was a scratch in the paintwork; it stretched from the bonnet to the boot. His voice thickened. 'My baby,' he muttered. 'My poor baby.' He flinched as he touched the scratch; he prodded it gently, as if it were a wound.

Jon looked into the car. 'They haven't taken anything. Radio's still there.'

'Fucking bastards. It's envy, see. Just because they're fucking useless pricks.' His voice rose. 'I worked my balls off for this car. My baby. *Shit*!' He opened the driver's door and threw in his briefcase. 'The bastards didn't even steal anything. What's the world coming to?'

'You're right. It's envy.' Jon roused himself and indicated the building. 'You going to report it?'

'To that wally?' He laughed, chokingly. 'Terrific bloody security here, eh?' He got into the car and started the engine. It roared into life. The car jerked forward. There was a crunch. Jon heard a muffled oath and the car reversed and swung round. It roared off, leaving a cloud of exhaust smoke and a lopsided sign: 'MANAGING DIRECTOR'.

St Alban's Abbey rose up, blocking the sun. The fiery sky spread around it; the shadow of its bulk lay across the street. Jon dismounted in its darkness and pulled off his helmet. He thought of God gazing down at a car, long ago in Dean Street – a beautiful red Ferrari mutilated with scratch-marks. *And the sinners will be punished and burn in everlasting torment.*

He rang the bell. It was a large, red-brick house; Flat A was on the ground floor.

The door opened and a young woman stood there, wearing a nurse's uniform. She didn't seem surprised to see him. 'Have you brought the money?' she asked.

His heart jolted. He said: 'What money?'

'Are you Special Delivery?' She had a twangy voice – Australian or something. 'I've just got in from work. Did you try earlier?'

He removed his helmet and shook his head. 'I'm a friend of the family. I'm looking for Mr Price.'

'Morris? He'll be back in a bit. Wanna wait?'

He suddenly felt terribly tired. He realised he hadn't eaten all day.

She looked at him. 'Wanna come in? It's a bit crowded. I'm Kimberley, by the way.'

He stepped in. The hallway was stacked to the ceiling with crates – blue plastic crates full of bottles.

'I thought you had some money for us,' she said over her shoulder. 'He's owed some from this restaurant.'

'Can I have a drink of water?'

'Water?' She laughed, gesturing around. 'Oh, there's plenty of that.' She opened a door. 'See what I mean? My flatmates used to live in there.' The bedroom was crammed with crates. 'They've gone now. Carbonated or non-carbonated?'

'I want to find out where his daughter is.'

'Come in. I'm bushed.' She led him into a kitchen. 'Which daughter?'

'Hannah.'

'This one's carbonated.' She unscrewed a bottle top; it fizzed and spurted over the table. 'Whoops. So what do you want with her?'

'I'm – well, somebody she used to know.'

'It's like that, is it?' She poured some water into a glass and passed it to him. Then she collapsed into a chair, sighing.

'Not really. I've got something of hers, that's all. I want to give it back.' He looked around. 'Why have you got all this water?'

'Morris has set up this business. Mate of his down the road has this well in his garden. Roman or something.' She yanked off her shoes, pulled a chair towards her and put her feet on it. 'So they're flogging the water to restaurants. Trust Morris not to sit on his butt. Busy busy, always on the go. You know him? I've hardly met any of his friends.'

Jon shook his head. He gazed at the wholesome girl. He thought: it's because of me that Morris has moved in with this nurse and the room is filled with bottles. His head span.

'His son's helping him,' she said. 'He's the London connection. Well, it keeps him out of mischief.'

She tipped back her head and drank. Her accent made her seem refreshingly disconnected from all that had happened; maybe that was why Morris had run away with her. Jon realised, with interest, that both he and Morris had been drawn towards somebody in uniform – a professional, disinterested woman to care for them and put things to rights. He had a sudden urge to lay his head on this nurse's lap and confess everything. She would say *there, there*, and give him a pill to help him sleep.

He drank the water; the bubbles busied themselves in his throat. Outside a bell tolled. It felt sanctified, to cleanse his system like this.

He said: 'Do you know Hannah's address?'

Her eyes narrowed. 'Hey, who are you exactly?'

'You know Julia, her old schoolfriend?'

Kimberley shook her head.

'I'm Julia's older brother. Hannah lent me some art books and I want to give them back.'

Kimberley seemed to accept this.

'It's somewhere near Ladbroke Grove. I went there once to see them but I don't know the number.'

'Them?' he asked.

'Her and Tobias.'

So Hannah had a boyfriend. That was why she had run away from home. He felt a wave of relief – so it wasn't just his fault. It was reassuring to know she wasn't living alone. This was followed by a small, surprising tweak of jealousy. He felt proprietorial – unhealthily so. He had a right to know about his successor.

'What's this Tobias like?' he asked.

'A real sweetheart.' She drained her glass. 'Adorable. I wanted to squeeze him until he squeaked.'

'He's fat, then?'

'He was when I saw him. He was crawling then.'

'Crawling?'

'Apparently he's walking now. Or at least shuffling about.'

He looked at her over his glass. Hannah's boyfriend must have some sort of disability. This girl talked about it so casually, almost heartlessly, but then she was a nurse. They must be inured.

He put his glass on the table. 'What do you mean, walking?'

'They're supposed to be walking, aren't they, at fifteen months?'

It's a strange thing, about time. He couldn't have been silent for long because the nurse didn't seem to notice anything odd. *My God*, he thought, over and over. *My God . . .*

He got to his feet. He had to get away, fast. His voice, to his surprise, sounded quite casual. 'Better be pushing off. Thanks for the water.' He picked up his helmet. 'So you don't know her address?'

'Morris knows.' She lifted up the watch on her chest. 'He'll be here in a tick.'

He moved towards the door. 'Could you possibly find it out and send it to me?'

She gave him a felt-tipped pen and a piece of paper.

He scrawled down his address. 'I don't have a phone. And – well – could we keep this just between ourselves?' He tried to look conspiratorial. 'Her father – well, it's a long story.'

She grinned. 'With this family, I'm used to secrets.' She looked at the paper. 'Eliot. I've never set eyes on you.'

He smiled. 'I'm the Invisible Man.' He thanked her and left. She closed the door behind him.

Night had fallen. He was a father.

He stepped into a world that had changed, for ever.

2

Eva hated it when a man she didn't know tried to come in her mouth. Why did she have to swallow all that stuff, practically choking to death? This bloke, Didi, had pushed her head down and rammed it in. His hand found her clitoris and started to rub it vigorously; it reminded her of her mother, polishing people's doorknobs.

'Yes . . . yes!' he moaned, thrusting against her palate. *No*! She pulled back and, rolling over, yanked him on top of her.

He was one of those guys who kept a woman fully informed. 'It's coming . . . yes . . . *yes* . . .' He sounded like the commentator at Aintree. 'Nearly there . . . yes . . .' Why should she be interested? The brass bed creaked, rhythmically. She and Jon, they used to get the giggles.

Don't think. She squeezed her eyes shut, blacking it out.

'Boy oh boy!' He groaned and shuddered. She pulled him against her and, pressing him into her, felt a wave of warmth between her legs but it was too late, the bastard was already sliding out.

'Wow, you're a little firecracker,' he said.

She climbed out of bed and pulled on her wrap. She didn't want him to see her naked.

'Nice place,' he said. 'Must've cost you.'

'My husband bought it,' she said. 'He's a gynaecologist.'

She went into the kitchen. She kicked aside a pizza box, pulled off a piece of kitchen towel and wiped her crotch. She poured herself a shot of vodka and drank it.

The weather was stifling; a clammy, June evening. She poured herself another shot and went into the lounge. The turretty building rose up against the yellow sky. She stepped out on to the balcony and lit a cigarette. She hadn't got round to planting anything this year. The tubs were empty, except for the bay trees. Now she looked at them, she saw that their leaves had turned brown.

The lavatory flushed. She flinched. They walked into the bathroom as if they owned the place. They got themselves cosy in the bed, too, cock of the roost, that satisfied look on their faces. It wasn't their bed. This bloke last week, he had said: 'Why don't you clean this place up?' It was none of his fucking business.

This guy, Didi, she had met him this afternoon in Kensington Gardens. She had been watching the kids playing. He was Moroccan or something but he spoke with an American accent. He had started telling her about what he did, selling machine parts or something, but she had been watching a little boy trying to pull in his boat with a stick.

She poked her cigarette into the earth. All the other ones stuck out, it looked like one of those war cemeteries. She hoped he was getting dressed. He was a lousy fuck. She was just there to be jerked-off into. Sometimes, just sometimes, it worked. If they were good at it, then she squeezed her eyes shut and her head exploded, she forgot everything. Just for a moment.

She listened. No sound. Maybe he had fallen asleep and she would be stuck with him all night. She shouldn't have brought him back here; she should have learnt her lesson by now. It was an invasion of her privacy; once they knew where she lived they pestered her. Or else they acted as if they owned the place and tried to sort her out. This bloke, back in the spring, he had even taken out the Hoover. Trouble was, they usually lived out of town, or they were married, or both. And she was usually so totally bolloxed she just said let's go back to my place.

She didn't like this Didi. Maybe he was snooping around. The guy in the spring, when he was looking for the Hoover he had found the gun. 'That's my son's,' she had said. 'Little Trevor. He's just out with his daddy.'

She drained her glass and went into the bedroom. She stopped in the doorway.

'*I'm a lumberjack and I'm OK!*,' Didi sang. He jiggled about, naked except for a tartan work-shirt. '*I work all night and —*' He stopped. 'Hey, what's the matter? You like Monty Python?'

'Take it off,' she said.

He raised his eyebrows. 'Sorry, sorry. It was only a joke.' He unbuttoned the shirt. 'Don't look like that, it's scary.'

'Get out,' she said.

'Hey, stay cool —'

'My husband's coming home.'

'But you said —'

'He'll be here in a minute,' she said. 'Get dressed.'

Her stomach cramps began. They took away her breath. She sat down in a chair.

'You OK?' he asked, pulling on his jacket. 'Can I see you again?'

'No. He's back for good.'

She saw him out. She closed the door, waited until she heard the hiss of the lift doors opening, and walked back into the flat.

She went into the bedroom and picked up the shirt – the woolly, tartan work-shirt. She pressed it against her face. Even after a year she could smell him – woodsmoke and sawdust. She lifted the arm and sniffed. She could smell his stale sweat.

Her legs felt weak. She sat down. It was nothing to do with Jon; it was because Elaine had given her a massage

286

that morning. Elaine worked in the health club. She was always twittering on about her boyfriend, how he wrote her poems. It was enough to make anyone puke.

After a while she managed to get up. She showered herself; that felt better. Then she poured herself some cornflakes, but when she looked at them heaped up in the bowl she felt sick. It was nine thirty. Only nine thirty! Somebody slowed the clocks, she was sure of it. Hours before she could go to bed. Hours more before she would sleep, even with the pills. They were no bloody good.

That shirt business had really freaked her out. Stupid, really. She didn't have the energy to open her TV guide. She shifted, on her bottom, towards the pile of videos; they had fallen out of the shelf weeks ago and she hadn't got round to putting them back. The video recorder said 9.32. At least it said the right time again – all winter it had been an hour wrong but when Summer Time arrived it was OK again. See? You just waited, and things happened, all by themselves!

She sat there for a while. The videos looked as if somebody had dropped them from the ceiling. Some of the cassettes still had his writing on. She hadn't touched those; he might want to watch them again. She picked up one with her handwriting on it. *Body Heat*. She had recorded it months ago and she hadn't watched it yet. She had seen it at the cinema once – she had gone with Lyle, long ago. William Hurt and Kathleen Turner, mmm, sexy . . .

She slotted it into the machine, pressed 'Play' and curled up on the settee. Outside the sky darkened; it started to rain. The picture came on. The News was just finishing – an old news from months ago.

' . . . so the battle continues in this sleepy Sussex town, and for the environmentalists it's a fight they're determined not to lose . . . This is Ian Leslie, Newsroom South-East, Horsham . . .'

Eva lunged forward. She pressed 'Stop'. She pressed 'Rewind'. She replayed the video.

On the screen a reporter stood, wrapped in an overcoat, talking to the camera. He was standing in a street. As he spoke Jon came out of a shop behind him. He crossed the pavement, waited for a car to pass and walked across the road.

Eva's hand shook. She pressed the wrong button – 'Fast Forward'. She jabbed 'Stop'. 'Rewind'.

Jon came out of the shop again. She pressed 'Pause'. He stood there, frozen. He wore his leather bomber jacket, jeans and a red scarf she had never seen before. She pressed 'Replay'. He came out of the shop and went in again, backwards. It was a hardware shop; planks of wood were stacked outside.

She paused him again. She knelt in front of the screen, staring at him. His foot was lifted, ready to take the next step. Beaky profile; tousled, longer hair. It was Jon all right.

She made him walk. She made him stop. She made him walk again. She sat back on her haunches, gazing at the screen. Her insides had collapsed.

Horsham. So that's where he was living. He must be living there; he was bloody buying things.

She pressed the button again. It was weird, seeing this winter scene in the middle of June. She watched, mesmerised. She moved him backwards and forwards across the pavement. Such power she had! It was like that virtual reality place near Piccadilly Circus – you moved them about and then ZAP! They exploded.

Horsham. She had got him.

3

It had taken Jon over a week to withdraw the money. He had deposited it in so many building societies in various nearby towns that it took him a while to work out where they all were, like a squirrel forgetting where it had buried its nuts. He had not wanted to arouse suspicion by depositing large amounts. Still he had to give notice that he was withdrawing such significant sums in cash.

He thought he would feel noble, reversing the transaction like this. He hadn't even spent the money. In fact he felt the opposite – the old fear returned, the criminal's jumpiness. His skin prickled with unease as he scanned the cashiers' faces. The recent months of honest citizenship vanished as if they had never happened and he hurried to his motorbike, clutching his carrier bags as if he were a thief. He *was* a thief, still.

This was the Friday. He rode up to London. Hazel was away for a few days on a long-haul flight to LA; this made the whole business both more urgent and more possible to carry through. He found a hotel in Notting Hill, a moderately-priced place called The Albion which he could hardly visualise later, such was his strange state of mind over that weekend.

Up in the bedroom he heaved his travelling bag into the cupboard and shut the door. He pictured a chambermaid unzipping it and gazing at £200,000 in banknotes. *Che sarà, sarà* . . . He felt curiously fatalistic about the whole enterprise, as if the weight of responsibility were already slipping off his shoulders.

He asked for directions. *Flat 23, Borrowdale, Mandela Estate*. Kimberley had sent him Hannah's address; it danced in his head. He had only known it for ten days but by now it felt as familiar as a nursery rhyme. He walked there that evening. The Mandela Estate was only a few streets away. He had waited for night to fall but as far as Hannah was concerned he would always wear a mantle of darkness. Unless he revealed his identity, which he had no intention of doing, he would always remain her Invisible Man.

Voices rang out. It was a warm night; the streets smelt of curries and perfume. He arrived at the estate – big concrete blocks of flats. Lights shone in the windows and along the walkways. The buildings looked like liners, sailing through the night; darkness glamourised them and amplified the clamour of TVs. He read the names . . . DERWENT-WATER . . . AMBLESIDE . . . he had been on holiday to the Lake District once, alone with his mother when his dad had been suddenly called away on business, a euphemism which had fooled nobody. Figures leaned over balconies, calling out to people below. Cigarettes glowed like fireflies. He thought of the wheel of fortune rolling him from childhood into his own son's infancy in a concrete Lake District; rolling him from the rackety streets of Tottenham, round through the hush of Kensington and back full circle into the shabbiness of this place. He realised, with a shock, that Eva was only a mile away; it seemed like another country. He mustn't think about her now.

BORROW ALE said the sign; someone had removed the 'D'. *Wheelclamping in Operation*. He looked up at the block of flats. Behind one of those windows his son was growing up. Tobias – did he like the name? – Tobias didn't gaze over the lush gardens of Stanmore; he gazed on to a single tree. A plastic bag, caught in its branches, glimmered in the lamplight. But if this were Stanmore his son would not exist.

The lift was broken. He climbed the stairs and emerged on to an upper walkway. *Flats 21–33.* The windows of the flats cast lozenges of light on to the concrete – treacherous spotlights through which he had to pass. It was ten o'clock. He hurried past twenty-one and twenty-two then he paused.

Outside the door of twenty-three a plant hung in a plastic holder. Two empty milk bottles sat on the step. The window nearest him was faintly illuminated, but the blind was pulled down. It was a yellow blind, printed with teddy bears. He felt a spreading sensation under his ribs. This must be his son's room. A few inches away, Tobias was sleeping – a little boy who was afraid of the dark.

He moved across the front door and looked into the other window. The blind was half-open; he could see into the room.

Hannah sat at a table. A single lamp shone on to a pile of books. She was bent over, writing. She paused, leafed through a book, and held it open with one hand. Copying from it, she went on writing. She looked studious; in fact she was wearing glasses.

Glasses. He never knew Hannah wore glasses. But in the hut, of course, she hadn't needed them.

He didn't go back to the hotel. He walked the streets. Men walked the streets like this in Tottenham; men with a fixed look on their faces who walked fast, their heads down. They looked purposeful but he had realised, once he saw them reappear along the same route, that in fact they were caught in a loop like muzak, doomed to their own repetition.

He wanted to go back to the flat and look into the bedroom. He thought: I'm as invisible to my son as I am to his mother; sometime during his life he may sit next to me in the bus and he won't recognise me.

Jon walked past a butcher's shop. Its empty trays gleamed in the streetlight. He thought: and *I* won't recognise *him*.

He thought: maybe Tobias isn't my child. Maybe the moment she was released she broke loose and flung herself at the nearest bloke . . .

He tried to work out what to do. Whether he should dump the money, ring the doorbell and run, like he used to ring doorbells when he was little. Whether to announce himself and, for the first and last time, look into Hannah's eyes and see his own face received there.

He had to see his son, see his face. He walked through the streets of Holland Park. Pillared houses loomed up. He wondered how the people who lived in them had earned their money. Had they taken away happiness from others to do it? He thought: I have visited that life, briefly. I just borrowed it for a while. BORROW ALE. There was something innocent about this minor act of vandalism. In pubs' Gents the graffiti said: '*You don't buy the beer here, you rent it.*' He had just borrowed the money, through weakness and desire, and in doing so he had caused a family to disintegrate and a child to be born. It didn't bear thinking about, yet he thought about it all the time. It returned to him, distorted, in his dreams. He thought: two years ago, in a chilly park in north London, my son really began.

It was dawn when he returned to the hotel. He climbed into bed. He thought: just one day. I shall spend just one day with them before I say goodbye.

And so began the most extraordinary day of his life. He kept that Saturday in a cupboard in his heart. Years later he would open it like a miser, gazing at his hoard that was more precious than gold – more precious than anything money could buy. Except, in a sense, money had bought it.

He didn't sleep. At nine in the morning he stationed himself outside the block of flats. He pretended to read the *Guardian* though the words danced. Nobody noticed him, or if they did, they didn't think him unusual. The place was full of unused-looking men who just hung around, and youths who huddled in the '*Max Headroom*' entrance to the underground car park, oblivious to anything except what they were inhaling. Besides, it was hot – the first true day of summer. He stripped off his shirt and sat, his back against a wall, soaking in the sun. Through slitted eyes he watched the stairwell exit. By late morning the seats around the trees were filled with women abandoning themselves to the sun and jerking their heads forward to shout at their kids.

Maybe he had missed her. Maybe she had gone out early. He was just starting to worry when Hannah came out. It was one thirty. She emerged from the stairwell, carrying her son under one arm and a pushchair under the other. He wanted to jump up and help her.

Instead he watched as she unfolded the pushchair. She did it with the casual expertise of long practice, kicking down the bar and shaking it open. She strapped her son into it. At this distance he couldn't see the child's face, just blue dungarees and some dark hair.

She walked off. He followed at a distance. Hannah's hair was cut short. She wore a blue skirt and floppy blouse; from the back she looked matronly. He was the cause of this transformation. She no longer walked with the everybody's-looking-at-me stiffness of adolescence. She was a mother, engrossed with her child. Sometimes she stopped and bent down to say something to the boy in his pushchair. Jon relaxed. There seemed little likelihood of her noticing that he was following her; the rest of the world didn't exist.

She crossed a street and walked down to the Portobello Road. It was Saturday; the market was crowded. She queued at a vegetable stall. The man loaded potatoes into her carrier bag. She chatted to him; she obviously shopped here regularly. She fumbled in her purse for coins; the man counted out her change. Her profile, when she put the coins back into her purse, wore the focused look of somebody calculating how much they have left to spend.

Jon followed her to a fruit stall. He thought: two years ago she was being stalked through another market. Two years ago she was a teenager buying clothes. Now she's a mother buying potatoes. He suddenly remembered sitting in the Toyota, playing one of Eva's awful Orbital cassettes to calm his nerves. Crowds of people had shuffled past, glaring at him because he kept the engine running. That car was so clapped-out that once he had switched off the engine it wouldn't start again. He had been surprised, at the time, how he thought of these practicalities whilst at the same time disowning what he was doing.

He edged nearer to look at his son. Tobias was sucking two fingers and fingering the sari of the woman standing in front of him in the queue. He had a round, dreamy face. It was focused on his fingers, drawing nourishment from them. He himself had sucked his thumb; Jon suddenly remembered the sensation, after all these years. He could recognise nothing of himself in the little boy. In a curious way this lifted his spirits.

Hannah was leaving the market. Two carrier bags swung from the pushchair handles. She walked past a stall which sold ethnic cardigans, like the one she used to wear, but she passed it without a glance.

He followed her to a park. It was just a playground, really, with some trampled grass and a few seats. It was surrounded by tall, peeling houses. Kids sat dipping their heads to their ghetto blasters. An old man slept face-down on the grass.

Hannah no longer had the ink-stained Indian shoulder-bag. She had a capacious, child-sized, canvas thing. She took out some bread, sat her son on her knee and tore him some pieces. Tobias flung them on the ground. The old man stirred and turned over. He wasn't old, in fact; he was Jon's age. He was surrounded by a collection of carrier bags. It looked as if the boy were throwing the bread for him to eat.

Jon sat down on the next bench. Pigeons, as if waiting for a signal, flew down. They pecked at the bread; they shook it and flung it about irritably. The boy threw them some more pieces. The man shifted his position and touched his bags, reassuring himself that they were still there. He rolled back on to his stomach, burying his face in the grass. His trousers were stained.

Jon felt the strangest sensation. He was only a few yards from Hannah; he was visible to her, yet invisible. He felt clothed in his own non-existence, yet here he was blowing his nose with a wet honking noise – watching his son moved him profoundly. Somebody shouted; Hannah turned and her eyes passed over him without recognition.

He felt weightless. He was nobody; he was anyone. He was the man lying on the grass with his possessions packed into bags so old that the writing was worn away. His twin spirits sat on either side of his son: a man with nothing and a man with everything. Or he could look at it the other way round: a man with a collection of carrier bags and a man with empty hands. Neither of them had been noticed by the small boy who was pulling at his mother's sleeve, pointing to the swings.

They got up. But Tobias wasn't struggling towards the swings. Hoisted on his mother's hip he was leaning towards the see-saw, pointing and whining something Jon couldn't hear.

'We can't,' Hannah said, and started to carry him towards the swings but he yelled in her arms.

Jon jumped to his feet. Later it struck him as a foolhardy thing to do, but he couldn't stop himself. He walked up to the see-saw and sat down on the bucket seat. In doing so, he crossed the border into Hannah's consciousness. He raised his eyebrows and pointed to the other seat.

Hannah, carrying the child, looked at him warily. She sized him up. *Do I trust him*? *What does he want*?

He shrugged and smiled. *I don't want anything from you.* He didn't dare speak, in case she recognised his voice. She probably thought he had been thrown into the care of the community.

She shifted Tobias on to her other hip. Then she smiled. 'Thanks.'

She lowered the child to the ground – look, he stood! She reached for the see-saw. Jon pushed himself into the air and she grabbed the other seat. With surprising strength she pulled it down and settled herself on it. She hoisted her son on to her lap.

She nodded at Jon to start. He pushed up. They landed with a thump; Tobias squealed. Hannah flexed her legs and propelled them up, up above Jon who sank to the ground with a bump. Their weights were equal; they set up a rhythm . . . up . . . down . . . Up rose their faces, Hannah's smiling, the boy's rigid with concentration . . . they sank . . . they rose . . . up they soared into the sunshine . . . Exhilaration swept through him. The sounds of the traffic faded away.

He pushed harder . . . up he swooped, they landed with a thump . . . Tobias squirmed and Hannah laughed . . . She pushed harder . . . up they soared . . . Jon landed with a bump, the force of it lifted his bottom off the seat, weightlessly . . . Grinning, he pushed hard with his legs and up he flew . . . down they bumped. Look! He could float up . . . up . . . forever . . . Hannah tried to stop but Tobias yelled, protesting.

He lost track of time. Five minutes, an hour . . . they

seemed to have been see-sawing all afternoon. At last Hannah called breathlessly: 'Stop!' She pushed herself up one last time. He climbed off his seat and held it, easing them gently down from the sky.

Gripping the child, Hannah climbed off the seat. Grounded, she suddenly seemed clumsy. Her face shone with sweat.

'More!' Tobias whined.

'Ssh, darling. We'll come back tomorrow.' She smoothed down her skirt. 'I promise.' His dungaree straps had fallen down; she hooked them back over his shoulders. Her hands were still inkstained. 'Thank you.' She smiled at Jon and then said to her son. 'Say thank you to the nice man.'

Tobias frowned up at him. Jon bent down and ruffled his hair. It was surprisingly thick. 'You take care of yourself,' he said.

He walked away. The park seemed wider, as if the people had receded. The grass was empty; the man with the carrier bags had packed up and gone.

Jon walked to the road. Pigeons flew up around him, their wings creaking. A fan of mottled clouds had spread into the sky. He only turned back once.

4

It was funny, how calm she was. Now she had him –
Horsham – she took her time. On Saturday she went to the
hairdressers and had her roots done. The girl, Donna,
said: 'You look great today. I could hardly recognise you.'

'My husband's coming home,' said Eva.

'How lovely! How long's he been away?'

'A year. He's been in Hong Kong.'

'A year?' Her fingers stopped. 'And you haven't seen
him?'

'We fax each other every day,' Eva replied. 'He sends
me flowers – like, roses and orchids.'

'How romantic! When's he coming?'

'Tomorrow.' Eva gazed at her reflection in the mirror.
She spoke to her own lips. 'Tomorrow I'm going to get
him.'

That afternoon she cleaned the flat. Six black bags, that's
how many she filled. Such strength she had! She heaved
aside the settees like they were made of cardboard. She
shovelled stuff into the bags – fag-ends, chicken bones,
amazing what she found. She even managed to carry the
espresso machine into the kitchen. It seemed only yesterday that it had been dumped on the lounge floor. A year, it
had sat there. Wasn't time funny? It was like, all these
months everything had been frozen. 'Happy anniversary,' she whispered to the machine, and kissed its
chrome.

She had a long bath. She poured in sandalwood oil and
a squirt of Badedas. She lit candles and lay there,

submerged, watching the light flickering on the tiles. 'Horsham,' she chanted. 'Horsham Horsham Horsham . . .' She hadn't sung for ages; her voice sounded cracked. She sang the Simon and Garfunkel song about the couple in the coach: 'We're all going to look for Hoooor-sham . . .' She lay there until the water was cold and the candles had guttered, one by one.

She went to bed early. She didn't even have a drink – look, she could stop just like that! One drink led to another and she wanted to be in peak condition tomorrow. She ate two bowls of Crunchy Nut Cornflakes and went to bed.

Trouble was, she couldn't sleep. Not surprising, was it? By five thirty in the morning she was dressed and ready. She wore black leggings and her tight black sweater he had always liked. She looked like she worked for the SAS.

She poured herself one last cup of coffee. Her hand shook but that was only natural, wasn't it? She watched the cigarette smoke wreathing between her fingers. She turned her hand this way and that. She stubbed out her cigarette in the ashtray; it was already overflowing with stubs. Funny, she thought, I can't remember smoking any of them.

She waited until eight. Then she let herself out of the flat and pressed the bell for the lift. She stepped inside and pressed 'B'; how smoothly it sank, down to the underground garage! She climbed into her Merc, her baby. The steel door slid open; she drove up the ramp, into the silent street.

London was still asleep. It was Sunday morning. The roof was open, she heard church bells ringing. She drove through Streatham, past shuttered shops. The map lay open on the seat beside her; its pages stirred in the wind. Under her fingertips the engine felt perfectly tuned, a powerful machine at one with her own body.

She drove fast through the suburbs and out into the countryside. HORSHAM 5 MILES. It was cold, with the roof open, but she didn't care. She hardly felt it. HOR-SHAM 2 MILES.

She arrived at Horsham, parked in a side street and switched off the engine. Next to her was a white-painted cottage. *Let's go and live in the country*, he had said. He could be standing behind those windows, wasn't it strange?

It was a grey, chilly day. She got out of the car and walked down the main street. The one angle of it was so familiar; she must have watched the video forty times. She walked across the street and stood in the spot the reporter had stood all those months ago. Further down the pavement was the hardware shop. She walked up to it. SORRY! WE'RE CLOSED.

She walked down the street and stopped at a newsagent's shop. A man came out, carrying Sunday papers like a tray in front of him. He looked at her and got into his car. Somewhere, a church clock chimed ten.

He had walked on this pavement. *He* had bought newspapers here. She went up to the window and looked at the postcards. *'Baby Belling for Sale.' 'Mare needs hacking.'* Jon was watching her. She could feel his eyes; he was here somewhere. She looked at the reflection in the glass; behind her, the street was empty.

She looked at the window again. It was then that she saw the card. *'Eliot Parker, Carpenter and Joiner. No job too small.'*

Eliot. The girl called Jon 'Eliot' once, in the hut. And Parker . . . Jon's hero was Charlie Parker.

It was Jon all right. It was his writing. He had changed his name, wasn't that sweet? The ink was faded from the sun; the card must have been there for weeks. *'4 Church Cottages, Minstead, Near Horsham.'*

She found the village on her road atlas. Jon had given it to her when they bought the Merc. She had never had a road atlas before. She had pictured them sitting side by side, the wind blowing their hair, roaring around Britain and screwing each other senseless in luxury hotels. Signing in as Mr and Mrs because that's what they would be.

She arrived in Minstead. The engine purred as she slid through the village. She felt wide awake, more awake than she had ever been in her life. More alert, even, than when she had been hunting the girl. She slowed down at a pub. It was still closed. Cottages stood back from the road, their windows watching her. She braked – whoops! a bit jerky – and read their names. Honeysuckle Cottage . . . The Old Forge. On the village green two kids sat on a see-saw. Their parents pushed them – Dad one end and Mum (a fat cow) the other. The Dad looked at her car as she passed.

She slid past a caravan showroom . . . past a post office . . . she slid along in her shiny black Merc, she slid like an oil slick . . . She wore her dark glasses and she had wrapped a scarf around her head – Hannah's blindfold, in fact. She suddenly realised this and giggled out loud. The roof was open, people were staring at her. They thought she was a film star. She heard the church bells . . . louder . . . there it was, down the hill . . . it was like the church was pulling her towards him, like a magnet.

The row of cottages stood opposite the church. She coasted past number four. It was the end cottage. The upstairs curtains were closed. She parked on the verge, further down the lane. A row of cars were parked there; people were going into the church. She switched off the engine. The bells pealed, what a racket! She closed the hood, sealing herself in.

She sat there for a while, breathing deeply. When she was trying to give up smoking, years ago, she had been to a hypnotherapist. *You're lying on a beach . . . relax . . . relax your fingertips, your hands . . .* She opened her eyes and looked in the driving mirror. She adjusted it, so she could see the cottage. Nobody went in or came out; there was no sign of life. No sign of his motorbike.

She got out of the car and walked towards the cottage. Some planks lay in the front garden, covered with tarpaulin. It was anchored with bricks.

'Looking for Eliot?'

She jumped. An old man had come out of the cottage next door. For a moment, she didn't know what he was talking about.

'He's not here.' The man carried a black rubbish bag. He opened a dustbin and shoved it in. 'He's gone to London.'

He went back into his cottage and slammed the door. Then he opened it, let out a cat, and closed it again.

A plane roared overhead. Eva felt the blood drain out of her body. She nearly laughed out loud.

Gone to London. He had gone back to the flat to get her. On the very same day that she had come to find him, too! Wasn't that typical. But then they were like that, her and Jonny. They had this thing between them – telepathy.

She opened the front gate. She walked across the front garden; the heels of her boots sank into the grass. She walked round the side of the cottage. Now she knew he wasn't here she felt bold. At the back was a vegetable patch – rows of vegetables, not a weed in sight. She thought: he's been growing them for us. All this time, he's been getting the place ready.

She walked up to the back window and peered in. She took off her Raybans and pressed her face against the pane. It was a kitchen; in the gloom she could see one of those old electric cookers, formica shelves . . . a crappy little kitchen but it would do. If you were happy, who gave a toss? He knew that she could be happy here; it was what he had always wanted for them.

Postcards were propped against the window, above the sink. This side, she could see the writing. She leaned closer, squinting in the light.

They all seemed to be from 'H'.

Just been to a son et lumière at this temple. Even the naff soundtrack can't quite destroy its mystery. . . etc. etc. Love H.

80 degrees here, eat your heart out. Hotel full of Germans, all sunlounger bandits . . . etc. XXX H.

This is a wonderful medieval wall-painting. Why is hell always more interesting than heaven? Answers when I return, please, one side only . . . etc. etc. Miss you, H.

Big, bold writing. *Miss you . . .*

Eva stood there. The church bells tolled like they were her stupid heart. They were drowned by a plane roaring overhead; its shadow went over her.

One of the postcards was in different writing.

Dear Eliot. It was great meeting you. Here, as promised, is Hannah's address: Flat 23, 'Borrowdale', Mandela Estate, London W10. Please give her my love. All the best, Kimberley.

Eva sat in the car. She gazed at the address. She had written it on the flap of her book matches; her writing was all jerky.

She couldn't swallow. Her throat felt dry, like she had been smoking dope. *Kisses from H.*

It had given her a shock, of course, but now she understood. It was Hannah, of course. That fat, spotty schoolgirl, she had the hots for him. It happened – like there was that Patty Hearst in America. She fell for the bloke who kidnapped her; they made a film about it.

The stupid little bitch. She'd got about, hadn't she? Hotels, swimming pools, foreign places. Life seemed to have been one long holiday as far as Hannah was concerned. Jon needn't have worried about them. The Price family was obviously loaded; half a million was bugger-all as far as they were concerned. Shit – they should've got more out of them – two million, three.

She knew what had happened. Jon had been embarrassed by Hannah's schoolgirl crush. He was such a softie, so kind. He had gone up to London to tell her the truth. *I love Eva. I've spent a year, preparing her this big surprise. Eva's the only woman I could ever love.*

Then he was going to go to the flat. *Surprise surprise!* he'd say. *You thought I was gone? How could I leave you? Silly-billy, I was only fooling.*

Her hands were shaking; they seemed to have a life of their own. Silly, when everything was going to be all right. At this very moment he was sitting Hannah down and talking to her. *Eva and me, we're going to be together for ever. Nothing can part us now, not even death. She's coming to get me, now.*

She slid the stick to R. She revved the engine and reversed the car, slewing around in the mud. She moved the stick to D, and drove back through the village.

Mandela Estate. This time she drove fast.

5

Hannah had spent the night with her mother. The flat was only ten minutes' walk away from her own place. She had slept in the double bed with Becky, while her mother slept in the little room. They often did this on Saturday nights, when the rest of London was out and about. There was a girlish confederacy about it that reminded Hannah of her Stanmore sleepovers.

In the morning Val wanted her to come to church. 'Just this once,' she said. 'You might like it.'

Hannah opened her mouth. *But I'm half-Jewish*, she was about to say. *I'm an atheist. I've got my A levels in a week.* But then she looked at her mother and nodded. 'OK.'

Val had found God. To be accurate, she had rediscovered Him – a childhood sweetheart who had been patiently waiting whilst all those years she had been married to someone else. How could Hannah deny her mother this comfort? After Val's breakdown – her own big sleep when she had lain in the dark for a week, pumped with drugs – after she had emerged into the daylight she had seemed more composed. Cheerful, even. She had sloughed off the bitterness. Her new-found Christianity seemed to make sense of things. Hannah had not yet discovered whether it was the forgiveness aspect of it that soothed her mother, that she had come to terms with those who had wreaked havoc in her life, or whether she was invigorated by the more robust satisfaction that after death they would burn in hell. It seemed ill-mannered to enquire.

All she knew was that the worldly, amusing Val had changed; she had become a more assiduous grandmother than she had ever been a mother. She babysat Tobias while Hannah went to college. She had moved into this flat nearby and worked part-time at a Citizen's Advice Bureau, negotiating with the poor rather than the rich. Only last week she had said: 'In a funny way I'm grateful for what's happened. Don't ask me why.' So Hannah hadn't asked.

They went to church – a heavy Victorian place in Bayswater. Becky, the contemptuous teenager, refused to accompany them and stayed behind, looking after Tobias. Hannah knelt in a pew. Beside her Val's strong voice joined in the Creed. 'I believe in God the Father, God the Son and God the Holy Ghost . . .'

Hannah, her lips closed, recited silently: '*Here's the smell of the blood still. All the perfumes of Arabia will not sweeten this little hand . . .*' She was learning lumps of *Macbeth* by heart.

'. . . the Apostolic Church,' murmured the congregation, 'the forgiveness of sins, and life everlasting . . .'

'*There's nothing serious in mortality,*' Hannah mouthed. '*All is but toys.*' She thought: we study A levels too early, before we have a clue what it's all about.

She thought about her son. Yesterday, on the see-saw, she had clamped him between her legs. Up they had soared into that treacherous blue sky. Already he was struggling to grow up and leave her, to launch himself into a world so out-of-kilter that his grandmother had turned to God for solace and his grandfather was trying to wash away his sins with mineral water.

'Hymn Forty-Seven.'

They climbed to their feet. In the past year either Hannah had grown or Val had shrunk; whichever, she was now taller than her mother. Far taller than her father, if he were here.

The voices rang out around her. Years ago, in the first

form, she and Emma had sung their own versions to carols ... *'While shepherds washed their socks by night ...'* They thought they were hilarious, that nobody had ever done it before. They creased up with mirth at their own wit. How long ago it seemed, when they were innocent of the world's knowledge ... before pimples and bras, before they had inhaled Marlboros and French-kissed. Emma's chest was flat then, her parents were still married. Hannah's own parents were still married and would be married forever ... And Julia ate her pudding before her main course in case the world ended. Which it hadn't. See? It hadn't, yet.

6

Eva drove straight from Sussex to Notting Hill. She nearly crashed the car a couple of times – stupid fuckers, couldn't they see where they were going? When she parked outside the sign saying 'MANDELA ESTATE' she was damp with sweat. She adjusted her driving mirror and applied her lipstick. Whoops! Try again. She rubbed it off and had another go.

The pavement glinted with glass. What if some bastard vandalised her car? This sort of place, they did it for kicks. But she couldn't drive through the entrance; the sign said 'RESIDENTS ONLY; WHEELCLAMPING ZONE'. Anyway, she didn't want Jon to see her – not yet. She wanted to surprise him.

She took out a tissue and wiped the mud off her heels. She must look smart for him. Opening the door, she dropped the tissue into the gutter. Rubbish was strewed along the pavement, like somebody had emptied bags of it; a mattress lay propped against the wall. She looked up at the blocks of flats. High-rise concrete, like the place her mum had moved to after she was put into care. He was in there, waiting for her.

She locked the car and walked through the gates. She thought: aren't I clever, to have found him before he has found me? She thought: God I love that man. I love him to death.

When she had just moved in with him, remember? Christ he'd loved her. He'd said: 'Each day this week I'm going to devote to a different part of your body.'

'OK. Where're you going to start?'

'Your knees.' He had dropped to his own knees and kissed hers. 'Each day I'm going to concentrate on a few square inches of you.'

'You daft thing.'

They lay on the carpet, laughing. He made up a poem, *knees* rhyming with *cheese*, something like that. Oh yeah –

> *These are the bee's knees,*
> *May I have more of them please?*

He put his face so close to them that his breath tickled her skin.

'Mmm, they smell like hay,' he said.

He took out a felt-tipped pen and drew on them. He drew a big smile on one of her knees and a frown on the other. They had gone to the pub and he had addressed his conversation to her knees, under the table. The blokes at the next table had stared at them like they were bonkers. They *were* bonkers.

'Who's the bee's knees?'

Eva stopped dead. A man, polishing his car, grinned at her.

'Just for a moment, I thought this was my lucky day,' he said.

Shit. She must have been talking out loud. She hurried on.

'And who's bonkers?' he called, laughing.

The lift was broken. She had to walk up the stairs. They were concrete – what a clatter her heels made! She walked on tiptoe. See? Not a sound. It was one o'clock. Her back ached, from driving all morning, but she didn't care. She felt powerful; she felt as strong as a horse.

She arrived at the flat. '23' on the door. The blinds were closed. She cocked her head, listening. No noise – nothing but the thumping of her heart.

They were in there, she knew it. She could feel Jon, just

beyond the door. He was waiting for her; she could hear him breathing. She closed her eyes and touched him – his soft throat.

Shame there was no back door. Then she could spring on him unawares. Watch his face!

She rang the bell. Nothing happened. It must be broken. She picked up an empty milk bottle and rapped it against the door.

What a racket! She jumped back. She waited. From the flat next door came the smell of roasting meat. How quiet it was! She stroked the milk bottle. If she broke it – easy-peasy, smash it against the railings – if she broke it, how smoothly it would slide into his throat, like a knife into butter!

She rapped again. Silence. Nobody was home.

7

Val's flat was a two-bedroom attic overlooking the rooftops of Westbourne Grove. It was cramped – the kitchen was a cupboard in the living room – but it had a studenty charm. They had just arrived home from church. As her mother lit the gas ring Hannah thought: divorced people, they shift back decades. My father is living with a student nurse; my mother has a geezer in the bathroom – not a bloke: a geezer, one of those Ascot things.

They ate pasta for lunch, and drank orange juice. Hannah pointed to the carton. 'That's the nearest you'll ever get to Florida now.' Her parents, all those months ago, had given the holiday tickets to Rhoda.

'To tell the truth, I never wanted to go,' said her mother.

'I did,' said Becky.

'I thought it would be full of muggings and old people wearing polyester,' said her mother. She smiled, and doled out second helpings. 'After all, we'd already been mugged at gunpoint.'

Hannah caught Becky's eye. Was this bitterness, or just a joke? Nowadays they couldn't quite gauge their mother. Though she lived with Becky she was no longer quite a mother anymore. She was beginning a new voyage in her life, a step apart from them.

At two o'clock, on the dot, the doorbell rang. The air weighed heavier. Val got up and carried the plates to the sink.

'Hallo chaps.' Morris stood in the doorway. He was breathless, from climbing the stairs. 'How's things?

How's my grandson?' He stepped inside and turned to Becky. 'You ready, Princess?'

Their father never stayed long. There seemed no room for him, somehow, in the flat. Anyone could see that he was uncomfortable. He wore a maroon sweatshirt with a drawstring waist; his stomach bulged over it as if he were pregnant. Hannah couldn't say this, of course. Even Becky could no longer tell him he looked a wally; their easy intimacy had long since gone.

He was taking Becky to the Queensway skating rink. 'Maybe a McDonalds after, eh?'

Becky pulled a face. Hannah knew what she was thinking. One – that she would rather be with her friends. Two – why did her father treat her as if she were younger than she was? Becky reluctantly got to her feet. Hannah thought: Why? Because he wants her to stay eleven years old, as if none of this has happened.

Val turned; she smiled a wintry smile. Morris gave her a carrier bag.

'Carbonated, just as you like it,' he said.

'Thanks.' She pulled out the bottles of water.

'Theo and I, we have a meeting on Monday. Trust House Forte. Fingers crossed.'

'So the business is going well?' Val spoke to Morris pleasantly, as if they had just met at a cocktail party. Morris, on the other hand, sounded jauntily artificial. When they were together for a while they were more natural, more like their old selves, but they usually weren't together for long. They never mentioned Kimberley.

Hannah's guilt about her parents had largely disappeared. Their separation had gathered its own momentum, blame was being dredged up from events that had occurred before she was even born, by now it no longer felt her responsibility. She worried about her parents, but like a grown-up would worry about her contemporaries.

And now they had settled into an uneasy routine, but a routine all the same. Hannah thought: amazing, how we adjust.

Val said: 'Could you get Becky back by six?' She wiped her hands. 'She's got a lot of homework.'

'Have I ever been late?'

Hannah got up and said she ought to go too.

'You want a lift?' asked Morris. 'Let me take you home.'

It was a grey, cold day; it felt as if a lid had been clamped down over London. Yesterday's sunshine seemed as impossible as a foreign holiday, once one has returned from it. Morris drove down Ladbroke Grove. Even then, before it all happened, Hannah had the feeling of a city stilled, waiting for something that would crack it open.

Morris chatted to Becky about her school – she went to Holland Park Comprehensive. 'So they frisk you at the gates?' he joked. He had made this remark several times.

'No,' said Becky languidly. '*We* frisk the teachers.'

They sat squashed together in the front seat. Nowadays Morris drove a van. When he braked, the bottles of water rattled in the back. He turned to Hannah and asked her how she was getting on with her revision.

'It's not for my sake you're doing this?' he asked. 'Or your mother's? I mean, your A levels?'

'No,' she lied. 'It's not for you. I'm doing it for me.'

'Oh.' She didn't know if he was disappointed or relieved. It saddened her, that she couldn't tell.

He drove along Mandela Street. He stopped the van and reversed into a parking place; the crates shifted. He said: 'Allow me, young lady, to escort you to your front door.'

Her heart sank. This laboured tone meant that he wanted to talk. She needed to keep her head clear. She was going to revise her *Macbeth* while Tobias had his nap.

313

Then she would take him to the swings as she had promised. Her son's needs were blessedly simple.

They got out of the van. They left Becky twiddling the radio knobs, trying to find Capital FM. Morris helped strap Tobias into his pushchair. They walked towards the entrance to the flat.

He cleared his throat. 'The fact is, my dear, I need your advice.'

'Mine?'

'There's nobody else I can ask.'

'What about Theo or Becky?'

He shook his head.

'Shoe!' Tobias shouted. He had kicked it off. Morris picked it up from the pavement.

'Dad Dad Dad,' said Tobias. It was the first word he had spoken. Hannah had felt rebuffed.

'The fact is – Kim, she wants to get married.' He addressed the small, red sandal in his hand. 'So she wants us to start a family. It's only natural of course. She's young, she has her life ahead of her. So what shall I tell her?'

'You think you're too old?'

'Too old? Sure I'm too old. I'm nearly sixty.' He strapped on Tobias's sandal. Tobias tried to kick it off again. 'But it's more than that. Me, how can I bring a child into the world like this?' He straightened up and pointed. Nearby a car was parked. It was a shiny black Mercedes. 'That car, it's a work of art. 350 SL, if I'm not mistaken. Now, when I see a car like that there are two thoughts going through my head. You know what they are?' He wagged his finger at her. 'I think – what did someone have to do, to buy a car like that? That's one thing. And I think – how long will it stay so perfect in this wicked life?' He paused. 'Something beautiful, it's there to be spoiled. How can I believe this, and bring a child into the world?'

Hannah looked at the Mercedes. Somebody was inside.

The driver's window was open, just a slit; cigarette smoke wreathed out.

'I just think – nice car,' said Hannah.

They walked on. 'There's nobody I can tell this to,' he said. 'I thought – my Hannah, she'll understand.'

'But I don't,' she said. 'Look! I've had a baby.' Her face heated up. She felt embarrassed, that he had confided in her. They walked towards her block.

'Dad Dad Dad,' Tobias spoke to the passing wall.

Hannah said: 'Mum says in a funny way she's grateful it all happened.'

'Your mother says that?'

'She says she's changed. She says she's learned things she would never have learned.'

They arrived at the stairwell. He folded up the push-chair and started to climb the stairs. 'And such a good job I made of it first time round,' he said bitterly, over his shoulder.

'You were fine.' Gripping Tobias, she climbed the stairs behind him. 'You found me irritating. It wasn't your fault. I probably *was* irritating.'

'And now it's Theo and Rebecca I'm disappointed in.' He paused, to catch his breath, and continued up the stairs. 'But mostly it's me.'

'Don't be an idiot.'

They arrived on her landing. She thought: isn't it strange, that I feel wiser than my own parents? She rummaged for her doorkeys. 'I'm glad you asked my opinion.' In fact, now the surprise was fading she felt deeply touched. For the first time in months she felt close to him. 'You want my advice? The people who did this – don't let them ruin the rest of your life. If they manage to do that, then they've finally won. Like, evil's won.'

She unlocked the door. Her father kissed her forehead. 'I'm proud of you,' he said. 'The way you've coped, it's made me proud to be your father.'

'See? If it had never happened, I'd never have had to cope at all. I'd be a student in Sussex, whining for you to buy me a car. You'd have never known how wonderful I was.'

He laughed. For once it wasn't a forced laugh, it sounded quite natural. Then he left.

She let herself into the flat. The closed blinds gave the place a peaceful, twilit look. 'Time for your sleep,' she said to Tobias. 'Then we'll go to the park.'

She put him to bed. He removed his fingers from his mouth. 'Dad Dad,' he said.

'Mummy,' she corrected.

She sat at her desk. She thought of her father, driving his van around London; in the back, the bottles of water rattled. Her poor father. She opened her *Macbeth*. '*Will all great Neptune's ocean wash this blood clean from my hands?*'

Morris crossed the street and walked to the van. There was a dent down the side; Theo had made a delivery to Covent Garden on Friday and had scraped against a bollard. Morris had had to conceal his annoyance; he needed Theo to work with him, for both their sakes. He had to tread so carefully. 'It's only money,' he had said.

He climbed into the van. Becky had wound down her window. Still, the scent of cigarette smoke hung in the cab. He opened his mouth to reprimand her; he stopped. He couldn't speak to Becky either; he was in no position to tell her not to smoke, not to do anything.

He started the engine and drove off. He was suddenly struck by the irony of it. In the old days, when nothing much happened, he could talk with ease to Becky and Theo. Now, when so many huge events had taken place – he had left home to live with another woman, his wife had divorced him and married God, he had a grandson whose unknown father had destroyed their family – now, after these two tumultuous years, the only person to whom he could open his heart was Hannah – the one daughter with whom, in the past, he had found such conversations difficult.

He drove towards Bayswater. He wanted to ask Becky a thousand questions. One of these, the smallest one, was: do you really want to go skating? Becky, his golden girl, his darling.

He said: 'Speak to me. Tell me something.'

'What?'

'Anything.' He was suddenly desperate. 'Say anything.'

She fiddled with her earring. 'Want to hear a joke?'

He nodded. A joke was better than nothing.

She said: 'What did the dyslexic devil-worshipper do?'

Oh no. It was going to be something sick, something she had picked up at that school.

'I give up,' he said. 'What did the dyslexic devil-worshipper do?'

'He sold his soul to Santa.'

Morris laughed. How innocent! He suddenly, irrationally, felt that everything was going to be all right.

'Where did you hear that?' he asked.

'Hannah told it to me.' They had arrived at the skating rink; she unbuckled her seatbelt. 'She learnt it from the man in the hut.'

8

Three o'clock and still they hadn't arrived. There were no children in the park. It was cold and windy; after the carefree sunshine of yesterday the weather had changed, as if it understood the solemnity of his task. Jon had been sitting here since one o'clock. He wore his leather jacket and motorbike gloves; still he felt chilly. On the ground, between his boots, sat the Tesco's bags.

'We'll come back tomorrow, I promise.' Hannah had told her son. Their son.

The only people here were people with nowhere else to go. At chucking-out time various men had drifted into the park. They sat, one to a bench; they rummaged in 'Euro Food and Wine' bags and took out cans of lager. Under a bush somebody lay in a sleeping bag; all this time they hadn't stirred. A black guy dressed in rags, with what looked like ashes smeared in his hair, wandered from one litter bin to another; he kept up a stream of girlish chatter.

Ten past three. This area was heavily policed. Several times a pair of officers had strolled through the park. They passed him now. He looked at his watch and frowned, pretending he was waiting for a date.

Three fifteen. A large woman stood in front of him and said: 'They pressed his little tummy.' She moved off and addressed the black man, who was standing on the rim of the sandpit. 'You know what they did? They pressed his little tummy.'

Jon looked at the plastic bags, slumped against his boots. They were heavy with the weight of his conscience.

He didn't think about Hazel; Hazel began tomorrow. He thought about his father. Towards the end his dad had started to hide his bottles. Once, startlingly, Jon had unearthed one in his toybox when he was searching for his tractor. One evening his mother had searched the house for bottles. Thin-lipped, she had shoved them into carrier bags. Jon was twelve then. He had heard her in the kitchen, shoving them into the bin. When she had gone to bed he had retrieved them, let himself out of the house and staggered down the street. The bags were so heavy! He had shoved them into the dustbin outside someone else's house, disowning them.

'Got a pair of nail clippers on you?' The woman stood there. Her voice was surprisingly educated. Jon shook his head. 'Only asking,' she said.

She sat down on the next bench. Her position was upwind from him but he didn't like to move, it would look rude.

Three thirty. Across the gravel stood the see-saw. Its blue bucket seat, the one he had sat in, was suspended in the air like a question. Paper bowled along the ground. The area around the swings was littered with spare ribs, as if an act of cannibalism had taken place.

Beneath the swing, rubber mats had been set into the gravel to break the children's fall. Jon thought: so many dangers Tobias will have to face without me. '*Take care of yourself.*' One feeble sentence to last his son's lifetime.

Between his boots sat a house. Two houses – more. Airline tickets to anywhere existed between his ankles. Within those bags lay all the possibilities he had dreamed about and never taken. Jon took out a Kleenex and pressed it to his nose. He had identified the woman's odour; he had smelt it once when he had passed a glue factory. It clung to the lining of his nostrils.

Hannah wasn't coming. He couldn't bear it any longer;

this place exhaled despair. He didn't *want* his son to come here.

He looked at his watch. Three forty-six. He would wait until four. Then he would give it up and leave.

9

Hannah nearly turned back. God it was cold! She looked down; Tobias sat in his pushchair, clutching the bag of bread slices. His hands were bright pink. When she slowed her steps he bounced up and down.

'Birds!' he whined.

They would just go there for five minutes – a quick swing, feed the pigeons. She crossed Portobello Road. Being Sunday, it was deserted. The spaces for the market stalls were painted on the road. She thought of Camden Lock – how, released from suburbia she had giggled through it with her gaggle of friends. She still kept in touch with some of them, despite the divergent paths their lives had taken. Emma was at Hull University; she was sleeping with her Pastoral Care Supervisor. Rachel and Tanya had taken a year off and were backpacking through South America, an enterprise which now she had a baby seemed, to Hannah, insanely dangerous. She herself hadn't been to Camden Market since that Sunday – that grey Sunday like this one – when she had gone there alone.

Not alone, of course. Somebody else had been there, following her. If she turned she would have seen her – a chestnut wig, a determined body pushing through the crowd.

Hannah pushed her son towards the park. That bitch had followed her all the way from Stanmore; she had watched her and dodged when Hannah turned ... Thinking back, Hannah was sure she had felt it ... the

malevolence of it, exhaled . . . someone was watching her
. . . walking behind her, tap-tapping on tarty heels . . .

The perfume, she could almost smell it now, blowing on
the wind. The scent that had filled her nostrils when she
had lain in the hut, her face to the wall . . .

A chill, grey day like today . . . too cold for early
summer . . . the iron lid of the sky clamped down . . . all
this Sunday the city had felt hushed . . . waiting, watching . . .

Hannah shivered. She wanted to go back but she didn't
turn, something stopped her. She walked briskly. She
spoke to Tobias, to reassure herself with the sound of her
own voice.

'Nearly there . . . look at the nice dog.'

The hot breath of the tube . . . tap tap . . . the heels
crossing the platform behind her . . .

'Nearly there, darling . . . round this corner.'

The skin at the back of her neck prickled. She tried to
concentrate on her father's news. Kimberly wanted to
have a baby; her Dad might soon be pushing a pushchair
too. Wasn't that weird? A stomach-shifting sensation that
hadn't caught up with her . . . the realisation, it was trying
to catch up . . . tap tap, hastening behind her, drawing
nearer . . .

'Here we are! Look.'

Ahead lay the park. The bushes rustled; the saplings
bent in the wind. Beyond the houses, in the main road, the
traffic roared.

'Dad Dad Dad,' said Tobias.

10

Eva's lungs hurt. They felt raw, like a layer of skin had been stripped off. Too many bloody cigarettes. She leant against a wall, catching her breath.

Ahead of her, Hannah walked across the street. She was heading for the playground. That waddling walk. Big legs, in blue jeans. And the *baby*.

Eva hadn't expected a baby. It had thrown her, at first. All this time, following Hannah, she had been trying to work it out. Basically, she was trying to convince herself that it couldn't be Jon's.

But it was. She was sure about it now. Why? Because there he sat.

She could see him quite distinctly; she knew Hannah would lead her to him. There he sat – battered leather jacket, curly brown hair. He was sitting on a bench near the swings. He was leaning forward – like, resting his chin on his hands. He was looking at some shopping bags. Shopping for the two of them.

Eva's insides tightened. A car crammed with black guys passed; its music thumped through her. Vomit rose in her throat.

She pulled her eyes away from Jon. Across the grass she watched Hannah. She walked past Jon, like she didn't know him. Why didn't they greet each other? For a daft moment Eva wanted to call out *Hey*! *There he is*! Stupid, eh?

Hannah stopped the pushchair at the swings. Jon stayed sitting on the bench.

Eva felt in her handbag. She fingered the knife –

Sabatier, nothing but the best. The most expensive that money could buy. It nestled there, wrapped in her tissues. She stepped across the street.

Also available from Deborah Moggach

Extract taken from

Close Relations

One

You had a problem? Gordon Hammond was your man. He was a jobbing builder, a man with a van. He was good with his hands, cheerful and reliable. He was his own boss, beholden to nobody; he was not the sort to knuckle down under someone else's orders. No job was too small for Gordon in those days. This was forty years ago, when he was just starting in the business and struggling to make ends meet. He had a wife, Dorothy, to support. And then his daughters were born, one closely followed by another, and though you could scrape by on £10 a week, especially with a wife like Dorothy who could conjure up a meal out of nothing, you still had rent to pay and as time progressed money to put down on a house.

Gordon called his business Kendal Contractors, for he had a romantic streak and it was on a holiday in the Lake District that he had proposed to his wife. He stayed a one-man band for years and he worked all the hours God gave him. While he hammered and plastered, the Russians sent the first sputnik into space, 3,000 anti-war protesters marched on Aldermaston and Christian Dior, a man unnoticed by Gordon alive or dead, died. For Gordon was busy.

By the late fifties the two daughters had arrived, and though people thought that he and his wife were trying for a son next time, a strong young lad to join the firm, Gordon said he was proud of his daughters and wouldn't want it any other way. His tone silenced any further questions, even from his wife. By 1959 another daughter had been born. She was born on February 3, the day Buddy Holly was killed; if it had been a boy, Gordon would have called him Buddy but as it was another girl they called her Madeleine. In that year the Mini car was invented, heralding the start of the swinging sixties. It was a decade that passed Gordon by as if it were happening in another country. He kept his head down; he was busy elsewhere.

In 1960 he and Dorothy bought their first home, a maisonette in Chislehurst. They even made a down-payment on a caravan but there was precious little time for holidays, Gordon being rushed off his feet and having to hire an ever-increasing work-force to cope with the demand. Word of mouth did it. He boasted that he had never advertised his services, there was no need for it, he kept his customers because no job was too small, small led to big, one recommendation to another. There was always a demand for a reliable builder who gave a fair estimate, turned up when he said he would, did a first-class job and cleaned up afterwards, not one of those cowboys–wally jobs on the cheap and the next month the ceiling falls in.

In those days the world was a hopeful place. The Russians thrust Gagarin into space, Kennedy was elected President and in 1963 Martin Luther King had a dream. The housing market was booming too. By the mid-sixties Kendal Contractors had a ten-strong work-force of chippies, plasterers and plumbers, in addition to a fluctuating number of labourers Gordon called in on a casual basis. Flat conversions, local authority work, private speculations – in those days property developers were two a penny and in partnership with a firm of local architects he ploughed his profits into some terraced housing in Putney, divided them into flats and made a larger profit which he ploughed into another speculation. And so on.

He put the girls into a private school, St Agnes, in Croydon. Though he winced at the size of the fees, his heart swelled with pride as he wrote the cheque. He bought a larger house, detached, up the road from the maisonette. The Vietnam War ended; the Watergate hearings began. In 1974 Gordon moved his family into their final home. It was a five-bed Tudor-style property in Purley, woods out the back, garaging for two cars and a dream kitchen at last for his wife, bless her. By the time Nixon had resigned Gordon had built an office extension on the side of the house, there was even room for a small yard for storing materials.

So the girls went to school, benefiting from the sort of education neither he nor his wife had enjoyed. While they did so, his wife, Dorothy, sat in the office and answered the phone. Over the years she had taught herself book-keeping, she discovered that she had a flair for figures, and though they had their ups and downs, particularly when the property market collapsed in the late seventies, there was always work for a good builder, for if people cannot afford to move house they have to adapt the place they are living in, and by now he was the oldest-established builder in the neighbourhood.

The girls grew up. Louise was the first-born. She was blonde and pretty and vague; from infancy she charmed those around her. She daydreamed her way through school, preferring to play with her dolls in a rehearsal for mother-hood. Everybody loved Louise and she accepted this with the equanimity of the beautiful. Even her sisters' intermittent bouts of jealousy were disarmed by her obliviousness to their existence, for those who are favoured by nature have an innocence about them, a protective envelope that seals them into their own sunny climate. She grew up into a willowy teenager with long silky hair. Lovelorn young men laid siege to the house; bricklayers hung around on payday hoping for a glimpse of her. In her sisters' eyes she always seemed to be disappearing, roaring off in some sports car leaving empti-ness and a smell of exhaust behind her. She enrolled in secretarial college but she never completed the course, she was far too disorganised. By that time, however, it no longer mattered for she had fallen in love with a young venture capitalist and soon she was ensconced in a flat in Chelsea, pregnant with her first child.

Prudence, the middle sister, was the intellectual. 'Always got her nose in a book,' boasted Gordon. With Louise it was 'bees round a honeypot'. Not a reflective man, he spent little time analysing his daughters and, when asked, summoned up the same phrases throughout their teenage years. He set each daughter in the mould of his own catchphrase. Prudence was the quiet one, the bluestocking. Prudence, whose self-esteem was low, considered herself plain but when removed from Louise's proximity her face gained in definition. It was a face one could gaze into with pleasure, like a painting of a Dutch interior.

Prudence was the only sister to go to university. She led a separate life inside her head and on graduation day it gave her a shock to see her parents in the audience, so alien did they seem in the mock-medieval hall. In their different ways all three sisters grew away from their parents but it was Prudence who was educated out of her background. Though she knew her mother and father were proud of her, the very shininess of their pride showed up their incomprehension of what she so easily took for granted. They had worked so hard to get her there, and in doing so they had lost her.

She remained a dutiful daughter, however, the peace-maker between her father and her unruly younger sister and the one to whom her parents turned when Louise moved away to her new house in a favoured part of Buckingham-shire. Prudence was the reliable sister, one of life's baby-sitters, who held the fort whilst others were having fun. If she rebelled against this she did it in such a well-mannered way that nobody noticed. Her parents were too busy with the daily dramas of the business and their two grandchildren. And Maddy, her younger sister, though a loyal ally – she would fight to the death for Prudence – had never got on with her father and absented herself by moving away from home and finally out of the country altogether. Meanwhile Prudence got a job in publishing, bought a flat in Clapham and lived there with her cat for company, and a row of African violets, the spinster's houseplant, on the windowsill.

From an early age siblings are assigned their roles and through the years they settle into others' expectations. Louise was the beautiful earth mother and Pru was the clever one. Maddy was the tomboy. When their mother recollected their childhood the same scene repeated itself. Louise sat in the garden, tucking up her dolls on the lawn. Pru lay on her stomach reading a book. And along charged Maddy, vroom vroom, pushing her toy bulldozer over Pru's pages, vroom vroom, pushing it over Louise's dolls. The yells! Maddy was a fierce, sturdy little girl. Sometimes her sisters wondered if her destiny was to act the part of the son her parents had never had, and maybe secretly desired. A truculent girl, she grew up at odds with her surroundings, 'a square peg in a round hole,' her father said. Even the name she was given, Madeleine, didn't fit; she never grew into it and remained Maddy from an early age. Photos showed her with a round face and pudding-bowl haircut, glaring at the camera and standing halfway out of the shot.

Despite her glowering, somewhat humourless exterior, she was deeply loyal to her sisters and fought with anyone who criticised them. She was a strong girl, good at sport, and won swimming trophies which her father proudly showed visitors. When he did this she grew red-faced and abrupt; her father considered this rude but her sisters knew she was simply embarrassed. When she was sixteen she dropped out of school. Her father was furious; hadn't he slaved away all these years to get her into the best school in Surrey? But she left anyway and went to live with a group of people in Stockwell who were running an adventure playground. For years she all but disappeared from view. She met Prudence from time to time, but she seldom saw Louise because she disliked her husband. He was a handsome, caddish man called Robert about whom Prudence, too, had mixed feelings but she was more tactful about showing it.

During the late eighties Maddy travelled a great deal,

backpacking, and for a while she lived in Canada where she worked with disadvantaged kids. Though she had never been a student there was a studently feel to her life – footloose, impermanent, at odds with not only her upbringing but with the Tory government, the felling of the rainforests and the conspicuous consumption of many people including Louise's venture capitalist husband. Her face remained curiously youthful, like a nun's unmarked by the passage of time. By the age of thirty-three, when she left to work in Africa, she could still be mistaken for a girl of twenty. 'You must have a picture in your attic,' said Prudence, who was feeling her age. Maddy, however, didn't understand; she had never heard of Dorian Gray.

Gordon, too, was feeling his age. That day in September, was his granddaughter's sixteenth birthday, he and Dorothy were driving down to Buckinghamshire for the lunch party.

'Sixteen,' he said. 'Seems only yesterday she was a baby.'

'Seems only yesterday the girls were babies,' said Dorothy.

It was true. His daughters were three great creatures, practically middle-aged. It seemed only yesterday that they were playing together in the garden. They seemed to have grown up while his attention was momentarily diverted. It was as if he had nipped out to buy the evening paper and come home to find them women. They had mortgages and opinions. Maddy was in Nigeria, speaking Ibo or whatever, how about that?

Birthdays always gave him pause for thought. His granddaughter Imogen was sixteen – practically capable of breeding herself. They drove towards Beaconsfield. Dorothy sat beside him, a parcel on her lap. She had bought it, she saw to that side of things.

'What is it?' he asked.

'Wait and see. It goes with her big one, from her parents.'

'Why won't anybody tell me?' he whined. He swerved out to overtake a lorry.

'Gordon!' Dorothy clutched the door handle. 'It's a secret.'

A secret – the story of his life. Girlish giggles behind closed doors. A houseload of females, mother and daughters, closeted together. Mood-swings, whispers. *Don't tell Dad, he wouldn't understand. He's just a man.*

'Gordon! It's a thirty-mile zone.'

Gordon was a restless, impulsive man. He drove too fast, he smoked too much. He was probably a stone overweight if he ever thought to stand on the scales. His wife was always nagging him about his health; he was sixty-five, he should have more sense. But it was his drive, his own blind energy, which had got him where he was today. It was part of the package.

In fact he resembled a parcel. He was a short, sturdy man – Maddy was the only daughter who had inherited his physique. He was getting bald, no denying that, but the extra weight was all solid, he spent his days on the go, he was as fit as a bull. There was a pugnacious set to his jaw, a forward thrust to his stocky body. But he was a cheerful man, too, a whistler. None of the young lads who worked for him whistled, they didn't have the tunes any more, but he had a repertoire of standards which used to get on his daughters' nerves. He was a robust man, he liked a drink and a joke; he was a man of action rather than a thinker and though he grumbled about the business he was happiest haring from one site to another, bawling out orders and bantering with his lads, he was a male animal through and through.

Women were by and large unfathomable. He should be used to them by now, he had had enough practice, but to tell the truth his daughters had always bemused him. Their preoccupations seemed beyond him, in another dimension entirely. And why couldn't Prudence and Maddy each find themselves a man, get married and give him some more grandchildren before it was too late?

His wife, now she was a different matter. He could rely on Dorothy. She twittered and fussed, like all women, she couldn't tell one end of a car from the other, but her femininity was of the old school, it was comprehensible to him.

They had been married for forty-four years, they held no secrets for each other. His childhood sweetheart had become a plump matron of sixty-three; when he looked at her properly, which wasn't often, it gave him a mild shock. His familiarity with her hadn't caught up with her age. Her hair, tinted now, was set in the same soft waves she had set it in for years. They were old companions, they had weathered their storms, they understood each other. If people had asked him about his marriage – which they didn't, it was too settled an institution and besides, nobody of his acquaintance talked in that language – if they had asked he would have replied that he and Dot rubbed along, what else was there to say? Conversations about relationships always made him fidget.

So Gordon Hammond and his wife drove through Beaconsfield in their Mercedes estate car, its back heaped with bags of cement. They passed the Queen Anne homes belonging to captains of industry and TV personalities. Set behind grass verges, the shops in the high street displayed designer clothes and photographs of desirable properties. The prosperity of the place – the width of the street, the manicured lawns! This was the heart of the Home Counties, sealed off from the brutish outside world. Nothing terrible could ever happen here, that was the message. Intruders beware! Wealth breathed from its renovated façades. Soon Gordon would be sitting down at Louise's table. It made his heart swell, to think that his daughter's sweet face had gained her entry into this privileged world. She had always been his golden girl, touched by the Good Fairy's wand. The reward for her beauty was two healthy children, a handsome husband and a life her sisters must surely envy.

He braked at a zebra crossing. Dorothy jerked forward. In the back of the car, paint cans shifted.

'Gordon! One of these days you'll give me a heart attack.' She replaced the package on her lap. 'Unless you have one yourself first.'

Six miles from Beaconsfield, in a fold of the hills, lies the village of Wingham Wallace. Set amidst rolling pastures and beechwoods it is in an area of Outstanding Natural Beauty. The village itself was recorded in the Domesday Book and its core remains – a pub, rows of cottages and a church dating from Norman times, with Victorian additions. The beauty of the village has been enhanced by age and wealth, the first needing the second for its own preservation. Within easy commuting distance of London, the place has attracted those high-fliers who wish for rural relief at the end of a demanding day. It is also convenient for Heathrow Airport, a mere thirty minutes' drive away. As a result of this several of the larger houses are inhabited by people so rarely glimpsed that they have become rumours. The smaller cottages have long since been gentrified, too, and their outhouses converted into garages that are too short for the 5-Series BMWs whose bonnets jut into the lanes and cause the passing traffic to swerve.

At its heart, however, this is still a real community inhabited by real people. Pebble-dashed council houses prove this, and bunches of youths who gather at night in the bus shelter, shifting restlessly like heifers, their cigarettes glowing in the dark. There is still a primary school – just – and a store-cum-post office run by a man called Tim, who does all the work, and his depressed wife Margot. And how could the rich live without the local people to service their households, cleaning and gardening and minding the place when they are away in the Caribbean?

On Sundays the church is well-attended, mainly by women with carrying voices and organisational skills who make jam and who campaigned successfully against a proposed development of starter homes which would have ruined the views and brought down the property prices. The vicar has long since moved into the next village; he now has five parishes in his care and the vicarage itself was sold back in the sixties. In a village of desirable properties it is one of the most enchanting – a Georgian house burdened with wisteria, grand but not imposingly so, with sunny rooms overlooking a walled garden and a view of the Chiltern Hills from the master bedroom. Successive owners have improved the lace, adding *en suite* bathrooms, a Smallbone kitchen and that essential accessory of the seventies, a conservatory. When Robert and Louise moved here with their children, six years ago, there were no more improvements to be made. This suited Robert. He hated DIY and said he had better things to do on a Sunday than stand on a ladder covered with dust.

This particular Sunday was their daughter Imogen's birthday. It was one of those early autumn days that already possess their own nostalgia; like petals packed into a bud, the dewy garden held within itself the future memories of a perfect day – the sort that makes England in general, and Wingham Wallace in particular, a satisfactory place to live. Robert and Louise's visitors, of which there were many, remarked how it always seemed sunny at the Old Vicarage, as if one of Louise's many skills was to create her own weather for her guests.

Today's lunch was to be a family occasion – Louise's parents and her sister Prudence. Unaided by her adolescent children she was cooking the meal. She was hampered by the dog, an overweight labrador called Monty, who lumbered to his feet whenever she moved and who stood in front of the kitchen units, strings of saliva hanging from his jowls, whining as she unleafed the salami from its wrapping paper.

Louise was forty-two and still beautiful. In fact age had improved her, revealing the bone structure beneath her soft face. Twenty years of marriage had also strengthened her character, sharpening the edges that had been blurred when she was younger. Robert was a demanding husband, easily bored. He expected her to amuse him and to be a sophisticated hostess when their guests came to stay. She had always wanted to please him – too much, according to her sisters. They suspected that deep down she felt that her background and intellect were inferior to his and that she had to stay in trim, mentally and physically, to keep up with him. They despised this lack of self-confidence, this female compliance. Didn't Robert realise how lucky he was to have her?

Louise carried some muddy lettuces in from the garden. Her son had appeared. His face was bleary with sleep. He leaned against the sink eating a bowl of Nutty Cinnamon Shapes.

'Jamie, it's twelve o'clock.'

He raised one eyebrow. It was a new mannerism, caught from his father. 'Chill, Ma.'

'They'll be here in a minute.'

'It's only Granny and Grandad.' His withering tone, too, resembled his father's voice. She hoped that he wasn't growing up to be a snob. Jamie was eighteen. Next year he was going to university. He was tall and bony, with thick fair hair. Judging by the number of phone calls for him he was becoming attractive to girls. This wasn't improving his character. They spoiled him. One would have imagined that in these post-feminist times this would be a thing of the past. But then Louise had spoiled her son too. Her sisters had always accused her of being slavish with men.

'Budge up,' she said, dumping the lettuces in the sink.

Imogen came in, yawning. 'Where's my black top?'

'Is nobody going to help me?' asked Louise.

'It's my birthday!'

Jamie, still eating, sauntered away into the living room. Sound bloomed from the TV.

'Why does he always leave the room when I come into it?' asked Louise.

'Because he thinks you're boring.'

'Gap year my foot. Gap from what?' She pointed to the potatoes. 'Scrape these, will you?'

'That's sexist. What about Jamie?'

'He's not here. Where's your Dad?'

'He went to buy some lemons.'

'That was hours ago.' Louise thought: the trouble with the

country was that you spent the whole time running out of things and the rest of the time in the car.

Her daughter popped a slice of salami into her mouth and wandered off. She paused to pat the dog. 'How's my sweetie today?' she crooned. It often struck Louise that her children were nicer to their pets than they were to her. Yet neither the dog nor the rabbits had ever lifted a finger to help them, they had never been bored rigid by playing card games with them, nor had they nursed them through the night. Imogen had a sugary voice that she only used with Monty. When Louise pointed this out Imogen showed no surprise. 'But he's so sweet,' she said. 'So if I rolled on the floor with my legs in the air you'd be nice to me?' asked Louise.

Imogen was a small, wiry girl. Her hair was dark, like her father's, but she hadn't inherited his good looks. The person she most resembled was Aunty Maddy, a fact that her brother pointed out when he wanted to upset her. Like Aunty Maddy she was no intellectual; she was a direct, loyal girl whose slow responses irritated her father and caused Louise to jump to her defence. Robert wanted dazzling children. When Louise pointed out that success could be measured in quieter, more internal ways – didn't niceness matter? – he said that niceness was the most tepid word in the English language and should be banned. Besides, Imogen was never nice to *him*.

Upstairs, Louise brushed her hair. The arrival of her parents always filled her with trepidation. She could trust neither of the men to behave themselves; they brought out the worst in each other. Her father's pride in her and her lifestyle made him look foolish and Robert, who had a cruel streak, goaded him on, much to Louise's and her mother's embarrassment. Gordon was a simple soul. He was putty in his son-in-law's hands and became a caricature of himself – legs akimbo, rubbing his hands like a north country mayor in a play by J. B. Priestly. Louise despised him for this and then hated herself for despising him; she hated Robert turning her father into an object for his own amusement and hated herself more for finding it amusing. For her husband could always make her laugh.

It was a quarter to one. Louise went downstairs. Where was Robert? Trust him to disappear when she needed him most. He would breeze in, late; he was never late for his friends, only for her parents. Sometimes she suspected that he was jealous of her family. He had no brothers or sisters. He had been brought up in some style, a lonely little boy on whom lavish amounts of money were spent but who was shamefully neglected. His mother had been too busy marrying her various husbands to take any notice of her son, who had been sent off to boarding school at the age of four. When Louise and Robert were quarrelling he brought up this fact, embellishing it with pitiful descriptions of himself sobbing in the dormitory, clutching a sodden teddy bear. This always did the trick, reducing Louise to tears. The bastard.

There were two composers who made Prudence cry: Brahms and Schubert. Other composers could, with certain passages – Bach, during the slow movement of his double violin concerto, the violins soaring up and entwining, making love to each other with such tenderness it seemed they must break. It was Schubert and Brahms, however, who spoke to her heart. Not the symphonies – Prudence found symphonies windy and self-important, there was a look-at-me feeling about a symphony. She was a chamber music person; there was a spareness and precision about a string quartet that suited her. Prudence needed order. It was essential to her life, it was the structure upon which she depended.

As she drove out of London the road blurred. Brahms was playing – her cassette of the Piano Quartet No 2. On their first date together she had taken Stephen to a lunchtime concert at St Johns, Smith Square. The Brahms had been played then, the Lindsay Quartet had performed it. For months afterwards whenever she read the name *Lindsay* she had felt a foolish jolt of electricity. During the concert she and Stephen hadn't touched each other. She had kept her hands in her lap, resting on her handbag, like a dowager, but she had felt the heat of Stephen down her right side. Her skin had been drawn towards the magnet of his shoulder and his thigh. It was the strangest sensation, as if her soul were being removed into his body.

Later, when the whole thing had started, he said that he had felt it too. They had lain in bed, and with the luxuriousness of all new lovers they had gone back over the preceding weeks, charting their progression into intimacy moment by moment. 'Did you feel that then, really?' 'What about that time when we bumped into each other next to the photocopier?' They described each others clothing – 'You were wearing your white blouse' – all those months of working together in the office were re-run, their own tender videotape, as they lay under her duvet. Hindsight made their most mundane conversations charged with significance. It was during the Brahms, he said, that he had felt his soul removing itself from his wife and finding its home in Prudence.

Her Metro was a mess. Her box of Kleenex was buried under a tea towel, a box of fisherman's lozenges (empty) and a packet of Silk Cut (also empty). She pulled out a tissue and wiped her nose. People's cars are often a surprise. Those who lead orderly lives can have chaotic vehicles, and vice versa. Those whose lives are disintegrating can drive around in spotless cars smelling of air freshener, with a single hardback road atlas on the back seat. Cars, supposedly an extension of our personalities, in fact reveal something more interesting – the contradictions that lie within us all. Prudence kept her flat tidy but in her car she became a different person, liberated and powerful, in control of a destiny which in normal life eluded her. She drove fast too – fast and skilfully. Yet she looked like the sort of woman who bicycled around London with a basket full of Kit-e-kat. Which she did do, too.

Stephen was her editorial director. He had a wife, a Dutch woman called Kaatya. He also had two sons. Prudence's affair with him, conducted for th e most part with little physical contact, at lunchtimes, had been going on for a year.

Prudence wasn't the sort of woman who fell in love with other people's husbands. The revelation of her own capacity for deceit had been one of the more painful experiences of the past twelve months. She drove along the fast lane of the M40; she turned up the Brahms. Stephen had given it to her two days earlier. 'Our first anniversary' he had said, lifting her chin towards his face.

She rummaged for a cigarette and lit it. She was the only Hammond sister who smoked though she hid the fact, out of some vestigial childish cowardice, from her parents. She didn't look like a smoker; she wore navy-blue cardigans to work, white blouses, flat shoes. It surprised some of her authors when she took them out to lunch and lit up. She smoked; she committed adultery. She thought how none of us are what we seem. Explore deeper and a person disintegrates, just as newsprint, when viewed close-up, disintegrates into tiny dots. How could you trust a word when it was just a collection of spots? Yet her life consisted of working with words, she had to believe in them.

At times she believed that she only existed in other people's expectations of her. When she was a child, for instance, her parents had assembled the dots to create Prudence, the nice, steady sister, the middle one, the swot. These dots clotted together to become her personality. But she knew better. She knew that she was a shifting collection of atoms trying to shape themselves out of chaos. Stephen didn't suspect this; neither did her sisters. Only her cat knew the truth; she could see it in his eyes.

The front of the Old Vicarage was knotted with wisteria. It had been planted many years ago, before the arrival of Robert and Louise. Its thick branches were twisted around each other like lovemaking limbs; their marriage had lasted so long that nobody could prise them apart, even if they had thought to do so. To the right of the vicarage rose the church, St Bartholomew. In its graveyard, beneath the silence of the yew trees, stood headstones. They slanted this way and that, as if blown on by the breath of God. Depending on the mood of the onlooker the mellow brick house and the ancient place of burial suggested either the permanence of love or its transitoriness.

Louise, hearing cars arriving, stepped out of the front door. Later, months later, she remembered that moment. A leaf from the wisteria spiralled down in front of her and came to rest on the gravel. She looked up, beyond the knotted limbs of the trunk. Did it have some sort of blight? The leaves were dying already; they usually didn't fall until October.

It was five to one. The cars arrived – her parents' estate car followed by Robert's BMW. They stopped in the driveway. As they did so Prudence's car appeared along the lane and drove through the gates. Louise hurried to greet them.

'Hello!' called her mother. 'We've all come together.'

'Glad some people do.' Robert grinned at his wife. 'Just kidding.' He shook Gordon's hand and kissed his mother-in-law

Gordon pointed to the house. 'Should get that guttering seen to.'

'Gordon –' said Dorothy.

Robert smiled: 'Want to fix it while we're having lunch?'

'Don't, love,' said Dorothy. 'He will.'

'One of my lads lives out this way. I'll get him to drop in –'

'Come on!' said Robert.

Robert carried two Tesco bags. A new superstore had opened a couple of miles away. Though he had only gone out for some lemons he had missed the village shop, which only opened briefly on Sundays, and had driven to Tesco with the pleasant sensation that he was both doing his duty and skiving off helping with lunch. Once in the superstore he had succumbed to impulse buys, he was a man who seldom resisted temptation. He had picked up exotic, whiskery fruits from Penang and a bottle of such extravirgin olive oil that he had practically remortgaged his house to buy it. He had headed to the wine section where he had been seduced into buying various obscure New Zealand vintages. How could such a boring country produce such interesting wines?

Maybe, once they had finished polishing their Vauxhalls and filling in their crossword puzzles, they had nothing better todo. Then he had lingered at the magazine rack and leafed through the more lurid Sunday tabloids, admiring the girls' breasts and the catastrophic lives of lottery winners.

Robert went into the house with his parents-in-law. Louise paused with Prudence. She looked at her sister's reddened eyes.

'You all right?'

'Blame it on Brahms,' said Prudence.

'Only Brahms?' Louise hated it when Prudence cried; she did it so seldom. Prudence was the one she relied on, who would always be there. The trouble was, other people thought so too.

'How's everything with . . . you know?' she asked.

'Same as ever.'

'That's why you look so awful.' Louise accompanied her to the front door. 'Listen, I don't want to sound like an older sister but shouldn't you –'

'No.'

Louise looked down the hallway. Sunlight slanted onto the tiles; it shone onto the rear portion of Monty as he wagged his tail, greeting the guests. A champagne cork popped; Imogen laughed.

Louise stood there, seeing it through her sister's eyes. She felt a wave of hatred for Stephen, a man she had never met, for Prudence kept him a secret and their parents didn't even know about his existence. Stephen wasn't entirely to blame, of course, but it is easier to put the responsibility onto somebody unknown, particularly if he is so visibly making your sister unhappy.

The dining room was squar e and masculine. Its french windows opened into the conservatory where geraniums glowed blood-red in the sunshine. There was a marble fireplace; there was a grandfather clock and a large mahogany table which Robert had inherited from one of his uncles. They ate salami and tinned artichokes, Imogen's favourite starter. Robert poured out more champagne. He was a generous host; he looked at home in this room, doling out wine and chatting, a man at ease with himself and his possessions. Today he wore a striped silk shirt from Turnbull and Asser and a plum-coloured cravat; he looked exactly what he was – a City whiz-kid who had loosened up for the weekend.

'So how're you doing, Pru?' he asked. 'How's the literary scene. Discovered any geniuses?'

'Well, I'm working on a book called *My Favourite Microwave Recipes*. It's written by that newscaster, what's his name.'

'Yeah, and really written by you. Why don't you tell them? I would.'

'It's what I'm paid for.'

'Don't be such a wimp' said Robert. 'You're wasted in that place. You should be managing director by now.'

Prudence shrugged. She was immune to Robert's flattery; to his attractions too. He had a handsome, wolfish face and thick black hair. He was a small man – it always surprised her that he was shorter than Louise. At some point in his childhood he had contracted TB and spent months languishing in bed, that was probably the reason. Like many small men he had grown up to be intensely competitive. He played tennis in a London club, thrashing what he called merchant wankers and boasting about it afterwards to Louise. Prudence was both fascinated and repulsed by his hairiness – dense black hairs on his slender arms. She pictured him in bed with Louise, gripping her like a monkey. When other people were talking a muscle twitched in his jaw; there was a restlessness about him, an impatience to be amused. Next to him Prudence, in her floral dress, felt like a head teacher.

Jamie had inherited his father's restlessness. His leg was jiggling under the table. His grandmother was talking to him.

'So what are you going to do in your year off?' she asked.

'Try to find a job.'

'Should be easy, with your A levels.'

'Not round here.'

Jamie was bored with the country; he had grown out of it. His days of tadpole-collecting were over and though he sometimes joined the local youths in the bus shelter they seemed like bumpkins to him. Like most adolescent boys he was unwillingly drawn into family gatherings and looked as if he would rather be doing a hundred other things. The question was: what?

Louise came in, carrying a platter. It contained a large salmon strewn with herbs.

'Look at that,' said her father. 'Is there nothing this girl can't do?'

'Woman, Dad,' said Louise. 'I'm forty-two.'

'A moment's silence.' He tapped his fork. 'Let us gaze upon this masterpiece.' On these occasions Gordon was inclined to grow flushed and jovial. It embarrassed his daughters but amused his grandchildren, who were at one remove. Louise sliced into the flesh of the salmon. Gordon raised his glass to Imogen. 'To the birthday girl. Sweet sixteen! You'll be giving me a grandchild before your aunties, unless they pull a finger out.'

There was a silence. Louise glanced at Pru, then she laughed hastily. 'I thought I was starting the menopause last week. Then I realised I'd just left my diaphragm in, all through my period.'

Prudence laughed. Dorothy indicated the teenagers: 'Louise!

Robert turned to his father-in-law. 'Some potatoes? So how's the business doing?'

'Worked off our feet,' said Gordon.

'I wish he'd take it easy. Haring around London like a twenty-year-old. He won't admit he's getting older.' Dorothy turned to Louise. 'You tell him. He never listens to me.'

'He never has,' said Louise.

'And what's that supposed to mean?' demanded her father.

'You've never listened to Mum,' said Prudence, joining in.

'Oh-oh, they're ganging up on me.' Gordon turned to Robert. 'Same as always.'

The doorbell rang.

'Shit,' said Louise. 'Send them away, whoever they are.'

Robert left the room. They heard murmurs in the hall, the surprised tone in Robert's voice. There was the bumping, dragging sound of luggage being brought in.

A woman came in. Though she was thirty-seven she looked younger. She had a no-nonsense, tanned face. It was bare of make-up. She wore jeans and a T-shirt and when she entered the room she paused, startled, as if she had emerged from the darkness to popping flashbulbs.

'Aunty Maddy!' cried Imogen.

Forks clattered onto plates. Her sisters hugged her.

'When did you arrive?'

'I've come straight from the airport.'

'Why didn't you tell us?' asked Louise.

'Are you all right, love?' asked her mother. 'You look so thin.'

'Wicked tan.' Jamie grinned at his aunt.

'We would've come to the airport,' Louise protested.

'She always was a law unto herself,' said her father.

Maddy looked at the teenagers. 'You're so enormous!' She hadn't seen them for four years.

Robert dragged forward another chair. Maddy, who didn't like kissing, who shrank from any show of affection, turned to Imogen and said gruffly: 'Happy birthday. See? I got back in time.' She looked around. 'I didn't know it was going to be, well, everyone.'

'Shall we go home then?' asked her father.

'Gordon.' Dorothy shot him a warning look.

'A letter would have been appreciated,' he said. 'Just one.'

'Dad.' Prudence frowned at him.

Louise gave Maddy a plate of food and a glass of orange juice – her sister didn't drink alcohol. They asked her questions: why had she decided to come back to England? How long was she here for?

'I don't know,' said Maddy. 'I just wanted to come home.'

Maddy had been working for an aid organisation in Nigeria. She had worked in a remote village helping to drill bore-holes and teaching women to read. Her letters had been infrequent and her life there was mysterious to her family. Like all people who have returned from living abroad she didn't know where to start; the experience was both too familiar and too amorphous to be made digestible for others. Besides, she was not by nature a talkative person and she felt exposed with her parents there. For years she had lived in places that were incomprehensible to her family and she felt grateful that even her sisters' curiosity was limited and would peter out after a few days. She needed to keep something to herself, otherwise her family consumed her. That was one of the reasons she had had to get away from them in the first place.

They gazed at her. Dorothy was right; she was thinner. Her face had sharpened; her arms looked muscular. Though far from a glamorous person, to the teenagers she was exotic – only yesterday she had been sweltering under an African sun.

Maddy couldn't eat. She was still living in another time-zone and was filled with airline food. She got up and pulled a wooden object out of her baggage. She gave it to Imogen. 'Happy birthday.'

'Gosh' said Imogen. 'What is it?'

'An Ibo fertility truncheon.'

Imogen paused. 'Wow.'

Robert burst out laughing. 'So if they don't shag you, you can beat them to death.'

Maddy said: 'I thought – you could make it into a lamp or something.'

'Thanks, Aunty.'

'Don't call me Aunty' said Maddy. 'It sounds so . . .'

'Auntyish,' agreed Prudence.

Louise pointed to the salmon. 'Eat up.'

Gordon indicated her plate. 'Bet you didn't eat that in Wogland.'

'Dad!' said Prudence and Louise together.

Gordon raised his hands. 'Only joking. I employ one of them myself. First-class chippie –'

'For God's sake –' said Maddy.

'– very sunny disposition.'

'Nothing's changed, has it?' said Maddy.

' – and he's got a lovely sense of rhythm,' said Gordon.

'Can't you stop him, Mum?' demanded Maddy. She turned to her father. 'We're human beings, Gordon –'

'So I'm Gordon now? What's wrong with Dad?'

'Know your problem?' said Maddy. 'It's ignorance and fear –'

'He's only winding you up,' said Louise.

'Forgot the Thought Police was back,' said Gordon. 'Better watch what I say –'

'Anybody different from you –'

'Jesus, Maddy!' Robert raised his voice. 'It's Imogen's birthday. Can we postpone the lecture about race relations?'

There was a pause. It reminded them of the debris settling, after a minor explosion. The grandfather clock struck three.

'I'm sorry.' Maddy turned to Imogen. 'I'm terribly sorry.'

'It's all right,' replied Imogen. 'You sound just like Mum, with Dad.'

'What?' said Robert.

'They're always having rows.' Imogen looked at her father. 'You're incredibly racist.'

'I'm not!'

'Sexist too.' Jamie joined in. 'When Janet Jackson came on TV –'

'That wasn't racism,' said Robert. 'That was lust.'

'Shut up, everybody!' shouted Louise.

There was a silence. In the hush, they heard the sound of a lorry arriving.

There is something about a horse that stills the heart. She was a grey mare, heart-stoppingly beautiful. She pricked her ears and gazed at them with her liquid brown eyes, could she really be as intelligent as she looked? She was 14.2 hands high, the perfect height – just taller than a pony, just a horse but not alarmingly so. She was six years old, still darkly dappled like a rocking horse. In the years to come she would grow whiter.

The lorry had driven away. The horse stood on the gravel, her nostrils expanding like sea anemones as she breathed in the air of her new home. Louise held the rope of her head-collar. She put out her hand and stroked the horse's muzzle; it felt velvety, like a raspberry.

'Where'll we put her?' asked Louise.

'In the kitchen,' said Maddy.

'What? Robert'll have a fit.'

'Don't be a sissy.'

Louise laughed. Suddenly the years fell away. After all this time one word could reduce them to giggles.

The others waited in the dining room. Robert called out: 'What's happening?'

'Wait! Don't come in!' yelled Louise through the kitchen door.

'We're not ready!' called Prudence.

Their mother smiled. 'Nothing's changed, has it.'

'Instant regression,' said Robert. 'How thin is the veneer of maturity. They're always like this when they get together.' He knocked on the door. 'What on earth are you doing in there?'

Suddenly they heard the muffled neigh of a horse. They jumped. Louise opened the door.

It was a large kitchen. The horse stood in the middle of the floor. Her tail and mane were plaited with red ribbons.

'Happy birthday, darling,' said Louise. 'She's called Skylark.'

Imogen stepped up to the horse. She looked as if she were

sleepwalking. Her mother passed her the rope. For a moment she was beyond speech.

'She's the most beautiful ... the most ... oh Mum ... Dad ...' She gazed at the horse. Her eyes filled with tears. Just then there was the sound of soft thuds.

'Ugh, gross!' said Jamie.

'Her first dung.' Imogen gazed at it, entranced.

'Want to embalm it?' asked Robert. 'Louise, I really think –'

'We'll clear it up,' said Prudence.

Imogen flung her arms around the horse's neck. She buried her face in the fur, breathing the scent.

'Love at first sight,' said Gordon.

'Steady on,' said Robert. 'Any closer and we'll have to call the Horse Helpline.' He went to get his camera.

Imogen lifted up her face. It was radiant. 'This is the most wonderful day of my life.'

The shutter clicked. It was a moment of pure happiness – pure, distilled joy. For months afterwards, whenever she smelt horse dung, Louise would remember it. Later she would frame the snapshot and put it in her bedroom. When their lives had changed out of all recognition she would look at it and feel a blade through her heart.

Maddy, standing apart from the rest of them, felt confused. One minute they were quarrelling, the next laughing. She had forgotten the tumultuous ebb and flow of family life. She felt buffeted one way and another like a stick in a stream. She had forgotten how to cope with it. How peaceful it had been to live abroad, even in a war zone. For years she had been amongst people to whom she was not related, with whom codes of manners and distance applied. Most of them didn't even speak the same language as she did; apart from the Nigerians, her closest European colleagues had been a French doctor and a Swedish project manager. She watched Louise sweeping up the droppings. Thrust back, jet-lagged, into the intimacy of family life she wanted to crawl away and pull a duvet over her head.

Gordon's heart swelled with pride. Imogen led the horse

outside. Through the window he watched her saddling up with casual expertise. He had a granddaughter who could buckle a bridle, who could talk with authority about fetlocks and gymkhanas. The sun shone on the yellow, rag-rolled kitchen units. Here he was, in the autumn of his years, surrounded by the fruits of his loins. For over forty years he had worked all the hours God had given him to arrive at such a moment. It was worth the wait.

His heart thumped. Pain shot along his arm. He sat down heavily on a chair.

Dorothy looked at him. 'What's the matter, love?'

'Nothing.'

Gordon took a breath – once, twice, breathing deeply. At the time, he just thought his heart was bursting with pride.

The three sisters sat on the lawn eating birthday cake. The sun was sinking; clouds were building up over the church spire. At the end of the garden was a vegetable patch, its poles trousered with runner bean plants. Beyond it lay the paddock. Imogen cantered round on her horse. Her hard hat rose and fell as she passed the brick wall. She wore the new hacking jacket her grandparents had given her.

A ladder had been erected against the house. Gordon stood on it, fixing something or other. He could never sit still. At the foot of the ladder stood Dorothy. From time to time she passed him a tool.

Maddy lay on her back, looking up at the clouds. 'I'm sorry. I've forgotten how to do this.'

Louise said: 'It comes from being amongst all those savages.'

Prudence listened to their father whistling. 'Nothing's ever going to change him.'

'Or her.'

Prudence licked her fingers. 'Wouldn't it be interesting if something happened which really shook them up?'

'It won't.' Louise, lying on her back, turned to Maddy. 'Where are you going to live?'

'Somebody's lending me a flat.' Maddy's friends were mostly unknown to her sisters. Maddy was not a social sort of person; neither Pru nor Louise could remember her ever holding any sort of party, or if she had, she hadn't invited them. From what they gathered, her friends worked for the sort of good causes that made Pru and Louise feel guilty.

'How's work?' Maddy asked.

Pru said: 'We were taken over in the spring. Maybe I wrote to you about it. A big German media group.' She didn't bother telling her sisters the name; neither of them would have heard of it. 'They're going to move us into a state-of-the-art monstrosity down by the river. It's all accountants now, they keep talking about the bottom line. Everybody's very jittery.' She lay back and closed her eyes. 'Mmm, it's so peaceful here.'

'Everybody says that,' said Louise. 'They come down from London and fill up here, like a garage. Robert does too. Then the next morning he buggers off again.'

'He always wanted to live in the country, didn't he?' said Maddy.

'That's because he's hardly ever here.'

The three women lay on the grass. The sun slipped behind a cloud.

'How are you two getting on?' asked Prudence.

'Oh, fine,' said Louise. 'It's just . . .'

'What?'

'Nothing. We're fine.'

Her sisters were silent. A long marriage is closed to outsiders, even to sisters. It seals off a couple from the world. It is only when the marriage is in trouble that the curtains open for a moment and people glimpse the astonishing drama that has been playing on the stage all those years. At that moment they can step inside with their consolation and advice – '*To be honest, I never liked him*', or '*I always thought she was selfish.*' Two things can then happen. The marriage can split apart for ever, baring its soul and loosening its secrets into the world, or the couple can make it up. When this happens the curtains are closed again and those who have offered their advice feel foolish, especially when they have been frank about the person's spouse. The words hang embarrassingly in the air, everyone tries to pretend they have never been said.

Prudence was a discreet woman; she didn't like to pry. Besides, she had never lived with a man and felt unqualified to offer advice. Maddy, on the other hand, wasn't that interested anyway. She turned on her side and pressed her ear to the ground. She could hear the faint, rhythmic thuds of the horse cantering around the paddock. It reminded her of the village where she had lived. The old men could remember when messages were sent, miles through the bush, by their fathers banging their staves on the earth. How simple, how satisfying, this method of communication seemed. How preferable to words, so treacherous and prone to misunderstanding. In Maddy's opinion, if people communicated with knocks the world would be a better place.

'Imogen says she's never going to get married,' said Louise.

'Don't worry, she will,' Prudence replied automatically. Then she thought: why should she? We all want people to marry. We think it will solve them. We have been brought up to think that this is the end of the story. In fact the entire romantic fiction list at her publishers, one of the few imprints that made a healthy profit, was based upon this lie.

She thought: I want to marry Stephen more than I have ever wanted anything in my life. I want it so much I feel sick.

It was cold. Maddy went into the house to find a jacket. She glanced through the front door. Robert was washing his car in the driveway. The dog stood watching him. Suddenly Robert swung round, grinning. He turned the hose on the dog. Monty yelped and ran away. Maddy watched as the dog shook himself in a glittering cloud of spray. As she turned back Robert caught her eye. He smiled.

Maddy glared at him. How dare he? She moved away, abruptly, out of his line of vision. Upstairs she could hear the thump of music. She went up to Jamie's room and knocked on the door. She had always been fond of her nephew and niece; in fact, she preferred teenagers to adults.

Jamie was taping a cassette for one of his friends.

'Can I borrow a sweater?' she asked. 'I'm freezing.'

He opened his cupboard. His room was the usual adolescent chaos but Maddy didn't notice; she was blind to her surroundings and she could live in chaos herself. She could live out of a suitcase, it made no difference to her.

Jamie passed her a sweater. 'Africa sounds great. I want to go there.'

'You'd like it. You're the only person here who would.'

'Why did you come back now?'

Maddy pushed her head through the sweater and pulled it down over her shoulders. 'Because I needed to start my life.'

'So why did you stay so long?'

'I just – didn't fit here,' she said. 'England didn't fit me.'

'I know what you mean.'

'That's because you're eighteen. With me, it was more than that.'

'Why?' he asked.

'Because –'

She stopped. Her father's face had appeared at the window. He waved at them, through the glass, and started hammering at the gutter.

When someone is in love with a married man, evidence of family contentment is too much to bear. His own home life, of course, is beyond thinking about. But the domestic lives of others are painful too, being a shadowy reminder of his. Oh the easy intimacy, so casually taken for granted by those enjoying it! Prudence tried not to be affected by her sister's house but so much stopped her in her tracks – scrawled notes stuck to the fridge, shopping lists with items on them such as Coco Pops, that only people's children want . . . Below this, a layer below, lay the evidence of the past, things that belonged to a younger Jamie and Imogen and that no doubt littered the boys' rooms in Stephen's house – abandoned rollerskates, battered boxes of Cluedo. Prudence didn't envy Louise's marriage – she herself wouldn't want to be married to Robert – but the sight of their bedroom filled her with self-pity.

She had gone upstairs to fetch a magazine. Louise was a magazine-addict and had kept a copy of *Elle* that contained an interview with one of Prudence's authors. Their bedroom was a large, corner room, its walls washed peachy-pink. Robert and Louise's clothes were strewn over the chairs; the disordered intimacy made Prudence feel like an intruder. *Master bedroom*. The words rebuffed outsiders. Master bedroom with *en suite* bathroom. The phrase implied a life of sensuality behind closed doors, of frequent couplings and sluicings. Prudence gazed through the door. The towel-rail was hung with lace knickers and black stockings; Robert liked to buy Louise fancy underwear for her birthday. Louise's bedside table was heaped with magazines. Robert's side was piled with heavy new hardbacks – the latest bratpack American novelist, a weighty volume called *Plunder and Plenty: The New World Order*. The chest of drawers was crammed with photographs of their wedding, their children, and snapshots of parties with friends of theirs that Prudence had never met.

As she stood there, thunder rumbled outside. It started to rain. She went to look out of the window. Down in the driveway she could see the abandoned hosepipe next to the BMW. Robert sat inside his car. From this angle she could see his legs. She remembered thinking, vaguely, that he must have got into his car to escape the rain. If she had really thought about it she would have realised that he could have easily run into the house – that nobody, a few yards from their own front door, would choose to take shelter in their car.

In fact, Robert was making a phone call. He kept his head bent, as if he were rummaging in the glove compartment. But Prudence couldn't see this from her angle and besides she was too busy speculating about her own painful and unsatisfactory state of affairs to think about those of anybody else.

Later, she gave Maddy a lift to London. It was still raining. The oncoming headlights blurred and smeared as the windscreen wipers slewed to and fro. They didn't talk; somehow, after three years' separation, there was too much to say. Maddy told her sister the address of a flat in Tufnell Park, the place she was going to stay. When they arrived Prudence unloaded the luggage and helped her with it to the door.

She drove home to Clapham. It was eight o'clock. On Sunday evenings she felt a loneliness that stretched beyond Stephen, beyond even him. In the houses lamps glowed behind closed curtains. Attic rooms bloomed with the nervy flicker of TVs. Everyone in the world was utterly alone, all those people who believed themselves companioned, they lived alone and they would die alone. Yet simultaneously Prudence felt that she was the only person who was really lonely. This sensation was peculiar to Sunday nights.

She arrived in her street, Titchmere Road, and parked her car. It was a long road of redbrick Victoriana, those claustrophobic façades and surprisingly spacious interiors that are characteristic of Clapham. Commuters used the street as a rat run, a short cut from the southern suburbs to the City. Various traffic-calming devices – humps, narrowed bits – failed to calm the traffic in the rush hour; in fact, just made it more impatient. In twelve hours Prudence herself would be joining them; only twelve hours to go before she could rejoin the human race.

She climbed up to her flat. It was on the first floor. The man upstairs was engaged in his nightly spring-clean, an operation which seemed to consist of dragging heavy items of furniture across the floor. She had a recurring fantasy that Mr Witherall, a timid bachelor, was in fact a serial killer and that every night he had to clean up the evidence and conceal dismembered limbs behind the wardrobe.

She went into the kitchen. Her cat, Cedric, brushed against

her shin. Long ago she knew a man who used to brush her cheek with the knuckle of his hand. He had married and gone to live in Vancouver. On the draining board sat the morning's washed-up cup and plate, exactly where she had left them. Her African violets sat moistly in their pots. Her flat had the stilled, Marie Celeste air of all flats belonging to single people; sometimes, in the past, she had found this comforting.

She went into her living room and switched on the lamp. A pile of manuscripts lay on the table, waiting for her. The top one was called *Commuter or Computer: Work in the Second Millennium*. Upstairs there was a thud. Mr Witherall had felled his latest victim.

She looked at the answerphone. It said '1'. She switched it on.

It was Stephen's voice. *'Listen, she's taken the boys swimming.'* His voice was low and urgent. *'If you're back before five, phone me. I'll come right over. We can have an hour. Oh darling . . .'*

Prudence was a methodical woman. Before she did anything she walked across the room and closed the curtains. Then she sat down on the arm of the chair. She gripped her stomach; the noise was wrenched out of her guts. Coming from this composed person it was a shocking sound – a howl of animal pain.